SHADOW OF A
DEAD MAN

Aquaphor

A SHOTGUN JOHNNY WESTERN

SHADOW OF A DEAD MAN

WILLIAM W. JOHNSTONE
AND J. A. JOHNSTONE

P

PINNACLE BOOKS
Kensington Publishing Corp.
www.kensingtonbooks.com

PINNACLE BOOKS are published by

Kensington Publishing Corp.
119 West 40th Street
New York, NY 10018

PUBLISHER'S NOTE: Following the death of William W. Johnstone, the Johnstone family is working with a carefully selected writer to organize and complete Mr. Johnstone's outlines and many unfinished manuscripts to create additional novels in all of his series like The Last Gunfighter, Mountain Man, and Eagles, among others. This novel was inspired by Mr. Johnstone's superb storytelling.

Special book excerpts or customized printings can also be created to fit specific needs. For details, write or phone the office of the Kensington Sales Manager: Kensington Publishing Corp., 119 West 40th Street, New York, NY 10018. Attn. Sales Department. Phone: 1-800-221-2647.

PINNACLE BOOKS, the Pinnacle logo, and the WWJ steer head logo Reg. U.S. Pat. & TM Off.

First Printing: June 2020
ISBN-13: 978-0-7860-5001-7
ISBN-13: 978-0-7860-5002-4

10 9 8 7 6 5 4 3

Printed in the United States of America

CHAPTER 1

A whistling bullet gave Johnny Greenway a clean shave across his left cheek before it hammered into a fir tree just behind him with a loud *thwack!*

The blue whistler was followed by the hiccupping report of a Winchester rifle followed in turn by a man shouting, "There he is!"

Johnny leaped down the steep forested slope. He dove forward as two more bullets plumed dirt and pine needles around him, these shots coming from the slope on his right.

He rolled up off his left shoulder, smoothly gaining his feet.

A large granite boulder with a V-shaped crack in it stood between him and the two men running up the slope toward him. He unsheathed both of his sawed-off, ten-gauge, double-barreled shotguns, which he wore in custom-made holsters on each hip, thonged on his thighs. Taking each savage popper in each gloved hand—he lovingly called the matched pair of handsome, walnut-stocked, Damascus-steeled death-dealers "the Twins"—he rocked the heavy rabbit-ear hammers back with his thumbs and stepped into the crack.

He grinned savagely as he extended the left-hand shotgun through the opening. The men running toward him, within fifteen feet and closing fast, breathing hard, dusters whipping around their legs, stopped suddenly. Their lower jaws dropped to their chests when they recognized their own annihilations in the ten-gauge's round, side-by-side maws, as black as death and as deadly as a lightning bolt.

Johnny squeezed the shotgun's left trigger.

Ka-boom!

The man on the left screamed and threw his rifle straight up in the air as the pumpkin-sized blast of ten-gauge buckshot picked him up and threw him down the slope as though into the jaws of hell itself.

"Nooo!"

The objection of the second man hadn't entirely left his lips before the cannonlike blast of the Twin's second barrel picked him up while blowing a big bloody hole through his middle and sent him hurling down the slope with his pard, his cream, bullet-crowned Stetson with a snakeskin band dancing along the ground beside him.

Two more bullets came whistling in from Johnny's right, one bullet nipping the brim of his black slouch hat, the other hammering the face of the boulder before him and setting up a ringing in his ears. Johnny turned to see two men running toward him across the shoulder of the slope, black suit coats buffeting in the wind.

Both men jacked fresh cartridges into their Winchesters' actions at the same time.

Johnny moved quickly to the far end of the

boulder, away from the approaching ambushers. He edged along the rock, heading downslope, then turned right to move around behind the boulder, putting it between him and his pursuers. He heard the two men's running footsteps on the boulder's far side, and the anxious rasping of their breaths.

"Where'd he go?" one asked the other, keeping his voice low but not so low Johnny couldn't hear it.

Johnny moved quietly toward the V-shaped crack in the middle of the rock.

"I don't know," said the second man. "I think he headed downslope."

"No, he didn't." Johnny angled his second Twin through the V-shaped crack and grinned. "He's right here."

Both men, standing a few yards upslope from him and slightly to his right, whipped around in surprise, one cursing and raising his rifle. The curse hadn't entirely left his lips and he hadn't entirely gotten the rifle aimed at Johnny before Johnny's right-hand Twin spoke the language of death.

It spoke it again, a second time.

The thundering echoes of the double blasts were still vaulting around the canyon as both men lay in shredded, bloody piles against the incline, shivering out their last breaths, their blood-splattered rifles flung out on the ground around them.

"There he is! There's that Basque devil!"

The voice had come from up the forested slope, maybe fifty yards beyond the dead men. Johnny looked up that way to see two horseback riders moving toward him, weaving through the pines and fir trees. They had to hold their horses to lurching trots on account of the trees and deadfall debris around them, but they'd seen him and they were making their way toward him, one just then raising a carbine and firing.

The bullet smashed against the cracked boulder, to Johnny's right, kicking up a fresh ringing in his ears.

Johnny stepped behind the boulder and, keeping the large rock between him and the men moving down the slope toward him, ran down the declivity toward a creek meandering along the bottom of it. While he ran, he quickly broke open his left-hand Twin, thumbed out the spent wads, and replaced them with fresh ones from his cartridge belt. He snapped the savage popper closed, returned it to its holster on his left thigh, and gave the same treatment to the right-hand gun.

He'd no sooner clicked the second shotgun closed than hoof thuds rose sharply behind him. He turned to see the two riders swinging around opposite sides of the cracked boulder. One flung a pointing arm toward Johnny running down the slope through the pines, and shouted, "There he is! Kill that son of the devil, dammit!"

He triggered a shot that went screeching over Johnny's head to splash into the creek beyond him.

Johnny leaped two deadfalls and wove around a large spruce as the riders thundered toward him, their horses rasping and wheezing, the hooves clattering and crackling on the debris-littered slope. Neither took much care for himself or his horse, so determined were they to snuff the wick of Shotgun Johnny.

They came roaring down the slope, horses leaping shrubs and deadfall, zigzagging crazily around the tall columnar pines. One man, the younger of the two, was sort of groaning and yowling with his fear of the treacherous ride. The older man, whom Johnny had recognized as Trench Norman, a former saloonkeeper who'd taken to the owlhoot trail when he'd been run out of business in Hallelujah Junction by a more moneyed competitor, was cursing a blue streak and whipping his horse savagely with his rein ends.

They were still roughly fifty yards behind Johnny, who broke out of the trees now and dashed across the clearing to the deeply cut creek bed. He leaped into the cut, landing on relatively dry ground beside the water, then hurled himself forward to sit back against the bank.

He drew both Twins and raked all four hammers back with his buckskin-gloved thumbs.

Beyond the clearing he heard his two pursuers thudding and crashing through the forest. There was a great crunching and cursing din as Trench Norman must have run into a snag. The man's horse whinnied shrilly, above Norman's curses. Then the thuds of another horse rose sharply as the other, younger man tore out of the forest.

Johnny swiped his hat off his head and edged a look over the lip of the bank as the younger man, wearing a battered cream hat and dirty rat-hair coat, reined his tired, wide-eyed horse to a halt between the trees and the creek bed. He was tall and lean, with a goat-ugly face complete with a fringe of colorless whiskers drooping off his pointed chin. A wad of chaw bulged one cheek.

He looked around wildly, waving his cocked six-shooter out in front of him.

"Hello, Frank," Johnny said, raising his left Twin above the lip of the bank.

Frank Tenor's eyes found Johnny and snapped even wider when they found the double-barreled Twin bearing down on him. He yelled and jerked his Colt toward Johnny but fired the piece into the air as the fist-sized spread of double-aught buck cut through his chest and belly and threw him howling off his sorrel's right hip.

Hooves crashed in the forest to the right of where Tenor was still rolling in the brush, his screaming horse lunging forward and leaping into the creek bed to Johnny's left. Johnny drew his head and shotgun down when he saw Norman explode out of the forest, firing his Winchester carbine one-handed, cursing loudly.

"Die, you greasy, damn, sheep-diddlin' Basque!"

The man appeared on Johnny's left as Johnny put his back to the bank. Horse and rider flew straight off the lip of the bank, an arcing blur of man and mount angling out over the narrow stream. Norman's carbine stabbed orange flames as he triggered the rifle straight out from his right shoulder a half second before his pinto's front hooves splashed into the creek.

Johnny snaked his right-hand Twin across his body and tripped both triggers, sending two pumpkin-sized blasts of the double-aught steel punching through Norman's upper torso and throwing him sideways off his horse. The pinto's saddle was empty when the mount lunged off its rear hooves, screaming shrilly, and leaped up and out of the stream and onto the opposite bank, its saddle hanging down its far side.

Johnny leaned forward from the bank and raised his left-hand Twin, tightening his trigger finger. He forestalled the motion.

The twin barrels of buckshot had taken decisive care of Trench Norman, whose hatless body just then bobbed back to the creek's surface, the water around the man bright red and glistening in the early-morning sunshine.

"No name-callin' now, Trench. Ain't one bit nice."

Johnny leaned back against the bank to reload the Twins.

As he did, he listened for the approach of more attackers.

If there were more, he didn't hear them. He thought he'd seen one other rider behind Norman and Tenor, but maybe that man had seen what the others had gotten for their attempt at stealing the gold bullion Johnny was hauling down from the Reverend's Temptation Gold Mine at the base of Grizzly Ridge, and had decided that even twenty-six thousand dollars' worth of freshly smelted, high-grade gold wasn't worth a fatal case of buckshot poisoning care of the former deputy U.S. marshal and now bullion guard, Johnny Greenway, aka "Shotgun Johnny."

Johnny snapped the second Twin closed and lifted his head sharply. He narrowed his dark brown, raptorial eyes to each side of his long, hawklike nose as his concentration intensified. His thick, dark brown hair curled down over his ears to touch the long, bright red kerchief he wore sashlike around his neck, the ends of which trailed down his broad chest toward his flat belly.

The rataplan of galloping hooves sounded in the far distance, from up the ridge on his right. Johnny

caressed the Twin's triggers with his gloved thumb,
and his heartbeat quickened with anticipation.

"One more . . ." he said half to himself.

He shuttled his gaze to the heavily forested ridge
down which he knew a switchbacking trail dropped.
It was off this trail he'd camped last night. It was while
he still lay in his blankets early this morning, not in
his camp but nearby—only a fool slept near his cook
fire in outlaw country—that his camp was attacked by
one party of the many countless gold thieves that
haunted this northern neck of the Sierra Nevadas.

"One more coming fast . . . heading this way . . ."

Johnny peered up the creek's opposite bank and
into the forest beyond.

The trail dropping down the ridge to his right
angled along the slope ahead of him, roughly following the line of the creek, before climbing another
steep pass on his left. A shrewd smile quirking his
mouth corners, he pushed himself off the bank, rose
to his feet, splashed across the creek, then ran up the
bank and into the forest.

He ran hard, holding his shotguns down snug in
their holsters. He'd been raised in these mountains
and moved in them as easily as any native creature.
Swift as a black-tailed deer, he climbed the ridge,
hearing the galloping rider closing on him, on his
right, following the gentle curve of the creek as it followed the crease between steep mountain passes.

Johnny's breath rasped in and out of his lungs,
and his mule-eared boots crunched pinecones and
needles topping the thick, aromatic forest duff. As
he followed a zigzagging course around pines and
aspens, he saw the trail ahead of him, straight up the

steep slope, sixty yards away. Through the trees on his right, he glimpsed the galloping rider, who'd descended the northern ridge now and was racing along the flat.

Soon he'd be directly above Johnny.

Johnny grimaced as he pushed himself harder, breathing harder, wincing against the pull in his long legs . . .

The trail was ten feet away.

Five . . .

The rider was a sun-dappled figure galloping toward him on his right, twenty feet away.

Johnny leaped onto the trail, drawing both his stubby cannons from their holsters and raking all four hammers back as he aimed straight out in front of him. The rider came around a bend and, seeing Johnny before him, gave a startled cry and leaned far back in his saddle, reining his horse to a skidding halt.

He was trailing a pack mule, and the mule stopped abruptly, as well, braying up an indignant storm.

It was especially hard for the beast to stop, with all the gold it was packing. At least, the thief *thought* the mule was packing gold.

Gold that belonged to the lovely Sheila Bonner, owner of the Hallelujah Bank & Trust . . .

Johnny smiled as he aimed down both shotguns' double maws at the thief's head. "Hello, Rance. Long time, no see. Where you off to in such an all-fired hurry? With my mule, no less . . . ?"

CHAPTER 2

Rance Starrett's eyes blazed with both fear and fury as he stared over his horse's twitching ears at Shotgun Johnny Greenway bearing down on him with his savage Twins. Starrett held his reins up taut against his chest. His horse, a fine gray brindle, had turned one-quarter sideways to the trail, so Starrett's six-shooter, holstered on his right hip, faced Johnny.

When Starrett glanced from Johnny toward the bone-gripped Colt, Johnny said, "Go ahead. Give it a try, Rance. See how far you get before I muddy up the trail with your bloody hide."

Johnny wouldn't hesitate doing just that any more than he'd hesitated before perforating the other men in Starrett's raggedy-tailed pack. Starrett, a good-looking cuss in his late twenties, belonged to a moneyed patriarchal family headed up by Garth Starrett, one of the largest ranchers on the northeast side of the Sierra Nevadas. Starrett's Three-Bar-Cross sprawled across nearly an entire county, and what land he didn't own in and around Hallelujah Junction, he was likely making a play for.

Not a legal play, either . . .

Starrett had no truck with legality, only money and power. He'd passed along his own values to Rance, who hadn't amounted to much. From the time the kid was old enough to wield a gun and ride a horse, both of which he did pretty well, he'd been a fire-brand who'd gone from cattle rustling to stagecoach holdups to rape and murder and now, finally, to robbing the gold run from the Reverend's Temptation to the Bank & Trust in Hallelujah Junction. Garth Starrett's wealth and power had always been able to get his worthless son out of even the deepest trouble—even two murder charges backed up by eyewitnesses, and the rape of a pretty young schoolteacher. Not to mention the rapes and killings of several parlor girls.

Such crimes had been covered up before they could be reported. But Johnny had heard about them. Most had heard about Rance Starrett's black-hearted dealings.

His father wouldn't get him out of the snag he'd just landed in here, however.

Johnny had been reading Rance's mind. He could see the wheels turning in the man's shrewd, amber eyes set deep beneath sun-bleached blond eyebrows. He was thinking that not even Shotgun Johnny would kill Rance Starrett. Not Garth Starrett's oldest son. Not even Shotgun Johnny had the oysters to pull such a stunt, even after Rance had been caught with his proverbial hand in the cookie jar—or leading Johnny's mule packing twenty-six thousand dollars in freshly milled gold.

Or so Rance thought.

At least, Johnny would hesitate to kill him. Hesi-tate long enough for Rance to drag that smoke

wagon out of its hand-tooled black leather holster
and shoot Johnny from point-blank range.

"Not worth it, kid," Johnny warned. He shook his
head, a thin smile tugging at his mouth. "Them panniers aren't even packin' gold."

The churning of Starrett's cunning mind paused
and incredulity ridged his brows. "Huh?"

"What? You think I'd actually leave the gold in the
camp when I myself had skinned out away from
the fire?" Johnny grunted a caustic laugh. "You damn
tinhorn."

"You're lyin'," said Starrett, cocking his head to
one side and narrowing a skeptical eye.

"Go on," Johnny said, glancing at the mule standing behind Starrett's edgy horse. "Check it out for
yourself."

Starrett turned back to Johnny, and he narrowed
his eyes again. "All right. I just will!"

"Go ahead. Slow. One fast move, and your pa will
have one helluva time recognizing your shredded
carcass."

"Stand down, you Basque devil. You so much as
muss the part in my purty hair, my pa will have you
run down and whipped like the sheep-dip-smellin'
greaser you are!"

Johnny ground his molars at the insult. But, then,
he was used to such condescension. He'd been born
Juan Beristain and he and his Basque parents and
brother—of Spanish and French descent—had
herded sheep around the Sierra Nevadas until a venal
cattle rancher had murdered his family and made
Juan an orphan. Juan had been homeless until another cattleman, Joe Greenway, had adopted him,
changed his name to make his life easier, and given

him a good home on his Maggie Creek Ranch between Reno and Virginia City.

Still, Johnny had to use every ounce of his self-control not to jerk young Starrett out of his saddle and bash his head in with one of the Twins.

"I'm not goin' anywhere, Starrett. I'll be right here, holding my purty Twins on you while you take a look inside them packs. If you so much as sneeze in the direction of your pistol, you'll look mighty ridiculous with your head rolling around in the brush."

Starrett spat in disgust then swung down from the saddle. He cast Johnny a glare of raw disdain then walked behind his horse to the mule, who brayed its apprehension at the whole affair.

"Shut up, you broomtail vermin!" Rance yelled at the mule.

Angrily, he freed the straps of the pannier mounted on the wooden pack frame and peered into the stout canvas sack. He froze, scowling. He glanced at Johnny, his amber eyes hard and cold, then reached into the pack. He pulled out a rock a little smaller than his head and slammed it onto the ground so hard both horse and mule jumped a foot in the air.

The mule brayed its indignance.

The horse tossed its head and whickered.

"A half-dozen men are dead for nothin', Rance," Johnny said. "Not that they wouldn't have gotten their tickets punched sooner or later. I don't think there was a one of them I hadn't sent to the territorial pen when I was still packin' a moon-and-star."

Rance turned to face Johnny square. "Where is it?"

"I'll show you." Johnny smiled. "Just as soon as you throw down that hogleg . . . nice an' slow . . . and put your wrists together so I can tie 'em. You'll be joinin' me back to Hallelujah Junction."

"You think so, do ya?" It was Rance's turn to grin.

Johnny's spine tightened. At the same time he'd seen the mocking grin enter Starrett's gaze, he'd heard the faint crunch of a stealthy footstep behind him.

Rance lifted his chin to shout, "Back-shoot the son of a buck, Chick! *Back-shoot him!*"

Johnny dropped like a wet suit off a clothesline.

As he did, a rifle barked behind him.

He rolled onto his back and, half sitting up, fired a barrel of each Twin into the man who'd stolen up to within fifteen feet of him.

Chick Ketchum's torso turned to bloody pulp as both loads sawed into him. He danced away as though taken by a sudden, catchy tune he'd heard on the morning breeze, and waltzed straight off to the pearly gates while his potbellied body, clad in greasy buckskin trousers and a patched hickory shirt, collapsed on the trail.

"Ah, *hell*!" were Chick Ketchum's last words cast out on a loud, deeply disgusted exhalation.

"Now, that was plumb stupid!" Johnny whipped around to where he'd expected to see Rance Starrett bearing down on him with his Colt. Only, Rance wasn't bearing down on anything except possibly a meeting with ole Saint Pete.

Johnny climbed to his feet. Holding his Twins straight down by his sides, he stared down at Starrett. The firebrand lay sprawled on his back in the middle of the trail. He looked as though he'd been staked out by Indians, spread-eagle. He had his pistol in his right hand, but he hadn't even gotten it cocked before

Chick Ketchum's bullet had plowed into the dead center of his chest.

Heart shot.

One that had been meant for Johnny and likely would have hit its intended target if the witless Starrett hadn't given Ketchum away.

Now Starrett stared, wide-eyed in death, straight up at the sun angling down through the high crowns of the pines lining the trail. The sun reflected off his pretty, thick, strawberry blond hair and his amber eyes. He had a dumbfounded expression on his face, but then, that was nothing new to Rance Starrett. Johnny believed Starrett had been born with such an expression, so it was only fitting he'd go out with one, too, not having learned one damn thing on this side of the sod.

And now he wouldn't.

Kind of a shame in a way—to die little smarter than how you'd started out. But it wasn't like the kid, having been born into a wealthy family, hadn't had plenty of opportunities. He'd just chosen the wrong fork at every turn in the trail.

Bad seed.

"Well," Johnny said. "Let's get you back to Hallelujah Junction. I reckon the least I can do is turn you over to your pa for a proper burial."

He'd be damned if he'd waste time on gathering the others. The predators could dine on them. That's what the tinhorns got for running with the lowly likes of Rance Starrett.

The next day, Shotgun Johnny reined his cream horse to a halt on a promontory-like shelf of rock jutting out over the Paiute River in the Northern Paiute River Valley, and was glad to see that the little boomtown of Hallelujah Junction hadn't missed him while he'd been gone.

At least, if it had, it showed little sign. Even from here, on a high shoulder of Mount Sergeant from which the town was little larger than Johnny's open hand, he could hear the tinkle of pianos and the occasional roars of the mostly male crowd being entertained in the two opera houses that abutted each end of the bustling little settlement, like bookends.

It was late in the day, almost night, and the light had nearly faded from Hallelujah Junction's dusty streets. That which remained owned a dull yellow patina edging toward salmon. Smoke from cook fires swirled like diaphanous white snakes amidst all those purple-green shadows and yellow and salmon sunrays, sometimes obscuring shake-shingled rooftops.

The sun had fallen behind the high western ridges of the northern Sierra Nevadas, and those crags, along with the slightly lower ones in the east, caused the sun to rise and fall later in the day, and for shadows to linger. Now those shadows had swallowed the town, and that was just fine with the burly miners, hardy shopkeepers, enterprising market hunters, professional gamblers and cardsharps, wily prospectors, oily con artists and snake oil salesmen, and coquettish soiled doves who'd settled in for the year, facing the long mountain winter ahead.

Settled in but not settled down.

They were all stomping with their tails up, judging by the din that Johnny could hear from his high perch, by the clumps of men milling on the streets between the saloons and gambling dens and parlor houses, of which there was virtually one for every man who'd come out here, braving the remoteness and relative lawlessness to seek wealth and adventure or to at least have a damn good time trying for either or both.

There were a few pistol shots, as well, rising above the low roar of generalized boomtown cacophony.

Those would likely either mark the unrestrained appreciation of the acting abilities of whatever troupe was in town, entertaining the crowds in one of the opera houses, or possibly a not-so-friendly dispute in a smoky, ill-lit gambling den tucked back in one of the less-than-respectable watering holes or houses of ill repute.

A girl's terrified scream vaulted up from the smoky, darkening settlement, reaching Johnny's ears high above and on the opposite side of the wide, black river. A man's angry shout followed, followed in turn by yet another pistol shot.

Silence returned.

A piano had fallen quiet during the apparent dustup but now it started again, and the general revelry continued in Hallelujah Junction, as well—life moving on as it always did even if a dead man and/or possibly a dead woman was being hauled out of one of the saloons or parlor houses to one of the town's three undertakers. Possibly, a crazy drunk with blood on his hands was now being led away to Town Marshal Jonah Flagg's jailhouse. The poor deceased Jake or Jill would be fitted with a crudely nailed together wooden overcoat and buried quickly the next day in the town's bone orchard on a knoll to the southeast.

The culprit would soon follow after a celebratory

hanging on the main street of the town, complete with barking dogs, laughing children, and a four-piece band. Six feet under he would go, another hastily erected wooden cross on Boot Hill.

Out of sight and out of mind.

Why ruin a good time with thoughts of death when it could occur so quickly, and so often did? Gentlemen, ladies—enjoy yourselves! The next round's on the house! Shuffle those cards, place your bets, roll those dice, spin that wheel!

Like clockwork, another raucous roar rose from a darkening roof, just then catching the last salmon rays of the now-defunct sun as it sank into the deep waters of the distant and unseen Pacific. A dog barked somewhere down there among those darkening streets. In the shadowy mountains on the town's far side, Johnny heard the mournful wail of a single wolf and the ratcheting cry of a late-hunting eagle.

He glanced over his shoulder at Rance Starrett's blanket-wrapped carcass resting belly-down across the saddle of Starrett's brindle gray, to the right of the mule packing twenty-six thousand dollars in gold bullion from the Reverend's Temptation. The gold was headed for the bank owned by the becoming Sheila Bonner.

Sheila.

Just the thought of the beautiful woman warmed Johnny's heart. He'd been in the mountains for six long nights—three nights up and three nights down—camping under the stars, only the night wind and the distantly howling wolves and the mule and his horse, Ghost, for company.

Well, last night he'd had Starrett's horse for company, as well. And Starrett himself, though the dead firebrand hadn't said much up there where Johnny had hung him upside down from a tree, so predators couldn't get at him. Johnny was glad he hadn't said anything. When the dead would start speaking to him, he'd know he'd been alone in the mountains too long.

"Come on, Starrett," Johnny said, nudging Ghost on down the shelf and back onto the trail that would take him down the mountain, across the wooden bridge spanning the river, and into the nocturnal town. "Let's get you settled in for the night. I gotta check in with the boss."

CHAPTER 3

Ghost and the mule and Starrett's horse clomped across the wooden bridge and onto the bank on the east side of the Paiute River, swinging to the left as the trail became the main street of Hallelujah Junction. Johnny put the horse westward along the street, muddy from a recent rain—it rained often at this altitude of nearly seven thousand feet—and wove his way through the clumps of men drinking beer or whiskey out front of the many saloons and parlor houses.

Both sides of the broad street were lined with tall front facades, brightly painted, most of the windows, except for those of the closed shops, now lit against the deepening night.

Signs jutted into the street from pine posts, and oil pots lined the boardwalks, filling the air with the smell of kerosene, which mixed with the smell of man sweat, whores' cheap toilet water, overfilled latrines, horse manure, and woodsmoke. Here and there boards had been laid across the street to make for easier crossings in the ankle-deep mud.

Two brightly painted and garishly adorned doxies

were just then making their way along a pair of such boards. They were holding hands and laughing, more than a little intoxicated, trying to negotiate their way across the narrow two-by-eights without getting the hems of their lacy skirts overly caked with the claylike mud.

As Johnny passed the Saw Mill Saloon, a man stepped away from a five-man group of smoking drinkers gathered around a single blond doxie, and turned to Johnny. He glanced grimly at Starrett's horse, then to Johnny and said, "Who you packin' tonight, Johnny-boy?" It was Louis Buchanan, a Scottish bouncer from the Saw Mill.

Johnny stopped Ghost as well as the mule and Starrett's horse. Buchanan was holding a half-filled beer schooner in one hand, a half-smoked cigarette in the other hand.

He stuck the quirley between his bearded lips and stepped over to the packhorse. He reached into a fold of the blanket in which Johnny had wrapped Starrett and pulled up the young man's head by his pretty blond hair, until the face was revealed, the features slack in death, Starrett's eyes half-open beneath lazy lids.

Buchanan's thick shoulders tightened as he whipped an astonished glance at the bullion guard sitting the fine cream horse ahead of the mule and the dead man's mount. The bouncer wagged his shaggy head, and said, "Gonna be a wee bit of hell to pay for that one, though if ever a man deserved to be kicked out with a cold shovel, it's that one there . . ."

Johnny said nothing. Buchanan let Starrett's head drop back down against the side of the horse. He gave the bullion guard a grim, drunken salute, his eyes still wide with incredulity, and Johnny booted Ghost on ahead.

The bank shone on the right side of the street. As Johnny approached, angling toward one of the two hitchracks fronting the low brick building, a figure moved in a dimly lamplit, curtained window, behind gold-leaf lettering announcing HALLELUJAH JUNCTION BANK & TRUST.

The curtain parted and a heart-shaped face appeared, staring out. Johnny's loins warmed as they did every time he saw her. A rare beauty was the unlikely bank owner and president. Her fine head was silhouetted against the light behind her, but he saw her eyes drift to the mule and then to the packhorse. The eyes shifted back to Johnny and held for a second before she pulled her head away from the window.

The curtain fell back into place and then the glass-paneled front door opened with a groan of the hinges, and Sheila Bonner stepped out, drawing a cloak around her shoulders and around her pretty, chestnut-haired head.

The mountain night was cold, as it was late in the year, and for a few seconds she stood on the bank's small stoop, regarding him silently, her breath frosting in the air around her pretty face. Her dark brown eyes, a shade darker than the chestnut of her hair, slid to the dead man tied to his saddle, then back to Johnny.

"Are you all right?"

"I'm fine."

She glanced at the dead man again. "Who is it?"

"Rance Starrett."

She just stared at him again but he thought he could

hear a long, slow exhalation of deep consternation leave her lungs.

"Who you got there, Johnny?" came a man's raspy voice to his left.

Johnny turned to see an unlikely pair of men walk down the steps fronting the Silver Slipper Saloon and into the street, heading toward him. One was large and hulking, standing even taller than Johnny's six feet four. That was Silent Thursday. If Silent had another first and last name, he'd never said. But then Silent hardly ever said anything at all, and that was no exaggeration. Thus the moniker. Silent spoke so little that some opined that he might have bit out his own tongue in one of the bare-knuckle fights he'd been so famous for all across the West a few years back, when he was a younger man and could take the abuse.

Now he was somewhere in his forties, and he'd stopped fighting. He worked as a bouncer over at the Silver Slipper and as a bank guard for Sheila. Johnny himself, longtime friend of the pair, had put in a good word for both Silent and Silent's longtime partner and business associate, Mean Mike O'Sullivan, who was a few years older than Silent and who, walking alongside the towering, thickset Silent, appeared nearly a dwarf.

In fact, Mean Mike was around five-six. His head came up only to a little above Silent's elbow. Mean Mike had come by his nickname as honestly as Silent had, for Mike was truly mean. He was as mean as he was skinny. Johnny didn't think Mike could have weighed more than 110 pounds fully clothed and dripping wet and holding the old Spencer repeating rifle he always carried.

He was an ill-tempered little reprobate, as poison

mean as a stick-teased rattlesnake. His pugnacious nature had come in useful when he'd been barking up fights for Silent in rough-and-tumble frontier towns and mountain boom settlements, and demanding the payouts when Silent came out on top, his fists dripping with other men's blood, which had usually been the case.

Those who chose to cheat the little man merely because he was little were quickly shown the error of their ways. When Mean Mike's temper was aroused—and it didn't take much of a slight to arouse it—he could do almost as much damage as Silent Thursday could do in the ring against his bare-knuckle opponents. In fact, Mean Mike had done *more* damage at times, laying waste to an entire saloon with little more than a bung starter and a broken whiskey bottle, flailing his blue tongue vividly enough to make even the most hard-bitten of Irish gandy dancers blush and run upstairs.

Both men, Mean Mike and Silent Thursday, worked part-time for Sheila as bank guards, and they came on duty whenever Shotgun Johnny pulled down out of the mountains with a fresh load of ore, as he'd done tonight, to help Johnny and Sheila safely store the ore away in the Bank & Trust's iron vault. They'd likely been watching for Johnny out a window of the Silver Slipper, which sat nearly directly across the street from the bank.

Actually, Silent was usually the one to haul the ore into the bank and stow it away, with Johnny and Mean Mike keeping watch, Johnny with his Twins and Mean Mike with his Spencer rifle, his stubby pepperbox revolver housed over his belly, and keen, suspiciously probing eyes and ears.

Mike was extra handy because, having been in the rough-and-tumble fighting profession for nearly thirty years, he could observe the minutiae of a town's workings and weed out trouble where most men wouldn't think to look. The nasty little bandy-legged man, who constantly had a quirley dangling from between his thin, colorless lips, could predict when trouble was brewing often hours or even days before it exploded.

"Trouble, Mike," Johnny said.

"You don't say?" Mean Mike gave a knowing little chuckle, as though he and trouble were old pards. He and Silent ambled around behind the pack mule then came up on its far side, approaching its grisly cargo.

While Silent held back, staring down in customary silence at the blanket-wrapped body, Mean Mike puffed his quirley and reached into a fold of the blanket to pull up the body's head by its pretty hair. Even Mike, on intimate terms with trouble, gave a start and snapped his surprised little eyes to Johnny, smoke unspooling from his pitted little nostrils.

"Whoo-ee, you sure said it, pardner. And then some!" Mean Mike's voice had a womanishly high pitch to it.

He glanced up over his spindly shoulder at Silent Thursday, who stared expressionlessly down at the dead man's face, customarily silent and with as much reaction as a well-seasoned oak knot.

"Who is it?" someone asked from the street's dark shadows.

A woman down the street behind Johnny answered, "Rance Starrett!"

Johnny turned to see a small crowd of men moving toward him along both sides of the street. Most of them held drinks in their hands. A few doxies in gaudy gowns were moving along with the men, also drinking and smoking and stumbling a little, drunkenly.

One man on a boardwalk on the street's south side shouted to a group of men on the north side of the street, "Johnny brought in Rance Starrett!" The man's voice echoed loudly in the quiet mountain night.

"*Who?*" a man on the street's north side said, cupping a hand to his ear.

The only response was a growing rumble as the word spread through the crowd, as it was likely doing through all of the saloons and gambling dens and whorehouses. The crowd kept coming along the street, the men's eyes flashing brightly in the lights from the surrounding saloon windows and the burning oil pots.

Johnny turned to Mean Mike and Silent Thursday and said, "Get the gold inside, fellas. We got company."

"Right, right," Mike said, nudging Silent with his elbow then loudly pumping the Spencer's triggerguard cocking mechanism, seating a fresh cartridge into the old rifle's action. "That's far enough, you drunken buggers. Just stay back or I'll pop you a pill you won't digest!"

The crowd, ever respectful of Mean Mike's venom as well as Silent Thursday's brute strength, held back, staring in wide-eyed disbelief toward the body of Rance Starrett. Meanwhile, Silent back-and-bellied the twenty-six thousand dollars in gold ingots off the mule's back and onto his own shoulders, as though the two panniers weighed little more than light feed sacks of cracked corn.

As Silent trudged toward the bank, Sheila came down off the stoop and walked up beside Johnny, regarding him with concern in her eyes. With a question, as well. One she didn't need to ask.

"It wasn't even me who shot him," Johnny explained. "One of his own curly wolves drilled that .44 round through his heart."

Sheila's eyes held on Johnny. She'd splayed the fingers of one hand across her upper chest, near the cameo she wore on a silk choker. "His father will still blame you."

"That's Starrett's problem." Johnny glanced at where Silent was hauling the gold into the bank. "You'd best open the vault. I'm gonna get Rance over to Flagg's office."

Sheila placed her hand on Johnny's thigh. "Come over to the house? I had Mrs. Godfrey put a chicken in the oven."

Johnny hesitated, glancing at the crowd of men who'd formed a half circle around Starrett's horse and whom Mean Mike was holding back with his narrowed eyes and cocked carbine not to mention the threatening oaths that came spewing off the little man's acidic tongue, from around the smoldering quirley clamped between his lips.

Mike hated everyone and everyone hated Mike. Except possibly Silent though Silent had never said enough for anyone to know how even he felt about his pugnacious pard. Johnny had to admit that even he didn't like Mike much, even though he called him a friend. It was hard to like a viper. Even a pet one, though Mike was no one's pet. Try to pet Mike, and he'd take your hand off . . .

Returning his gaze to Sheila, Johnny said, "Might be a good night for me to stay clear of the house."

The words pained him. He purely did ache to hold this woman in his arms again, and her eyes were telling him she felt the same way. But not tonight. He'd gotten his wife and boy killed in a situation similar to this one, and he wasn't going to take that chance again. Not with Sheila—the woman who'd saved him from drunken wretchedness . . . who'd almost literally picked him up out of the gutter of the muddy streets of Hallelujah Junction . . . who'd given him a job as well as the self-respect he'd thought he'd never know again.

No. He owed her too much to endanger her life. He wouldn't do it. Even if it meant not sharing a meal as well as a quiet and much-longed-for conversation this evening.

Johnny manufactured a smile but knew it probably didn't reach his eyes. "I'll see you tomorrow. Maybe join you at the bank for a cup of coffee."

Sheila drew her mouth corners down with worry. "Do you think it's that bad?"

"I don't know. It might be."

She gave a reluctant nod. "You be careful."

"I will. Good night."

She tried to smile, but hers didn't reach her eyes, either. "Good night, Johnny."

As she entered the bank behind Silent Thursday, with Mean Mike standing guard with the Spencer on the stoop, Johnny cursed under his breath, then booted Ghost up the street toward the jailhouse.

Chapter 4

The crowd followed Johnny the block and half northwest along the main street, staying a few yards behind the mule that was braying anxiously at all the commotion.

Word had leaped forward, like a forest fire casting sparks out ahead of it, so that more men and a few women of the street variety were moving toward Johnny from ahead of him, as well. Men and doxies had come out of the saloons and parlor houses to stand on boardwalks or verandas or second-floor balconies to gaze with speculative fascination at the grisly cargo Shotgun Johnny was carrying over the back of the horse he was leading.

Starrett's name was being bandied about, mostly in whispers but in occasional shouts that vaulted above the crowd's general, low, rumbling din, in answer to shouted or whispered queries.

"Pshaw!" one man exclaimed in disbelief. "I don't believe it!"

"It's true, I tell ya!" said his friend walking along beside him. "Leastways, that's the word goin' around!"

"Well, if it's true, hell's sure to pop!"

Johnny stopped his horse at the hitchrack fronting

the town marshal's small, stone, barracklike office, which sat back behind a sagging, unpainted front veranda. A sign announcing JONAH FLAGG, TOWN MARSHAL was mounted above the door.

One of Flagg's deputies, a short, stocky man named Phipps was just then shoving a handcuffed prisoner up the veranda steps. Flagg himself was coming up behind Phipps, a double-barreled shotgun resting on his shoulder. Flagg had turned his head to regard the one man and two horses moving toward him and flanked by a good half the town. Now he stopped near the bottom of the veranda steps, nudged his battered, funnel-brimmed Stetson back off his domelike forehead, and spat a wad of chaw into the mud.

Regarding Johnny with characteristic disdain, the local lawman said, "What the hell's this all about?"

Johnny booted Ghost up to Flagg and tossed the man the lead ribbons of Starrett's horse. "Got a dead one for you."

"*Another* dead one for me," Flagg said, spitting the words out like bad raisins.

Starrett's bunch hadn't been the first to try to take the Reverend's Temptation gold from Johnny Greenway, and they hadn't been the first to pay the price for doing so. Not all of Johnny's five runs had been hit, but three of them had. The first one had cost him the life of his best friend, the old mountain man Bear Musgrave. It had almost cost him Sheila, as well, for she'd ridden along on that trip—Johnny's first after she'd hired both him and Bear.

"Not just another one."

"What?" Flagg said, his disdain for Johnny still plain in the curl of his lip and the flare of a nostril.

He was tall, and he had been lean until recently, when he'd gained nearly thirty pounds, so that his cheap, three-piece suit no longer fit him. It grabbed at the potbelly bowing out his brown leather vest. His broadcloth trousers were too tight at the thighs. He no longer had much of a neck, either, and even his eye sockets had gotten fleshy around his shallow eyes.

Flagg was an idiot, plain and simple. He'd been a shotgun guard for the local stagecoach line, but he hadn't been much good at it, so he'd resigned instead of enduring the disgrace of being fired. He'd been awarded the town marshal's job mainly because no one else was fool enough to take such a dangerous and underpaid position and most laughed at him for doing so. He drank and mongered whores and left most of the law work up to his two deputies, former miners, and he hated Shotgun Johnny because of the fool he'd been exposed to be when Johnny had had to foil an attempted bank robbery for him.

That's when Johnny had won the respect and confidence of Sheila Bonner—two things that Flagg wanted in the worst way possible. Well, that was only partly true. It was no secret that Flagg wanted the lovely woman's heart, as well. He hated Johnny even more because Johnny had obviously won it, judging by how much time the two spent together during nonworking hours.

"Take a look," Johnny said, canting his head toward his grisly cargo.

"It's Rance Starrett!" said one of the men in the crowd that had gathered closely around Johnny and Starrett's brindle gray.

Flagg jerked an exasperated look at Johnny. *"What?"*

"Go ahead," Johnny said. "Take a look. He won't bite. Not anymore, he won't."

Flagg looked at the two men who were crowding close to Starrett's horse, curious as well but also wary, as though they thought maybe Johnny was packing rattlesnakes inside that blanket roll. No telling what the former Juan Beristain, the crazy-eyed Basque, might do just for kicks and giggles. All Basques were known to be hot-blooded, unpredictable sorts with strange ways about them.

"You men get the hell away from there!" Flagg berated them as he strode over toward the packhorse, the horse's reins in his left hand, his shotgun in his right. "This is official business. I need some room here!"

Several of the men muttered mockingly though Flagg ignored them. He stopped by the blanket-wrapped bundle then, as though he himself was worried about getting snakebit or some such, used the barrel of his twelve-gauge shotgun to part the blankets. He peeled them away from the side of Rance Starrett's face, exposing the man's left cheek and ear and his enviable, thick, strawberry blond head of hair.

It was enough of a look for Flagg to recognize the man.

Flagg pulled the shotgun away, letting the blanket ends fall back into place. He took a step back, saying, "*Ho-lee kee-rist!*" He cast an openmouthed look at where Johnny still sat his tall cream stallion. Flagg didn't say anything. He didn't need to. The gravity of the matter was plain in his eyes.

"All I can tell you, Flagg, is I gave him a chance. It wasn't even me who shot him. It was one of his own men. Starrett's wick was trimmed by a bullet meant for me."

"That don't matter an' you know it," Flagg said, wagging his head slowly, his eyes nearly as round as his open mouth.

"Oh, I know." Johnny reined Ghost around, preparing to head back in the direction he'd ridden from. He looked at Flagg again. "Leastways, it won't matter to Garth Starrett. But it makes a big difference to me."

Johnny booted Ghost ahead, the crowd parting for him.

"Hold on, Johnny! Where the hell you think you're goin'?"

"Oh, we all know where he's goin'," said a snickering voice in the crowd to Johnny's right.

Another man laughed.

Johnny turned to glare at the man. The man flushed and looked away, sheepishly brushing his fist across his nose. Johnny knew that his relationship with his comely boss was the subject of much ribald gossip in and around Hallelujah Junction, but it still burned his drawers to hear the sly remarks. He might have deserved it, but Sheila didn't.

Turning back to Flagg, Johnny said, "I *think* I'm gonna go grab a hot bath and a warm meal."

"What about Starrett? I mean . . . who's gonna tell *Mister* Starrett?"

"You are. I'll ride out an' talk to him later, but you'd best take the man his son's body. It's not my place to give him the news."

"*Me?*"

"I did my part. This part's up to you." Johnny winked at the man. He touched spurs to Ghost's flanks, and the crowd parted as horse and rider trotted back down the street the way they'd come.

"I don't care if he was tryin' to rob you or not," Flagg yelled at Johnny's back. "This is still your fault, Johnny!"

Again, Johnny halted the cream. He glanced over his shoulder at the raging town marshal, one eye skeptically arched. "*My* fault?" Johnny chuckled.

"Ever since you took out Harry Seville and Louis Raised-By-Wolves, every damn wannabe gunslick in western Nevada and northern California has drawn a target on your back. Now they wanna be the one to take you down. Make a name for themselves. It's like goin' up against a big gambler. All the little gamblers wanna beat him so they can pull on his boots, *be him*! Now that you've killed Rance Starrett, more and more would-be firebrands are gonna be climbin' into them mountains, waitin' to kick you out with a cold shovel and carve your notch on their gun butts!"

"I'm just so damn sorry I took down Seville and Raised-By-Wolves. How shortsighted of me!" Johnny chuckled again, dryly, and booted Ghost forward.

As he rode eastward, the crowd split, and the men and women stood off to each side of the street, gazing at him warily, speculatively. They were staring at the man who'd killed the notorious Rance Starrett of the highly respected and feared Starrett family led by old Garth Starrett himself, a man who himself had killed a good many men in his time and was still killing those who crowded his cattle empire northeast of Hallelujah Junction.

Garth had exterminated the Indians in this neck of the Sierra Nevadas, with help from the army sent by friends of his in the federal and territorial governments. And he'd hunted down and killed men and families who'd dared squat on the land he'd sent his men out to homestead and prove up on and then sell to him for pennies on the dollar once their two-year obligations were up.

It had been wrong, but other cattlemen had done it though it was not letter-of-the-law legal.

It would be wrong, of course, to kill the man who'd killed his son. Especially since his son had had it coming for a long time. Rance Starrett, obviously the bearer of a black heart from his earliest stages, probably should have been shot as soon as he'd left swaddling clothes—"Shoot the boy and spare having to hang the man later," as the saying went—but they'd left that job to Johnny Greenway.

Johnny hadn't even shot him though he'd likely have had to. The whole thing was a joke. A very bad joke but Johnny couldn't help smiling, anyway, especially at how all the drunken rascals around him were regarding him like some African king of the jungle who'd broken out of his circus cage and was stalking the town for an easy meal.

He passed a saloon, and the cool air scented with the malty smell of fresh ale and the molasses-like aroma of good whiskey made him want a drink. Unfortunately, he'd had to give up the bottle, and he wasn't going to add diving back into that sewer to the list of his current troubles.

As he approached the bank, he couldn't help stopping. A light still burned in the window to the right of the door. Sheila was still inside. He could see her sitting at a desk near the window, writing with an ink pen in a large open ledger book. A lamp burned on the table before her, the light shining richly in her chestnut hair gathered up in a loose bun atop her head, a few sausage curls angling down to caress her alabaster cheeks.

As much as he wanted that drink, he wanted to swing down and go inside and tell her that he'd join her at her house at the north edge of town for roasted chicken and probably a slice or two of whatever dessert her maid, Verna Godfrey, had baked this week. Smothered in a healthy dollop of freshly whipped cream.

They'd talk quietly together on the sofa in her sparsely but elegantly appointed parlor, making sure the curtains were drawn against Sheila's voyeuristic neighbors. Maybe later, if it seemed right, and it usually did, they'd take each other's hand and climb the stairs together to her second-story bedroom, which had been her father's bedroom before old Martin Bonner had died of a heart condition just last year, not long after Sheila had come from back East to help out with the bank that had been brought to its knees by her father's ill-advised investments and general faulty business practices as well as a string of bullion robberies.

Sheila had gone to a fine college and had become a nimble accountant. In fact, without her help, the bank—and the Reverend's Temptation, which she and her father also owned—likely never would have been saved. Now she was the rarest of small-town curiosities—a well-bred, educated, unmarried woman in her late twenties who was also proud of her independence and not afraid to invite her male employee into her home whenever she wanted.

She even insisted Johnny leave by the house's front door. Even in broad daylight.

No sneaking around for Sheila Bonner. She didn't care what the neighbors or anyone else thought or said about her. She was her own woman, and if anyone didn't like it, they didn't need to deposit their money in her bank—even though it was the only one around. She was shrewd that way. Maybe a little superior with a touch of wild rebelliousness that had made her even more attractive to Johnny.

Now, staring in through the bank window, he felt the warmth of his need to hear her voice, to see the light sparkle in her eyes and in her hair, to feel her soft, warm flesh pressed up taut against his.

But in his head he heard the blast of the shotgun that had killed his son as the killers had stormed into his house in Carson City, leaving his son and his wife dead and Johnny only a ragged shell of himself . . .

His breath rattled in his throat when Sheila suddenly looked up from her ledger book to stare out through the window. It was as though she'd sensed him here. She canted her head to one side, as though seeing him out here, staring in at her from the saddle of his big cream horse.

Just as she started to rise from her desk, Johnny said, "No, no . . ." and booted Ghost on down the street, quickly slipping into the shadows of a southward-arcing bend as he heard the bank door's latch click and the hinges groan.

"Johnny . . . ?" he heard her say quietly into the night.

He did not turn back.

CHAPTER 5

As Johnny rode downstream along the Paiute River, the outlying shacks of Hallelujah Junction falling back behind him, he felt good to be shed of the town and its sweaty wash of snarling humanity once more. He didn't like people. Never had. Of course, there were a few he'd loved, but people in general and in numbers of more than four or five, he didn't care for. His blood father had once told him, while drinking Picon punch around their campfire one night in the mountains, that more than two people in a room was a society, and societies were hell with the fires out.

Like his father before him, Juan didn't care for society. He had no place in it; it had no place in him. His Basque parents, itinerant sheepherders—Joseba and Yolanda Beristain—had been loners. Johnny's adoptive father, old Joe Greenway, had been a loner. Johnny was a loner, too.

He swung off the old mine trail he'd followed out of town and onto the shaggier two-track trail that led to Bear's old cabin. After Bear Musgrave had died, butchered by Harry Seville and Louis Raised-By-Wolves when he'd been guiding Johnny and Sheila down the mountains from the Reverend's Temptation, Johnny had taken over the cabin in a picturesque little clearing by Goat Creek. Mean Mike and Silent Thursday lived out here with Johnny, but those two were either off working or carousing most of the time.

Mostly, Johnny was alone out here.

He liked it out here, off the beaten path a couple of miles from town, no one else around except birds, deer, elk, and the occasional roving griz, most of whom left Johnny alone as long as he left them alone in turn. He liked bears. Since Bear Musgrave's death, he thought he recognized the old mountain man's spirit in those grizzlies that gleaned berries from the brush around the cabin, and fish from the creek, as if in them Bear was paying a visit to his old friend who'd taken up residence in his old haunt there by the stream, in the open wash of mountain sunshine by day, under the pearl glow of the stars by night, wolves howling and owls hooting from near ridges.

Johnny put his horse up in the stable flanking the cabin and then followed the well-worn path—the path worn by old Bear himself—around to the front of the stout, brush-roofed log shack. Moonless, it was nearly pitch-black out here tonight.

The stars sparkled across the firmament like glitter spilled across black velvet, but little of their light made it down here to the clearing sandwiched between two steep, forested ridges, the creek angling along the ridge behind the cabin and that Johnny could hear now in the ethereal mountain silence. He thought he could even feel the coldness of that water fed by springs and glaciers from the mountains' higher reaches, adding to the bladelike chill of the night air.

His saddlebags draped over one shoulder, his blanket roll sandwiched under his other arm, Johnny shivered. He placed a boot on the stoop's bottom step and stopped. He dropped the blanket roll, and instantly his right-hand shotgun was in his hand, his thumb raking the hammers back.

His heartbeat quickened as his eyes probed the shadows under the stoop's low roof from the rafters of which iron pots and pans hung as did a water bucket and dipper. The sun-bleached skulls of deer, elk, wolves, moose, and even a few bears shone pale in the thin wash of starlight, tacked as they were to the porch's awning post and to the cabin's front log wall. The dark eye sockets stared malevolently at Johnny, the fleshless mouths sneering.

"Who's there?" Johnny said, his voice sounding inordinately loud in the heavy silence.

Were they already after him? Perhaps someone wanting to get a jump on the bounty Garth Starrett would surely place on his head . . . ?

Johnny slid the sawed-off shotgun to the left and the right as his squinting eyes probed the shadows for a target, his spine drawn taut and his flesh crawling as he waited for the rose flash and the burn of a bullet.

Ahead, nothing moved.

He turned his head slowly, gazing into the darkness around him, suspecting that others were out here, moving in on him, trying to catch him in a whipsaw.

But nothing. No sounds except the infrequent hooting of a near owl and the faint rustling of some burrowing creature in the woodpile at the end of the cabin.

Slowly, Johnny moved up the porch's creaky three

steps. He looked around at the narrow stoop then moved toward the Z-frame door. He'd taken two steps, his finger drawn taut against one of the Twins' eyelash triggers, when something moved to his right, dropping straight down past his shoulder.

A sharp thud sounded, echoing loudly inside his head.

He gave an exclamatory grunt and swung the shotgun around and down . . . but held fire when a cat's meow reached his ears. Two soft green eyes stared up at him from the porch floor, near the barrel in which Bear had collected rainwater.

"Louie!" Johnny said. "You're gonna give ole Johnny a heartstroke, you infernal polecat!"

He depressed the shotgun's hammers, returned the Twin to its holster, then reached down and picked up Bear's liver-colored puss. Instantly, Louie started purring, his entire body quavering and digging his claws affectionately into Johnny's arm.

"How you doin', you old skudder?" Johnny said, jostling the friendly critter against him. "Were you lonely while I was gone? Why, I guess you were, weren't you? Don't seem to have lost any weight, though. In fact, I think you might've even gained some. Been terrorizin' the mice, have you? Well, good . . . good on ya, pal."

Johnny loved all animals—most more than people. Like Bear, he had an especially soft spot for cats.

He dropped Louie to the floor then retrieved his blanket roll from the base of the porch steps. "Come on inside, an' I'll see if I can rustle up some milk and maybe a few bits of jerky." Returning to the stoop, he tripped the door latch and Louie hustled through the door beside him, rubbing his fat, furry body up against Johnny's right leg and purring so loudly that Johnny thought he could feel the reverberations through the cabin's earthen floor.

He stumbled around in the heavy darkness until he lit the lamp hanging over the small eating table by a length of twisted wire. The lamplight spread a weak, watery yellow glow, casting shadows like scuttling black rats around the cabin's single room. Tripping over Louie, who clung to his ankles like a second pair of boots, Johnny found a can of milk on a shelf, pierced the top with his barlow knife, and poured the milk into a small tin pan.

He set the pan on the floor, and Louie crowded close, loudly slurping.

"There you go, pard. Drink up, you champion mouse-killer!"

With Louie taken care of, Johnny got to work building a fire in the small range that sat in the kitchen area of the cabin. As the range ticked and groaned, heating up, Johnny took a lantern to the keeper shed out back. He cut a couple of thick steaks off the deer hanging there. He, Mean Mike, and Silent Thursday always kept a food critter of some kind hanging in the keeper shed—usually deer as well as rabbits. He grabbed a potato and an onion from a burlap sack and returned to the cabin.

He tossed the steaks into a pan, added the chopped potato and onion, a big scoop of pork fat, and set the pan as well as a dented coffeepot, filled with water from the rain barrel, on the stove. When the pot boiled, he added a big handful of coffee from an Arbuckles' sack.

While the coffee returned to a boil, he stirred the potatoes and onion around in the pan in which the steaks sizzled, the mixed grease of the meat and the pork fat popping jubilantly. While the steak and potatoes continued to cook, and the leaping flames inside the range drove the penetrating chill from the cabin, he poured himself a cup of coffee and sat at the table, sipping the coffee and smoking a cigarette he'd taken his time rolling.

It was good to be home. He liked the peace and quiet and the sense of belonging he felt here, in the cabin in which he'd lived with Bear after Bear had taken him in when Johnny had been at his worst with the bottle. This was his home now.

And forevermore.

Still . . . he sipped his coffee, drew on the half-smoked quirley, and blew the smoke out against the dark window on the other side of the table from him. Still . . . he missed her. He'd seen her and spoken to her briefly, and that short meeting had made him want so much more.

Maybe someday they'd be together. Out here. He couldn't live in town, in her nice, civilized house. If they ever lived together, it would have to be out here in the mountains. He'd give Mean Mike and Silent the boot.

Johnny gave a dry chuckle at that as, the quirley dangling from between his lips, he stirred the potatoes around in the pan. Who was he trying to kid?

She'd never move out here with him. The cabin was cozy by his standards, but by the standards of a woman like Sheila Bonner, with all the old rusting traps and moldering hides on the walls and hanging from rafters, the ancient weaponry and wools and leather from Bear's earliest hunting and trapping days, it would be a virtual grizzly cave!

No, she'd never move out here. And he'd never move to town. Lying with her in her father's old, big, four-poster, canopied bed was pure bliss. But he'd never felt at home in that house. With her, sure. But not in her house.

He loved her with all his heart, but he had to stop kidding himself that they had any kind of a future together. She was far from his unschooled, rough-hewn ilk. He was a former mountain boy, former ranch hand turned deputy U.S. marshal turned town drunk turned bullion guard. She was an eastern lady with an education he couldn't even fathom. A high-bred girl with a golden future back East when she finally got tired of the crude lifestyle of Hallelujah Junction, and sold her business interests out here for a small fortune.

It probably wouldn't be all that long now. She'd be here another year at the most, and then she'd be gone.

No, there was no point making it harder for either one of them. He had to end it now. She probably realized the same thing. They were from different worlds. Besides, his life was dangerous. He'd made a lot of enemies, and recently he'd made one more. A big one.

Garth Starrett.

He didn't want anyone else he loved getting caught in a blast of lead meant for him.

He scraped the nicely charred potatoes and onions over the top of the steaks and shoveled the whole works onto a pie pan. He ate the succulent food and washed it down with the strong black coffee. He would have enjoyed it more if he hadn't started thinking about her. The lack of her. Of the impossibility of him and her together.

When he was finished, he tossed his dishes into the wreck pan on the dry sink, then set to work stoking the range again and heating water for his bath. He hauled Bear's old tin tub from where it hung from a rusty nail on the outside of the cabin and set it down at the foot of his hide-covered bed. While Louie napped on a folded trade blanket on Bear's old elk-hide rocker, curled into a tight, purring ball, Johnny peeled out of his trail-grimed duds—white cotton shirt, bright red neckerchief, black leather vest, black frock coat, black broadcloth trousers, low-heeled cavalry boots, and wash-worn balbriggans—and eased himself into the steaming, near-scalding water.

He scraped and scrubbed and rinsed with fresh warm water then, rolling and smoking another quirley while sitting back in the tub, he started to fall asleep until Louie woke with a chortling start. The cat rose and arched his back, looking from Johnny to the door, flicking his tail and moaning deep in his chest.

Johnny was never far from the Twins. Both poppers were in his hands now, drawn from the holsters he'd draped over a near chair back. He clicked all four hammers back and aimed the shotguns across the low-ceilinged, shadowy room toward the front door, which he'd remembered to bar.

Hoof thuds sounded. A rider approaching from the trail.

Whoever it was was heading here, because there were no other cabins out this way.

Johnny waited, caressing the shotguns' hammers, his heart beating slowly but heavily.

The hoof thuds grew louder. The horse stopped in front of the cabin.

Johnny slowed his breath, held the Twins steady, all four barrels aimed at the door, ready to blow it to smithereens and anyone standing outside of it who was foolish to shoot through it.

Someone was coming up the porch steps, the risers squeaking softly. His visitor crossed the porch, paused, then rapped lightly on the door.

"Johnny?" Sheila called.

He let out his held breath.

He let the shotguns sag in his hands. He drew on the quirley clamped between his lips, exhaled through his nostrils.

"Johnny?" she said again. "Let me in."

"No," he said, just loudly enough for her to hear on the other side of the door. "Go away. It's not safe here."

She knocked again, three times, harder. "Let me in."

"Go away."

"You don't mean that."

"Go away," he said, louder.

"Not until I've talked to you."

"It can wait till tomorrow."

"No, it can't." She paused. "I . . . can't . . ."

"Go away!" Johnny leaned forward, resting his head on his knees.

Damn her. Why did she have to come just when he was trying to get her out of his head?

In annoyance, he lifted his head and shouted,

"Dammit, climb back onto your horse and ride the hell out of here!"

She didn't say anything for nearly a minute.

Then her voice came again—soft, gentle, intimate. "If you're not careful, Johnny, I will leave."

Again, he rested his head on his knees. He hardened his jaws, ground his back teeth.

Another minute-long silence.

Then she said in a faintly mocking tone, "All right, then . . ."

Johnny waited. He lifted his head from his knees, and suddenly his yearning for her was a raging stallion inside himself.

What the hell had he done?

"Wait!"

He rose quickly, stepped out of the tub, and looked around for his clothes. He'd tossed them into a dirty bundle in the kitchen, ready to take to the Chinese laundry in town. There was no near towel.

"Oh hell!"

Wet, water dripping off his naked body, he strode quickly, urgently to the front door. She was probably gone by now. Damn fool! What was he going to do without her? He'd been a moron to think he could end it so quickly. For good or bad, he loved the woman!

He fumbled the locking bar out of its brackets, leaned it against the wall. Clumsily, knowing she was riding off into the darkness, he worked the door latch, finally got the door open, and poked his head into the chill night air, yelling, "Sheila!"

He jerked back with a start. She stood before him, smiling up at him from a foot away. She had one foot cocked confidently forward, her arms crossed on her breasts.

"Don't worry," she said, reaching up to place a hand against his face. "I'm not going anywhere, Johnny Greenway."

He closed his arms around her and swept her off her feet. She squealed with delight as he hauled her inside and kicked the door closed behind them.

CHAPTER 6

Garth Starrett lifted his head abruptly from his pillow and reached for the old LeMat he kept loaded and ready for battle on his nightside table.

Only, it wasn't the LeMat he'd grabbed. He blinked now, clearing sleep and alcohol fog from his eyes, to see that instead of the old nine-shot in his knobby hand, he'd grabbed a whiskey bottle.

An empty one.

He cursed, set the bottle back down, knocking it over so that it tumbled off the table to the floor—making a helluva racket, dammit—and then grabbed the LeMat. But by the time he'd gotten the old piece in his hand, his mind had clarified somewhat.

It was not twenty years ago, and he was not camped down by the Avalanche River. War-painted Paiute warriors were not sneaking into his cow camp, intent on freeing his topknot and drilling a stone-tipped arrow through his ticker.

His ticker . . .

He winced and leaned back against the pillow propped against the headboard as the old claw grabbed hold, sending sharp pains spasming against his breastbone. His breath grew shallow, and he could feel a strange, painful numbness leaching down his left shoulder and into his arm.

He cursed and fumbled a nitro tablet out of the little tin box on the table. He leaned out over the bed to grab another bottle off a shelf beneath the table and quickly popped the cork, nearly rendered breathless by the minimal effort. He washed the tablet down with a couple of deep pulls of his favored forty-rod whiskey.

Most men who'd made as much money as Garth Starrett preferred something with a label—Spanish brandy, say, or a well-aged Scotch. Not Garth. He still preferred the kind of home-brewed tarantula juice you found in remote roadhouses, corn distilled in a knocked-together contraption to which a few handfuls of strychnine and a diamondback's head were added for a little extra pop and sizzle, so that the bottle smoked a little after you popped the cork.

And it smelled like brimstone and moldy leather. With a burn that spread into your toes, reminding a feller that he was alive, by God.

An acquired taste but one that, once acquired, some men always preferred over any other.

"There," Starrett said, feeling the skull pop and the nitro going to work, knocking the old crab on its head so that it eased its hold on his heart. "There, now . . . damn you," he addressed the crab.

He took another pull off the bottle, set it on the table, and climbed heavily out of bed. In his nightgown, his bloated feet bare, the toenails as thick and yellow as small clamshells, he made his way over to the big window. He slid the green velvet drapes aside and stared down into the yard.

So that's what he'd heard. He had a visitor. A man had come into the yard trailing a packhorse. A market hunter selling a deer, maybe. The man was talking to Starrett's foreman, Milo Channing, down by the breaking corral and the windmill, both standing there holding what appeared to be a solemn conversation.

As they talked, Channing kept shaking his head and glancing at whatever the visitor had hauled in over the horse's back. Then he lifted his chin to shuttle his gaze up the hill to the Three-Bar-Cross's big main house, which was a sprawling mess of a structure, the main log cabin, originally one room and a loft, having been added onto several times and then remodeled so that it looked more like a barn than a house.

Not much to look at from the outside, but Garth Starrett had built an empire from this headquarters. He'd raised a family here, of sorts, though so far the halls sadly wanted for the echoing laughter of his grandchildren's play . . .

Garth heard a breath restrict itself at the back of his throat.

Wait. The visitor was no market hunter. It was the useless town marshal of Hallelujah Junction. Starrett saw the star on potbellied Jonah Flagg's vest flashing in the midmorning sunshine. And the horse over which the animal lay . . .

Rance's brindle gray . . .

Starrett's gaze returned to what the brindle was carrying. His head grew light, and he shuffled back away from the window, his logy heart increasing its pace and straining with the effort. He drew a deep breath, swallowed, drew another, then stumbled around the room, drawing his buckskin trousers on, looping the snakeskin suspenders over his arms. He shrugged into his traditional blue wool shirt, sat down to pull on his black leather boots into the wells of which he shoved the buckskin's cuffs. He didn't bother to tuck in his shirt.

Trying to keep his anxiousness on a short leash but having trouble doing that—he felt as though he'd been pushed up close to a deep precipice, and the very bowels of burning hell were flailing their flames at him, the devil's hounds down there grinning and snarling up at him, snapping their jaws—he pulled his long, grizzled, gray-brown hair back behind his shoulders then fumbled the door open.

He shuffled out into the hall, trying to ignore that crab clamping down on his heart again, and headed toward the stairs. As he passed his daughter's room, the door of which was open, he glanced inside to see Bethany standing at her window, gazing down into the yard. Bethany Starrett was the proverbial "old maid." Sloppy and unattractive. Pale and overweight.

She was the sole survivor of a pair of twins, one born dead, having been strangled by the other's, Bethany's, umbilical cord. Surely, the dead one would have been the lovely one, if she'd lived. The poor girl had taken after Garth's side of the family, not having been given a lick of Murron's rare beauty. Thus she lived here as she would throughout her days, long after Garth and Murron were gone, most likely. She'd be the old maid aunt residing here with the family Garth prayed that Rance would one day find the settlement and courage to raise . . . with a good woman . . . taking over the business . . . filling the halls

with the echoing laughter of many children . . . all
Starretts . . . passing on the name . . .

Garth remembered that . . . that *thing* . . . slumped
over the saddle of Rance's brindle, and the crab tightened its stranglehold on his heart.

Oh God—no. It couldn't be . . .

He must have made a noise. Bethany turned from
the window, her pale, plump, coarse-featured face
expressionless, both hands laced loosely together in
front of her. She wore a shapeless gray housedress, a
frock that could have been worn by any pauper's
daughter, and her lusterless hair was pulled behind
her head in a tight, schoolmarm's bun.

"Visitor, Father," she said. The corners of her
mouth quirked in a—a what? A grin? Almost a self-
satisfied smile, as though she'd known this was
coming and even might have welcomed it, taken
some weird, sick sort of pleasure from it . . . ?

Starrett cleared his throat, drew another calming
breath, and nodded. "I, uh . . . I was just going
down . . ." He steadied himself with a hand on the
unadorned pine-paneled wall then moved heavily
forward, his boots as heavy as lead weights.

"Feeling all right, Father?" Bethany called from
her room, her voice bland, maybe even vaguely mocking, concern in her words only.

"Fine," Starrett said, breathless. "Fine, dear . . ."

He grabbed the banister and then started down
the broad stairs that cleaved the house in two, separat-
ing the parlor area from the kitchen area to his left.
The high, wide, wraparound veranda shone beyond
the large windows Starrett had outfitted the lodge
with, shipped around the Horn from the East Coast, so
that from anywhere on the first floor he could look

out over his vast holdings sloping away in all directions
from the bluff upon which his big timbered lodge
stood—sprawling, dark, and bleak, and as prideful
and stalwart as any Norman castle.

The Chinese couple who cooked and kept house
were moving around stiffly in the kitchen, the woman
Ling, kneading bread dough at an end of the long
eating table, her husband, Woo, down on his knees
adding split cordwood to the range. Both paused in
their toil to glance at Garth, as though they themselves had seen through a window the marshal of
Hallelujah Junction in the yard below the house.

Garth turned away from the pair and continued to
the front door, which was cracked. When he opened
it and stepped through it, he saw his wife, Murron,
standing out there, staring down the slope toward
where Flagg and Milo Channing were now walking
slowly up the hill along the cinder-paved path, toward
the steps that had been cut into the hill for a thirty-
foot stretch just below the house and where two stock
troughs and two wrought iron hitchracks stood, their
ends forming the Three-Bar-Cross brand.

Murron swung her regal head sharply to Garth.

Older now, of course, than the young woman he'd
married—the well-bred daughter of one of Garth's
Scottish business partners—she was still a beautiful
woman. Gray liberally streaked her once–coal black
hair, but it was still thick and rich. It shone with frequent brushings. She took as much pride in her hair
now as she had when, only nineteen years old, she'd
married the thirty-five-year-old Garth. Her figure was
still high-busted, firm, and sound, her face attractively
if severely sculpted, with a slightly hooked and defiant

nose. Her eyes were the dark blue of the stormy Scottish seas.

Because of Garth's weak heart, they no longer shared the same bed. At least, that was the reason she'd given him three years ago for kicking him out of their bedchamber on the house's second story, relegating him to the room of their oldest son, Wallace, who'd drowned in a bog while trying to free a cow and a calf when he was only fourteen. Still, Garth had stolen peeks into her boudoir while she'd been dressing, so he knew her body was still nearly as fine as that of the girl he'd married.

Nearly as fine but off-limits, and there wasn't a damn thing he could do about it. She was stronger than him, and it was his most deeply held secret that he feared her while living in fear that one day she would leave him.

A similar heat as before, as well, blazed in those stormy Scottish eyes regarding him now in silent horror. Murron squeezed the timber rail of the veranda with one hand while digging the long, finely tapering, beringed fingers of her other hand into her upper arm. Her plump, red lips moved, but she didn't say anything. It was as though she'd suddenly been rendered mute.

There was someone else on the veranda. Garth's gaze flicked over him briefly—his second living son, his youngest—the scrawny weakling named William but known since a small child as Willie. A bookish dandy who suffered from debilitating asthma and a generally weak constitution.

A beautiful child, or so Murron called him. Willie should have been the daughter, for he looked more like a girl, a pretty girl with thick, curly black hair and a pale, fine-featured face with plump pink lips and cobalt eyes. He stood at the rail, beside his mother, whom he hovered around as though for protection from his father and even from life itself, even at the age of nineteen, constantly with a book in his hand. Reading. Forever reading and coughing and taking to bed for days at a time—a generally worthless and embarrassing creature who Garth doubted had ever felt the warmth of a girl's lips.

Garth doubted the boy would have found any pleasure in a girl's lips even if he'd had the opportunity to experience such a sensation. He'd tried to ship him back East to schools, once even to a military academy, but after only a few weeks Willie had always ended up back home, homesick, sickly, and anxious, due to the overly good graces of his fawning mother whom he could not make the break from, nor she from him.

Giving Willie only a passing glance and unconsciously noting his customary aversion to the child, he turned back to Murron, still regarding him with blazing periwinkle eyes, still rendered silent by the explosion of emotion inside of her. He gave his wife a tight, fleeting smile, a weak attempt to reassure her as he tried to do to himself, as well.

Of course, it couldn't be what they both thought it was. There was a simple explanation for Flagg returning Rance's brindle gray. He'd probably gotten into some trouble in town again, and Flagg had had to turn the key on him for a few days. He'd let him out in a couple of days. That's what he was here to reassure Garth, because, of course, Flagg feared no one like he feared Garth Starrett.

Knowing Garth's reputation, everyone in the county did. Except his own wife, of course. And his own oldest son . . .

Trembling a little but trying to feign some nonchalant spring in his step, he started down the wooden steps terracing the hillside below the veranda. He kept a steadying hand on the wrought iron rail paralleling the steps. Flagg and Channing had stopped at the bottom, and they were still talking in low tones as Flagg tied his horse and the brindle gray at one of the tie rails.

Hearing Starrett's clumsy descent, they both turned to look up at him, and he stopped cold in his tracks. He saw it in their eyes.

His son was dead.

And there would be holy hell to pay.

CHAPTER 7

Garth tightened his grip on the wrought iron rail. His entire body had gone cold. As though he were caught out in a midwinter blizzard. He suppressed a shudder as he stared down at the two men and the two horses, including Rance's brindle.

Garth forced himself to continue down the steps. Flagg and Channing stared up at him, neither man saying anything. They knew he knew. They'd seen it in his eyes, in his whole demeanor. Awkwardly, Flagg removed his ragged, funnel-brimmed Stetson and held it against his chest. Channing merely stared up at Garth, his round, beefy face sallow behind his thick walrus mustache.

Garth gained the bottom of the steps. He stepped between the two men, moving like a man in a trance now, and walked over to the brindle. He stared at the blanket-wrapped body. Anguish gripped him. And shock and exasperation. Fury. It was likely too much for his logy heart, which would probably explode from the overwhelming wash of emotion. It was beating fast, too fast, and it was skipping beats.

It felt as though it had come unmoored and was bouncing crazily around in his chest.

He looked at the hands dangling down the side of the horse, the hands already pale and stiffening with death. Rance's hands. Garth didn't remember ever taking particular note of his son's hands, but he recognized them as Rance's, all right. He lifted his quivering hands to a slight gap in the blanket enshrouding his son's blond head. Through the gap he could see the young man's thick blond hair. It was Rance's hair, all right. He'd gotten the thick head of hair from Murron's father, who used to brag that he had the blood of Viking conquerors in his veins. Still, Garth had to be sure.

He widened the gap in the blanket and dropped to a knee to stare at the exposed face. He could see only the side of it, but he could see that both eyes were half-open and opaque with death.

He sucked back a sob, drawing his jaws so taut he thought they would break. He slid his shaking hand to Rance's head, closed his fingers over the side of the young man's face, as though he could somehow return life to it with the warmth of his own flesh.

All was lost. All hope for the continuation of the Garth name was gone. In this one dead young man, all that Garth had fought and nearly died for many times, all that he had built by the sweat of his brow and the blood of the many men who'd helped him fight off the Indians whom he'd seen as no better than coyotes and wolves—all that had been for nothing.

In a flash, he saw it all—the house, the barns, the corrals, the blacksmith shop, the tack shed, the windmill and stock tank—as it would look only a few short years after he, Garth Starrett, had been planted on the hill to the north, where his other two children were buried. Dilapidated ruins quickly being retaken by the range on which another man's cattle grazed.

Even though Rance had turned out bad, and even worse than bad—worthless—Garth had still clung to the hope that when Rance had finished sowing his wild oats, he'd return to the ranch and take over for his father. That he'd marry and raise a family here.

Rance had been Garth's only living son capable of doing just that. He'd been strong and tough and capable. But for some reason, he'd gone bad early on and taken to the outlaw trail.

He'd just been wild and turning his wolf loose. Garth knew that. He understood. Garth himself had nearly done that a few times himself. Instead, however, he'd turned his wolf loose right here on the Three-Bar-Cross, fighting off Indians and other white men who crowded him, trapping and breaking wild horses, building all of this he saw around him now and stocking his range with some of the finest cattle in the world, the seed stock shipped all the way from England.

He'd married a beautiful, well-educated woman from a fine family—a woman who was better than him, if the truth be known—and she'd borne his children.

The Three-Bar-Cross was a product of Garth Starrett's own wild blood. Rance had rebelled against all of this because it was in a boy's nature to rebel against his father, to refuse what his father had built. By doing so, he gained a sense of himself as an individual. But when the boy matured into manhood, that rebelliousness left him and he realized the value in kinship. He saw what really mattered.

And what really mattered for Rance Starrett was family and the Three-Bar-Cross.

Only, now he wouldn't live to realize it.

The ranch would soon be a ruin and Garth Starrett would molder to dust in his grave. It would be as though he'd never lived at all . . . never fought and built and suffered at all.

"Who?" He'd turned to Jonah Flagg standing nearby, holding his hat in his hands, his eyes respectfully lowered.

Flagg looked at him, frowning. So did Channing.

"Who?" Garth asked again, louder, his voice quavering with the rage that threatened to swamp his heart and kill him. "Who . . . killed . . . my . . . son . . . ?"

He'd barely gotten that last word out before a reedy voice said haltingly behind him. "Pa . . . ?"

Garth turned to see Willie standing on the bottom step of the terraced slope. A skinny little freckle-faced thing with those girlish lips and cobalt eyes framed by thick, curly, dark brown hair spilling to nearly his shoulders. Clad in a white silk blouse with puffy sleeves, cut low down his pale, skinny chest. Not something a man would wear. Not a real man.

"Pa?" Willie said again, tears in his eyes. "Come away now, Pa. It'll be all right. I'll take care of you."

Garth sucked a sharp breath through his teeth, feeling a fresh boil of rage inside him. "It will? *You* will?"

Willie stared at him, swallowed. The sadness in his eyes was replaced by apprehension.

"Your brother is dead, Willie."

"Yes, I know, but . . . Pa, Rance . . . he was no good, Pa." Tears spilled out of his eyes and dribbled down his cheeks. "I mean . . . you had to know this was comin' . . . sooner or later . . ."

An even newer, rawer wave of fury blew like a tornado through Garth. He lurched forward, almost stumbling over his own feet, and grabbed the young man's skinny left arm and jerked him forward. "How dare you say one bad word about your brother, you damned Dorothy!"

"Garth!" gasped Murron, standing several steps up the slope, cupping her hands to her mouth.

"You damned *Dorothy!*" Garth swung his open right hand against Willie's left cheek.

Willie screamed and fell backward against the slope.

"Garth!" Murron screeched. "Oh, *Garth!*"

Garth grabbed Willie's arm again and smashed two more loudly smacking blows against the boy's face before Willie could bring his hands up to ward off the attack.

"At least Rance was a man!" Garth bellowed, pummeling the screaming, sobbing boy's head with both his open hands, swinging his arms out broadly, raging, "You're not even *half* a man. You're nothing but a damn *sodomite!* Now I have no son to carry on my name. Only *you*—a cork-headed fool and a wailing sissy, to boot!"

Garth swung his right hand back behind his shoulder but before he could send it smashing against the boy's face again, Murron threw herself into him. Garth had been kneeling, and now his wife's unexpected and surprisingly fierce attack sent him falling backward, Murron on top of him, smacking her open hands against his face and head, driving him back against the ground.

He looked up in shock to see his wife straddling him on her knees, cursing and screaming as she gave him as good as he'd given their son, lashing him with her open hands—fast, powerful, stinging blows to his cheeks and lips and to both temples. He reached up to ward off the attack but he realized with more than a little chagrin that his wife was stronger than he was.

He glanced up past her flailing hands at Jonah Flagg and Milo Channing staring in wide-eyed, hang-jawed fascination at the woman pummeling the older man with unbridled fury, Murron's hair coming free of its bun and spilling down around her shoulders, framing her wild-woman's wide-eyed face.

"Stop!" Garth yelled up at the two men. *"Stop . . . her . . . !"*

The two men glanced at each other. Channing was the first to edge forward and grab one of Murron's arms. It took him several tentative attempts before making more of an effort, and then he grabbed one of her arms and then both of them, pulling her back off her husband.

"Please . . . please, Mrs. Starrett . . . my God . . . you'll *kill* him!"

When he got her sort of half pulled off her husband, she relented. Channing released her, and she lowered her arms. She turned back to Garth, whose face was battered and bleeding, his lips cracked. She spat at him wickedly, distorting her face so that she resembled nothing so much as a witch.

A crazy, beautiful Scottish witch.

She heaved herself to her feet, breathless, her face still red with rage. Rearranging her green velvet skirt and adjusting her wide, black patent belt with its large, brass buckle, she glared at her husband and said, "You lay a hand on him again, I'll kill you."

Starrett just lay there, his head reeling and aching, his wife's shrieks resounding in his ears, staring up at her in shock.

She adjusted the collar of her disheveled white blouse, buttoned to her throat, and turned to Channing. "Please have a couple of your men haul my deceased son into the house. We shall prepare the body for internment." She turned to Willie, who sat against the slope, also staring at her in disbelief, his own lips bleeding and one eye beginning to swell.

She took one of his slender wrists and helped him to his feet. "Come on, son. Let's get your face tended. Then you will assist me and your sister with your brother."

As she helped Willie climb the steps to the house, Channing and Flagg gazed down at Garth. "You, uh . . . you okay, Mr. Starrett?"

"Not sure yet." Garth drew a breath and lifted his hand toward the two men. They helped him to his feet.

When he'd regained a modicum of composure, though his pride was still reeling and humiliation still burned his cheeks, he turned to Flagg. "Not a word of this." He glanced at Channing, as well. "Not a word of any of this to anyone—understand?"

"Oh, of course not! Of course not, Mr. Channing!" assured Flagg.

"Not a word, boss."

"If I ever hear otherwise, I'll have you both flogged."

Flagg swallowed, nodded. "I understand, Mr. Starrett. Not a word. I assure you, sir."

"Sure, sure, boss," Channing said. "I would never say anything. You know that." He scrutinized Starrett. "Are you all right?"

Starrett brushed his fist across his bloody lip. "Shut up, Milo. Shut up about it!"

"You got it, Mr. Starrett."

He drew a calming breath. His former rage returned, making for a caustic brew of fury and humiliation.

"Now, then." He drew another breath, trying to quell that damned crab at work in his chest. He turned squarely to Flagg, and again his eyes blazed with barely bridled rage. "Who killed my son?"

CHAPTER 8

Shotgun Johnny Greenway followed the two-track trail up the top of a pass between high, pine-clad ridges and drew back on Ghost's reins, stopping the horse. Four riders were just then dropping down a hill straight out away from him maybe a hundred yards, and galloping in his direction, lifting a tawny cloud of sunlit dust behind them.

They were well-armed men, guns flashing in the light of the midday sunshine.

Ghost whinnied anxiously and shook his head.

"Easy, fella," Johnny said, keeping a taut hold on the reins. "Easy, now. All is well." He leaned forward to pat the sleek mount's sweat-lathered right wither.

At least, he hoped all was well. He'd been expecting to see riders heading toward him since he'd spied the lookout a half hour ago, glassing him from atop a haystack butte. The sun had reflected off the lenses of the binoculars. Not long after, Johnny had spied more, sharper reflections being sent in the direction of the Three-Bar-Cross headquarters.

The lookout had been sending Morse code signals back to Starrett's compound. The army used the same heliographic signaling method in their war with the Apaches down in Arizona. Johnny knew that Garth Starrett's men communicated in the same fashion, for the Three-Bar-Cross covered a vast territory, and Starrett ruthlessly and shrewdly protected every square mile of his nearly fifty thousand acres. This was not Johnny's first visit to the Starrett ranch. He'd visited a few times, on business, when he'd been a deputy United States marshal and Starrett had been suspected of hanging squatters.

Johnny had arrested several Three-Bar-Cross men who'd actually done the hanging. They were likely still doing hard time in the territorial pen. Starrett himself, however, had never been charged, though Johnny had wanted to charge him. His bosses had refused. Starrett had rarely if ever been charged with anything, though it had been well established that he was a brutish and savage killer.

The problem was, like most rich killers, he had the money to hire the best attorneys. Time and time again, he'd bought his way out of a hang rope.

There was no question that he ordered his men to hang squatters on sight. To not only hang them and their families, no matter how young the child, but to leave the bodies to hang there, to rot or for their bones to be picked clean by birds, as a message to others who might have the same idea as they'd had— to settle on open range that Starrett had unlawfully declared his own.

"Easy now, Johnny," Johnny told himself aloud, watching the riders gallop up the hill toward him, within fifty yards now and closing fast. "You're not here to restart old battles. Besides, you're not a lawman anymore. You're just a lowly gold guard."

The lead rider of the four men drew his horse to a stop roughly thirty feet down the hill before Johnny. The man was Starrett's foreman, Milo Channing— a tall, round-shouldered man in his late forties, going to tallow around his middle and with a thick walrus mustache and wedge of a whiskey-red, pugnacious nose cleaving his face splotched by the sun. Hard eyes regarded Johnny with bald disdain as the three others, flanking Channing, did the same.

Channing's men held rifles across their saddle-bows. The foreman, whose own Winchester rode in a leather scabbard under his right knee, had a big Colt .45 with gutta-percha grips holstered high on his left hip, for the cross-draw.

Channing settled his bulk in his saddle and studied Johnny darkly from beneath the brim of his dark brown slouch hat trimmed with a red hawk's feather poking up from behind the band. He used his gloved hands to indicate an object the size of a grapefruit and said, "You either got cojones this big, or you ain't near as smart as you used to be."

With an easy smile, Johnny said, "Just wanna have a chat with the man, Milo."

"My God, Johnny—you killed the man's son!"

"Nope. I did not."

"Let's not split hairs. If it wasn't for you, the worthless pile of dog dung would still be alive."

"Let's split 'em finer. If he hadn't tried to rob the gold, he'd still be whoopin' and stompin' with his fool tail up."

Channing placed his gloved hand on the handle of his .45. "If I shot you right now and dragged your lifeless carcass back to the ranch, I'd get a big pay bump. He might even build me my own house, stock it with a Mexican hooker, and plant a tree in my front yard. He'd give me a plot in his family cemetery!"

Again, Johnny gave an easy smile. "Don't doubt it a bit. But you're not gonna shoot me."

Channing rose in his saddle and jutted his chin with customary belligerence, his large-pored face swelling and turning deep rose. "Why in the hell ain't I?"

"Because, while you are a snake in the grass, Milo, you are an honorable snake in the grass. Unlike your boss, I might add." Johnny raised both his arms, winglike, to display his upper thighs and hips. "I ain't armed. Don't even have a slingshot in my saddlebags."

"Where's the Twins?"

"All wrapped up cozy-like, layin' on my bed at home."

"What the hell are you up to?"

"Like I said, just wanna have a chat with the man."

"About *what?*" Channing said with a dry, exasperated laugh.

"About peace and love and eternal happiness. About forgiveness. Do you know what the Good Book says about forgiveness, Milo?"

"No, can't say as I do. I just know what Garth Channing says about forgiveness." Channing studied Johnny warily, his thick brows knitting together above the bridge of his thick nose. "I don't get it. Somethin's off here. This ain't like you—ridin' out to powwow with a man whose son you killed. To talk about *burying the hatchet*? You? Why, you ran down and killed all the men who raped and murdered your wife and shotgunned your son!"

"And I'd do it again in a heartbeat. Those men

deserved to die. They were killers. I'm not a killer. I was merely doing my job. Rance Starrett was trying to separate me from gold that did not belong to him, and he ended up crow bait for his trouble. I just want to explain that to his father, express my regrets for his death, offer my condolences, and pass along a small offering of peace to him and the rest of the family, so we can all go about our lives without harassment."

"You mean so you can go about *your* life without harassment."

"Yes."

"What a load of horse dung. You don't one bit regret Rance Starrett's passing!"

"Will you work with me here, Milo?" Johnny said with impatience.

Again, Channing studied Johnny. It was almost as though he hadn't quite understood what he'd said, or that he'd been listening to a madman spew nonsense. "Johnny," he said in disbelief, "you know Garth Starrett. You know how he is."

"Just wanna powwow with the man, Milo. Come on." Johnny leaned impatiently forward in his saddle. "It's hot out here. My nose is peelin'. Lead me in."

Channing blinked, shook his head, and glanced at the other men sitting their mounts behind him. None said a word but only smiled incredulously, maybe a little delightedly. Turning back to Johnny, the foreman said, "All right, I'll lead you in. But first, you lift the flaps of that coat, let me see up under your arms."

Johnny lifted his coat flaps shoulder high.

"Naked as a jaybird," he said.

"I'm gonna come over and look in your saddlebags."

"Be my guest."

Channing rode over, stopped his horse off Ghost's right hip, and opened the flap on the near saddlebag pouch. He leaned out from his horse to peer inside, frowning. He glanced at Johnny, then dipped a hand into the pouch, withdrawing a spray of dark red roses wrapped in paper and bound with string.

He held them up to show Johnny and then the other three riders still sitting their dusty horses on the trail. They all smiled. One snickered.

Johnny grinned, shrugged. "An olive branch."

Channing stuffed the flowers back into the saddlebag pouch then rode around to the other side of Johnny's horse. He opened the flap and peered into the other pouch. Again, he frowned and withdrew something wrapped in burlap.

Again, he looked at Johnny, frowning curiously. Johnny said, "That's a smoked river trout caught and smoked by none other than Stuttering Bob Schwartz on the Avalanche River."

Channing snorted. "Stutterin' Bob, huh?"

"If you haven't had one of Bob's smoked trout, Milo, you haven't really lived."

"Sorta like that mulatto doxie at Miss Kate's place in Winnemucca," said one of the three cowboys sitting their horses on the trail. "They say a man hasn't truly lived till he . . ."

He let his voice trail off under the foreman's scowl, and shrugged. "Just thought I'd mention it," he added, sheepish eyes averted.

Channing shoved the trout back into the saddlebag pouch and said to Johnny, "You sure come out here with your tail between your legs. It ain't like you,

Johnny. Am I correct in sayin' you seem a might . . .
well . . . a might *fearful* these days?"

"You'd be correct in sayin' I'm a might *careful* these
days," Johnny corrected with a crooked smile and
one arched brow. "I've become a more seasoned,
peace-lovin' man, Milo. Go ahead an' take points off,
if you like."

"Okay, peace-lovin' man," Channing said, throwing
an arm out in the direction of the Three-Bar-Cross.
"Let's go powwow with Garth Starrett. It's your funeral. I might even sing for you."

"No, thanks. You don't look like you can hold a
tune."

"I can't."

"See?" Johnny booted Ghost into a trot down off
the top of the hill. "Let's fog a little sage, boys."

"Say, Johnny?" Channing asked.

"Yes?"

"I don't believe I ever seen you without the Twins
before. You miss 'em?"

"I purely do."

"I bet you do!" Channing laughed as he and the
others galloped behind Johnny.

CHAPTER 9

Twenty minutes later, Johnny and his new trail pards rode through the Three-Bar-Cross's wooden portal proudly straddling the two-track trail. Starrett's brand was burned into the crossbeam.

They clomped into the compound that sprawled at the bottom of the hill on which Starrett's large, timber lodge stood proud and tall, a bulky sentinel watching over the beef-peppered wash of tawny hills and bluffs and cedar-clad hills that stretched beyond every horizon and that Garth Starrett had wrestled out of the Paiutes' grip.

Stolen from the Indians, more like. But, then, that was the tale of the entire West. Starrett was no different from a hundred, maybe a thousand, other landowners occupying similar spreads across the frontier. Venal, rapacious men who, by comparison, made the Indians they'd pummeled into submission and saw hazed off to reservations on some of the worst land west of the Mississippi, look like Sunday-morning churchgoers clutching Bibles to their breasts.

No, Starrett was no different from most of the other

western conquerors. No different from the Romans or the Vikings or the Pilgrims who'd booked passage on the *Mayflower*. Such men as they were the way of the world.

The only difference here—at least for Johnny— was that it had been Starrett's son Johnny had hauled back to Hallelujah Junction, belly down across his saddle.

Several horses whinnied greetings from a couple of the stock corrals, stomping around with their tails arched and ears pricked. The men working around the place and taking smoke breaks in the shade under the bunkhouse's brush ramada, all paused in their work or idle conversations to the give their attention to the newcomer on the tall, cream horse.

Two big, bare-chested, bullet-headed fellas— bare-knuckle fighters who likely offered welcome distractions on Saturday nights at the ranch—were taking time to practice their boxing moves in the gap between the bunkhouse and the cookshack. Three others looked on, one offering advice. A shaggy shepherd dog lounged in the shade nearby, tongue drooping over its lower jaw.

Among the ranch hands, there were whites and blacks and even a few half-breeds, Johnny saw. Some Mexicans, too, in straw sombreros and nattily decorated chaparajos. One such willowy, boy-sized Mexican, so brown he was nearly black, was riding a humpbacked bronc in the breaking corral. Even this man paused in his perilous work, drawing back on the bronc's rope reins, to turn a wary look at Johnny from beneath the brim of his palm-leaf sombrero.

One man under the brush ramada had been idly

fingering a guitar's strings, but now he stopped and also turned his head toward Johnny. It was as though they were all suddenly frozen in time, just standing or sitting there, staring toward where the man who'd killed the boss's son had just ridden in under the portal.

Their surprise at seeing him here was almost palpable. Finally, one man turned to another and said something that caused his listener to grin.

Then the others started looking around at one another, as well, also conferring in hushed tones and quiet laughter.

"The fellas are right happy to see you again, John," said Channing as the foreman rode around Johnny to lead the way over to the hill the house sat on, atop a long stretch of hillside terraced with wooden steps.

A couple of the three men remaining behind him chuckled.

Johnny reined up beside Channing at one of the two wrought iron hitchracks that stood at the base of the terraced steps. He swung down, looped his reins over the rack, slipped Ghost's bit, and loosened his saddle straps. He pulled his saddlebags down off the cream's back and draped them over his left shoulder.

A nettling apprehension had followed him out from town, but it had grown until he felt his skin pricking across his shoulder blades. He felt obscenely light without the Twins adorning his thighs.

Channing grinned at him with not-so-vague mockery, reading his mind. He beckoned, said, "Right this way, John," then started up the steps.

Johnny glanced at the other three standing behind him. They grinned, as well, taking unabashed delight in his discomfort and no doubt anticipating with some relish how his meeting with Starrett would go.

Johnny couldn't blame them. The Three-Bar-Cross was a long way from town, so Starrett's men didn't regularly frequent Hallelujah Junction's parlor houses and watering holes. Having spent his teenage years on Joe Greenway's Maggie Creek Ranch, he himself knew the torpor of life on a remote spread. These men no doubt welcomed any kind of diversion. This was sure to be a good one.

Johnny just hoped it wasn't *too* good.

He climbed the steps behind Channing, the other three climbing along behind him, spurs chinging, breaths rasping with their effort. The late-summer sun blazed down, and the air had a piney tang.

The other men had resumed talking and working in the yard below. The clang of a blacksmith's hammer rang in the dry air. The bronc's hooves again thudded around the breaking corral. There were the occasional soft smacks of the bare-knuckle fighters' fists striking home. The guitar player was plucking his strings again, but this time there seemed an ominous pitch to the chords . . .

Johnny followed Channing up the broad veranda's half-logged steps. As he crossed the veranda to the front door, Johnny saw several figures with pale oval faces moving behind the tall, deep-set window on his left. His apprehension weighed heavier.

Here he was, armed with only roses and a smoked trout. He'd clearly lost his mind.

Channing knocked two times on the big door, then stepped back and to one side, making way for Johnny, giving him that smug, mocking grin again.

Hushed voices sounded on the other side of the door—three women, Johnny thought. His heart thudded heavily against the backside of his sternum. It increased its pace when the door suddenly opened, drawing back quickly, and a handsome, dark-haired woman in a black dress with a white collar and sleeve cuffs appeared, smiling broadly, dark blue, severely almond-shaped eyes flashing in the sunlight pushing inside from over Johnny's shoulders.

"Marshal Greenway," intoned Mrs. Starrett. "What a wonderful surprise! How good of you to visit! Come in, come in!"

The woman's reaction to his visit almost literally rocked Johnny back on his heels.

She stepped back into the house, drawing the door even wider and turning slightly to one side. Two others stood to the left of the door. Johnny had been wrong about the three women. There were only two women in sight. The third voice he'd heard must have belonged to the Starrett's youngest boy, whose name, if Johnny remembered correctly, was William. Willie for short.

He was a prissy lad whom no one saw very often and thus had remained a bit of a mystery around the county. The daughter, Bethany, stood a few feet from Willie, nearest the door. She, too, was rarely seen. A figure of mystery. While Willie favored a pretty girl— and a dainty one, at that—Bethany was as plain, dour, expressionless, and downright sloppy as a young woman could be. The plain gray or brown frocks she usually wore—at least on the few times Johnny had seen her—seemed purposely intended to accentuate her lack of visual appeal.

Both she and her brother stared at Johnny in openmouthed shock. Willie was holding a book down by his side, closed around the index finger marking his spot. His delicate face was cut and swollen, and one of his eyes was black. He'd either had one hell of an accident or he'd been in a fight.

Their mother, Murron, was beaming and blushing like a whorehouse madam welcoming the lucky Jake who'd just laid down a royal flush in the nearest gambling parlor.

"Please, please! Come in, come in, Marshal Greenway!"

Both of her children appeared to be as baffled by her behavior as Johnny was. He'd be damned if she didn't actually mean the warm welcome. Of course, she didn't, but she sure as hell was doing a good job of selling it.

Haltingly, removing his hat and holding it over his heart, he stomped the dust off his boots and stepped over the threshold. In the periphery of his vision, he could see Channing and the other three men regarding one another skeptically, as taken aback by the woman's greeting as Johnny was.

"Mrs. Starrett, I'm sure my appearance here comes as a bit of a surprise."

"Surprise? Surprise? Whatever are you talking about, Marshal Greenway?"

"Uh . . . it's just *Mister* Greenway these days, ma'am. I'm no longer a lawman."

"Oh, that's right." She frowned with what appeared to be genuine concern and even sympathy. "I think I heard . . . your family was killed, weren't they?"

"Yes, ma'am."

"And you hunted down and killed the men who killed them. Shotgunned them down, didn't you?"

"Uh . . . well, yes." He glanced quickly at Bethany and Willie still staring at him, aghast at his appearance but also confounded by their mother's reaction to it.

"My Scottish ancestors would applaud your fury," Murron Starrett said. "Blood for blood. I do myself. Sometimes, when a man . . . or a family . . . has been wronged, the only satisfactory remedy is blood."

"Sometimes, ma'am," Johnny said, meeting her gaze with a cold, hard one of his own. "*Sometimes*, in certain situations, that's the only remedy. When you've been wronged."

She held his gaze for one, slow, cold blink of her tempestuous Scottish eyes, then manufactured a smile so broad that it was actually only a caricature of a smile. It was a likeness formed as though in wax by an insanely raging artist. "We had a funeral here yesterday. Buried our son. Our oldest boy—Rance. We have few friends—we are a clannish, reclusive people—but those who did come brought far too much food for my own small family to consume before it spoils. Would you care for a roast beef sandwich? Maybe some crumb cake and a cup of tea?"

"Ah . . . well, no, ma'am. Actually, I, uh . . ." Johnny dipped into a saddlebag pouch and pulled out the roses that were a little ragged from the ride out here but nevertheless in full, bright red flower. "I brought these . . . as a token of my condolences. Also . . ."

He opened the flap of the other pouch and pulled out the burlap sack. "I have this. I know you don't need more food, but it's only proper to bring something to a grieving family. It's a smoked trout. Should keep just fine for a few weeks in your root cellar or keeper shed."

"Oh, he brought flowers!" Murron exclaimed as though in unabashed delight to her stony-faced children, shoving the gifts at each of them and then sandwiching her own face in her beringed, long-fingered hands. "Look, children—he brought smoked trout. How thoughtful, Marsh . . . er, I mean, *Mister* Greenway! Purely, you are so kind to ride all the way out here, bearing gifts. I mean, considering your less-than-friendly past with my husband, and now . . . well, now, with me, too, of course."

Her face stiffened, her death's-head mask of a smile in place despite her glassy eyes. Eyes as cold and dead as any cadaver's. "Which is to be expected, isn't it? Under the circumstances of my son's murder . . . ?"

Again, Johnny returned her gaze with a frank, hard one of his own. He would give her no ground. Her son had not been murdered. He'd been killed while he'd been trying to rob the gold from the Reverend's Temptation. Johnny could understand the woman's grief, but not her fury. Her rage was misdirected.

"Mrs. Starrett, is your husband around? I'd like a word if he's available."

"No tea and peach cobbler?" she said. "No German chocolate cake?"

"No."

The boy, Willie, stepped forward to place a soothing hand on his mother's left arm.

Ignoring him, keeping her bizarre gaze on Johnny, Murron Starrett said, "Simply a cup of coffee? I believe you're no longer drinking the hard stuff, or I'd offer you whiskey or brandy."

"I'd just like to speak with your husband, Mrs. Starrett."

"All right, then. If you must. As you can probably understand, he's still rather grief-stricken. His oldest boy and all. The hopes and dreams for the ranch gone—snuffed out irrevocably when that bullet ripped into Rance's heart."

Behind her, Bethany Starrett gasped and placed a hand over her mouth.

"But it's done now, isn't it?" Mrs. Starrett said. "And now each of us must do what we need to do to go on. To make life bearable for ourselves from here on in."

A faint glaze of tears in her eyes, a faint tremble in her lips, she turned and stretched her arm toward the stairs that split the parlor area from the kitchen area—both vast areas amply but unostentatiously appointed. The long table in the kitchen was covered with cloth-covered pots, pans, and bowls. "So . . . yes, please do go on upstairs. Take the next set of stairs at the end of the second-story hall. My husband's office is on the third floor, at the top of the stairs. You can't miss it. You'll smell his infernal cigar."

"Thank you, ma'am." Johnny nodded to her, stepped past her, and mounted the stairs.

Channing and the other three men came in behind him and followed him up the stairs, their boots on the risers sounding like the thunder of a stampeding herd. Behind Johnny, the other men were silent, as though still stricken by the bizarre display by the grief-crazed woman, as was Johnny himself.

That had not been the reaction he'd expected.

Possibly a door slammed in his face, yes.

Screams and gunfire, yes.

But not what just happened down there.

He continued up the next set of stairs to another timbered door that was open a crack. He knocked on the door and waited, Channing and the other men flanking him, breathing hard from the climb, one nervously clearing his throat.

"Come," came a phlegmy-throated voice on the other side of the door.

Johnny drew a deep breath then shoved the door open. He stepped inside.

Garth Starrett stood in front of a long window in the room's left wall, looking out over his sun-bathed, fawn-colored range to the northeast. He turned his head toward Johnny and dropped the tumbler he'd been holding in his hand.

Chapter 10

Starrett gazed in hang-jawed shock at Johnny, the tumbler lying on the bare wood floor, the whiskey pooling around his deerskin-clad feet. His hands hung straight down at his sides. They trembled violently, as did the man's knees inside his baggy buckskin trousers.

He appeared on the verge of a seizure.

As Channing and the three other hands filed into the office behind Johnny, Johnny said, "Mr. Starrett, I know this is . . ."

He let his voice trail off as Starrett turned full around to face him, eyes blazing. "You . . . you . . ."

He stumbled backward, falling. An armchair was behind him. He tried to reach it but collapsed before he could get himself seated. He hit the floor in front of the chair.

"Oh, fer mercy sakes, Mr. Starrett!" Channing and the other men rushed into the room from behind Johnny.

Starrett and one of the others managed to get Starrett back on his feet and then seated in the brocade-upholstered armchair while the other two stood nearby, staring in shock at their obviously infirm boss. Starrett kept his enraged eyes on Johnny, who stood awkwardly in front of the open doorway, his hat in his hands, empty saddlebags draped over his left shoulder.

Starrett clutched his chest, bunching his soiled undershirt in his fist—he wore only the undershirt and suspenders, with an old quilt draped over his shoulders—and rasped, "Bot . . . *bottle!*"

He waved one shaking hand toward the giant oak desk that sat in the middle of the badly cluttered room whose high walls were adorned with game trophies from every species of beast in the West, as well as maybe fifty or sixty wolf and coyote skins. An amazing array of weaponry was displayed there, as well— old blunderbusses and breechloaders in soot-stained glass cabinets.

The office was a veritable museum displaying the checkered history of a frontier land baron. Not a neat or clean one, surely. The room was filthy, coated in dust and soot from a massive fire-blackened field-stone hearth before which lay several sewn-together wolf skins forming a rug.

Account books were stacked several feet high on the floor against the walls, as were miscellaneous folders and loose papers. There were rolled maps stacked on shelves and filing cabinets; rusty traps, mining equipment, and long-since-time-yellowed ammunition boxes and now-archaic traps and hand tools. On shelves were leather-bound tomes on western ranching, including one whose gilt lettering read: *Economic Aspects of Beef Cattle Raising.*

There were small model clipper ships on display tables, flint Indian knives and arrowheads and feather-trimmed spears lying around as though tossed there by a rambunctious child. What were obviously Indian scalps hung like black ristras from ceiling beams. They added a pungent musk to the pent-up, smoky air of the office. A ratty Indian headdress hung from a large wooden peg in the wall by the door. There were old saddles and Indian blankets and what Johnny assumed were bones dug up from ancient burial mounds residing in open wooden crates stacked against the wall to his right. They were conversational curiosities no doubt displayed during the storied germans, or dances, that had once been held at the Three-Bar-Cross, with guests hailing from all over the world.

The room stank of old leather and sour hides and bones and mouse droppings and sickly sweat and whiskey and, just as Mrs. Starrett had warned, of cigars. One burned in an ashtray on the desk even now. Starrett gestured toward the stogie as one of the men shoved a freshly poured glass of whiskey into his quivering hand.

"The smoke . . . bring me the smoke," he said, and, returning his gaze to Johnny, chugged down half of the whiskey in his glass.

Channing held the ashtray out to the rancher. Starrett took the cigar and drew on it several times, sucking the smoke deep into his lungs and blowing it out his nostrils, as though it were some magic elixir. Placing the cigar back on the tray, he held up his hand, dismissing the stogie, and tipped back the glass, draining it.

Channing set the ashtray back on the desk.

The three other men stood around their seated boss, who sat leaning forward in the chair, still a little breathless, pasty-faced, and glassy-eyed, the empty glass in his hand. Like his son Willie, he appeared to have been in a fight. His lips were cracked and one cheek bruised.

He glared at the tall, dark, hawk-eyed visitor in the black suit and red neckerchief with its two long red tails trailing down his broad chest, over a crisp, recently laundered white cotton shirt and black leather vest. The old man's eyes flicked to Johnny's hips, no doubt surprised to not see the notorious sawed-offs usually housed there, snug in their custom-made holsters.

He glanced at Channing. "He's not armed?"

"No, sir. Rode in without the Twins. I checked him out. He's clean."

"Left a trout and a spray of flowers downstairs," said one of the other men out of the corner of his mouth, sneering at Johnny.

"Roses," added another with a similar look.

Starrett kept his own hard, incriminating gaze on his visitor. His eyes fairly blazed and a rosy flush began to leach up into his craggy, sagging cheeks, battling away some of the sickly pallor stemming from his initial shock at seeing Shotgun Johnny enter his office. He was stoop-shouldered and long-haired and old, sad, sick, and exasperated. In short, he was a drunken mess.

Starrett sucked a sharp breath, hardened his jaws, narrowed his eyes, and said, "Milo, I want you to unsheathe that big Colt of yours and shoot this lying murderin' devil in both knees."

Johnny felt a tingling in his knees.

All four of Garth's men turned to him. Three grinned. Channing frowned, his lower jaw sagging a little in his suety face. He brushed a hand across his big, gray-flecked walrus mustache and glanced from Starrett to Johnny and back again. "Uh . . . say again, Mr. Starrett . . . ?"

"You heard me," Starrett said, flaring his left nostril. "Shoot him. Go ahead. Do it now before the Basque coward turns tail and runs."

Johnny held his ground in front of the closed door, boots spread a little more than shoulder-width apart. He placed his fists on his hips, highlighting the fact he was unarmed. "Don't worry, Mr. Starrett. I'm not going anywhere."

"Do it, Milo." Starrett gritted his teeth. "Shoot the son of Satan!"

The other three men looked at Channing. The foreman appeared stricken. Again, he shuttled his gaze between his boss and Johnny and back to the old man again. "He's unarmed, Mr. Starrett."

"Shoot him in the knees! Both arms!"

"Sir, he's unarmed."

"He killed my son. I want him down on the floor, bleeding and howling. Do it. *Now!*"

Channing studied Johnny. Johnny kept his face hard and expressionless despite the anxiety sparking in his blood. Channing's hands hung straight down at his side. Johnny saw his right index finger twitch. His own gut tightened.

Silence.

The only sounds for nearly fifteen seconds were the piping of the swallows wheeling past the windows and the shrieking of a jay. It was so quiet that Johnny thought he could hear the thudding of Milo Channing's heart.

"No, sir," he said finally, with quiet defiance, keeping

his eyes on Johnny. "I won't do that, Mr. Starrett. I won't shoot an unarmed man."

"Berger!" Starrett said, flaring his nostril again, keeping his glare glued to Johnny.

The tall man standing nearest Starrett's chair stopped smiling. His eyes widened slightly, and he glanced at Channing, who gave his head a very slight shake in the negative.

Berger cleared his throat. "Uh . . . like Milo says, Mr. Star—"

"Phelps!" Starrett barked. "Shoot this son of a low-down, dirty cur! Shoot him now!"

Standing next to Berger, his own eyes wide, Phelps said, "I'd love to, Mr. Starrett. But he ain't armed, sir. That'd be a low-down, dirty—"

"Then fetch me the LeMat from my desk!" shouted Starrett, his entire face red and swollen, his pale blue eyes blazing like exploding stars. He glanced at the third hand, standing near the desk, to Channing's left. "O'Ryan!"

O'Ryan, a young redhead, lurched with a start, his own eyes snapping wide. He turned and started to reach for the old cap-and-ball pistol residing atop a stack of moldering yellow newspapers atop the desk, but stalled the motion when Channing shook his head.

"There's not going to be any shooting here today, Mr. Starrett," he said levelly. "You can fire me if you want, but I'm not going to let you shoot Johnny in cold blood. Now, when he's armed again, that's another matter." He gave Johnny a flinty stare that said he meant it. "But not here, not now. You'll thank me later, Mr. Starrett."

Starrett scowled up at him, lips bunched with fury.

Slowly, he took a deep breath, then, apparently resigned to his defeat, he turned his red-rimmed eyes back to Johnny. His voice was an angry snarl. "Why are you here?"

"I came to explain the situation, Mr. Starrett."

"I know the situation. You murdered my boy."

"I did not murder Rance. He tried to rob the gold I was hauling from the Reverend's Temptation. I intended to bring him in, but one of his men stole up behind me and fired the bullet that killed Rance."

"Tried to *rob* you?" Starrett's face was bunched with total disbelief. "That's a bald-faced lie, an' you know it."

"I'm not the first one he tried to rob, and you know it, Starrett."

"That's *Mister* Starrett!" Channing objected, starting forward.

Starrett threw up a hand, stopping the foreman, and said, "My son had no reason to rob nobody. When he needed money, he came to me. I always gave him whatever amount he asked for. He never asked for that much, because he lived cheap. As parsimonious as I am, Rance was!"

Tears glazed his eyes. Deep lines creased his broad, high forehead, and for a few seconds Johnny thought the man was going to break down in tears. A pathetic-looking old bag of bones and sagging flesh, sitting there in the chair, his gray hair long and grizzled, hanging down past his shoulders, framing his long, craggy face. A ghost's face.

The man was completely in the dark about who his son really was.

"You knew a far different Rance Starrett than the man I knew," Johnny said. "But whatever you believe about your boy, you have to understand that I'm not responsible for his death."

"The hell you're not!" Starrett pounded the arm of his chair. "You didn't like Rance. He got under your skin when you was out here accusin' my men of murder. I remember you two had words. Rance said somethin' about you bein' a lowly Basque, insulted your bloodline, said there was sheep in it, and I remember the look you got. You held a grudge. You prob'ly encountered Rance and his friends in a back-country waterin' hole somewhere, or maybe a parlor house—yes, Rance enjoyed the ladies, just like his pa did at Rance's age—an' you goaded Rance into a fight an' killed him!"

Again, he hammered the arm of his chair, tears shimmering in his eyes, threatening to spill over and wash down his cheeks.

Johnny shook his head in exasperation. "Where in the hell did you get that notion? Did you come up with that one yourself, or did somebody else plant the seed in your head?"

"You watch how you talk to the boss, mister!" Phelps said, thrusting out an arm and admonishing finger at Johnny, closing his other hand over his holstered pistol's handle.

"Did Jonah Flagg tell you that?" Johnny asked the old man, ignoring Phelps.

Starrett glared back at him. Johnny could see the rocks rolling behind the old man's eyes. Sure enough. Flagg had planted the seed. Merely because Flagg was afraid of Garth, as was most everyone in the county and beyond, and there was no love lost between him and Johnny. Flagg had known that Starrett would want an easy answer to his son's death.

That easy answer was Shotgun Johnny murdering Rance in cold blood.

Garth didn't really believe it, though. Johnny saw that in the faint chagrin showing in the man's gaze, the slight tightening of his eye corners, the firm set of his mouth. And in his brooding silence.

Johnny walked slowly forward. Channing and the others closed their hands around their pistol grips but left their guns in their holsters. Johnny stopped in front of Starrett, who leaned his head back to stare up at the six-foot-four, hawk-faced bullion guard.

"Don't believe easy answers," Johnny said. "I'm not the reason Rance is dead."

"I say you are."

"All right." Johnny drew a ragged, fateful breath. "I see I wasted my time riding out here."

"Why did you?" Starrett asked, incredulous. "That ain't like the Shotgun Johnny I remember."

"This one appreciates peace and quiet a little more than the old one did."

"That ain't it." Starrett turned his head slightly to one side, regarding Johnny searchingly. "What is it? What trick you got up your sleeve, Johnny? If you got a hideout on you . . ."

Johnny chuckled. "No hideout, Starrett. Just the truth."

"Well, Johnny, I don't believe you. I think you rode out here to cover a guilty conscience. I think you murdered Rance, all right. And you'll pay for that transgression. You will. And you know you will. You'll pay hard."

"Don't send anyone after me, Starrett. If you do— I don't care who"—he shuttled a fleeting glance at

Channing—"or how many. I'll kill them. And then I'll ride out here and I'll kill you, too."

Starrett's lower jaw dropped and his eyes grew wide and hard in fury once more. "How dare you threaten me in my own house, you blackhearted Basque son of the devil!"

Johnny swung around and headed for the door.

"How dare you!" Starrett fairly shrieked, pounding his chair arms.

Johnny went out and descended the stairs. He heard Channing and the other men following while Starrett continued to bellow and roar like an old, dying lion, lurching up and down in his chair and pounding the arms. Johnny could still hear him ranting and raving as Johnny walked along the second-floor hall, the other four men clomping loudly along behind him.

They didn't say anything. They just followed Johnny down the second set of stairs toward the first floor.

Murron Starrett sat at the long kitchen table to the left of the stairs. Her shapeless daughter, Bethany, stood in front of the range, staring expressionlessly toward Johnny and the hands flanking him. To Johnny's right, in the house's large parlor area, Willie stood before the horsehide sofa he'd been sitting in until a few seconds ago, reading.

The book was in his hand again, index finger marking his place. He stood with his brows furled over his cobalt eyes, his fine-boned, bruised, and battered face framed by a feminine mop of curly, long, dark brown hair. He wore tight black slacks, black boots, and a white silk shirt with a ruffled front, cut deep down his pasty chest. His red, swollen lips were parted as though he was about to say something if only he could find the words.

Had Willie fought with his father? Johnny couldn't imagine it, but then all families were mysteries to outsiders.

Mrs. Starrett held a steaming teacup to her mouth. She lifted her eyes to indicate the ceiling from which Garth Starrett could still be heard, raging like a locked-away madman though his words were severely muffled. They were accompanied by violent thumping sounds, as though he was bouncing his chair on the floor.

Mrs. Starrett arched a brow. "How did it go?"

Johnny didn't answer. He reached for the knob of the main entrance but stopped when she said, scowling her disdain and curiosity, "What on earth were you thinking?"

"I was trying to prevent a war."

"Why?" Her lips widened with an incredulous smile. "That's not who you are."

"Maybe I changed."

"Why?"

Johnny shrugged. "Just getting old and sentimental, I guess."

"I admire you for your bravery, Mr. Greenway. Truly I do." She set her cup down in its saucer. "But there will be a reckoning."

"I know that now," Johnny said with a nod. "I'm sorry. Please remember that I tried to prevent a bloodbath." He glanced at each of her children in turn, then returned his stern gaze to the woman and placed his hat on his head. "Good day, Mrs. Starrett."

She turned her head away quickly.

Johnny went out and descended the veranda steps.

CHAPTER 11

As Johnny walked down the terraced hillside toward his horse, Channing said behind him, "I should've let the old devil drill you one with his old LeMat. Save us trouble later."

"That's not who you are, Milo." Johnny grabbed his reins off the hitchrack and turned to the thickset, walrus-mustached foreman walking toward him, the three other hands in their places behind him. "Why don't you do him a favor and talk him out of it?"

"Of what?" Channing untied his own reins from the other hitchrack. "Of exacting revenge for his son?"

Johnny swung up onto Ghost's back. "Since that's how he sees it, yes."

Channing laughed, hocked raucously, and spat phlegm into the dust by his horse. "He kills men who steal hay from him. He had a whore in Reno killed for giving his best horse-breaker a nasty case of the pony drip. You think he's gonna let you get away with killin' his son? Even if you didn't?" He grinned.

The foreman heaved his middle-aged bulk into his saddle. His three hands had already done likewise. "You see, Johnny, the old man believes what he wants to believe. He don't believe Rance went after your gold because he don't *want* to believe it. He wants to believe you killed him in cold blood because he *wants* to believe it, so he can kill you and make himself feel better about havin' to plant that blond-headed little piece of worthless Starrett dung in the family cemetery the other day, while prissy Willie sang 'The Old Rugged Cross' an' 'Bringin' in the Sheaves.'

"You see, Johnny, the old man don't want to believe Rance went crossways with him a long time ago . . . and amounted to little more than a pile of goat dung . . . because you can imagine how awful it would make him feel to believe that. That his oldest boy, the one he hung so much hope on, wasn't ever gonna take over this ranch and carry on the Starrett name. He's believed all these years, since Rance first started ridin' with curly wolves, that Rance just got off track a ways and someday soon a little nudge of realization would bring him back here. That he'd move into the house with a good strong woman and take over for the old man, and his good strong woman would drop good strong kids left an' right, and all would be well for the next three or four generations at the Three-Bar-Cross."

Channing hocked and spat again, wiped his mouth, and turned again to Johnny, squinting. "When you killed Rance, you showed that lie for what it was—a lie. That lie was pretty much the only thing that's been keepin' the old devil alive. That an' the nitro tablets. And he's gonna kill you for it."

The foreman glanced over his shoulder to gaze up the terraced hill to where Mrs. Starrett and her two children, boy and girl, stood on the veranda, staring darkly down the hill toward Johnny and Channing and the three hands. Keeping his voice low, Channing added, "And if he don't, she will."

"Well, that's too bad."

"No use cryin' over it."

"You tell that to her if he . . . or she . . . sends men after me."

"Oh, he . . . or she . . . will. You can count on that."

"Will you be one, Milo?"

Channing grinned. "If they send me, I will be."

"Why's that? Knowin' what you do . . ."

"Because this is my home. Has been for damn near twenty years." Channing winked and dipped his chin. "I ride for the brand, Johnny. You know that. You get crossways with the Three-Bar-Cross, you get crossways with me. An' you're crossways with me right now."

"All right." Johnny reined Ghost around and started down the rest of the hill toward the main compound and the trail back to Hallelujah Junction.

"I'll see you out," Channing said as he and the other men flanked him on their own mounts.

As Johnny followed the trail down the hill, he saw that the other hands were now no longer going about their business as they had been when he'd first ridden into the yard. They'd gathered near the south end of the bunkhouse, including the two bare-chested men who'd been practicing their boxing moves. All eyes were on Johnny now as he angled across the yard toward where the trail snaked in from the portal, entering the yard between two hitch-and-rail corrals kept in good repair.

The group edged over in Johnny's direction, stepping into his path about a hundred feet ahead of him, their eyes hard, dark, and threatening, more than a few mouths twisted in amusement and mockery.

"Looks like the boys wanna give you a little send-off, John," Channing said behind him, and chuckled.

"Ain't that nice of 'em?" Johnny said.

Approaching the group, Johnny checked Ghost down, and his gut tightened. Nevertheless, he shaped a smile and said, "Hello, there, Tom. Red, Tiny, Mulligan. Is that you, Kinch? Hi-dee, Clell! How you fellas been, anyway? Stayin' out of trouble, are you?"

He knew a good half of the men gathered before him. He knew them either from previous times he'd ridden out here to investigate homesteaders' or prospectors' disappearances or from when he'd hauled them to federal court for other sundry sins carried out away from the Three-Bar-Cross range. That was true for two of the men he saw here, at least. He'd arrested Dave Applewhite and Mix Dundee for selling whiskey on the reservation. If Johnny remembered correctly, both men had gotten eighteen months for their indiscretions. That was a long time in the federal lockup.

They were two of the men smiling darkly at him now.

Sidling up close to Ghost, Applewhite waved. "Hey, Johnny!"

Holding back on the cream's reins, Johnny grinned and said, "Hey, App. How in the hell you doin', anyway, you old sidewinder?"

"Never better, John. Never better. Say, John, would you mind settlin' a bet for me an' the boys?"

"A bet?" Johnny frowned with mock curiosity and scratched the back of his head. "Well, I certainly like to help where and when I can. What kind of a bet are we talkin' about?"

Mix Dundee glanced at one of the big, bullet-headed, bare-chested fighters standing to his right. "Johnny, this is Gunther Langendorf."

Johnny grinned again and pinched his hat brim to the big man. "Pleased to meet you, Gunther. Say, you're a big fella. You must weigh close to three hundred pounds."

"Two-eighty-six, judging by the scale at the feed shop in town!" bellowed another man standing farther back in the crowd, funneling a hand around his mouth.

"Two-eighty-six," Johnny said. "And I bet there's not more than a pound or two of fat in any of that."

"No, sir," said Dave Applewhite, standing on the other side of Dundee from Gunther Langendorf. "All muscle. Same with his cousin Fritz Schneider!" He canted his head toward the other big, bare-chested man standing grinning on his left. "A few pounds lighter, but that means he moves a lot quicker. Do you remember Harry 'the Hammer' Costigan from Reno?"

"Sure do. Used to fight every Saturday night in the main saloon of the Plaza Hotel. Helluva fighter!"

Applewhite said, "Fritz punched him so hard last year that the Hammer is now a babblin' idiot livin' in the Odd Fellows Home of Christian Charity in Winnemucca. Can't even feed hisself and has to go around wearin' rubber pants on account of how he dribbles down his leg!"

"Now, see!" Johnny exclaimed with phony shock. "Happens more often than not to such men. Let that be a lesson to you both—Gunther, Fritz—it's best to quit while you still got your marbles."

"Now, about that bet we need settlin'," Dundee said, grinning from ear to ear. "One of the boys made a bet when he saw you ride into the yard. He bet that you, big man that you are, could not only hold your own against our pal Gunther here, but that you could knock him out in five minutes."

"Oh, I don't know about that," Johnny said, chuckling, sizing up the big man before him.

Langendorf appeared nearly as stout as a good-sized rain barrel, with broad, rounded shoulders, bulging biceps, and two massive pectorals standing out, slablike, from his upper chest. He was mostly pale but lightly tanned from where he'd obviously been working out in the sun, and his chest was lightly carpeted in ginger hair, which also mantled his mouth.

The mustache and body hair was all the hair he had, for his head was as bald as the bullet it was also shaped like. Two small, pinched-up, grinning eyes were set too close against a broad, lumpy nose that had obviously been broken a few times and not set correctly.

It was a tough nose, Johnny could see. It had likely taken some tough fighters to break it. He'd have bet a full month's pay that Gunther Langendorf had broken other men's noses more times than his own had been broken.

The man wore loose buckskin trousers secured to his stout hips by a wide, black leather belt. His legs inside those pants were thick and solid, stout as tree trunks. He'd likely give about as much ground as a full-grown mule that had been fed oats and corn all winter and been harnessed to a stone boat all summer.

"Nah," Johnny decided aloud, chuckling dryly.

"Nah, I don't think so. He's a big man, ole Gunther is, an' he looks kinda mean, too, if you ask me. No offense, Gunther! Nah, nah . . . I think I'll just ride on back to town. By the time I get there, it'll be time for my glass of milk and a nap."

"Oh, come on, Johnny," encouraged Dave Applewhite. "Won't you do us this favor? Just take you five minutes. I'm sure you'll blow ole Gunther's lamp out in no time, settlin' the argument for us boys, an' then you can get back on the trail to town and your glass of milk an' your nap."

He glanced around, and the other men laughed.

Gunther's smile broadened, and he stood with feet widely spread, swinging his arm and smashing his right fist into the palm of his roast-sized left hand with loud, smacking thumps, each one making Johnny's nose ache.

Johnny looked from the grinning Applewhite, Dundee, and Gunther to the three hands standing in front of his horse, one holding Ghost's bridle bit in both his gloved hands as though he had no intention of letting it go.

Johnny drew a deep breath. He'd known he wasn't going to get off the Three-Bar-Cross without a bruise or two. He'd figured there'd be some price to pay. Could be worse, however. He could be having his lifeless carcass tossed out of the back of a buckboard wagon into a deep ravine over which buzzards were eagerly churning.

Of course, not to say that wasn't still going to happen, but . . .

"All right, all right," Johnny said, laughing with feigned joviality. "I reckon life does get a little dull

out here at the Three-Bar-Cross. You prob'ly don't get
visitors very often, and when you do, you wanna have
a little friendly interaction. All right, all right." He
swung down from Ghost's back. "I get it. I reckon the
least I can do for you fellas is settle your bet."

He doffed his hat and hung it on his saddle horn.
"I reckon I got five minutes to spare." He turned,
smiling, to Applewhite, Dundee, and Gunther Langendorf now standing facing him from eight feet away.
The big German had his fists on his hips, the twin
slabs of his impressive chest stuck out toward Johnny,
as though he were a door he was silently daring
Johnny to open.

Johnny said, "I'll settle the bet for you fellas an' be
on the trail back to town an' my glass of milk an' my
nap in three jangles of a doxie's bell."

"Thanks, Johnny," said the grinning Applewhite.
"I had a feelin' you'd be agreeable."

"Yeah—thanks, Johnny," said the grinning Dundee.
"We sure appreciate it."

"Gentlemen, don't mention it."

Dundee hurried up to him. "Here, I'll help with
your coat!"

"Thanks," Johnny said as Dundee peeled his coat
off his shoulders, "I appreciate that, Mix."

"Not a problem, Johnny. Not a problem."

When Johnny had removed his neckerchief, he set
it on the coat which Dundee had folded neatly and
set atop his saddle. Slowly, looking again at his stocky
opponent, Johnny rolled his sleeves up his own long,
heavily muscled arms. Langendorf was dodging and
weaving and shadowboxing a few feet in front of
Johnny. He was roughly Johnny's height, but a good

bit wider and bulkier. He appeared to have been carved out of granite.

Johnny grinned through a wince. The big man looked like nothing so much as a large pile of raw, unadulterated hurt.

Yep, that's what he looked like, all right . . .

CHAPTER 12

"All right, then," Johnny said. "I reckon I can settle you fellas' bet."

He stepped out away from his horse and into the open semicircle of ground the other men and Gunther's cousin Fritz had cleared for the two fighters. The shaggy dog was running among them, barking and wagging his tail, excited by the festival atmosphere that had fallen over the Three-Bar-Cross headquarters. The hands were exchanging money, Applewhite taking the bets while Dundee scribbled the names and amounts in a small notebook.

"I think it's only fair to warn you, Gunther," Johnny said, crouching and raising his fists, pivoting slightly from side to side on his hips, "this ain't my first rodeo."

"No? It's not?" his opponent said in a heavy German brogue. "*Ja*, well, then let's see how you do— huh, Marshal Man?"

"You can call me Johnny, Gunther," Johnny said as he and the big man closed slowly on each other, dodging and weaving, slowly rotating their fists, each fighter looking for first entrance on the other. "I done hung up my badge a few years back."

A fleeting glance in the periphery of his vision told Johnny that some of the hands were passing over pretty-good-sized wads of money to Applewhite. Some of those wads looked like a whole month's wages, in fact. Judging by the calls, most if not all of the men were not betting on how long it would take for Johnny to knock out Gunther Langendorf, but how many minutes Johnny could hold out against the big, bullet-headed German.

Not that Johnny blamed them. Glancing at the big, roastlike fists rotating in the air before him, the size of the German's forearms and almost obscenely bulging biceps, Johnny himself would have bet in the same direction. He'd probably give himself a minute. Possibly two. Three on the outside but only if those fists didn't turn out to pack as much punch as they appeared to.

Yeah, Johnny would probably be upright for a minute and then he'd be on the ground with a broken nose and a few missing teeth.

Oh well. He didn't regret the ride out here. He'd been compelled to do it and now he'd done it, and he was satisfied that he'd tried, anyway. Maybe, in fact, this wouldn't turn out so bad. He wasn't as big or heavy as the German, so maybe he'd be a little quicker on his feet. If he could move fast enough and surprise the German with a few quick, reeling blows, maybe he stood a chance.

Maybe.

Johnny made his move, lunging forward. He swung his left fist to distract the German. When Gunther glanced at the fist coming toward him, Johnny lowered it and swung a right haymaker toward the man's left cheek. This wasn't Gunther's first rodeo, either. Somehow seeing or sensing the ruse, Gunther dropped his own fists and leaned far backward so that Johnny's fist barely grazed the point of the man's spadelike chin.

Wham!—Wham!

Gunther nailed Johnny's face with two quick but thundering jabs that sent Johnny staggering back on his heels. If not for his spurs, he would have taken a seat in the dirt. His mouth felt as though it had been stung by five giant bees. Behind the throbbing, burning pain, he felt the oily wetness of blood bubbling out of the cuts.

Gunther bunched his mustached mouth as he shot toward Johnny like a pale boulder fired out of a giant sling. The man's dark eyes grew as large, round, and as hard as the rest of him. The man buried his fists, one after the other, in Johnny's solar plexus and then, when Johnny bowed down as though to kiss the man's ring, he hammered both fists, one after another, against Johnny's temples.

Johnny flew backward, head reeling, and would have fallen had not several of the other hands caught him and heaved him upright. He stumbled forward, shaking his head to clear the cobwebs, gasping and sucking air back into his battered lungs.

The men around him laughed and yipped. Humiliation burned in him and when he saw the smugly grinning opponent standing before him, slowly swinging his fists in the air before his stout chin, ready to attack once more, the humiliation inside Johnny was edged aside by anger.

By fury.

It burned like a cool blue flame just behind his eyes and behind his heart.

That's what he also had in addition to quickness. He had a temper. The kind of hot-blooded fury that had driven him to hunt down and kill every man responsible for his wife and son's murders. It was that kind of unbridled fury that ran free in him now.

Glancing around at the men laughing at him, some throwing their heads back and roaring in unabashed delight, he regained his wind, and the pain-fog cleared.

He raised his fists again. He returned his grin to his cracked and bleeding lips, not wanting the big German to see how riled he was, wanting it to come as a surprise.

"You okay, Mr. Johnny?" asked the German, grinning, showing several large, square, off-white teeth. He was missing more than a few of them, so it was a gap-toothed grin to rival that of a seven-year-old. "You don't look so good. I hurt you, I think. *Ja!*"

"I think you might have knocked some teeth loose, but I'll be all right. I'm gonna make short work of you now, Gunther. You ready? I'm a-comin'!"

That evoked another roar of unrestrained laughter, the hands slapping one another's backs.

"Look out, Gunther!" shouted Gunther's laughing cousin Fritz. "He's gonna get you now! Maybe you should make it easy on yourself and surrender!" He clapped his big hands together, roaring. "Haw! Haw! Haw!"

Johnny swiped blood from his lower lip with his fist and moved toward Gunther. The man's little, close-set eyes were dancing merrily as he stepped up to Johnny, dodging and weaving.

He threw his left foot forward and brought his

right fist up from his knees, intending to decapitate Johnny. He likely would have if Johnny hadn't ducked. Gunther's fist swung through the air where Johnny's head had just been, making a *whooshing* sound!

Gunther grunted as the force of the swing-and-miss surprised him and momentarily threw him off-balance, sent him stumbling sideways.

Johnny rose from his crouch and jabbed the man once with his left fist, once with his right at the blunt end of his nose. That stunned the big German, who went stumbling backward. Johnny followed him, staying close, relentlessly ramming his left fist against the man's stony jaw, his right against the nose again, his left against the man's right brow.

Gunther stumbled backward, seesawing from side to side and grunting, surprise showing in his eyes, dust rising around his high-topped boots.

Johnny did not relent. He knew that if he gave the big man time to recover, the man's own rage would fuel an offensive Johnny might not have the fuel left to fend off again. He swung with his right, with his left, again with his right, with his left, following the man through the crowd parting for them, working him toward the stock trough at the base of the windmill.

Somehow, the powerful German managed to regain his balance amidst Johnny's onslaught. He ground his boots into the ground beneath him and, deflecting Johnny's blows with his thick arms, leaned forward on his thick waist.

Ah hell, Johnny thought. *Here it comes. I'll be needing those rubber pants soon . . .*

With a raging, elklike bugling roar, Gunther heaved himself forward, leading with his big, rocklike head, bulling into Johnny's chest, slamming his head against Johnny's own head. The man wanted to drive Johnny to the ground and finish him.

Johnny wouldn't have it.

With his own bellowing wail, Johnny ground his own heels into the dirt, stopping himself and the man bulling into him, and slung his fists up from his waist and into the man's bare belly, grinding his knuckles deep into the German's hard midsection. It was like punching slabs of freshly butchered beef.

But it worked.

The German grunted under the onslaught to his belly and chest. He couldn't draw a breath. He lowered his fists and arms to fend off the attack.

As he did, Johnny stepped back and went to work on the man's head again, throwing rights and lefts with almost blinding speed at the man's eyes, temples, cheeks, nose, and lips. He was a veritable windmill, grinding his teeth as he punched . . . and punched . . . and punched, hearing his breaths raking in and out of his lungs, his own groaning wails of rage and bottomless determination.

He didn't realize that he'd worked the man backward again until he saw the black water of the windmill moving up toward him from behind his battered and bloody and now-wailing opponent. He hammered another right cross to Gunther's jaw, hearing the big bone break with an audible *crack!*—seeing it sag loose beneath the upper one. He stepped back as the man, whose broad nose was now turned sideways behind a mask of thick red blood, fell backward over the stone coping ringing the water trough and into the trough itself with a great splash.

The German disappeared beneath the surface of

the churning water for a moment, then, thrashing back to the surface, yelled and coughed and got his feet beneath him. He swung around and flung his arms over the side of the trough and lay there, pressing his bloody face to the top of the stone coping, choking and grunting in beaten, battered exhaustion.

Johnny stumbled backward, his own exhaustion suddenly weighing heavy in him. Blood dripped from his cut knuckles; it was a mix of both his and his opponent's bodily fluids. He set his boots beneath him. His knees buckled and dropped to the ground. He fell forward, on his hands and knees, raking great drafts of air in and out of his lungs.

He saw the ranch hands moving around him on each side. Another man stepped up from behind him and walked around him. It was Fritz. The second big German walked over to peer down at his cousin still slumped over the windmill's stone tank. Fritz spoke in what Johnny assumed was German to his ailing cousin. Gunther grunted out some German of his own, in angry tones.

Staring with no small bit of acrimony in his frosty blue eyes, Fritz turned to Johnny.

Footsteps sounded behind Johnny still down on all fours, trying to regain his wind. He glanced to his left. Applewhite and Dundee walked up beside him. The muttering crowd of incredulous hands moved up behind them.

"Hey, Johnny," Dundee said, planting the toe of his boot against Johnny's side. "Can you settle a bet for us?"

Johnny chuckled in spite of his misery. "Another one?"

"You see," said Applewhite. "We got us a bet goin'—

the fellas an' me. I say you can take ole Fritz in under five minutes, just like you did ole Gunther."

"I say you can't," Dundee said, grinning down at Johnny. "What do you say you give him a go?" He squatted on his haunches beside Johnny. "Please, John?"

Johnny looked up at Fritz.

Fritz, who was a slightly shorter but just as muscle-bound a fellow as his cousin, with even harder, meaner eyes mantled by a severe ridge of a single black brow, grinned down at Johnny. Eagerly, he ground his right fist into his right palm and toed the dirt like a bull.

Johnny gave the brute a weak smile.

Murron Starrett gazed down into the ranch yard from her perch atop the house's front veranda. A grin of rare delight pulled at her mouth corners and made her stormy Scottish eyes glint.

Shotgun Johnny Greenway was getting his hat handed to him down there. So to speak. The big German's fist just then connected with Johnny's left cheek. Johnny went stumbling backward and dropped to one knee. The German closed on him quickly, stout as a lumber dray, and drove his right boot into Johnny's side.

Murron could hear the thud of the kick and the grunt of the man being kicked. Johnny struck the ground and rolled. Several of the other hands grabbed Shotgun Johnny's arms and hauled him to his feet. They shoved him toward the stout German, who went to work on him again, punching his face and his belly.

Johnny tried to fight back. He managed to land a

blow here or there, but he was too weak to put up much of a fight.

When Fritz was finished with him, Gunther, who'd recovered somewhat from the beating Johnny had given him, and hauled himself out of the stock tank, walked over to where Johnny lay in a heap surrounded by Garth's cheering, jeering men. The German spat a gob of blood. He crouched over Johnny, pulled the half-conscious man to his feet, and began beating him savagely.

Murron glanced to her children standing to either side of her—Bethany on her left, Willie on her right. They winced as the smacks of the beating reached their ears from the yard below.

"And that, dear children, is what happens when you cross the Starretts."

A few minutes later, they watched several of the hands drag the half-conscious heap of Shotgun Johnny to his horse. They heaved him onto his saddle. He crouched forward over his horse's pole, barely able to hold on, it appeared. One of the men tied the cream's reins to Johnny's wrists and then to the saddle horn, and led the horse to the edge of the yard.

The man stepped back and triggered a pistol into the air. *Crack!*

Murron smiled again as horse and slouched rider galloped out of the yard, through the portal, and into the rolling country beyond, heading back in the direction of Hallelujah Junction.

"Why, Mother?" Willie asked. "Why . . . why did he . . . take such a chance? He must have known what would happen when he rode out here. To the family of the man he killed . . ."

"Oh yes." Murron nodded as she stared after the horse and slouched rider dwindling into the distance. "Yes, I'm sure he did. It was a chance he was willing to take."

"Why, Mother?" Bethany asked, frowning curiously.

Murron drew a breath, regarding the horse now just before it disappeared around the far side of a haystack butte, its hoof thuds fading quickly. "There can be only one reason for a man like that to endure a beating like that."

Willie shook his head, scowling. "What reason, Mother?"

Murron stretched her arms around her children, drawing them close against her. She smiled thoughtfully, devilishly in the direction of Hallelujah Junction. "Love."

CHAPTER 13

Seated at the kitchen table in the old cabin they shared with Shotgun Johnny, Mean Mike O'Sullivan dealt out a hand of five-card draw to him and his friend and partner, Silent Thursday. Each man studied his cards under the light from the sooty, rusty lantern hanging over the table, from a braided wire wound around a nail in a ceiling beam.

It was a cold, early-autumn, Sierra Nevada mountain night, and they had a fire popping in the potbelly stove. The cabin's liver-colored puss, Louie, was curled up in the elk-horn rocker in the cabin's parlor area, nose to tail, softly purring. The cat, sated on fresh mouse and a bowl of canned milk, was sound asleep and oblivious of the large wildcat head snarling toothily down at him. The puma had been killed long ago by the cabin's previous owner, the now-deceased Bear Musgrave, who had rescued Louie, a stray he'd found in the stable, from the chill winds of a previous winter.

Mean Mike arranged his cards in his bony hands, a grin slowly twisting his thin lips around the corn-husk cigarette clamped between them, in one corner of his knife-slash mouth. He glanced across the table at Silent, who, at nearly seven feet tall and as wide as an ore dray, was customarily as quiet as a church mouse with the preacher on a holy tear.

"You want another one?" Mean Mike asked impatiently.

Silent studied his cards in his large, thick hands, dirt crusted beneath the thick nails. "Nah."

"What, then?"

"Raise." Silent placed his index finger on a quarter by his right forearm, nearly covering the whole coin. He slid the quarter to the middle of the table.

Mean Mike snorted a laugh. "Well, ain't you the confident one? Hah!" He matched the bet and said, "Show."

Both men laid down their cards.

"I got me three of a kind, sonny boy," Mean Mike crowed with a grin, drawing on the quirley and letting the smoke slither out his bladelike nose cleaving his small, long, badly wizened and liver-spotted face sporting a patchy gray beard. "What you got over . . ."

He let his raspy voice trail off as he stared down at the hand Silent had laid down in the middle of the table. Mean Mike's face grew as lumpy as a relief map of Arizona Territory. He studied his customarily silent and stone-faced partner's poker hand, his deep-set eyes glinting his exasperation. "What the hell you packin' there, you son of three-legged snipe? Is that a—?"

"Full house," Silent finished for him, his face implacable. He reached for the quirley resting in the ashtray cut from an airtight tin near his coin sack and narrowed his hazel eyes as he inhaled deeply on the coffin nail, which dripped gray ashes.

Mean Mike leaned forward to more closely scrutinize

Silent's hand. "Full house, my—!" He stopped and fingered Silent's cards, spreading them out so he could more clearly see them.

Sure enough, there were three queens and two kings. Mike scowled angrily at the big man who dwarfed him. Silent sat casually there with his thick arms crossed before him, staring dully down at his cards. "Where in the hell did you get that extry queen?" Mean Mike wanted to know.

Silent only shrugged and reached for the pot.

Mean Mike slapped the big man's paw away and said, "No, no, you don't! I wanna know where you got that extry queen!"

Silent looked incredulously up from beneath his brows at his diminutive former boxing manager. "Huh?"

"Let me see your . . ." Mean Mike grabbed Silent's right hand, pulled it toward him, and raised it a little so he could see up the man's sleeve, along the underside of his wrist. "*Aha!* Just what I suspected!" Mike plucked a card out of the sleeve, beneath Silent's wrist, which was as thick as one of Mean Mike's biceps, if you could call them biceps, and tossed the queen of diamonds onto the table, where it shone glaringly in the guttering, lemon yellow lamplight. "Why, you four-flushin' son of a ten-cent doxie! You're *cheatin'*!"

Silent Thursday, uncommonly expressionless as well as speechless, merely flushed a little with chagrin, pulling his mouth corners down.

"Well, I'll be a boiled skunk!" Mean Mike lurched to his feet and pulled his pepperbox revolver from the holster he wore over his belly. Clicking the stubby weapon's hammer back, he aimed across the table at his mountain-sized partner's big square head capped with tightly curled, ginger-colored hair. "I oughta drill a hole through your thick head for that! That's what would happen if you tried that in Virginia City. Hell, you'd already be dead, and two bouncers—or maybe three or four, in your case—would be draggin' your lifeless side of beef into the street for the stray dogs to fight over! That's what would happen to most men who cheated Mean Mike O'Sullivan *even here!*"

Infuriatingly unresponsive, though Mean Mike had gotten accustomed to his partner's implacable demeanor in the nearly twenty years they'd been together, drifting about the frontier, as unlikely and as odd-looking a pair as you could find anywhere, Silent took another drag off his quirley, picked up the poker deck, and said, "Wanna play again?"

Mean Mike depressed the pepperbox's hammer. "Why not?" he grouched, returning the popper to its holster. "What the hell else we gonna do out here, away from the saloons and sportin' gals?"

He sagged back into his chair, facing Silent, who sat with his back to the cabin's front wall. Mean Mike peered out the window flanking Silent though he couldn't see much in the night-black window except his own ghostly visage. "I just wonder where in hell Johnny is. He don't frequent the saloons an' sportin' girls no more. Not since he stopped drinkin' an' went to work for—"

A horse's whinny cut him off.

"What the hell was that?" Mike said.

"Hoss," said Silent.

"I know it's a hoss, you cork-headed lout!" Mean Mike climbed to his feet and grabbed his Spencer repeating rifle from where it leaned against the front wall, by the door.

He cocked the old rifle, then jerked the door open. He stepped quickly outside and then to the right, putting the wall behind him, so he wouldn't be outlined against the cabin's inner lamplight. "Who is it?" he called, squinting into the night and pressing the Spencer's butt plate to his shoulder. "Who's there? Name yourselves or I'll start sendin' lead—"

Silent stepped out of the cabin, having to duck low to get his head through unscathed, and placed a big ham-sized paw on Mean Mike's rifle, shoving it down. "Johnny."

"Huh?"

Silent stepped off the cabin's small stoop.

Mean Mike squinted into the darkness. Sure enough, Johnny's pale horse, Ghost, stood at the edge of the light shed by the windows. Mean Mike was a little embarrassed that he hadn't seen the horse right away. He'd been too busy expecting pistol or rifle fire.

Force of habit. He and Silent had left many a frontier town and mining camp on the run, men cursing, pistols popping, and dogs barking behind them. When he and Silent had been working every frontier town from Calgary, Alberta, to Mexican Baja, they'd regularly been run out of towns by disgruntled gamblers who'd been fool enough to back their hometown boys instead of Silent. Sometimes those fellas would get liquored up and come after Mean Mike and Silent Thursday, loaded for bear.

Those had been rough-and-tumble times. So much so that Mean Mike was surprised that he and Silent had lived this long, well into their early forties (Silent) and midfifties (Mike). Though they'd both long since thrown in their fighting towels, Mike was still expecting to go out in a hail of hot lead some late night, the owls hooting and the wolves howling dirges for the doomed pair.

Yeah, that's why he hadn't spotted Ghost right off. It certainly wasn't because his eyes were dimming from old age. No, sir. Nothing like that.

Mean Mike lay his Spencer across the porch rails and hurried off the stoop and into the yard, heading for the tall cream in his bandy-legged, shuffling gait. Ghost had a big, dark lump on his back. Either that or Johnny, leaning so far forward that that's what he looked like. Just a big lump sprawled across the saddle.

"Johnny? Johnny-boy? That you?" Mike bellied up to the horse, beside Silent, who stood there silently inspecting the crouched rider. "Good Lord, Johnny! Don't tell me you took to drinkin' again." He turned to Silent. "Is he drunk?"

Silent only shrugged his big shoulders and stared at Johnny.

Mean Mike reached up and grabbed a fistful of Johnny's coat and jerked the man. "Johnny! Say, Johnny! Oh, Lord in heaven, help us all! You're pie-eyed!" Mean Mike fairly sobbed.

Johnny made a low guttural, grumbling sound. He lay with his face buried in Ghost's mane. He bobbed his head a little. It looked like he was maybe trying to lift it but it weighed too much. He tried again, finally got it a few inches off the horse's pole, and turned his head so that his face was pointed toward Mean Mike and Silent Thursday.

When he saw Johnny's face, or what was left of it, Mean Mike recoiled with a gasp. *"Jumpin' Jehoshaphat!"*

"Ooh," Silent said in his soft, toneless voice.

"Johnny . . . oh, Lordy, Johnny—what happened, you poor old lion-tamer? Lordy be, I ain't never seen a face so broken up since Silent cleaned the clock of Red Devine in Bannack, Montana, back in the late sixties!"

"M-Mike . . . ?"

"Yes, Johnny?" Mike couldn't tell if Johnny's eyes were open or closed. That's how swollen they were. In fact, his whole head was swollen up like a pumpkin, and he had blood oozing from cuts inside his cuts! It looked like someone had taken a club and an ax to him, and gave the devil the hindmost! "Yes, Johnny, what is it, you poor old wretched fool? Anything!"

Johnny's cracked and swollen lips moved a little. "C-could y-you h-help me down . . . from my . . . my hoss . . . ?"

Mike leaped with a start. "Oh, of course, Johnny! Sure thing!" He gave Silent a vicious swat, though it was like beating a horse with a feather duster. "Don't just stand there gawkin', you copper-riveted idjit! We gotta get Johnny inside an' then one of us has to fetch the sawbones!"

Almost two weeks later, Sheila galloped her filly along the Paiute River, heading southeast of Hallelujah Junction. Near the sawmill at Canyon Ford, from where she could hear the big steam saws chewing into freshly cut logs and smell the heady resin of green wood, she swung off the main trail. She put the horse onto a narrower, shaggier secondary trail that twisted around and climbed a low, forested ridge and then, twisting some more, traversed a low gap between mountains.

It was Sunday, and the pretty owner of the Bank & Trust was still clad in her Sunday finery—a conservative, dark orange frock with white lace and a thin ribbon tie knotted at her throat. Over the frock she wore a stylish black leather vest. Her hair was gathered into a French braid secured with a decorative gold clip. She'd worn a little straw hat to church, but that was gone now, as it wouldn't have endured the wind nor the jarring of the mountain trial.

Contrasting the tailored frock, her delicate side-button shoes, and the waistcoat, was the ratty and oversized buffalo robe she wore. It had been her father's robe. He'd mostly worn it in the fall and winter for yard and stables chores. When Sheila had gotten home from church an hour earlier, she'd grabbed the robe off the hook by the house's back door and hurried out to the stable flanking her house to saddle the filly.

She was no longer concerned with fashion.

She and the fine horse, bearing some Morgan and Arabian blood, and sporting a silky blond mane and tail, "lit a shuck," in the parlance of the western frontier, out of Hallelujah Junction. Now she crested a low hill and, coming down the other side, rode across a sun-washed clearing surrounded by aspens clad in the glittering golden gowns of full-blown autumn.

She rammed the heels of her shoes into the filly's ribs, and the horse lurched forward into a smooth, ground-eating lope, crossing the two hundred yards of clearing quickly then entering the yard fronting the humble gray cabin. As she did, a wiry little gray-headed and gray-bearded man stepped out of the front door, crouched over the old rifle in his hands.

"Put the rifle down, Mike," Sheila called, reining the filly to a halt near the cabin's stock trough and hitchrack just off the slanting stoop. "It's Sheila Bonner!"

She saw the little man's lower jaw loosen with incredulity as he let the rifle sag in his spindly arms. As he stood gawking toward where Sheila was swinging down from her horse's back, the hulking figure of Silent Thursday ducked out of the cabin behind Mike, towering over the older, smaller man.

She had been so preoccupied with worry that she hadn't noticed the buggy on her left. Outfitted with a single, red plush-covered seat and four high red wheels, the rig was hitched to a tall sorrel. She'd seen the buggy in Hallelujah Junction many times and knew that it belonged to the young woman who worked as an assistant to Dr. Kenneth Albright, the only medico in town—in this part of the county, for that matter. A badly overworked man was Albright, though he'd taken time for church this morning. That was where Sheila had last seen him.

"Oh boy," said Mean Mike. He stood on the stoop, flanked by Silent, who'd closed the cabin door behind them both. Mike wasn't wearing his usual old, ratty bowler hat, and his balding scalp shone through his wavy, silver hair that curled down over his ears to nearly his shoulders.

Sheila walked toward the stoop. "Oh boy, is right."

Mean Mike held his hands up, palms out. "Now . . . now, just hold on, Miss Bonner."

She stopped at the bottom of the three porch steps

and glared up at Mean Mike and his customarily tongue-tied partner, Silent Thursday. "Why wasn't I told about this?"

"Told about what?" Mike said, frowning, doing an awful job of playing dumb.

"You know what!" Sheila stomped her foot in fury. "I learned about it only this morning as I was leaving church. Dr. Albright asked me in passing how Johnny was doing. My response was: 'What on earth do you mean, Doctor? Johnny's been off hunting elk high in the Sierra Nevadas for the past two weeks. My loyal employee Mean Mike O' Sullivan told me that Johnny decided at the last minute he needed some fresh air and room to roam, and off he went.'"

She hardened her gaze at Mean Mike, who withered under the woman's rage. "It turns out I'd been lied to by said *loyal* employees!"

"Ah hell . . . er, I mean *heck* . . . Johnny made me do it. I had no choice in the matter, Miss Bonner. He didn't want you to know."

"Why on earth not?"

"I don't know . . . he just said . . ." Mean Mike glanced up at Silent Thursday towering over him as though for help, then realizing that he would, of course, get no assistance from that quarter, returned his deeply chagrined gaze to the enraged young woman confronting him with her fists on her hips. "He just said something about what you don't know won't hurt you."

"Oh, he did, did he?"

"He didn't want you gettin' your bloomers in— er, I mean, he didn't want you getting' all *upset*, ya see? He didn't want you to fuss over him. Johnny's prideful that way, he is. Notional, too. Them Basque folks are like—"

"What's the real reason, Mike?"

Mike winced, glanced up at the expressionless Silent again, then scowled in frustration at his partner before returning his gaze to Sheila. He glanced behind him as though making sure they were alone out here, then, keeping his voice low, he said, "He's afraid if you're near him, you might get hurt. He didn't say it outright, but I think he thinks what he got out at the Three-Bar-Cross is the first winds before the cyclone. He thinks ole Starrett is gonna send men for him . . . to hurt him real good. Even better than they done week before last." He winced again, wagged his head, and stared at the ground. "Poor ole Johnny."

"You mean he thinks Starrett is going to have him killed."

"I reckon that'd be right, ma'am. Yes." Again, Mike glanced behind him. "I'd appreciate it if you kept that just between you an' me, ma'am."

Hiking her skirt above her ankles, Sheila mounted the porch steps. "Let me see him."

"Best not, ma'am," Mike said, blocking her way at the top of the stoop.

Even on the porch's second step down from the top, Sheila stood taller than Mean Mike. She glared down at the long-faced oldster, two red apples of anger showing in her finely chiseled cheeks. Her eyes glinted with fury. "Out of the way, little man!"

"Johnny's gonna be awful mad!" Mean Mike wheedled.

"Out of the way!"

Sheila shoved Mean Mike aside. She glared up at Silent, who was almost two feet taller than she, but he put up no more resistance than Mike had. The big man grimaced, looked away, and took one step to his left. Sheila walked between the two men, opened the timber door, and walked into the cabin.

Chapter 14

Sheila's eyes went immediately to the bed in the cabin's rear left corner.

She saw Johnny lying there, all but his face buried under several quilts. She couldn't see him well from this angle and distance, but she could see the bright white bandage encircling the top of his head.

She turned to where Doc Albright's pretty, young assistant, Glyneen MacFarland, stood at the dry sink to Sheila's right, on the other side of the small eating table. The blue-eyed blonde, who filled out the plain gingham frock she was wearing annoyingly well, was washing out some rags and utensils in a bucket of hot water.

She was also looking over her shoulder at Sheila, smiling affably.

"Hello, Miss Bonner. I heard you talking outside with Mike." She had a fairly pronounced and fetching Southern accent to go with her comely figure. Sheila had heard she was from somewhere in the Deep South, possibly Georgia, though what had brought the pretty blonde, probably in her early twenties, to Hallelujah Junction, Sheila had no idea.

Sheila stepped forward, cast another glare behind her at Mean Mike, then closed the door. "Yes . . . I came as soon as I spoke with Dr. Albright in town earlier. I had no idea what had happened to John—" She stopped abruptly, her cheeks coloring with a vague embarrassment as she continued with, "To my bullion guard. Naturally I was quite concerned."

Glyneen MacFarland's smile broadened a little with understanding. "Of course." The cast to her sapphire blue eyes told Sheila that she was well aware of the nature of her and Johnny's relationship. That they were more than just employer and employee. They'd tried to be discreet in their associations, but Hallelujah Junction was a small town, and in a small town, gossip was the only thing that spread faster than fire.

Sheila felt a pang of jealousy edge aside her self-consciousness as she studied the young woman before her. She'd never seen Miss MacFarland close up until now, but only from a distance as the comely young woman made her way around town either on foot and carrying her black medical kit, or in her distinctive, red-wheeled buggy with its single, red plush-covered seat. She assisted Dr. Albright by checking on his patients, administering medications, changing bandages, and helping with births.

Sheila knew little about her, only that she lived with her mother in a small cabin at the edge of town, and that her skills were well regarded. Sheila had heard said she'd harbored an interest in medicine since she'd been a little girl and had had to act as nurse to an older brother who'd been badly wounded during the War Between the States.

Sheila had also heard that Miss MacFarland was

nearly as capable as Dr. Albright in many ways outside of surgery. The thick blond hair cascading like golden honey past her shoulders was trimmed with a dark blue ribbon that matched her eyes as well as the print of her dress. Sheila knew from past sightings that she turned many male heads on the streets of Hallelujah Junction.

Despite the annoying jealousy she couldn't help registering on account of the fact that Glyneen had been privy to Johnny's trouble long before Sheila had, Sheila instantly liked Miss MacFarland. There was a definite, earthy sweetness and honesty about her. It went well with her charming accent. Sheila thought it would have been hard for anyone not to have liked her right off. Including Johnny, no doubt . . .

As the young woman's eyes flicked from Sheila to Johnny, a little color touched her plump, heart-shaped face touched with a spray of very faint freckles.

She liked him, too. Of course she did.

An awkward silence had cluttered up the air between them. Quickly, Sheila said, "How is he?"

Drying her hands on a towel, Miss MacFarland regarded Johnny as she said, "He's out of the woods. Dr. Albright thinks he might have had a slight skull fracture. Definitely a severe concussion. He had a bad fever and he was out of his head for several hours after he'd arrived here—tied to his horse, I understand."

"Oh Lord . . ." Sheila was walking slowly toward the bed.

"There were multiple cuts and abrasions, some requiring stitches. He slept for three days straight . . ."

"But he's awake now." It was Johnny's voice. The pinched, raspy sound of the words took Sheila aback.

She saw now as she drew close to the bed that his swollen, blackened eyes were open. The whites of his eyes were nearly entirely red. He had cuts and bruises everywhere, stitches on his lower lip and on both brows. His head resembled a patchwork quilt—one put together by a crude quilter.

"Johnny." Sheila stood over him, her heart aching at the broken sight of him. He looked horrible . . . and miserable. "Oh, Johnny!"

He winced as he pushed himself up a little then settled back against the two pillows behind him.

Sheila sat in the spool-back chair angled beside the bed and which Glyneen MacFarland must have been sitting in a few minutes ago, when she'd been tending him. Sheila leaned forward, wanting to touch him, to put her hands on him, but she felt stiffly self-conscious with the other woman in the room . . .

"Why didn't you let them tell me?" she asked him.

He lifted his chin, stretching his neck and shoulders. "Didn't . . ." He paused, glancing at the doctor's assistant, who was now toweling dry the instruments she'd washed. She faced the table, her back to them, but of course she was within hearing distance. "I didn't wanna bother you. I know you're busy at the bank."

Sheila leaned close to him, placing her hand on his chest, the other on his shoulder. She didn't care who else was in the room with them. She no long cared a wit about who knew about her love for Johnny Greenway, nor about his love for her. He looked terrible, was obviously in terrible pain, and her heart was torn with worry.

"Johnny, I have a right to know! You should've

told me. Oh, Johnny, are you really as miserable as you look?"

"Nah, I'm feelin' better. Doc and Miss MacFarland say I'm well on the mend."

"He is," Miss MacFarland said from the table, smiling reassuringly over her shoulder, blue eyes sparkling. "Like I said, he's out of the woods. Doc said a beating like the one he took would've killed a weaker man. He's lucky he's young and strong, tough as an oak knot. Put up a good fight, judging by the cuts on his knuckles. There'll be a few scars but nothing really . . ."

The girl let her voice trail off when she saw Sheila regarding her over her shoulder, Sheila's features apparently betraying her annoyance. Sheila knew she should not feel annoyed. The girl had helped save Johnny's life, for God's sake. Still, she was peeved, for she sensed Miss MacFarland's attraction to the man she, Sheila, was deeply in love with.

Though Sheila couldn't blame her.

Miss MacFarland looked away, her pale cheeks flushing again.

Sheila turned back to Johnny, frowning. "Dr. Albright said you rode out there. That it happened out there, at Starrett's ranch."

Johnny didn't respond. He stared straight ahead, his expression unreadable.

"Why, Johnny?" Sheila asked. "Why on earth would you ride out to the Three-Bar-Cross after . . . after what happened?"

He gave a halfhearted shrug. "Just wanted to explain myself, the situation."

"You should have known the danger."

"Oh, I knew the danger, all right." Johnny chuckled

then winced as though it hurt his ribs to do so. Sheila saw that his hands were bandaged, as well. Yes, he'd put up a fight, all right . . .

"Then, why? Why, Johnny?"

He turned to her. His gaze held hers. It was hard to read his eyes with all the blood in them. His face was a swollen, discolored mask of misery. "I just did, that's all. Leave here, now, Shei . . . Miss Bonner. I'm tired."

"I'll be going." Miss MacFarland stood by the door. She wore a wool coat, had tied all of her thick blond hair atop her head now, with the ribbon—*why had she let it down in the first place?*—and she held her medical kit in one knit-mittened hand. "I'll be back in a few days, Mr. Greenway." Her eyes flicked to Sheila and acquired a fleeting, sheepish cast. "To check your ribs and head and to change the bandages on your hands. Don't forget to have someone"—her eyes flicked self-consciously to Sheila—"rub the ointment I left into the cuts a couple of times each day. It will help them heal."

She smiled.

"Yes, ma'am, I surely will." Johnny glanced at Sheila then back to Miss MacFarland, and he grinned despite the obvious pain it caused. "I'll be looking forward to your next visit." He winked.

Miss MacFarland flushed brightly, blue eyes sparkling again, and went out.

Johnny glanced at Sheila, then looked away.

"Pretty," Sheila said.

"Enticing accent, too."

She studied him critically. Then she ran her hands through the untrimmed hair at the back of his head and said, "I love you, Johnny. You realize that, don't you?"

"Yeah, well . . . about that . . ."

Sheila removed her hand from his head. "About what?"

Johnny cleared his throat and turned to her, his gaze direct. "Don't you think it's time we stopped foolin' ourselves?"

"What do you mean?"

"You an' me. I mean . . . there's no way."

"What do you mean, 'there's no way'?"

"There's no way you an' me—together—are ever going to amount to anything. I mean, where are we headed? *Marriage?*" Johnny laughed. "Look at me." He spread his bandaged hands and arms to indicate his battered body. "This is my life. You . . . why, you're *civilized*. In a year, maybe two, you're gonna tire of this rowdy minin' camp and head back to where you came from. Well, this is where *I* came from. I ain't goin' anywhere. I'm at home here. Even after havin' the stuffin' stomped out of both ends . . . I'm at home here."

"Are you saying we should just forget about each other?"

"That's exactly what I'm saying, yes."

"No, Johnny." Sheila shook her head. "I won't accept that."

He gazed at her with even more gravity. "You have to. The whole thing's a silly mess. We're playin' a fool's game."

"We don't need to think about the future, Johnny. What we have is right now, and that's enough for me."

Johnny sighed. "You're not hearing me, Sheila.

What I'm saying is—it's over. I've moved on. Look here . . ." He reached under the bed, and his bandaged hand came up clutching a half-empty whiskey bottle. He held it up to show her, grinning.

Sheila's belly tightened.

Johnny pulled the cork out of the bottle with his teeth and spat it onto the quilts. He took a long pull, groaning. When he pulled it down after lowering the level in the bottle considerably, he smacked his lips and ran the back of his hand across his mouth. "Damn, that's good!"

"Don't be ridiculous," Sheila said. "It's for the pain. You must be in horrible agony."

"It *was* for the pain. At first. Now . . . it's because I'll be damned if I haven't reacquired a taste for the stuff. Yeah, I know. I've crawled back into the bottle. And you know what? I don't know if I'm ever gonna crawl out again. What's the point of deprivin' myself? Life's short an' we're dead a long time. And you know what else I don't feel like deprivin' myself of anymore?"

Sheila just stared at him, her own anguish building inside her.

"Other women," Johnny said. It was like a slap across Sheila's face. "Did you see that pretty doctor's assistant? Yeah, you saw her." Johnny was grinning now, jeeringly. "I've taken a shine to her. It's my high-runnin' Basque blood, I reckon. The French an' Spanish in me. Damn hard to stick with just one woman. So . . . I reckon I've sorta moved on . . . Miss Bonner."

Johnny took another deep pull from the bottle. He lowered it, swallowing, and yelled at the door, "Hey, Mean Mike—I'm gonna need more whiskey soon, you old skudder. Fetch me another coupla bottles from town, will ya?"

He turned back to Sheila with his mocking grin, then shrugged. "I suspect I'll be confined to the old mattress sack for a while. Gotta have somethin' to do. I'm gonna lay back an' drink an' wait for that purty li'l blonde's next visit."

Sheila sat back in her chair, her body stiff, rigid. Emotion washed through her, threatening tears. She suppressed the building sobs though her heart was breaking.

She shook her head. "I know you don't mean it. You're trying to keep me away from you, because you think Starrett's going to send more men for you." Now tears washed over her eyes, and she lowered her chin and sobbed. "And you don't want me to get hurt."

"That *was* it," Johnny said. "Gotta admit. But now . . . havin' had time to do some woolgatherin' . . . and drinkin' . . . I've come to realize how silly this whole thing is. How silly we are. Makin' damn fools of ourselves. You know it. Deep down. I know you do. Soon, you're gonna wanna leave here and go back to society. What—you think I'm gonna go with you? Hell, by then, you won't even want me to go with you. You'll want a civilized man. The kind of man you were born for."

He paused. "Look at me."

Sobbing now, she would not, could not, look at his face. His poor, swollen, battered face with his blood red eyes.

With a groan of pain, Johnny reached for her, placed his bandaged hands on her shoulders, and shook her. She gazed up at him, his countenance angry, jaws hard, eyes narrowed. "We're through. Do you understand? We're through. I'm drinkin' again. I've taken a fancy to my nursemaid. As soon as I can, I'll be runnin' off my leash just like I used to. Like when you first saw me passed out on that loafer's bench outside the Silver Slipper. You'd best find another bullion guard right quick . . . before the Reverend's Temptation has enough gold for another run."

Johnny released her. With a wince, he settled his weight against the pillows again. "Now, go on. Get outta here. I got some drinkin' to do."

He picked up the bottle and took another long swallow.

"Okay." Nodding, Sheila rose from the chair. Brushing tears from her cheeks, she made her way to the door.

Maybe he was right, after all. She loved him with all her heart, but maybe he was right. Maybe they were playing a fool's game. She didn't doubt that he loved her. That was why he'd ridden out to the Three-Bar-Cross. To try to get Starrett to call off his wolves.

Still, they were just so different. And he was right. Some day she would leave the mining camp of Hallelujah Junction. There was no way Johnny would go with her. That would be like trying to take a wolf out of the wild and set it down on the streets of Boston or Philadelphia.

She paused by the door, her hand on the knob.

She turned back to him and nodded, his battered image clarifying now through the thinning veil of her tears. "Okay, Johnny. Have it your way."

Johnny just stared off into space. He took another long slug from the bottle.

She opened the door, went out, and pulled the door closed behind her. She winced as the latching bolt clicked home.

When he heard the hooves of her horse retreat into silence, Johnny smashed the bottle against a ceiling support post.

CHAPTER 15

"Trouble!"

Mean Mike had kicked open the cabin door and stepped out onto the stoop where Johnny was sitting on an overturned washtub and leaning back against the cabin's front wall, taking the cool night air and the last sips of his post-supper coffee.

"What're you talkin' about?" Johnny said, scowling at the bandy-legged old-timer who stood atop the porch steps, pumping a cartridge into the action of his old Spencer rifle. "I don't hear a . . ."

He let the words dwindle to silence as, pricking his ears, he picked up the distant thudding of a horse's hooves. His incredulous scowl turned to a look of skeptical surprise. "How in the hell did you hear from clear inside the cabin when I couldn't hear from out here?"

Mike's breath frosted in the cool air around his head. He pointed at his right ear. "Good ears and an uncanny sense for trouble."

"You are trouble, Mike. How do you know you're not sensing yourself?"

Mean Mike kept his gaze on the dark yard surrounding the cabin. "Mock me all you want, you young skudder, but we got a visitor, sure enough."

Johnny leaned forward to slide his twin ten-gauges from the holsters he'd draped over the porch rail. Slowly, he gained his feet. It had been two weeks since Sheila Bonner's visit, and he was feeling a lot better. At least, physically. Judging by his image in the looking glass he'd taken to shaving in again now that most of his cuts and bruises had pretty much healed, he was looking better, too.

Mean Mike turned his head to one side to call softly, raspily into the cabin. "Hey, Silent?"

"What?" It was Silent Thursday's turn to wash the supper dishes, which he was doing now, a hulking figure standing over the wreck pan mounted on the kitchen table, sending up steam around his tall, broad, silhouetted figure.

"Grab your rifle an' get out here, ya big galoot."

"Why?"

Mean Mike gave a caustic snort. "'Cause I said to!"

"All right."

Just when Silent ducked out through the door with his own rifle in his hands, Mean Mike, staring off toward where the trail entered the yard from the meadow, said, "Never mind." He glanced at Johnny standing to his right, both Twins' double sets of hammers rocked back to full cock. "Buggy."

Johnny scowled at the diminutive, gray-headed man again. "Huh?"

But then he heard it, too, the clatter of wagon wheels along the rough, rocky trail. Or buggy wheels, rather. This was a light rig approaching.

Again, Johnny turned to Mean Mike. "How in the hell did you . . ."

He didn't finish, for just then the horse and buggy took shape as they approached the edge of the yard.

They were both inky shadows until they entered the yard, and then the light from the cabin glistened in the eyes of the handsome dun hitched to the light, red-wheeled buggy. The wan yellow glow limned the buggy itself as well as the blond-haired rider sitting in the red, plush-covered single seat.

"Hmmm," Mean Mike said, lowering his rifle and smirking at Johnny. "Your, uh . . . nursemaid's come callin'. Kinda late, you ask me." He glanced at Silent standing behind him, towering over him. "Wouldn't you say?"

"I don't know," was the giant's customarily clipped response. "I got more dishes to scrub." Silent turned and ducked back into the cabin.

"Hmmm," Mean Mike said as Glyneen MacFarland drew the horse to a halt in front of the cabin. He glanced at Johnny. "I reckon I'd best go in and help Silent with the dishes. I know when a buggy has one too many wheels on it."

Chuckling to himself insinuatingly, he spat over the porch rail then turned, ambled back into the cabin, and closed the door.

Johnny off-cocked his shotguns and returned them to their holsters. Miss MacFarland sat on her buggy's red seat, staring at him, head canted slightly to one side. "I hope I'm not interrupting anything, Mr. Greenway."

"Not a thing, Miss MacFarland."

"Good."

"What can I do you for?" Johnny held up his hands, opening and closing them. "I'm pretty much on the mend. You even took the bandages off my hands—remember?"

Miss MacFarland had been back to the cabin one

time since the awkwardness between the three of them together in the cabin—Johnny, Miss MacFarland, and Sheila Bonner. Neither Johnny nor the young woman had mentioned the discomfort of the previous visit, nor Johnny's strange behavior, but it had hung there, a lingering awkwardness between them.

He felt it again now, a warmth touching the nubs of his healing cheeks.

Miss MacFarland said, "Dr. Albright sent me out to check on you one more time. I meant to come earlier but I got caught up at the woodcutters' camp back near the river. One of the men cut a couple of fingers off while sawing firewood."

"Ouch."

"Yeah." Miss MacFarland gave a throaty laugh. "That's what he said . . . in so many words—none of which I would repeat to my mother." Johnny liked the way she said *mother*. It sounded like "muthaww."

"I bet he did."

Johnny moved down off the porch steps and strode up to the side of the buggy. He lifted his hand to the pretty young blond woman standing now in the buggy, holding her black medical kit. She wore a heavy, purple cloak and knit cream mittens. Her honey blond hair, touched by the flickering lamplight from the windows, fetchingly contrasted the darkness of the cloak, as did her porcelain-pale features. Her heart-shaped face was delicate, eyes direct but smiling.

He noted that while she mostly wore her hair up, in a businesslike bun or French braid, as Sheila did during working hours, Miss MacFarland wore her hair down this evening. It flowed down over her shoulders, a pretty blond cascade billowing onto the cloak and caressed lovingly by the slight, cool wind murmuring down the valley from the west.

She looked at the proffered hand. "I don't need help down."

"I'm a gentleman above all things."

She chuckled. "You *must* be feeling better. When I first saw you, you couldn't have lifted a baby from a bassinet." She stepped up to the edge of the buggy, accepted his hand as well as his help down to the ground. Looking up at him, she said, "A couple of weeks ago, that would have stirred up those ribs."

"They're better. I think I'll be able to start chopping wood again soon. You've done a right fine job, Miss MacFarland."

"Let me be the judge of that." She smiled, vaguely coquettish, then lowered her chin, raised her free hand, and waggled her fingers, primly ordering him back onto the stoop. "You first, sir," she said, accentuating her accent.

Johnny climbed the steps and sat back down on the overturned washtub. She sat in the backless chair beside him and set her medical kit at her feet. She sighed as though breathless, braced by the long ride in the cool air. The coolness shone beautifully in her doll-like, heart-shaped face. She tossed her hair back and asked, "Well, then . . . how are you feeling? Overall, I mean."

"Like I said, much better."

She removed her mittens, leaned toward him, and placed her left hand on his cheek, turning his face to hers. She leaned into him, scrutinizing his healing cuts and bruises. "Hmmm. You're right. Healing nicely, I see . . ."

"I can even shave again."

"I can see that. You clean up well, Mr. Greenway."

"After all these visits I think you can call me Johnny, Miss MacFarland."

She narrowed her eyes at him, vaguely chastising. "I don't think so." She scrutinized his right brow, from which she'd removed the stitches during her last visit, then lowered her hand. "Does it hurt anymore when you breathe?"

"Only if I take deep breaths and only on the left side."

"There?" She dug her fingers into that side.

"Ouch!" he laughed. "You got it. Right there, exactly."

She rammed her fingers into him again, a little lower this time. "How 'bout there?"

"Yeah," Johnny cried, recoiling against her assault. "I didn't realize until now, but I'm tender there, too."

"Yes, I think those ribs were the most badly bruised. Doc thought so, too."

He stared at her in exasperation. "Thanks for reminding me."

"Just examining you, Mr. Greenway," she said, a tad of haughtiness tempering her playfulness. "Any more headaches?"

"Just now and then."

"Sharp or dull? Sporadic pains or steady ache?"

"Steady ache. Doesn't usually last long, though."

"Do you need anything for pain?"

"Nah, I don't think so," Johnny said with some chagrin.

Miss MacFarland arched a brow at him. "No whiskey?"

Resting his elbows on his knees, Johnny laced his hands together and studied his boots. "I gave it up as soon as I could manage the pain on my own. Sorta made me sick, truth be known."

"You certainly put on a good show for her, though, didn't you?"

He looked up at her sharply in surprise. "What's that?"

"The way you were swilling the who-hit-John when Miss Bonner was here, I mean. That was a show, wasn't it?"

Johnny was tongue-tied. He just stared back at her, his cheeks more than a little warm now. They were downright enflamed with chagrin.

When he said nothing, Miss MacFarland laid into him again. "Dr. Albright told me you'd had quite the problem at one time with the coffin varnish. I understand it. Several men from my own family back in the hills of Tennessee fell a little too in love with the corn squeezin's. The good doctor said you'd quit because of her—Miss Bonner."

Johnny's tongue was still in a knot. He wasn't sure where the young woman's line of query was leading.

Miss MacFarland shook her head. "Never mind. I have a confession to make, Mr. Greenway. A last examination was, in fact, my idea. Not Dr. Albright's."

"Oh?" The pretty young blonde was certainly surprising him tonight, making him feel about as comfortable as a rabbit at a rattlesnake convention . . . "Well, then . . ."

"I thought you should know that Garth Starrett visited Marshal Flagg in Flagg's office last week. It struck me as odd because, due to his heart condition, Dr. Albright has advised Starrett to stay home. No long horse rides, certainly, and only short buggy rides. He's to keep stress to a minimum."

"But he rode into town, anyway."

"Yes. On horseback. The county prosecutor, Warren Teagarden, and one of the county commissioners met him at Flagg's office. They had a rather prolonged conference."

"Oh . . ."

"Then," Miss MacFarland continued, "several days later, yesterday, in fact, a good dozen of Starrett's men rode into town. They rode out of town with Flagg and returned with old Winky Peters."

"Winky Peters?"

"Yes, an addlepated old . . ."

"Yeah, yeah, I know who Winky is," Johnny said, darkly pondering. "He was injured in a mine cave-in a few years ago. Almost died from lack of oxygen. He's out of his head most of the time. Sells game to the local mining camps and drinks up most of his earnings. Talks a lot but doesn't make a whole lot of sense."

"Flagg put Peters up in the Inter-Mountain Hotel last night."

"No kiddin'? Just like . . ."

"Just like someone important," the young woman finished for him.

"So, what's your take on this curious turn of events, Miss MacFarland?"

She shrugged, smiled self-effacingly. "I'm neither judge nor jury nor executioner, Mr. Greenway. Those are just the facts as I've seen them. I get around town . . . and I notice things. And that's just a series of curiosities I've noticed lately."

She drew a deep breath and rose to her feet. "Just thought you should know. If I were a bettin' gal, which I'm not—my mother and father raised me right and proper, don't' ya know—I'd bet that dark clouds were building on your horizon."

She favored him with a deep, dark glance.

"You might be right," Johnny opined aloud, lightly tapping his fingertips together. "You might be right, at that, Miss MacFarland." He rose from the washtub. "Thanks for letting me know."

Glyneen stood staring up at him, pensively studying him for a time.

"That was a nasty thing to do to both of us, you know," she said, drawing her mouth corners down. "Pitting us against each other like that. I hardly know the woman."

"I know it was a nasty thing to do, Miss MacFarland. I do apologize."

"Don't apologize." She gave a faint, fleeting smile. "If you weren't so doggone handsome, I likely wouldn't have minded."

Johnny blushed.

"Just don't do it again," she warned, but a faint, playful smile remained in her eyes.

She swung around, shook her hair back again, and walked down the porch steps into the yard.

Johnny started down the steps. "Here, let me—"

"No, no, I can manage." Miss MacFarland climbed into the buggy and set her bag on the seat. She sat down beside it and untied the reins from around the brake handle. "Take care of yourself, Mr. Greenway. If Garth Starrett still has it in for you, I don't think you'll get much help from around Hallelujah Junction.

As my father once said, 'When Starrett's mad, the whole county is nervous.'"

"Yeah," Johnny said from the stoop's top step, squeezing a ceiling support post in his right hand. "I know all about Garth Starrett."

She nodded. "Take care."

"Let me saddle my horse," Johnny said. "You shouldn't be out here by yourself this time of the night." He started down off the stoop.

"No, no," she said. "Don't worry about me." She reached over to pat the long, double-barreled shotgun stretched across the seat beside her. "Old Hazel here is all the chaperone I need. I'm a crack shot, too. When times were hard, I filled many a stewpot with squirrel meat." She winked.

Johnny chuckled. "Old Maggie isn't going to save you from trail hazards—rocks an' chuckholes an' such. Perilous trails out here."

"I've been on these trails many times. Often at night. I know them well. I appreciate the offer, but don't you worry about me, Mr. Greenway. I can take care of myself." The girl was pretty but no hothouse flower. She'd come from the oak-studded hills and mossy hollows of the Old South, and she was as independent as they bred them down there.

Johnny smiled, nodded. "All right."

Miss MacFarland gazed at him thoughtfully then pulled her mouth corners down again and sighed. "You sure are a handsome cuss—I'll give you that."

Johnny chuckled with embarrassment. She released the brake and shook the reins against the dun's back and rattled back down the trail.

CHAPTER 16

"Trouble!" Mean Mike rasped, still half-asleep as he sat up on the cot abutting the cabin's rear wall.

"Huh?" Silent Thursday grunted, sprawled belly-down over his own cot across a two-foot gap from Mike. He was too big for the crude, homemade cot, which he'd had to repair and reinforce several times since he and Mike had moved into Bear Musgrave's old cabin with Johnny.

Mean Mike sat up, his thin, grizzled gray hair slithering across his long, craggy face. He raised his black eyeshades—which was really a doxie's black garter belt—and blinked, gazing about the cabin, one hand reaching for the Spencer leaning against the wall beside him.

"Pull your horns in, Mike," Johnny said. "He was sitting at the kitchen table, smoking a cigarette and drinking a cup of coffee. "The only trouble here is me. For now."

Mike had woken when Johnny had risen a half hour earlier, but after peering out from beneath his "eyeshades" to see Johnny dressing and gathering his gear, had lowered the shades over his eyes and fallen back asleep. Now maybe it was the silence or the sense of Johnny's wakeful, watchful presence that had set him off.

Mike propped himself up on his elbows, squinting through the cabin's deep shadows at Johnny. Johnny had his saddlebags and bedroll on the table beside him. He was fully dressed, his black slouch hat on his head, the tails of his red neckerchief dropping down his chest. The Twins were holstered and thonged on his thighs.

"What you doin' up so early?" Mike asked.

"I'm pullin' my picket pin."

"Huh?" Silent grunted, still belly-down, his big face buried in his pillow.

"Go back to sleep, ya big galoot," Mike told him.

Almost instantly, Silent's deep snores resumed, charitably muffled by the pillow.

"Pullin' your picket pin?"

Mike swung his skinny legs off the cot, then rose, sweeping up two thick quilts behind him and wrapping them around his scrawny frame clad in only ragged longhandles through tears in which his bony, white knees shone, and dirty wool socks. He shuffled into the kitchen area, pulled a coffee cup down off a shelf, filled it from the steaming pot on the range, then dragged a chair out from the table, and dropped into it, across from Johnny, with a grunt.

He blew on the hot black liquid, swallowed, then blinked skeptically up at Johnny. His eyes were still rheumy and red from sleep not to mention the whiskey he drank last night before heading home, late, from one of the saloons in which he performed the duties of a gambling lookout. "Pullin' your picket pin? What're you talkin' about, Johnny?"

"Trouble's on the way."

"How do you know?"

"Miss MacFarland."

"Ah, hell." Mean Mike blew on his coffee again, took another pensive sip. "Starrett?"

"Yep."

"When?"

"They might be on the way here right now."

"Don't you worry, Johnny-boy." Mike narrowed a grave look at him, old eyes sparking confidently. "We'll back your play—me an' Silent. They'll be sorry they left their mattress sacks. They'll be howlin' like gut-shot coyotes by the time we're through with them privy rats!"

Johnny shook his head. "No. I'm not gonna involve you an' Silent. When Starrett and Flagg come, they'll have a sizable posse with 'em. Starrett's out for blood. He got a little taste a couple weeks ago and that likely tided him till now. They been up to something sneaky, sounds like. Something that involves the county prosecutor, Warren Teagarden, and Winky Peters. And Flagg, of course. I wouldn't doubt they called in some deputy marshals, to boot."

"Winky Peters is an addlepated old peckerwood!"

"I know."

"An' Flagg's no lawman!" Mike rasped, chuckling derisively. "Anyways, you can't run, Johnny. You're not a runner. Me an' Silent'll face 'em beside you. We'll back you to the grave, sure enough!"

Johnny sipped his coffee, took a drag off his quirley, blew the smoke at the ceiling. "I don't want to get you two killed, and that's what will happen if you help me face them here. I'm gonna lead them up into the high country and kill 'em by ones an' twos.

That's the best way. Here . . ." He looked around at the cluttered, crudely furnished cabin. "They'd just shoot, starve, or burn us out of here."

"We'll go with you, then."

Mike turned in his chair, about to rise, but Johnny said, "Keep your bony ass planted, Mike. This is my problem. I'll take care of it." He gave the older man a hard, pointed stare across the table. "Besides, the lady needs you."

Mike turned his mouth corners down as he studied Johnny through the steam unspooling from their two coffee cups and the smoke from Johnny's cigarette. "She needs you, too, Johnny. The woman's gone for you. Wasn't right how you treated her the other day. I don't know what you did, but when she came out of the cabin, she was bawlin'. Tried to pretend she wasn't, but she was."

"I ended it." Johnny took another pensive drag off the quirley.

"Why?"

"Never mind."

"Oh, I know you ended it. Starrett."

"I ended it, that's all, dammit." Johnny took another deep, frustrated drag off his quirley.

"What if you kill him?" Mike said. "What happens after that?"

"I'll have to leave. Starrett's king of the mountain. There'll be bounties on my head. I'm pullin' out, Mike. For good." At least, if he was still alive to leave the area after his battle with Garth Starrett and Jonah Flagg and likely the small army they'd throw at him. Leastways, he'd kill Starrett even if he died with the effort. Starrett would pay for his sins as well as those of his son.

Regarding Sheila—folks move on. Time heals all wounds. At least some wounds, anyway. A little.

Johnny took one last puff off his quirley then mashed it out in the ashtray.

"You sure about this, Johnny?" Mike asked. "I hate to see you go. You done so much for me an' Silent, gettin' us jobs at the bank, settin' us up out here. I wish there was somethin' we could do for you."

"There's one thing." Johnny tossed back the last of his coffee. "Keep an eye on her for me. A close eye. Make sure she's safe until this matter has been dealt with."

Mean Mike nodded slowly, pooching out his lips thoughtfully. "All right. We'll do that, Johnny. I promise."

"Thanks, Mike." Johnny rose and extended his hand across the table. "Been nice knowin' you, you rancid old bag of contrary bones." He smiled.

"You big handsome galoot," Mike said, grinning sort of cockeyed up at Johnny. "Been nice knowin' you, too. Maybe we'll run into each other again one day, before we're all three kicked out with cold shovels."

"I'd like that."

Johnny pulled his heavy buckskin mackinaw off a wall peg and shrugged into it. He had his pistol, a top-break Schofield, wedged behind his cartridge belt. He backed up the Twins with the hogleg. He grabbed his bedroll and saddlebags off the table, pinched his hat brim to the oldster sitting at the table regarding him sadly, then opened the door and went out.

Johnny stopped on the stoop, staring into the darkness, letting his night vision adjust. It was around four o'clock. He doubted Starrett's posse would make the ride into the mountains until at least false dawn, as the trail was treacherous to men and horses unfamiliar with it. He wasn't sure they'd even come today, but since Starrett's men had been in town yesterday, some kind of action must be imminent.

Whenever they came, he'd be ready for them.

When he spied no movement in the clearing around the cabin and heard nothing except the slight breeze and the occasional night bird, he headed back into the trees flanking the cabin. That's where Bear had built his small stable and corral, concealed from possible stock thieves. Johnny went into the stable, then fetched Ghost from the corral, where he'd been sleeping standing up with Mean Mike and Silent's mounts.

"Sorry to wake you so early, pard," Johnny said, running his hand down the stallion's long, sleek snout. "We got a little sage to fog, I'm afraid. Might be pullin' out for good. Well, no *might*s about it. I reckon you an' me are off to explore another territory. What do you say, boy? It's prob'ly time we did a little sightseein'. To push back the horizon a bit, as ole Joe used to put it."

But about as far as his foster father, old Joe Greenway, ever got from his sprawling Maggie Creek Ranch between Reno and Virginia City was a quick trip to Sacramento or San Francisco with his half-Basque *segundo*, Marcel. They'd visit the Barbary Coast parlor houses and saloons for a rowdy weekend of ribald fun and to drink with their California stockmen pals. Joe, who lost his wife roughly ten years before Johnny had entered his life, had said he knew it was time to

bleed off some sap when his dreams got too "pestered"
for a proper night's rest.

Joe and Marcel had taken Johnny along when
Johnny had turned sixteen, and memories of the trip
still brought a warm flush to Johnny's cheeks and
ears, just thinking of that first time with a French
doxie named Claudette. The talents that "lady" had
exhibited still pestered his own sleep from time to
time . . .

Ghost nuzzled Johnny affectionately and sniffed
his coat pockets for treats. Johnny slipped the mount
a couple of sugar cubes then threw his saddle blanket
and saddle onto the cream's back. Ghost stomped and
switched his tail, whickered a time or two.

The stallion was eager to hit the trail. Johnny
wished he could feel the same enthusiasm. The truth
was, his head was awash with bleak emotions. For one
thing, his heart ached for the woman he loved. For
another, his fury at Garth Starrett was a wild, raging
beast inside him.

There was no good reason for Starrett to harbor a
grudge against Johnny. He'd just been doing his job.
Now, the "incident" on the ranch had been none of
Starrett's doing. That had been Starrett's men. It was
Johnny's own fault for riding out there unarmed,
especially after all of those men's friends he'd sent
up the river, turning large rocks into small rocks for
years at a stretch.

They were just having fun, giving Johnny the reckoning they'd thought he deserved. That came with
the territory. Johnny realized that. He'd always taken
his licks, and he'd taken those though they'd damn
near killed him.

Starrett was another matter. If he really was forming

a catch party for Johnny, a so-called legal one, with the intention of stringing him up because of what had happened to Rance, Garth Starrett was a dead man. And so were as many of Starrett's men as Johnny could take before they rode him down. Which they no doubt would do.

He'd been a fighting man long enough to recognize long odds when they were stacked up before him, and he recognized them now. It was fun to think about the far future and further adventures in some other state or territory, but the truth was that, deep down, Johnny knew he was near the end of the line.

He led Ghost out of the stable and mounted up. He looked around again, listening carefully. The stars were still bright but he could see the first lightening of dawn in the east. Time to move out. He didn't want to involve Mean Mike or Silent Thursday. Neither was a young man anymore, and they wouldn't have a chance against Starrett's men. Besides, they had no dog in the fight beyond their friendship with Johnny. This was his battle. Not theirs.

Besides, Sheila needed them.

He booted Ghost past the cabin and into the clearing beyond it. Soon he was traversing the crease between ridges, where the darkness closed in around him. Then he was back to the Paiute River. He crossed the river and climbed a butte on the far side of the wide, shallow water reflecting the stars' glow.

He tied Ghost in a hollow at the crest of the butte, well hidden from the trail below, then moved back down the butte until he'd found a nest in rocks and brush about three quarters of the way up from the bottom. From here, he had a good view of the trail that led out from Hallelujah Junction, following the gradually meandering course of the river.

He settled in for the wait.

The breeze caressed him with its icy hands, making him shiver. The few remaining leaves on the aspens lining both sides of the river made scratching sounds.

The water chortled quietly over rocks. Somewhere far behind him a rabbit screamed as a hawk or other night bird dropped from the sky for a quick meal before sunrise. The rabbit screamed again . . . and again, its terror stark and vivid, until Johnny winced and just wished the damn hawk would finish the poor thing off. He was in no mood to listen to nature's cold brutality though he knew that brutality all too well.

He hunkered down in his chill nest and watched the stars fade. The sky pearled. When the first lemon rays of the sun touched the top of the butte above him, he heard the faint rataplan of riders.

He gave a grim smile and said, "Right on time."

He unsheathed the Twins, held one in each hand, caressing the eyelash triggers with his index fingers, the hammers with his thumbs.

The thuds grew louder until the men appeared, coming around a bend in the trail on the far side of the river—two riders, then three and four, then four and five . . . until the whole group riding stirrup to stirrup and tail to tail was laid out below Johnny and on the opposite side of the river and the nearly bare aspens lining it.

A hasty count told him there were nearly twenty men down there. Two of Starrett's men rode point. Garth Starrett himself and Jonah Flagg were the second two riders. The rest of the men were from the Three-Bar-Cross . . .

No.

Just then Johnny saw something flash on a coat lapel. A badge. He scrutinized the man wearing the badge—a chunky, dark-haired gent wearing a Boss of the Plains cream hat and a cinnamon bear fur coat, a ribbon tie whipping in the wind around his neck. He rode high in the saddle, leaning forward, holding his reins in one hand up high against his chest. His other gloved hand was draped over the ivory-gripped Colt Lightning that Johnny remembered he carried, identical to the hideout he carried in a holster strapped to the small of his back.

That would be Jack Whaley, the deputy U.S. marshal who had jurisdiction over this neck of eastern California and western Nevada. Johnny had worked with the man on several occasions and hadn't liked him. He was a blustering lout. Whaley had always been in the pocket of the highest bidder, which was usually a wealthy rancher. Obviously, Starrett had called him in to give his charade at least the appearance of legitimacy.

Riding beside Whaley, on his far side from Johnny, was another deputy U.S. marshal—Beech Skinner. The lean gent with a red, dragoon-style mustache in stark contrast to his round, pale face rode with one hand holding his crisp gray bowler hat on his head. He wore a heavy black wool dress coat with a mink fur collar. A stag-butted pistol bristled on his right hip, in a shiny black leather holster, a flap of the coat drawn up behind the pistol's grips, making an easy draw when the time came.

Johnny grinned, chuckled. "Two federals straight up from Carson City. Now, that's about as official as a vigilante committee is gonna get!"

He rose from his nest, raised the Twins high in the air above his head, and triggered a wad skyward. As the rocketing blast filled the canyon below, echoing off the ridges on both sides of the stream, he triggered the second Twin, adding another crashing report to the heels of the first.

The posse riders, directly across the stream from Johnny now, all hauled back on their horse's reins, bringing the mounts to skidding halts. They reached for pistols or rifles and looked around wildly, trying to follow the echoing reports to their source.

"There!" one of the riders said, pointing with his rifle.

Johnny grinned. When he had the attention of all of his pursuers, he turned full around, giving his back to the posse. He unbuckled his cartridge belt, lowered his pants, and bent forward.

CHAPTER 17

"Sheila, you haven't eaten a thing on your plate!" exclaimed Verna Godfrey. "What's the matter, my dear? Are you sick?"

The stout woman in a plain gingham dress, her liberally gray-streaked brown hair pulled into its customary bun, had just entered the kitchen from outside, breathless from fetching a pail of split firewood from the woodshed in the house's backyard. A gust of wind blew dead leaves into the kitchen around Verna's stout ankles, and she hurried to close the door, chuffing her disdain at the mess. As she passed the table, holding the large wooden pail by its handle with both of her plump, pale hands, she cast Sheila a curious look.

"Your color looks all right. Do you feel feverish?" she asked, setting the pail down near the black Hartford range.

Mrs. Godfrey had come with the house, so to speak. She'd been Sheila's father's housekeeper for several years, and Sheila had kept her on after her father had died over a year ago, to cook and clean and generally manage the house, which, because of her work schedule, Sheila had little time for.

She was glad to have the middle-aged woman—who lived just down the street and came over every morning at six o'clock sharp and left every afternoon at three o'clock just as sharp—working for her. Verna was a workhorse who kept the house spotless and was a good cook, besides. There were some mornings, however, when Sheila would have preferred to have the house to herself.

This was one of those mornings.

She hadn't realized she'd taken only a small bite or two of her fried eggs and none of her ham or toast, which Verna had set on the table precisely at seven o'clock, as she did every morning. Poking at a yolk with her fork, Sheila said, "I feel fine. Just not very hungry this morning, is all. I'm sorry, Verna. I think I'll just finish my coffee and head to work. I have a full schedule today, as usual."

She set her fork down and lifted her china coffee cup to her lips. Before she could take a sip, Verna moved quickly around behind her—Sheila was always surprised at how fast Verna could move, given her large size—and clamped her hand to Sheila's forehead. "Hmmm . . . no, you don't *feel* warm."

"I'm fine, Verna. Honest, I am."

Sheila sipped her coffee. Verna moved around to the other side of the table, pulled out a chair, and sank into it. She leaned forward, resting her heavy bosoms on the oilcloth, and reached across the table to take Sheila's left hand in both of her own.

She squeezed and patted the hand, giving a sympathetic smile. "It's your young man, isn't it?"

Sheila's eyes widened in surprise.

Verna's smile turned a tad shrewd, her soft blue eyes glinting in the light from the lamp hanging over the table. The sun had not yet found the deep valley in which Hallelujah Junction resided. At this time of the year, it wouldn't for another half hour. "You can't hide much from Verna Godfrey. Not that I'm a snoop or a gossip. No, sir—I can't stand the sort. At the first blab of gossip I hear in the grocery store or the post office, I turn around and close my ears!"

Sheila thought she did a serviceable job at not snorting a laugh at the obvious fib.

"I have, however," Verna continued, keeping her voice low, as though someone might be listening from another room, "recognized the signs of a man having been here a few times over the past couple of months."

Sheila's cheeks warmed. She hadn't gone out of her way to keep anything of her intimate life scoured from her house. She hadn't flaunted it, however, either. She was a single young woman, and her entertaining a man here in the house without a chaperone was, according to the rules of polite society, an indulgence that would get most women shunned.

Not the men, of course. Only the women.

But Sheila did not kowtow to society's double standards for women. At least, not here in her own house. This was her home. She would do what she wanted here, and if that meant entertaining a man she wasn't married to, she would do just that. And she had. And she didn't feel one bit guilty.

Well, maybe a little, she thought now, sitting across the table from her middle-aged and traditional housekeeper, who quickly added, "I am not judging you, my dear. Judge not lest thee be judged!" Her smile grew a little crooked, and a naughty glint entered her gaze as she added, "A handsome young devil like that young man of yours, so tall and dark, with those brooding hawk's eyes of his, would make me keep a light burning in my own window after dark!"

Sheila felt her lower jaw drop. "You know about John . . . I mean, Mr. Greenway?" she cried.

Verna gave an ironic chuff. "I know all about Johnny Greenway! Now, I'm no gossip, mind you. Certainly not! How you or anyone else chooses to live your life is none of my business. That said, I've happened to look out my window a time or two, early in the morning—just by chance, mind you!—and seen your Mr. Greenway walking down the street from the direction of your house." Verna sat back in her chair and said beside the hand she raised to her mouth, "A definite spring in his step, too, I couldn't help noticing!"

She winked, slapped the table, and sent a laugh booming toward the ceiling.

Sheila's flush grew redder, burned even hotter. She didn't know why she was so surprised that Verna knew. She and Johnny had had more than a working relationship for some time, and there was no way they could have kept it a secret. Not in a small town like Hallelujah Junction. Especially when Sheila had insisted they take no great pains to conceal it. Her pride as well as her innate stubbornness and rebelliousness had prevented her from doing so. It had even caused her to insist that when Johnny left her house he do it by the front, as opposed to the back, door, even though most times he'd left while it was still dark outside.

Oh well. It was over now. She needn't worry about being tarred and feathered any longer.

"Oh dear!" Verna exclaimed, reaching across the table again to take Sheila's hand in both of hers, squeezing. "I'm sorry . . . I shouldn't have . . . oh, please don't cry, honey!"

"No!" Sheila pulled her hand out of Verna's clutch and wiped away the two tears rolling down her cheeks, one beneath each eye. "I'm not crying. I'm, uh . . . I'm just . . ." Embarrassment now mixed with her shame. Here's the tough lady banker crying at her kitchen table over a man!

"What happened?" Verna's voice was gentle now, deeply sympathetic, her head canted slightly to one side. "You can tell me, dear."

"It's just that . . . well . . . it's over. That's all there is to it." Sheila pinched away another tear and placed her hands flat against the table, squaring her shoulders and drawing a deep, calming breath. "You're right, Verna. There was something between us. Emphasis on the *was*. Apparently, I didn't understand the depth . . . or the shallowness . . . of Shotgun Johnny's feelings."

"A wild one, eh?"

"You could say that, yes."

"Oh, that's been well known for years in these parts. My husband, Gordy, and I came here when Hallelujah Junction was only four shacks along the river. Ours became the fifth! We couldn't have children, Gordy and I, so we could afford to get caught up in the gold fever. Anyway . . . Shotgun Johnny Greenway was the U.S. marshal in these parts back then. He wore those two sawed-off double-bores on his thighs, and he cleaned up this neck of the mountains right well, he did! Claim jumpers and rustlers didn't stand a chance against him."

Verna gave an insinuating yet sympathetic smile. "And neither did the ladies, hah!" She shook her head in disgust.

"Yes, even after he was married . . ." Sheila immediately regretted saying it. Not that Johnny's betrayal of his wife was a secret, but it was a burden of shame he carried heavily on his shoulders. That betrayal had been what he and his wife, Lisa, had been arguing about the night the men had broken into their house in Carson City and murdered Lisa and their son, David.

Sheila was deeply ashamed of herself for bringing it up. Johnny might not have been what she'd thought he was, but he didn't deserve her dragging his name through the mud. Enough people had already done that.

"Heard about that, did you?" Verna said. "He's a wild one, that Johnny Greenway. Raised in the mountains by Basques then taken in by old Joe Greenway when his family was murdered. He didn't have a chance, with a history like that. And then living with a wild old codger like Joe and his just-as-wild Basque *segundo*, Marcel." Verna paused. "I suppose, though, given how he was raised, he turned out about as good as could be expected. I mean, at least he's not in prison though some say he should be. You know—for hunting down and killing the men who—"

She stopped when Sheila slid her chair back quickly and rose. "If you'll excuse me, Verna. I'm gonna head off to the bank, get a jump on the day."

"I'm just saying, Sheila, that—"

"You're just saying that, given Johnny's history, I should have known what I was getting myself into. Yes, you're right. And I'm fine, Verna. Really. My pride is a little sore, but I'll get over it." Sheila walked around the table and placed a hand on the woman's thick, fleshy shoulder, gave it an affectionate squeeze. "I do appreciate your concern. But I'm fine."

"No, you're not fine. You were in love with him, and now, for whatever reason, the cad has hurt you." It was Verna's turn to cloud up and begin to rain, as Johnny would have put it. "And I just feel so bad for you, dear. You, of all people—such a smart and beautiful young woman—deserve such great happiness. You deserve a good and kind man, not some wild man of the mountains who'll break your heart as quick as a peg pony can turn on a dime!"

Sheila sniffed back her own tears. "Thank you, Verna. But I don't need a man to make me happy. My work fulfills me better than any man ever could. And, speaking of work . . ." She shrugged into her wool coat and grabbed her leather satchel off a chair. "I need to get over to the bank."

"I'll have a roast in the oven for you, with plenty of potatoes, onions, and carrots." Verna smiled through the sheen of tears in her eyes. "Just how you like it!"

"Thank you, Verna." Sheila kissed the older woman's temple. "What would I ever do without you?"

"Ohh!" Verna said with her customarily scolding self-deprecation.

The satchel clamped under her arm, Sheila headed out the back door, taking a deep, bracing breath of the chill morning air. The sun was just then poking the top of its lemon head above the dark, sawtooth ridges to the east. Birds were piping as though they hadn't a care in the world, and the rings of a blacksmith hammer sounded cleanly on the cold, dry mountain air.

Sheila followed the stone path up the side of the house to the front yard in which her father had planted several trees and flowers that Verna still immaculately tended, just as she'd tended them when Sam Greenway had been alive. Sheila smiled at her father's love of flora as well as the sense of adventure that had lured him out here to this wild place in the years after Sheila's mother had passed.

As she moved through the gate in the picket fence and walked out into the dusty street that was really still more of a trail than a bona fide street, she wondered at her own fate—having followed her father out here from the myriad civilized comforts she'd known back home in Philadelphia. She'd come when the thefts of his gold, instigated by none other than his business partner and the bank's vice-president, George Poindexter, in cahoots with a savage gang of thieving killers led by Harry Seville and Louis Raised-By-Wolves, had so stressed him that he'd suffered a heartstroke.

To this crazy, wild mountain boomtown, clear across the continent Sheila had come . . . and fallen under the spell of the man she'd hired as her bullion guard, Shotgun Johnny Greenway . . .

Just the silent mention of his name caused a raptor's bristling claw to grab her heart and squeeze. Oh God—she really did love him, didn't she? She almost laughed at the notion. They were so different. Her, a city-bred and educated young woman. He . . . well, Verna had characterized him best.

A wild man of the mountains.

It simply wasn't meant to be. Johnny had been right about that. She would one day leave Hallelujah Junction. Not anytime soon, but one day she would have to answer the siren call of civilization and return to the East. She couldn't imagine living the entire rest of her life here in these rugged mountains, with these rugged people who ordered beer by the pail and triggered pistols off inside opera houses to show their disdain or appreciation, whichever the case may be, for a performance. Where would her eventual leaving have left him and any children they might have had, had it worked out between them and they'd . . . they'd . . .

Now she did laugh. *Had she really entertained the foolish notion that they would have one day been married?*

"Oh my God, Sheila," she told herself, wonderingly, scoldingly, "you really did let that wild man of the mountains get under your skin, didn't you?" *Well, you'd best clear your head. Forget about him. He'd been right. You couldn't be together. Now he was in the bottle, he'd set his hat for the doctor's pretty blond assistant, and you have to start looking for another bullion guard before the mine superintendent from the Reverend's Temptation sends word down the mountains that he has enough bullion for another run . . .*

Sheila turned her thoughts to that practical matter as she turned the corner onto Paiute Street and headed west along the boardwalks fronting the many business establishments, giving a wide berth to the dead game animals hanging out in front of Murphy's Grocery Store and which Cullen Murphy was just then butchering for his shop, tossing scraps to his two beastly slathering curs. He greeted Sheila in passing, pinching the brim of his bowler hat with a bloody hand, and Sheila smiled and nodded in turn.

She'd taken two more steps behind the two deer and one elk hanging obscenely from their metal tripods, when she stopped suddenly, dead in her tracks. She was on the boardwalk fronting a barber shop, and now she reached out and wrapped her hand around the unpeeled pine pole that acted as an awning support post, using the post to partially conceal herself as well as to steady herself.

A man had just entered Hallelujah Junction from the western trail, moving toward her from a block away and on the opposite side of the street. There was quite a bit of horseback and light wagon traffic on Paiute Street at this early hour, around seven-thirty, but this man did not yield to any of it. He rode his tall, black horse straight down the street, as though on a beeline, swerving for no one but letting everyone else give the street to him.

He was an impressive, formidable figure, this tall, dark rider on an equally impressive horse. The black— a stallion, Sheila thought—owned the high, proudly arched neck and tail of a purebred Arabian. The regal beast high-stepped along the street as though at the head of a Spanish military parade, the straight-backed, broad-shouldered rider lightly holding the reins in his black-gloved hands.

In fact, he was nearly entirely dressed in black. He wore a high-crowned black Stetson and the coat of a black wolf with only a little charcoal gray showing as the wind ruffled the fur. He wore Spanish-cut, black trousers stuffed into high-topped, high-heeled, silver-tipped boots with large, silver Texas spurs.

His face was long and pale. It could have been chipped out of limestone and set with two deep, coal black eyes on either side of a long, pale, oddly feminine but unforgiving nose. A thick, black mustache mantled his mouth, dropping around both sides to the bottom of his lower jaw.

Sheila could see the tip of a black holster, thonged on his left thigh, poking out from beneath his coat. Something told her he would likely have another, matching pistol holstered on his other thigh. A walnut-stocked rifle with a gaudy silver butt plate jutted proudly up from a black, hand-tooled leather scabbard strapped to his horse's left side.

A distinctive man, if Sheila had ever seen one. Having seen this one, her breath grew shallow and a cold hand of apprehension spread its fingers across the small of her back, chilling her to the bone. Even from across the street and with several wagons and horseback riders and pedestrians moving between them, she could sense the raw evil of the man.

It was like the fetid stench from the bowels of a deep cave filled with bats.

Others seemed to have noticed, as well. More than a few heads of men on the street had turned toward the black-clad rider, regarding him skeptically, awfully, some elbowing others to direct their attention to the straight-backed, coal-eyed stranger who'd just ridden into town—a dark wind rife with the fetor of hell's bowels.

CHAPTER 18

As Sheila watched, the stranger in the black wolf coat pulled up in front of the Silver Slipper Saloon nearly directly across the street from the bank, a half a block ahead of her now, on the street's opposite side. He swung down from his saddle, his movements as smooth as a cat's—he reminded her in size and litheness of Johnny—and turned toward her to look around the street. She was about to pull her face behind the support post but his gaze landed on her before she could.

He looked away . . .

Turned back to her.

Her breath caught in her throat as his gaze held on her. His lips widened in a smile, making his mustache rise. His long, black eyes rose up at the corners, as well. Those were another thing that was catlike about him. His eyes.

Slowly, he raised his right, black-gloved hand and pinched the brim of his black Stetson, gave his chin a cordial nod. His eyes flicked up and down as he stared at her, and she knew he was undressing her. She knew that look, had seen it a million times before,

and there was no way such a man was not doing what
she knew he was doing now.

Some men tried for more subtlety. Not this stranger.
In fact, he seemed to want to make it as obvious as
possible—assaulting her with his gaze.

Pure, unadulterated evil.

She'd seen that menacing visage before. Not in the
flesh. On a wall.

Which wall? Where?

Then she remembered: the post office.

He stood there as though reading the anxiety,
the dread he'd evoked inside her. He gave another
slow nod, as though in parting, then slowly turned
away. He looped his reins over the hitchrack fronting
the saloon, mounted the steps, again moving smoothly
with little or no hitch in his movements, no awkwardness at all. He not so much pushed as slithered through
the Silver Slipper's batwings.

The louvered doors rattled back into place behind
him, and he was gone.

The chill he'd stirred in Sheila remained.

She wheeled and retraced her steps back to Third
Avenue. She crossed the street and continued one
more block to the post office. The Hallelujah Junction postmaster said something as Sheila entered—
probably a greeting—but Sheila ignored it, for she
was barely listening to anything except the voices
of alarm shouting inside her head. She strode over
to the bulletin board covered in several layers of
wanted circulars that came weekly in the mail or via
stagecoach.

Sheila picked up the bank's as well as her own mail
after lunch every day, and she had the peculiar—at
least, it seemed peculiar to her—habit of perusing

the wanted circulars. She'd found an odd, discomfiting satisfaction in staring at all those names and faces of men—at least, mostly men though there were some women, as well—wanted for robbery or murder.

Mostly murder. Those were the ones with the most money on their heads. The most intriguing men.

Sheila supposed it was a grim fascination on the order of some folks' regular, voyeuristic scrutiny of the *Police Gazette* and other pulp rags devoted to crime, with their photographs and drawings of soulless killers and people killed violently.

She studied the penciled and inked likenesses staring back at her from beneath the large, black, blocky letters: WANTED. There were several layers of the circulars on the board, so Sheila flipped through them quickly, knocking several off the wall. She thought she heard the postmaster chuff in reproof of her haste and carelessness, but she paid him no mind. She continued flipping through one sheaf of dodgers after another, looking for the face of the man she'd just seen on the street.

She knocked several more flyers off the wall, and they tumbled around her ankles.

"Mercy sakes, Miss Bonner!" exclaimed the postmaster, Earl Atkinson, having stepped out of his cage to stand scowling at her with his fists on his hips, his gaze glassy with reproof beneath his green eyeshade.

One long circular on faintly yellowed paper fluttered up against Sheila's right ankle then fell flat against the hardwood floor. She gasped and felt herself recoil a little when a man in a high-crowned black hat and with two eyes like coals, a long slender nose, and thick, drooping mustache stared up at her with

much the same lewd expression he'd just favored her
with on the street.

WANTED

DEAD OR ALIVE

~ For Murder ~

By FEDERAL AUTHORITIES in the Territories of
New Mexico, Arizona, California, and *Nevada*

The killer's savage likeness split the dodger in
two, then:

JOSE RAMON CORDOBÉS
" E L   C U C H I L L O "
Deadly Killer from Sonora, Mexico
FEDERAL BOUNTY:
$ 6 , 0 0 0

Sheila bent forward and reached for the dodger at
her feet. Her fingers tingled, stiffened. She felt as
though she were reaching for a coiled serpent. She
plucked the yellowing leaf off the floor and held it in
front of her. She glanced from the foreboding image
of Jose Ramon Cordobés to Atkinson, still regarding
her like a schoolmaster who'd caught her stealing
someone's lunch out of the cloakroom.

Sheila rattled the sheet in the air, tapped it with
her finger, and rattled it in the air again before showing Atkinson the likeness penciled on it. "I've seen
this man, Mr. Atkinson. I've seen him. Recently. I
mean . . . he's in town this very moment!"

"Let me see." Atkinson stepped forward. He was
extremely skinny, and his wool clothes hung on him.

He always smelled like whiskey and cigarettes, and he even did so this early in the morning, as though drinking and smoking were part of his morning toiletry.

He took the paper and widened his eyes behind his small, round, steel-framed spectacles. "El Cuchillo?"

"I just now saw him ride into town and enter the Silver Slipper!"

"Yes, well . . ." Atkinson lowered the paper. "He does come around from time to time."

"He does?"

"He prowls these parts. Works as a regulator for the larger ranchers. Don't like seein' him in town. No businessman does. It means they're probably about to lose a customer."

"Don't you notify the authorities?"

"Who—*Flagg*?" The postmaster almost laughed at the notion that an empty sheath like Jonah Flagg could arrest such a man as Jose Ramon Cordobés, aka "El Cuchillo."

"If not Flagg, the U.S. Marshals Service. We do have a telegraph office, Mr. Atkinson!"

"Oh, that wouldn't do no good, Miss Bonner."

She stared in exasperation at the skinny man. *"What?"* She didn't wait for a reply but only groaned in frustration. Plucking the wanted circular out of Atkinson's hand, she strode back through the door and onto the boardwalk fronting the post office. She looked around the street, whose shadows were slowly being obliterated by sunlight angling between the eastern crags.

The door opened behind Sheila, and Atkinson stepped out. "If you're lookin' for Flagg, he's not in town, Miss Bonner."

She turned to him, frowning. "No? Where is he?"

"He left town early . . . with, uh . . . with a couple of deputy U.S. marshals and Garth Starrett."

Sheila's heart quickened. "Starrett?"

"Probably chasin' rustlers. Somethin' like that." The postmaster's tone was reassuring, as though he knew that concern for Johnny Greenway was foremost on the young woman's mind. "Garth Starrett—he don't stand for rustlin'. Or squattin'. Maybe it's squatters he brought in the marshals for . . ."

Sheila sighed and cast her gaze to the west along the main street before her. Her mind returned to the killer. Cordobés was here for a reason.

Could that reason be Johnny? What other reason could there be?

Why on earth was such a man, wanted for murder in nearly every territory on the frontier, riding into a town in broad daylight? So brash! He was obviously not one bit worried that someone would try to cash in on the significant bounty on his head. Not one bit worried that a lawman would do his job and arrest him!

Sometimes the rustic workings of the West—the lawlessness—exasperated her no end.

Starrett had likely brought the killer into Hallelujah Junction to assassinate the man who'd killed his son. At least, Sheila was going to find out if that was the case. And she was going to let Mr. El Cuchillo know that she knew who he was and that marshals were in the area, so he'd better not think his killing ways would stand. Not with her on the scout!

She was frightened but not overly so. Certainly not even El Cuchillo would kill a woman—an important businesswoman in and around Hallelujah Junction—in broad daylight. She'd probably have to go to bed tonight clutching one of her father's pistols to her bosom, but she'd cross that bridge when she came to it . . .

"Ma'am . . . uh, Miss Bonner . . . what you got on your mind . . . ?" Atkinson called haltingly behind Sheila as she stomped back down the street in the direction from which she'd come. "Uh . . . Miss . . . ?"

She wasn't listening. She crossed Third Avenue then drifted to the left, angling across the main street toward the Silver Slipper. She had to stop for a ranch supply wagon then two cowboys pulled up their horses abruptly to let her pass, pinching their hat brims to her. She gave them only a passing glance as she continued across the street, hearing one of the drovers say to the other: "Ain't that the bank lady?"

"Yep. Wonder what's got a bee in her bonnet . . . ?"

"Why, I think she's going into the . . . !"

His words faded from Sheila's ears as she mounted the Silver Slipper's three steps then pushed through the batwings. The doors rattled closed behind her as she took two steps into the shadows, thick with the stench of sour beer and man sweat, and looked around.

It wasn't even eight o'clock yet, but there were already several men in the place, mostly rough-hewn types standing at the bar running along the wall to Sheila's left. The owner of the mercantile, Mort Stanley, was there, as well, drinking his morning beer at a table far back in the room's deep shadows.

Sheila had entered the Silver Slipper only once in the past. That was the day she'd first encountered Johnny Greenway. He'd been reclining, drunk, on the loafer's bench just outside the saloon but had followed her inside when she'd entered, intent on reading the riot act to Sheriff Flagg and the now-dead deputy U.S. marshal Lyle Wallace. Both men had been drinking and frolicking with parlor girls instead of going after the men who'd been robbing her bullion at the time, and she'd wanted to shame them into getting off their lazy behinds and doing their jobs for a change.

She knew the mercantiler, Stanley, frequented the saloon every morning because she often saw him pass through the batwings on her way to work. Now the portly, bald man shifted his position in his chair, turning away from Sheila in apparent chagrin though she didn't give a damn what the man ate—or drank— for breakfast every morning.

Her gaze had already landed on the black-clad stranger, anyway.

He was sitting with his back to the red wallpapered wall to Sheila's right. He'd removed his high-crowned black hat and set it on the table, near a nearly full beer schooner and a half-filled shot glass of whiskey. He'd also removed his wolf coat and hung it from his chair back, making it apparent where his nickname of El Cuchillo—The Knife—had originated.

A large, pearl-handled knife jutted from a sheath on each hip. Another, smaller knife hung down his chest in a hard, shiny, black leather scabbard trimmed with three turquoise-encrusted silver conchos. The knife, probably what they called a stiletto, had an obsidian handle with a hilt and cap of glistening silver.

He sat kicked back in his chair, his long legs extended and boots crossed on another chair before him. He wore black leather slacks and high black boots. He looked like a long cat lounging there, a long black cat lingering over his liquid breakfast, a long slender black cheroot smoldering in an ashtray on the table near his drinks.

Sheila sucked back her instinctive fear of this predatorial man—a known murderer—and, dropping her valise on a vacant table, strode the width of the bar to the killer's table. As she did he studied her blandly, blinking slowly, smoke from his cigar unfurled in the air by his right cheek. His hair was startlingly black, in sharp contrast to the milky whiteness of his skin. If she hadn't known he was a killer, she'd have known just by looking at him, just by sensing the savage, predatorial air radiating around him.

Sheila stopped before him and slapped the wanted circular down on the table near his drinks and cigar. "I know who you are," she said, keeping her voice down though it had suddenly become so quiet in the saloon that there was no way the other customers and the lone bartender hadn't heard her. They would have heard her had she whispered.

The Mexican killer called El Cuchillo gazed back at her through his black, heavy-lidded eyes. Even in the shadowy saloon, his pupils were as small as BBs. He took a deep drag off his cheroot and, exhaling the smoke, said, "Then, señorita, you have me at a disadvantage. Or is it señora?"

"It's *Miss Bonner*," she announced tightly, flaring her nostrils at the killer, not quite knowing where her courage was coming from and not caring. *"Miss Sheila Bonner."*

"Miss Sheila Bonner." He spoke with a heavy Spanish accent. "That is a pretty name. What can I do for you, Miss Bonner?" He emphasized her name with no subtle mockery.

"Starrett brought you here, didn't he?"

El Cuchillo frowned. "Starrett?"

"I know he brought you here. There's no point lying. I know you hire your gun out to wealthy ranchers. Garth Starrett brought you here to kill the man he thinks killed his son."

El Cuchillo was every bit the cool customer she'd thought he'd be. "I don't know what you are talking about, Miss Bonner." Again, the emphasis with a faint jeering glint in his left, black eye. "Why don't you sit down and have a drink with me? You appear to need to have some of the edge filed off of your nerves. You seem extremely nervous. Are you always this hot-blooded?"

One of the men in the room gave a brief snort. She couldn't see the other customers, as she was facing El Cuchillo and the wall, but she knew they were watching and listening. Aside from that snort, they didn't make a sound. The only sounds were the sounds of wagon and hoof traffic on the street, and the muffled sounds of morning conversations.

Leaning forward with one hand on the table, a fire of barely bridled rage burning in her chest, Sheila said, "You'd best leave now, Senor Cordobés. *El Cuchillo.* There are U.S. marshals in the area. With Starrett himself, I'm told. I'll tell them about you. About your plans. And if they won't help me rid the town of you, you filthy killer, I'll send a telegram to the chief marshal in—*ohhh!*"

Fast as a striking snake, he'd shot his right hand forward to grab her wrist. He bent it sideways, mashing that hand down hard against the table. His grip was savagely taut, with no give in it whatsoever, and her hand instantly numbed while spasms of agony shot up her arm.

"Ow!" she cried, her knee nearest the table buckling as she tried to withdraw the hand he had a death grip on. "Let . . . let go . . . you're . . . you're *hurting me*!"

He did not let go.

He'd set his cheroot into the ashtray and now he leaned forward in his chair, over his extended legs, and looked up into her pain-racked face with a hard look of his own. His voice was low but stone-hard as he said, "How dare you come in here and insult me like this. And threaten me. The only reason I haven't slit your throat by now, the only reason I'm not watching you bleed out on the floor while I continue enjoying my beer and my whiskey, is because you are a beautiful woman, Miss Bonner. But, then, you know that—don't you? That's why you were so certain you could walk in here and insult me and threaten me, and I wouldn't stick you like I would have stuck a man by now." Slowly, he raked a gloved finger across his neck. "I could lay you open from one ear to the other and watch you bleed dry before me."

He widened his eyes, probing her eyes with his own. "Is that not right, Miss Bonner? Is that what you thought I wouldn't do to one so beautiful?" He pronounced it "Meese Bawner."

"Go to hell!" she sobbed as he continued bending her wrist at an odd angle, threatening to break it. The pressure on her hand kept her from falling, for if she fell, she was certain she'd snap the wrist. "Go to hell!" she fairly screamed in defiance of the brute's assault.

His nostrils flared, and he stretched his mustached mouth in a cold smile. She was sure he was about to go ahead and break her wrist. She almost welcomed it. At least then he'd release her, let her fall to the floor.

His eyes flicked toward the batwings, which she just now heard rattling behind her and to her right. El Cuchillo frowned.

A familiar, raspy voice said, "Let her go, you bean-eatin' sidewinder!"

There was the metallic rasping of two rifles being cocked.

"That ain't no way to treat a lady—especially our boss lady—an' you know it!"

Sheila glanced over her right shoulder to see the diminutive Mean Mike and the hulking Silent Thursday standing in front of the batwings, aiming their rifles from their shoulders at El Cuchillo.

CHAPTER 19

Sheila returned her gaze to the Mexican killer.

As Cordobés stared at the two men aiming rifles at him, his eyes turned even darker and flatter than before. For a moment she thought he was going to go ahead and break her wrist, anyway. But then he released it.

She groaned and dropped to one knee on the floor beside the chair on which his boots were crossed at the ankles. Her hair had come free of its French braid. It hung messily down one side of her face.

"You all right, Miss Bonner?"

Mean Mike hurried up to her, keeping his old Spencer rifle aimed at the tall Mexican still sitting in his chair.

"Easy, señores," said El Cuchillo, mildly, lazily holding up both of his black-gloved hands. "We just had a little misunderstanding—Miss Bonner and I. That is all. Nothing to get your pantaloons in a twist over."

He smiled and gave a slow, catlike blink.

"Yeah, well, I'll be the judge of that," Mean Mike rasped at the man, keeping his rifle aimed at the Mex while dropping to a knee beside Sheila. He raised his voice to call to his partner behind him, "Silent, if this bean-eater so much as twitches toward one o' them knives or pistols, paint the wall with him!"

"Okay," Silent said from the batwings, in his customary bland, toneless voice.

Sheila was massaging her left wrist with her right one. The pain was relenting though her heart was still racing. Rage still burned inside her every bit as hot as before. She looked at El Cuchillo still sitting smugly back in his chair, smiling, his black eyes slitted. "You savage!" she yelled. "How dare you!"

He plucked his shot glass off the table between his thumb and index finger and lifted the glass to his lips.

Mean Mike helped Sheila to her feet, with one hand keeping his Spencer aimed at the Mexican.

"My threat still stands," Sheila told the man.

Holding the whiskey before his lips, El Cuchillo arched a brow and nodded as though with merely a vague interest in a mildly noteworthy fact. "Hmmm . . ."

The man's insouciance was infuriating.

She felt herself about to lunge at him, wrap her hands around his thin neck, and drive her thumbs into his windpipe. But Mean Mike pulled her toward where Silent stood near the batwings, still keeping his rifle aimed at Cordobés. "Come on, now, Miss Bonner . . . this ain't no place fer a lady."

He glanced anxiously toward the black-eyed killer regarding them both now with glittering, baleful eyes, that sneering grin twisting his mouth and mustache. "Nope . . . it sure ain't . . ."

Still fuming, Sheila allowed Mean Mike to lead her toward the batwings. She grabbed her valise

off the table she'd dropped it on, then she and Mike
skirted Silent Thursday and pushed through the
batwings. Silent backed out through the louver doors,
keeping his rifle aimed at El Cuchillo. Once outside,
he lowered the rifle and stood towering over Sheila
and Mean Mike, glowering down at the pair.

"Uh, Miss Bonner . . . ?" Mean Mike said as she
stood staring into space, trying to figure out her next
move. For once she wished the local lawman, Jonah
Flagg, was in town. Certainly, he wouldn't be as cowardly as to turn his back on the knowledge that such
a notorious killer as Jose Ramon Cordobés was in
town. He'd certainly do something or have the U.S.
marshals do something . . .

"Miss Bonner?" Mean Mike said, waving a hand in
front of her face to get her attention.

She turned to him, frowning with annoyance.
"What is it?"

"Do you know who that hombre *is* in there?" His
voice was shrill with exasperation.

"Yes."

"That's Jose Cordobés! El Cuchillo they call him
on account of how he likes knives so much . . . and
knows how to use 'em, I might add!"

"I know who he is. He's a regulator. I think Garth
Starrett brought him in to kill Johnny."

"You think . . . ?" Mean Mike frowned curiously
up at Silent.

"Where is Johnny?" Sheila asked Mike. There was
no point in talking to Silent, for Mike did all of the
talking for both of them. "Is he still at his cabin? If so,
one of you should ride out there and warn him that

that . . . that . . . *animal* . . . is in town. Likely here to kill him."

Again, Mike and Silent shared a dubious look.

"What is it?" Sheila asked. "What's going on?"

"Uh . . . nothin'," Mike said, guiltily.

"Out with it," Sheila prodded the man. "Where's Johnny? If not at the cabin—where?"

"He's uh . . . he's uh . . ."

"Out with it Mike!"

Mike glanced at Silent again. "He's up in the mountains. He took off just this mornin', in fact. Now that he's feelin' better he felt like havin' a ride up there—you know, to take stock an' such."

"And maybe do a little hunting?"

"Uh . . . yeah . . . maybe . . ." Mike's wrinkled face flushed sheepishly.

"Listen, Mike," Sheila said, crossing her arms and cocking one shoe out in front of her. "This is the story you told me a couple of weeks ago, after he'd ridden out to the Three-Bar-Cross and had the holy life kicked out of him. Why do I sense that this is another one of your lies?"

"No, no, no," Mike said, wagging his head defiantly. "It ain't no lie. Johnny's ridin' up in the mountains even as we speak." Mike raised his hand, palm out. "I'd swear on a stack of Bibles. Heck, I'd swear on my ma's grave . . . though she was even meaner than me!" He chuckled then sobered quickly when Sheila narrowed a skeptical eye at him.

"If you're lying," Sheila said with threat, "I'll fire the both of you!"

"I am not lyin', Miss Bonner. Truly." Mike cast

another skeptical glance up at Silent, who just stood there, staring expressionlessly down at both of them.

"All right." Sheila looked away, thoughtful. "Good. That'll give me time to figure out what to do about that man in there." She glanced at Mike again, fiercely. "Until I do, just make sure that when you see Johnny again, you tell him that El Cuchillo's in town and likely out to kill him."

"Oh, I will, miss! I will do just that!"

"All right." Sheila drew a breath, canted her head to peer through the batwings, made a face, shivered in revulsion at the killer in there, then turned toward the bank. "I have to get to work. Whichever one of you is on guard duty this morning, let's go."

"Yes, ma'am—that'd be me," Mike said. "Silent's bouncin' over at the hotel. He's takin' over for me at the bank at noon."

As Sheila stepped into the street, she turned her head to one side in time to see the two men share another furtive glance. Again, her curiosity was aroused. What were they hiding?

Maybe something. Maybe nothing at all.

They were an odd pair. At least they worked for cheap.

Johnny ran crouching down a steep ridge high in the Sierra Nevadas, just south of Hell's Knob and the old New Penny Mine, and dropped behind a large fir. Voices rose from farther on down the hill. Two men were moving toward him.

He pressed his back to the fir and raised the Twins, one in each hand, his thumbs caressing the hammers.

"You sure he's up here?" asked one of the men moving toward him.

"Seen his sign. Climbed right up this hill here, mounted."

"Maybe we'd best get the others."

They were getting close to Johnny's position, just below him, maybe thirty feet. They were breathing hard from the climb. They'd likely tied their horses at the base of the slope.

Their horses would have had a hard time making it up through the slash littering the forested ridge. Johnny had eased Ghost through it, taking his time, knowing the posse members had split up and spread out to find him after he'd lost them near the source of Pine Creek. They were in smaller, more manageable groups than they'd been in earlier this morning, when he'd mooned them from that butte, and they'd given chase, infuriated by his mockery.

He'd tied Ghost to a branch at the crest of the ridge then come back down on foot to show these two shadowers the error of their ways.

"Forget the others. Starrett put a two-thousand-dollar bounty on his head. Cash on the barrel. I don't see no reason for one of the others to get it."

"We split it, no matter which one of us gets him?"

"A thousand dollars each would stake us to a winter in San Fran. I just love them slope-eyed doxies on the Barb'ry Coast!"

"Touché, amigo," the other chuckled. "Tou-ché!"

Johnny angled his right-hand Twin around the tree, narrowing an eye as he more or less aimed down the stubby double bores. Starrett's men took two more steps, climbing hard, breathless, before one lifted his chin, his flat hat brim coming up to reveal his shaggy-browed face, the eyes instantly widening. Johnny had seen him in the ranch yard the other day, cheering on Gunther and Fritz.

He didn't appear nearly as jubilant just now.

"Ah, mule fritters!"

Ka-boom!

As the first man flew backward into the slash, screaming, the other man, ten feet to the right of the other man, stopped, cursed, and raised his Winchester.

His back still pressed to the bole of the fir, Johnny pulled his right-hand Twin back behind the tree as his second shadower hammered two rounds into the face of the fir. Johnny felt the reverberations in his back as the bullets chewed into the tree.

On the heels of the second shot, Johnny stretched his left-hand Twin out from behind the bole, opposite the side he'd first fired from, and evoked another curse from the second shadower, who had just seated a fresh round into his Winchester's breech. The man yelled in terror, seeing the two black, round jaws of death gaping at him, and then went tumbling down the hill in a roiling cloud of dust and pine needles and buffeting chaps and ringing spurs as the second blast rocketed around the tree crowns.

Johnny rose, listening as he broke open one of the Twins.

Silence except for the wind.

Smoke curled from the open bores, and the smell of fresh cordite peppered his nostrils.

A minute later, the thudding of hooves was accompanied by men's voices raised in alarm from somewhere down along the base of the ridge. One man shouted loudly to another, but the wind garbled the words.

That was all right. Johnny knew they were just trying to get a bearing on the shots they'd heard. They'd be after him soon.

And they'd die for their trouble.

He reloaded the Twins, holstered them, and began making his leisurely way straight up the mountain toward his horse.

Garth Starrett brought his black Morgan to a sudden halt. He'd been studying the ground before him rising along the left side of Little Porcupine Creek, but now he turned to gaze out over the gauzy green-blue forest billowing out below him to the northeast.

A man's scream had just been cut off by the deep, resolute report of what could only have been a large-bore shotgun. The blast rocketed up from a slight crease in that rumpled green blanket of mountain forest, swirling as it echoed, dwindling.

Another shout.

Then a rifle cracked twice.

Another shotgun blast rocketed up from that crease in the mountains.

One of the men behind Starrett cursed.

"There it is," Starrett said, giving a sour smile. "Good ole Johnny's playin' his ten-gauge serenade." He glanced at the others. "Anyone know where it came from?"

Jonah Flagg had been riding ahead of Starrett, stirrup to stirrup with Deputy U.S. Marshal Beech Skinner. Three of Starrett's hands had been riding behind Starrett, and now all six of them had stopped to stare out over the forest from their high perch in the ravine cut by Little Porcupine Creek rising gradually toward Avalanche Pass above and ahead of them.

One of the hands now to Starrett's right pointed with a gloved finger and said, "The highest peak over there is Hell's Knob. Just below the knob is the old New Penny Mine. The valley below the knob and the mine is the one Happy Creek cuts through. Same creek last year them Germans tried to build a cabin in—"

"All right—that's enough, Horner, you gassy fool!" Starrett cut the man off, glancing incredulously toward the deputy marshal, Skinner, who returned Starrett's look with a faint grin. "Just lead the damn way!"

"Yessir, Mr. Starrett!"

Horner neck-reined his gelding around and trotted his horse back down the wash along the thread of muddy water cutting between the banks of the creek and making a sound like small bits of broken glass falling on a stone floor. The other hands followed Horner Indian file down the narrow wash. Starrett fell into line behind them, Flagg and Skinner riding drag, their horses' hooves thudding on the soft ground, their tack squawking, bridle chains jangling.

As Starrett let his Morgan, born and bred from one of the finest lines in eastern Texas, pick its own way back down the mountain, he reached into the pocket of his wool-lined buffalo hide coat for his travel flask. He uncapped the lid and took a couple of shallow pulls—just enough to keep the crab in his chest satisfied.

Behind him, Flagg must have seen him. "How you

feelin', Mr. Starrett?" the Hallelujah Junction town marshal asked in his customarily unctuous tone.

Starrett's ill health was widely known, for he'd suffered his first heartstroke several years ago. He knew folks were just waiting for him to die, like the herd surrounding an old bull buffalo, knowing the contrary old creature belonged to a wilder, earlier time and no longer had a place on the prairie. No one liked Garth Starrett, and he didn't blame them. Hell, he didn't like himself. But he took great satisfaction in keeping them waiting for his funeral, watching for signs that this day would be his last.

Starrett didn't like Flagg. He didn't respect any man who kowtowed to him with such wheedling subservience though he demanded nothing less. Nettled, peevish, he said, "Fine as frog hair split four ways, damn your useless hide, Flagg! Now, let's get that sidewinder and drag him back to town—dead or alive—before sundown!"

"Yessir, Mr. Starrett!" Flagg exclaimed.

Riding ahead of the local and federal lawmen as they all dropped down the declivity along the creek, Starrett gnashed his teeth with raw disdain. Wasn't it ironic that the only man he really had any respect for was the man he was about to kill?

Johnny Greenway. The former Juan Beristain. Damn Basque. Mountain people. Sheep people. Outsiders. Quiet, wild as the damn eagles hunting the highest ridges.

What cojones the man must have—riding out to the Three-Bar-Cross a few weeks back. Unarmed. He took his beating like a man, and now he was putting up one hell of a fight. He'd go down fighting, and that was just fine with Starrett.

Almost a pity such a man would die. A rogue grizzly hunted down by dogs undeserving of the kill.

Still, there it was. Rance was dead. Garth couldn't rest, couldn't die peacefully, until the man who'd caused his son's death was dead as well.

Blood for blood.

CHAPTER 20

Garth Starrett's tired old body was aching fiercely by the time he followed his men halfway down the mountain then eastward into the draw through which Happy Creek meandered.

Happy was the name to which the white explorers and mountain men had changed the old Indian name, *Hop-oh-hahh-hee-hee-oh* (or some such Paiute nonsense). There'd been little happiness here lately. Not when Starrett had ordered the German family hung from pine trees when the hoople-heads had refused to leave the Three-Bar range, or what everyone knew Garth Starrett had claimed as his private property despite what the government range plats indicated.

There would be no happiness here today, either. Not for Shotgun Johnny Greenway, anyway. Nor for Starrett. He'd long ago outlived happiness though fortunately not the satisfaction of seeing his enemies get what was coming to them.

Despite the aches in his back and the galls on his badly chafed rump—he hadn't sat a horse for this long, nor been on this harsh of a ride, in several years—he felt satisfied to know they were closing in on their prey. Near the German family's abandoned dugout cabin, dug into the side of the southern ridge and on the south side of Happy Creek, three riders sat their horses, apparently waiting for Starrett's bunch. One of those riders was Jack Whaley, the other deputy U.S. marshal, whom Starrett's friend and ofttimes business associate, Chief Marshal H. W. "Wild Bill" Casebolt, had sent up from Carson City. Whaley was a lout in a Boss of the Plains Stetson, but he took orders from Starrett, and he'd been relatively effective in fulfilling the rancher's wishes in the past.

As Starrett, Flagg, Marshal Skinner, and his three cowhands reined up before Whaley and two more Three-Bar-Cross waddies, Starrett said, "You run him down?"

Whaley, thickset and affected, was smoking a meerschaum pipe. He let smoke slither out around his lips and pipe stem as he wagged his head then narrowed an eye as he stared up the northern ridge. "I sent four men up there to pick up his sign and pin him down. I waited here for you . . ." He glanced over his right shoulder, where seven more of Starrett's riders, summoned by the shooting, approached at full gallops from upstream.

"All right," Starrett said, pulling back on the reins as the Morgan tossed its head, "what are we waiting for, then?" He glanced at his men, Flagg, and Skinner, and said, "Get after him, boys!"

He'd just planted the steel to the Morgan's loins when Whaley reached out and grabbed the cheek strap of the Morgan's bridle, pulling the horse up short. "You sure you should go up there, Mr. Starrett?"

He glanced up the ridge littered with dead slash and black, skeletal trees that were the result of a wildfire sometime in the recent past. There was also a field of black slide-rock. Above the slash and the talus was sparse, green forest, but the problem area appeared a good hundred, maybe two hundred, yards wide.

"What do you mean—am I sure?" Starrett was fiercely indignant, cold eyes glinting. "I didn't ride out here to sit in the brush. Unhand my horse and let's get after that killer!"

Starrett saw Marshals Whaley and Skinner exchange dubious glances. He cursed both men roundly as he savagely booted the Morgan up the ridge.

He pushed hard for the first twenty yards but then he had no choice but to slow down and let the beast pick the best route up through the snags of rock and charred, fallen trees. The slow progress infuriated him further, made his old ticker race, skipping beats. Sweat basted every inch of his body, and the raw wind at this high altitude chilled him deeply despite his own raging fire.

The other riders were spread out to both sides of him, also carefully picking their way. One rider's horse slipped on the slide-rock and fell out from beneath the man. The man cursed as he rolled free of the shrilly screaming horse then climbed angrily back to his feet, reset his saddle, and remounted his anxious, blowing mount. A couple of the other men taunted him, laughing, and he cussed them both as he resumed the climb.

A half hour later, Starrett sat his blowing, sweating Morgan, staring down at the bloody carcasses of Ray

Anderson and Vernon Wade—both men nearly blown in half by Shotgun Johnny's infamous twins.

Starrett was the last man of his bunch to reach the dead men, whom two of the other riders had laid out side by side, heads on the upslope, feet on the downslope, as though propped against a storefront for viewing. Anderson's eyes were wide open and staring straight up at the sun. His tongue curled out one side of his mouth, like a dog's. Vernon Wade's eyes were half-closed, and he appeared to be smiling, as though enjoying a ribald dream.

"He was up here." Whaley stood upslope a hundred feet, beside a wide-boled fir whose trunk had had two fist-sized gouges blown out of it, likely from either Anderson's or Wade's Winchester. Skinner held up two spent shotgun wads in the palms of his gloved right hand.

Starrett mopped his face with his sweat-soaked red handkerchief. "Where are the men you sent?"

Whaley turned to stare up into the more widely scattered forest stretching out above and reaching to the very top of the ridge, which was out of view from this angle on the slope. "Hard to say. I told them when they found him to send one man back to—"

A rifle crack cut him off.

All the men around Starrett, some standing, some sitting their mounts, whipped their heads to stare up the incline.

Another rifle belched from somewhere near the ridge. Or maybe from *on* the ridge or slightly down the other side. It was hard to tell. The shot echoed hollowly, rolling off down the canyon, dwindling. Two more shots followed.

Flagg, standing holding the reins of his horse beside Starrett, chuckled. "Now they got him!"

He'd barely gotten the *him* out before the cannon-like blast of a shotgun rocketed around between the near ridges. Another blast followed close on the heels of the first. A man screamed. It was a shrill, womanish cry of great terror and agony. It was drowned by a third blast and then a fourth.

The echoes chased each other across the forest slope, vaulting away over the ridge behind Starrett, who sat his saddle tensely, his heart jerking and quivering and skipping beats in his chest. His breath was short and he felt those eerie tentacles of pain reaching out from his colicky ticker into his left shoulder and down that arm.

All the men around the rancher turned to regard him with expressions ranging from disbelief to bright-eyed, taut-jawed rage.

"Well, what the hell you waitin' for?" Starrett barked, swinging his right arm and lifting his chin toward the northern ridge. "Get after that son of the devil!"

"You got it, Mr. Starrett!" said one of the men, swinging eagerly onto his saddle and putting his horse up the ridge through the slash.

A couple of the others were nearly as eager as the first, Rollie Ryan, but most of the others looked hesitant, maybe even a little scared as they mounted their own horses and continued on up through the perilous talus and slash. One of those was Beech Skinner, who cast Starrett a skeptical glance beneath the narrow brim of his brown bowler, which he had tied down on his head with a wool muffler. His bright, frowning eyes betrayed his apprehension.

Enraged, Starrett swung his arm forward. "What

the hell are you waiting for, Beech? For that devil to get clear up to Grizzly Ridge! Get after him!"

Skinner glanced at his partner, Jack Whaley, and then Skinner said, "All right. You got it, Mr. Starrett!"

"Try to bring him back alive!" Starrett wheezed after both men following Starrett's hands up the ridge, weaving their way carefully around obstacles. "Drag him back at the end of a rope. Dutch ride!" He choked out a laugh and then winced as a sharp pain blazed down his left arm. He punched his chest with his right fist, as though trying to loosen up the crab clutching his ticker.

"You all right, Mr. Starrett?"

It was Jonah Flagg. The town marshal paused about fifty feet up the slope, hipped around in his saddle to regard Starrett with concern. Or at least with a manufactured look of concern. "You look a might on the pale side."

Starrett drew a deep breath, wincing at the ache it kicked up in his chest, and wheezed out, "I'm gonna . . . I'm gonna . . . ride on over to the east shoulder of . . . of this here ridge. Flat spot there, as I remember. You bring that murderin' devil to me there. Go on ahead now, Flagg. Run him down! I'm countin' on all of you boys!" He gave a crooked, coyote-like grin. "If you bring him in, we might just be callin' you *Sheriff* Flagg come next election."

He broadened his grin and winked.

Flagg's thick-lipped mouth widened in his own delighted grin. His eyes sparkled like diamonds on a rich woman's neck. "Yes, sir, Mr. Starrett! Yes, *sir,* Mr. Starrett!"

He turned forward and booted his mount on up the slope toward where the others were now disappearing into the thinner forest up close to the crest. Starrett indulged a caustic chuff. He knew that Flagg, a little man—not physically but in every other way possible—had designs on the sheriff's job. The local lawman was just stupid enough to believe he could actually handle such a position, overseeing the law and order of an entire county.

Flagg wouldn't make a good sheriff at all, for he was cow-stupid and a coward. He knew that about himself, yet he didn't think anyone else did, and he aspired to more. In the shadowy recesses of his dull mind, he actually thought he deserved more, as so many dim-witted, power-hungry men did.

No, he wouldn't make a good sheriff, but he'd do Starrett's bidding, and that's all Starrett cared about. If Flagg was part of the group of men who helped drag Shotgun Johnny to Starrett at the end of a lariat, the rancher would be grateful enough that he'd be more than willing to make sure Flagg "won" the next election. He'd "won" many elections for many politicians, and he'd do it for Flagg, as well. It would take only a letter or two. Hell, maybe he'd even make Flagg territorial senator one day.

Why not? Anything was possible for the man who brought in the man responsible for Rance's death, the man responsible for setting Starrett's heart on fire with the rage that was killing him.

He reached inside his coat and fumbled a nitroglycerin tablet from a little gold travel box, and washed the pill down with another pull from his flask. He sucked in a breath and held it until the angry claw began to loosen its taut grip on his heart.

He felt washed out and dizzy, and sore all over, so he eased the Morgan slowly along the side of the ridge, heading toward the meadow he remembered taking his herds to every summer when he was a younger man. Now his hands ran the cattle up there in the summer and down again in the fall while he sat in his office, on especially bad days, or, on better days, out on the lodge's wraparound porch, taking the sun and furtive sips from a bottle and remembering the old days when he and this range were young and wild and churning with possibilities.

Back when Rance was still a young boy embodying all of his father's hopes and dreams for the future . . .

He rode in a half doze, lightly steering the Morgan around the eastern shoulder of the mountain and then into the meadow he remembered—a heavenly place of tall brome grass and scattered firs, spruces, and white-stemmed aspens and birch. The grass was awash with autumn wildflowers, their colors having dulled now so late in the year, but still pretty.

Staring at a patch of Sierra tiger lilies, he frowned, curious about why it had taken him all these years to concentrate his attention for even only a brief time on the flowers, and to appreciate them. The only reason he knew the name of this particular variety of flower was because it was Murron's favorite. When Garth had first brought her out here—a beautiful, precocious, half-wild Scottish beauty—she'd ridden through these mountains on her own half-wild broncs, picking wildflowers and identifying them with the help of her numerous leather-bound field guides she'd purchased on trips to San Francisco.

Garth wasn't at all sure why it was that he suddenly found himself clumsily dismounting the Morgan, sobbing. Crying, really—snorting and sucking back tears. It was a futile effort. They rolled down his cheeks and into his beard, turning ice-cold as they slithered down his neck and under his shirt.

Keeping one hand on the Morgan for balance, for his knees were mud and his feet lead, he moved to a saddlebag pouch from which he produced a fresh bottle of unlabeled rotgut whiskey. Cradling it like a baby, he shuffled to a near birch, leaned back against it, and slid down the bole of the tree to the ground. He dug the cork out of the bottle, spat it into the grass, and sobbed some more, openly now.

He couldn't hold back the tears and hoarse, raking sobs any longer, though for the life of him, he could not figure out what he was crying about. Wailing, practically—like a newborn babe or a mother who'd lost her youngest child.

Maybe he was crying for Rance. Maybe he was crying for himself and all the lost years. Productive years, to be sure, but what did a man really have when he'd attained so much without being able to fully appreciate it? Everything he'd attained had only made him want more.

More land. More cattle. More horses. More water. More money. More women. Better men. Better off-spring. A wife who truly loved him in a way that he'd known from early on that Murron never could. Not that he could blame her. He was not a lovable man. He hadn't really loved her, either, if the truth be known. He'd loved her body in the beginning, but then he'd preferred the parlor girls in his old haunts in Reno and Virginia City, and on occasional business trips to the California cities.

He was a very wealthy and a very hollow man whose life, for all he'd attained, had come to nothing. That knowledge was so alive within him it was almost like a

second birth into a wretched hell of his own making.
It threatened to swallow him whole.

He leaned his head back against the tree and wailed.
Between raking, guttural cries, he took deep pulls from
the bottle. After maybe twenty minutes of exhausting
himself with his unseemly but oddly exhilarating howling and sniveling, he must have slept, for he dreamt
of Murron riding toward him down a forested slope
on a tall calico stallion. She'd been a lovely rider,
and early in their marriage, after she'd first arrived
on the Three-Bar-Cross, they'd ridden together up
here and elsewhere in the mountains.

They'd usually brought a small, simple picnic
lunch and a demijohn of wine. After a long ride and
lunch and perhaps a bit of lovemaking in the sun-
dappled shade along a murmuring stream, Murron
would ride off by herself, leaving Garth to doze and
finish the wine. He watched her now as she looked
then, slender and pale and black-haired and beautiful with those stormy eyes, galloping toward him,
weaving through the pines and midsummer aspens.
The sun shone like liquid gold on her coal black
hair, which bounced thickly around her shoulders,
her crisp blouse pulled back taut against her proud
bosoms.

Only, when she drew rein before Starrett and lifted
her head, tossing back the thick tresses of her hair, it
was not Murron's young, smiling face and flashing
stormy eyes gazing back at him, but the puffy and
mannish face of their daughter.

Starrett yelled, startling himself awake and causing
the Morgan to leap with a start before it resumed for-
aging nearby.

Not the lesser of his life's ironies was that he'd married a beautiful woman much younger than himself for the sole purpose of producing attractive children, but his only living daughter had taken almost solely after Garth. Bethany had not been blessed with one iota of her mother's grace and beauty, nor of Murron's charm. Instead, she'd been struck by the same ugly stick as Garth. Rance had had some of Murron's physical attributes but also her stormy nature untempered by her intelligence. Rance's enviable head of thick blond hair had come from Murron's mother. Mostly, the boy had been cursed with the weaker, latent traits of Starrett's own bloodline—greed, lust, unquenchable thirsts for gambling and drink, sudden violence, and sloth.

God only knew what diabolical accident of nature had brought about Willie. Willie was the devil's own, final curse on the Starrett name—the embarrassing nancy boy being Garth's only living son and about as much good for the bloodline as the scrawniest of steers. If it hadn't been for Murron, Garth would have taken the lad on a one-way hunting trip several years ago.

The Morgan lifted its head suddenly and whinnied.

Starrett followed the horse's gaze toward the opposite side of the valley.

Slowly, his lower jaw sagged and his feeble heart gave a weak hiccup in his aching chest. His ears rang.

"Oh my God!" he wheezed as a tall, hawk-faced man on a rangy cream horse rode toward him.

CHAPTER 21

"Oh my God!" Starrett said again but no louder than before. It came out as a wheezy raking sound.

He stared in wide-eyed exasperation at Shotgun Johnny, riding toward him on his big cream stallion. A big, olive-skinned, dark-eyed man, Johnny wore a black slouch hat and a thick buckskin coat. The twin tails of his customary long red bandanna buffeted down his chest in the chill, late-afternoon breeze. His savage shotguns were holstered on his thighs, securely thonged to his legs.

Starrett's gaze drifted back behind the man and yet another hoarse exclamation raked out of his throat though with no more coherence than the previous one.

A dozen or so horses were lined out behind Johnny, the first one's bridle reins tied to the tail of Johnny's cream. Over the dozen horses, dead men were slouched over their saddle horns. Their wrists were tied to the horns, their ankles were tied beneath the horses' bellies. Starrett recognized the jostling but inanimate and blood-splattered figures of Marshals Whaley and

Skinner, Milo Channing, Rollie Ryan, and Jonah
Flagg and every other damn man in Starrett's posse.

Dead!

As Johnny and the dead men approached from a
hundred feet away and closing at a slow, thumping
walk, Johnny, gazing without expression at Starrett as
he rode easily in his saddle, Starrett glanced at his
Sharps rifle snugged down in the saddle boot strapped
to the Morgan.

Too far away. He'd never make it.

He tried to lift the flap of his buffalo coat to reach
for the handle of the old-model Colt holstered on his
right hip. But he couldn't get his hand to move. It was
frozen against his side. He tried to move his left hand
toward the LeMat wedged behind the buckle of his
cartridge belt, its handle poking out through a gap in
his coat.

That hand wouldn't move, either. It was raw and
sore and throbbing with the pain radiating up out of
his chest from his strangling heart. His left, gloved
hand had taken the form of a claw. For the life of him,
he could not straighten his fingers.

He sweated from every pore.

He shuttled his exasperated gaze to Shotgun
Johnny.

The man who'd killed his son drew rein and stared
down at Garth from beneath the brim of his black
hat. His longish, dark brown hair was mussed by the
breeze where it curved down behind his ears. The twin
tails of his red neckerchief billowed in the chill breeze.
His raptor's gaze pinned Starrett back against the
tree—frozen, helpless, sweating, enraged . . . terrified.

"Johnny . . . !" he wheezed, the word fluttering like
a dying moth on his lips.

Johnny swung lithely down from his saddle. He dropped the reins of his cream horse and smoothly, cleanly shucked his savage Twins from their black leather holsters on his thighs clad in black whipcord, and clicked the heavy hammers back.

"Johnny," Starrett wheezed again, his heart leaping around in his chest like a mad rat in a cage, "*spare . . . me!*" He suddenly realized, albeit vaguely, buried beneath his terror, how much death horrified him. Just the thought of his annihilation turned his blood to ice. It was even worse than continuing the cruel joke he'd made of his life.

Johnny stopped before Starrett, glowering down at the man.

"What—and disappoint Ole Scratch?" Slowly, eyes slitted, Johnny shook his head. "Nah, nah. The devil's been waiting for you for a long time, Garth. But, then, you know that, don't you, you worthless old peckerwood? That's what's been keepin' you awake at night . . . less'n you chug several bottles of that rat juice you love. Nah. I'm gonna send you down to the burning fires along with your son, who had his name on that bullet a long, long time ago. I'm just sorry Rance's bullet didn't come from my own gun."

"No," Starrett gasped, gritting his teeth, stretching his lips, and slitting his eyes in horror, pulling his head back away from the blast he knew would come and send his head rolling through the grass. "No . . . Johnny . . . *please* . . . *!*"

He watched the four round black jaws of death yawn at him from four feet away.

"*Johnny!*"

Just as all four gaping barrels turned bright red and

became shrouded in smoke, the Morgan whinnied again sharply, and Starrett jerked his chin up from his chest with a raspy cry—*"Johnny, please!"*

He gazed out before him, blinking, sweat dripping from his cheeks, his heart quaking and shivering as it raced and hiccuped in his chest. He blinked again, trying to clear the sweat burn from his eyes.

"Mr. Starrett?" a man's voice called. A hand shook Starrett's shoulder. "Mr. Starrett—are you all right, sir?"

It was his foreman, Milo Channing, down on one knee before him. Not Shotgun Johnny.

Looking beyond the middle-aged foreman with his thick, brown, gray-flecked walrus mustache, Starrett saw no sign of Greenway but only Jonah Flagg and Marshal Whaley and the rest of Starrett's party made up of his own ranch hands. They were all still mounted, sitting their horses in a broad semicircle before him, regarding him skeptically.

Sitting their horses. Not slouched forward, dead.

No, they were alive, all right. At least most were.

A dream. Johnny . . . the Twins . . . the dead men—all just a dream.

Remembering how he'd called out for mercy, the burn of humiliation rose into Starrett's already burning cheeks. "I, uh . . ." Starrett scrubbed his hand across his gaunt, pale face touched with the pink of embarrassment. "I must've . . . been . . . dreaming."

"Yes, sir," Channing said, staring at him skeptically.

Starrett cleared his throat, his humiliation changing back to anger. "Did you get him?"

Channing shook his head. "No. We lost his trail after . . ." The foreman looked down, toying with the ends of the spruce green muffler knotted around his thick neck, inside the collar of his red plaid mackinaw.

"After what?"

"After he killed two more men," answered Jack Whaley. His voice was low and coldly bitter. "One bein' Skinner." He glanced at where six horses were lined out behind the mounted men. Each of the six horses was packing a body draped belly-down across their saddles.

"Frank Wright bought it, too," Milo Channing told Starrett, grimly. "We spotted Greenway, gave chase. He went to ground in some thick forest and killed both Skinner and Wright as we rode past his position. Then he was gone. Just like that. Too dark in the forest to track him. Sun'll be down in a half hour. I figure we better make camp, if you wanna continue after him tomorrow . . . or head on back to the Three-Bar-Cross."

Starrett ground his back teeth. "What are you talkin' about—'head on back to the Three-Bar'?"

"I just mean . . . well, I mean . . ." Channing glanced at the other men staring darkly down from their horses. A couple had dismounted, and now a couple more did, as well, to start making camp for the night. They all held their cautious, vaguely expectant gazes on their obviously ailing, possibly insane boss. Turning back to Starrett, Channing said, "The men are tired, sir. It's been a helluva ride. Maybe it'd be best if we rested up an'—"

Starrett grabbed the front of Channing's coat and thrust his face up to within inches of the foreman's. His hateful gaze bored into Channing's eyes. "That's the killer of my boy. His trail will *not* grow cold. We got him on the run, we're gonna keep after him till we run him to ground and hang him. You understand, Milo?"

Channing drew a breath, nodded. "I understand, Mr. Starrett."

Starrett turned his burning gaze to the others, slowly, cautiously moving around now, unsaddling their horses. "Do you fellas understand? We won't go back home until that man has stretched some hemp!"

Flagg glanced around at the others, who were slow to respond. Turning to Starrett, he said in his typically unctuous way, "I understand, Mr. Starrett. I for one intend to get back after that murderin' devil at dawn's first blush!"

"Yeah, me, too," said one of the younger of Starrett's men.

Then the others all chimed in, nodding, agreeing, muttering that they, too, understood. All except the thickset Jack Whaley, that was, who continued sitting his strawberry roan gelding, staring obliquely down at Starrett from beneath his Boss of the Plains hat.

The rancher turned to him. "What about you, Jack? Do you understand?"

Whaley stared down at Starrett. Garth knew what the man was thinking. He was wondering if avenging Rance Starrett, the worthless son of Garth Starrett, was worth Whaley risking his own life and possibly costing him that life, as it had cost his partner, Beech Skinner.

Fury welled once again in Garth.

He reached under his coat and slid his big Colt pistol from its holster. Milo Channing rose and stepped back wide, as Starrett aimed the Colt at Whaley and clicked the hammer back.

"If you wanna leave, Jack," Starrett said, "that can be arranged. But you'll be leavin' in a pine box."

For a moment, Whaley's eyes blazed. He opened his mouth to speak then closed it. He looked at Starrett and, apparently reading the murderous intent in the old man's eyes, he opened his hands in supplication and said, "All right. I'm in." He swung down from his horse and reached under its belly to unbuckle the latigo strap.

The others had stopped dead in their tracks to regard Starrett in hushed, awful silence.

Channing turned to them and said, "Well, don't just stand around with your thumbs up your hind ends. Let's get these hosses tended and camp set up! Come on—let's go. You know how fast it gets dark up here!"

Starrett insisted on tending to his own horse though he was so drunk and out of breath and suffering from the general misery of his condition, that it took him twice or three times as long as the other men. By the time he'd finished and was dragging his saddle and rifle into the area Channing had deemed their bivouac spot, the others already had a fire going and two big coffeepots suspended over the leaping flames, steam curling from their spouts.

Channing had positioned four sentinels around the camp, in case their prey turned even deadlier than he already had, and decided to turn the tables on them and become the hunter. A fella never knew what to make of Shotgun Johnny. Starrett supposed that's what had made him such an effective lawman back before he'd turned his wolf loose, killed the men who'd murdered his family, and was stripped of his moon-and-star.

Starrett felt a little sheepish about how he was staggering and was so obviously unwell, but he tried not to show it. Instead, he overcompensated by being extra grouchy and demanding and giving unnecessary orders and generally making his campmates uncomfortable and belittling the men for little more than bringing in wood that wasn't seasoned enough or for hanging the coffee too low over the flames and then raising it too high.

They merely flinched and smiled and chuckled uneasily, exchanging furtive glances, and held their tongues.

Starrett berated Tramp Hintjen for burning the steaks and the beans though most men liked their beef and beans cooked just the way Hintjen had cooked them. Starrett told him his biscuits were undercooked and not salty enough when in fact Hintjen was the best biscuit cook at the Three-Bar-Cross and tonight's batch was no worse than any others he'd cooked.

The group ate in uncomfortable silence, speaking only when practically necessary and then in quiet tones, like children in a house in which the father was obviously, arbitrarily angry and spoiling for a fight with the first person who looked at him in a way he deemed wrong.

When they'd all eaten and the pickets were relieved so they could eat, too, Hintjen and a couple of the other men hauled the dirty dishes and utensils off to the near creek for scrubbing. Good dark had fallen over the valley. A few feet from the fire it was nearly as dark as at the bottom of a well.

Fresh coffee was brewed and the men sat around, spicing the coffee with a bottle they passed around, and sank down into their coats in sullen silence. There was little talking and no one broke out a poker deck. They merely sat around the fire, belching and sipping their coffee, smoking and sighing and occasionally shivering against the penetrating chill.

Starrett sat at the edge of the camp, near Milo Channing, taking deep pulls from his bottle and occasionally, when that ornery crab grabbed hold despite the whiskey, washed down another nitro tablet. His mood was as sour as before despite the food he'd eaten though he'd been able to choke down only a few bites.

Finally, as though he couldn't stand the silence any longer, Jonah Flagg poked his cream Stetson back off his broad, pale forehead and lifted his smoking coffee cup high as he turned to Starrett, smiling his groveling smile. He loudly cleared his throat and spoke loudly and clearly, as though making a great pronouncement: "To Rance, Mr. Starrett. May he rest in peace!"

He raised the cup higher in salute.

He turned to the others and again raised his steaming cup. They looked at him, scowling, the reflection of the orange flames leaping in their otherwise dark eyes.

Flagg glanced quickly at Starrett and then scowled back at the others. "To Rance," he repeated, louder, demandingly.

They each looked at Starrett, who glowered back at them.

"Yeah, yeah, sure," said the cook, Hintjen, and touched his cup to Flagg's. "Damn tootin'—to ole Rance!"

Then the others touched their own cups to Flagg's, saying, "To Rance!" They sipped and then sat back against their saddles and bedrolls, the silence now even heavier, uneasier than before.

CHAPTER 22

Johnny jerked his head up, automatically reaching for the Twins.

He shucked each from its holster where he'd positioned them and his cartridge belt over a tree stump beside him and swung the left one across his body, toward where he'd just heard the faint crunch of gravel under a stealthy tread. He tripped the Twin's left trigger just as a man dressed in a heavy coat and muffler stepped around a boulder and brought a Colt's revolving rifle to his shoulder.

The man cursed and dropped his rifle. He brought both hands to his bloody face as he stumbled backward, screaming.

Spying movement to the right of the first man, Johnny straightened and extended both Twins straight out before him. Flames stabbed from the end of a rifle, the bullet sizzling past Johnny's left ear to sputter off a rock behind him.

Johnny squeezed a trigger of his right-hand Twin and watched the shooter fly backward as the buckshot cut through his striped blanket coat. A third man stood two feet to the right of the second man. He'd taken some of the buckshot and stumbled backward and sideways, cursing loudly then setting his feet beneath him and raising his Sharps.

Johnny tripped two triggers, one on each Twin.

KA-KA-BOOMM-BOOMM!!

The two blasts nearly pulverized the man's upper torso, turning him red from the waist up, picking him up off the ground and blowing him back into a cranny in the rocks mounded behind him.

Only about six seconds had passed since Johnny had heard the men stealing into his camp. He'd been dead asleep though the thickening gray light told him it was well into dawn. Damn fool thing to do—sleeping in like a Russian princess in her bearskins when he knew Starrett and the man's posse would be after him early. He attributed his deep dolor to the fact he was still recovering from the dustup—if you could call it that; more like a beating—out at the Three-Bar-Cross. In his already weakened state, yesterday's hard ride had filed his fangs if not dampened his fire.

Adding insult to injury, he'd outsmarted himself by making camp up here on this craggy ridge overlooking the valley in which he knew Starrett's men had camped last night, because he'd watched their campfire. He'd thought he could sit up here this morning, having the advantage of the high ground, and pick the posse off as they made their way toward him, for he'd left clear sign the previous afternoon.

It might have worked if he hadn't overslept. He'd tied Ghost at the north base of the crag, opposite the side from which the posse would likely come and far enough away that the horse probably wouldn't sense trouble until it had come.

Well, it had done just that, catching Shotgun Johnny uncharacteristically flat-footed.

"He's up there!" a man shouted to the south.

More shouting erupted in the same general direction. They were up early and looking for him and now they'd found him. Johnny had tossed his blankets aside and gained his feet. He was fully dressed, even wearing his coat and boots. He grabbed his hat, quickly buckled the Twins around his waist, and scrambled across the small flat area here at the top of the crag.

A rifle barked behind him, the bullet screeching off a rock to his left and assaulting him with sharp stone shards. As he started down the side of the crag, a man behind him loudly racked a fresh round into his rifle's action and shouted, "There he is! Woke the devil up—*hah!*"

Another voice yelled, "We got him now!"

Another bullet sang off a rock to Johnny's right as he pulled his head down below the escarpment's crest and hotfooted it down the steep northern side, toward where he'd tied Ghost a hundred feet below. The horse watched him now, switching his tail anxiously, twitching his ears, fully visible in the pale, clean light of the late dawn.

At the bottom, Johnny dropped to a knee and quickly reloaded both Twins.

He glanced at the horse staring at him dubiously.

"Don't look at me that way," Johnny groused, snapping the second Twin closed. "A fella can oversleep a time or two. Don't mean he's a layabout." He saw the horse glance up the scarp then give its tail an extra-nervous switch. "Suicidal, maybe . . ."

He stepped out from the base of the scarp, turned,

and gazed up the way he'd come. One man was moving toward him, coming fast, holding a Winchester in one hand.

"But not lazy . . ."

Johnny leveled his left-hand sawed-off at the man who saw him a second too late. He tried to stop, but he was coming too fast down the steep grade. He raked his spurs into the ground, kicking up dust, and his eyes grew as round as silver dollars as he opened his mouth even wider.

His scream was cut off by the concussive report of Johnny's left-hand Twin.

Johnny didn't watch the man tumbling over the rocks, painting them red, but turned to his right to see several riders galloping toward him along the old mining trail winding its way up the forested ridge. He could hear more men coming up from around the scarp's opposite side, on a secondary trail, both trails having once seen the heavy ore wagon traffic of the now-defunct New Penny Mine cut into the next ridge to the north.

If Johnny hadn't been fully awake a few minutes ago, he was now. His heart was racing, blood sparking in his veins. He felt like a cow-killing wolf with a twenty-dollar bounty on his head and with a pack of angry waddies closing fast.

He glanced at Ghost and then at his saddle and blanket draped over a rock near where the jittery mount lifted his head to pull at his tied reins, whickering anxiously. Johnny had no time to saddle up. No time to even leap bareback onto Ghost's back. They were coming too fast—riders from both sides, and more men from above, a couple just then taking shots at him from the rim of the crag, the bullets thudding close around where Johnny stood, hesitating.

"Ah, hell!" he raked out, and bolted off his heels, rising and lunging into an all-out run. His only chance of escape was up that northern ridge bristling with widely spaced rocks and pines and at the top of which the mine had been cut but was now abandoned, the buildings and the old stamping mill now moldering gray relics of an earlier time.

Johnny followed the trail up the ridge, running hard, grimacing at the pain in his still-tender ribs. Men shouted and triggered rifles behind him. He kept his head low and ran, leaving the switchbacking trail and heading straight up the ridge, which wasn't as steep as the southern one, but it was no easy haul, either.

Especially not with men yipping and nipping at his heels, like coyotes with the blood scent, and sending a veritable hail of lead sparking and cracking off the rocks around him, whistling so close around his head that they drove cold nails of terror into his spine. He was certain it was only a matter of seconds before one of those bullets tore into his flesh and hurled him into the black well of death.

He was a goner, for sure. He was fully aware of that. They had him badly outnumbered and on the run.

His only chance . . . and a slim one . . . was if he could reach the top of the mountain, he could possibly hold the high ground and pick off Starrett's men one by one and whittle their numbers down until the rest were either dead or discouraged enough to stop the siege.

It was a long shot but the only shot he had.

It evaporated the second a bullet plunked into

his right calf. It felt as though he'd been kicked by a horse.

The impact of the bullet drove his right foot out from beneath him. He hit the rocky ground and rolled onto his back, bringing up the Twins. Two galloping riders were hot after him, whooping and hollering as their horses weaved around the rocks. One man held his reins in one hand while cocking his Winchester with his other hand. The other man was aiming his own Spencer in both his hands, the butt plate snugged up against his shoulder.

The Spencer licked smoke and flames. The bullet tore a crease across the top of Johnny's right arm a quarter second before he triggered his left-hand Twin and blew the Spencer-wielding son of a buck ass over teakettle from his horse.

Johnny tripped a trigger of the right Twin and felt a mild sense of satisfaction as the man who'd just cocked his Winchester one-handed went the way of his pard, rolling in the dust and gravel and painting the rocks around him dark red.

The others were still coming, some running on foot, a few more galloping their horses up the steep, perilous slope. One man's horse didn't make—it tripped over some obstacle unseen by Johnny and went somersaulting forward, grinding its screaming rider to a bag of pulverized bone.

That gent's violent end distracted a couple of the others, slowing them slightly. Johnny took advantage of the brief diversion by gaining his feet, trying like hell to suppress the nasty dog bite of agony in his right calf, and hurling himself up a steep shelf of ground, toward a gap between two boulders offering cover.

A bullet ripped his hat from his head.

A wink later, another bullet tore a hot line over the top of his left shoulder. He dropped belly-down and twisted around, a cold stone of dread dropping in his belly.

Two men were within twenty feet, both on foot, one triggering a rifle, the other a pistol. They were laughing. One was shouting, "We got him now! We got him now, Mr. Starrett. That two thousand dollars is all mi—"

A rifle had just belched loudly above Johnny and to the west.

The man who'd been shouting so jubilantly had now stopped running up the steep incline. He straightened, rising from the crouched position he'd been running in, releasing his rifle, and dropping his arms to his sides. He had a weird, puzzled expression. Both eyes rolled back in their sockets and in toward his nose, as though to scrutinize the quarter-sized hole in the middle of his forehead.

His chin lifted, his head listed toward the down-slope, and he fell straight back against the incline, making no move at all to break his fall.

He hadn't hit the ground before the man running up the slope ten feet to one side of him stopped, gasped, dropped his pistol, and clamped both hands over the blood geysering up from his upper left chest.

Johnny whipped his head upslope and to the east, from where he'd just heard another rifle crack.

His lower jaw drooped as he scowled in shock at none other than Mean Mike O'Sullivan cocking his Spencer repeater and cackling like a witch freshly loosed from the bowels of hell and shouting, "There you go, you copper-riveted dunderhead. How'd that meal go down? Not so good? Well, complain to the cook if you can find him. Hah!"

Mike shifted his rifle around, picking out targets, shooting and working the Spencer's trigger-guard cocking mechanism furiously, cackling and cursing and insulting bloodlines in some of the sharpest, most colorful language to ever reach Johnny's ears.

Johnny's pursuers were going down in bloody, dusty heaps. As the slaughter continued, Johnny looked up the slope on his left to see Silent Thursday shooting from around the boulder Johnny had been running toward. The boulder wasn't large enough to conceal Silent's hulking body and his big head with bullet-crowned black felt hat completely, but it didn't need to. Silent and Mike were picking off the attackers left and right, and those who weren't going down howling had turned to flee back down the slope and away from the lead nipping at their heels.

Movement drew Johnny's attention to the upslope. He blinked, incredulous.

"What the hell . . . ?" he muttered.

Sheila had just stepped out from behind a boulder farther up the slope, near the mine buildings. She came down the incline now, a Winchester carbine in her gloved hands. She wore a black wool coat and a black leather riding skirt. A long red muffler was knotted around her neck. On her head was a crisp brown felt hat with a flat crown and a stiff brim.

"What the hell are you doing here?" Johnny said as she drew within a few feet of him.

Mean Mike and Silent Thursday's shooting had tapered off to near nothing, though Mike was still cursing Starrett's posse's bloodlines. Silent didn't say anything, of course. Mean Mike was saying plenty for both of them—for a whole posse of shooters, in fact . . .

Sheila dropped to a knee beside Johnny, her brows furled with worry. "How bad are you hit?"

"Answer my question. You shouldn't be here. Why, I told—!"

"Yes, I know what you told Mike and Silent. Don't be mad at them. I have my ways of making men speak the truth. I know you wanted them to keep me in town and keep an eye on me, but when I learned that Starrett had ridden after you with a whole posse, I . . . well, I ordered Mike and Silent to take me to you."

"How in the hell did they—?"

Mike, who'd stopped shooting now, as had Silent, looked down around his covering boulder at Johnny. "Ah, don't get your neck in a hump, Johnny. She tricked us into tellin'. Then she made us ride up here to give you a hand. I figured you'd try to lead 'em up here, toward the New Penny. Good, high ground an' all. We got up here last night, an' then just waited an' . . ."

"And hoped you'd actually come this way," Sheila said. "And Mike was right."

Mike groaned. "Ah, hell, Johnny, it ain't our fault—mine and Silent's. She's got a way about her, Miss Bonner does. I tried to keep mum but then I just seemed to find my ole lips a-flappin' like a pair of ladies' underfrillies on a wash line, an' the next thing I knew, me an' Silent was leadin' her up here in the dark of the consarned night!"

Sheila placed a hand on Johnny's cheek, and her warm eyes bored into his. "I know you love me,

Johnny. I know you pretended you didn't, because you didn't want me hurt. I wasn't going to let you die for me. I swear, I've never heard of anything so romantic in all my life"—her eyes were shimmering now behind a veil of glistening tears—"but I just couldn't let you do it!"

"Ach!" Mean Mike groused. "All right, all right— that's enough for this old mick!" Mike stepped out from behind his covering boulder and beckoned to his partner. "Come on, Silent. Let's get out of here before we both get so sick to our stomachs from all this honey talk we take to our sickbeds fer the winter." He grabbed his belly and wagged his craggy, gray head. "I swear, I feel like I chugged a whole crock of sour milk!"

Silent walked up toward Mike, resting his rifle on his thick shoulder. Mike started hiking up the incline then swung his head back around to cast his gaze downslope again, toward where the dead Starrett riders lay sprawled among the rocks.

He frowned, staring. "Wait, now. What's that we got comin'?"

CHAPTER 23

Johnny and Sheila turned to gaze down the slope to the south.

At the bottom, near the high outcropping atop which Johnny had made camp last night, three men sat three horses. Two of the men faced one who rode slightly slumped forward in his saddle. The slumped rider wore a long buffalo coat and a black muffler. He was gray-headed beneath his cream Stetson, obviously old, and he rode a long-legged black Morgan. Long gray hair blew out around his once-square shoulders. Garth Starrett.

The rancher's horse was pointed toward the steep slope on which Johnny sat, Sheila kneeling beside him, Mean Mike and Silent Thursday a little farther up the slope behind them. At the bottom of the incline, Starrett and the other two men were arguing but Johnny couldn't hear what they were saying from this distance of two hundred yards.

But then he could, because Starrett straightened in his saddle, lifted his arm angrily, pointed a finger toward Johnny, and raised his voice to a screeching, phlegmy yell: "Milo—you get back up there! You, too,

Flagg! Turn tail? When my son's killer is still alive? *I won't have it!*"

`Milo Channing, the thicker, heavier of the two men facing Starrett, wagged his head and said something Johnny couldn't hear. Flagg said something, too, but Starrett was obviously having none of it. He had a pistol in his hand and now he raised it, pointed it straight out toward his foreman.

Channing raised both his gloved hands, palms out. "Hold on, now, Mr. Starrett. He's got help and we got the low grou—!"

Starrett's revolver flashed. The *crack* of the report reached Johnny's ears a second or so later, after Channing had jerked in his saddle.

Starrett's revolver flashed again, and another crackling report fluted around the ridges.

Channing slapped a hand to his chest then sagged to one side as his horse leaped with a start. The Three-Bar-Cross foreman was thrown from his saddle to pile up on the ground, the horse bucking as it wheeled. It inadvertently kicked Channing then galloped off to the south. Flagg followed suit, neck-reining his own mount away from the obviously crazy Starrett, and ramming his spurs into its flanks.

"Hi-hah!" he yelled. *"Hi-hahhhh!"*

Starrett bellowed a curse and snapped off a shot toward Flagg. Flagg just then dropped down out of Johnny's sight, so Johnny couldn't tell if Starrett's bullet had hit home.

Starrett cursed loudly then turned toward Johnny and the others on the long, rocky incline before the rancher. Starrett just stared for a time. He was too far away for Johnny to see him clearly, but Johnny knew there was a deep, raw, primal malevolence in the old man's eyes.

Starrett fumbled with his pistol, apparently reloading. He slid the gun into his left hand, slid a bottle from a pocket of his buffalo coat, took a deep pull, then returned the bottle to the pocket.

He returned his revolver to his right hand. With his other hand, he shook the Morgan's reins. He poked his spurs into the horse's flanks, and the horse started forward, leaving the trail and moving straight up the mountain.

Mean Mike laughed raspily behind Johnny and started forward down the slope, raising the Spencer in his hands. "Allow me."

"Get back, Mike."

Mike frowned down at him.

"Take Miss Bonner." Johnny glanced from Sheila to Silent Thursday, standing and staring expressionlessly down the slope at the rancher moving toward them up the mountain. "All of you, get back behind the rocks."

"Johnny, you're wounded," Sheila said.

"Help me up." Johnny reached for her hand and she supported him as he rose, moving tenderly, grimacing against his pains, old and new. He tried not to put as much weight on his right foot as on his left, for his bullet-torn right calf throbbed hotly.

He looked at Sheila. "Now get back."

"Johnny, you can't—"

"Get back!"

She closed her mouth and glared up at him from beneath her straight-brimmed hat. She turned to Silent and then to Mean Mike and started climbing the slope, holding her skirt above her booted ankles, moving up toward the mine buildings. "Come on, gentlemen. There's no arguing with stupid!"

When they'd all climbed the slope above Johnny, Johnny reloaded each of the Twins in turn. He squeezed the neck of each shotgun as he stood staring down the slope Starrett was riding up, the Morgan stepping carefully around clumps of rock and slide rock and twisted alpine shrubs. Magpies chirped as they raced around the debris.

Starrett was leaning slightly forward in his saddle, horse and rider slowly growing in Johnny's eyes, until Johnny could see the man's long, bony, hollow-cheeked face behind a scrubby patch of gray beard. He wobbled a little in his saddle, drunk and sick. In his right hand he held his Colt revolver down over his right thigh. His hair, white as cotton, fluttered like corn silk around his face and shoulders.

Johnny stood watching the man and the Morgan rise toward him, the Morgan's hooves lifting little puffs of dust, Starrett's breath frosting in the air around his craggy face. When Starrett was maybe two hundred feet below Johnny, he raised the Colt. In the thin, dry air, Johnny heard the man click back the revolver's hammer.

Johnny started to raise the Twins then lowered them again to his sides.

Starrett aimed the pistol straight out before him, and hardened his jaws, ramming his bearded chin forward, as though it were a fist and he was throwing a punch. His right hand trembled.

"Die, you devil!" he barked.

He fired. Behind Johnny, Sheila gasped as the bullet kicked up dust a good ten feet to Johnny's left.

Johnny glanced up the slope behind him. Sheila,

Mean Mike, and Silent Thursday stood about fifty feet above him, out in the open. "Get behind cover!" Johnny yelled, irritated.

Mean Mike took Sheila's arm, and all three stepped behind an overturned, rusted and splintering ore wagon long abandoned with several others sprinkled along the slope.

Johnny turned to the downslope up which the sick, enraged, old man rode toward him, again aiming his Colt, firing. "Die, you devil! Damn you—*die!*"

That shot had landed nearly as wide as the first one. Starrett blinked each eye in turn, then shook his head as though to clear his vision. Johnny thought the man probably saw two or three of him, and those two or three versions of Johnny were likely blurry as hell. Also, the man couldn't get his gun hand to stop shaking.

Starrett kept coming, gritting his teeth behind the fluttering screen of his hair, and firing.

That bullet plunked into the slope well below Johnny.

The next one flew well wide and up the slope behind him.

Finally, Starrett halted the Morgan twenty feet downslope from where Johnny stood defiantly, holding the Twins straight down at his sides. Starrett clicked the Colt's hammer back again, blinking his eyes again, trying to get his target into focus, and snarled, "You killed my son . . . my hope . . . my only living . . . *hope!*"

He squeezed the Colt's trigger.

The hammer clicked onto an empty chamber.

Starrett grimaced as he tried to fire again. Another worthless effort. He'd popped all his caps.

He ground his jaws as he glared through watery eyes at Johnny. Several knotted veins throbbed in his forehead. His face turned even paler than before. He became as white as snow and blue where the swollen veins rose close to the surface of his papery skin. He made a strangling sound, leaned forward, his left arm dropping down that thigh and stiffening.

Gasping, Starrett dropped down the left side of his horse and piled up on the ground, wheezing and gasping as though for air he could not seem to draw into his lungs. His left arm lay stiff on the ground. He clamped his right fist to his chest and lay staring up at the sky, grimacing. His gaze was sharp with pain.

Johnny holstered the Twins and walked up to stare down at the obviously dying rancher. He was a little dumbfounded to find that he no longer felt anger toward Garth Starrett, the man who'd twisted his life into knots for the past several weeks and had nearly killed him. What he felt now, if he felt anything, was pity.

To have piled all his hopes on one useless son . . .

Starrett gazed up at Johnny, the man's eyes now cast with beseeching.

"What do you need?" Johnny asked.

Starrett slid his right hand toward his shirt pocket.

Johnny dropped to his left knee beside the man and pulled a small pillbox out of the man's pocket. By now, Sheila, Mean Mike, and Silent Thursday had moved out from behind the wagon to stand over Johnny and Starrett, several yards up the slope.

Johnny popped the top on the pillbox, shook out a gelatin tablet he recognized as nitroglycerin. Joe Greenway had used the stuff over the last year of his life. Johnny dropped the pill into Starrett's partly open mouth. The rancher closed his lips and made a face as he swallowed with effort.

He grunted and gestured toward the right pocket of his coat from which poked the neck of his whiskey bottle. Somehow, the bottle hadn't broken in his tumble from the Morgan's back.

Johnny plucked the bottle from the pocket, uncorked it, and dribbled a little between Starrett's lips. Most of it ran down his cheeks to the ground but some of it must have made its way into his mouth, for Johnny saw the man's throat working as he swallowed. When Starrett's eyes met Johnny's again, urging more, Johnny poured a little more of the whiskey into the man's mouth.

Starrett blinked. His eyes looked a little clearer, his face less pale. He began breathing regularly again, and his right fist, still resting atop his chest, opened.

"Sit up," he raked out, driving both elbows into the ground.

"You best lay there," Johnny advised.

Starrett shook his head. "Sit up!"

"All right, all right."

Sheila dropped to a knee beside the rancher, opposite Johnny, and she and Johnny hoisted the man to a sitting position. Starrett drew his left leg in toward his right one, which he extended nearly straight out before him. He drew a deep breath, scrubbed his sleeve across his mouth, and grabbed the bottle away from Johnny.

He took two deep pulls of the rotgut liquor, scrubbed his mouth again, glanced at Sheila dubiously, then turned to Johnny, frowning. "Why?" He shook his head a little. "Why didn't you kill me?"

Johnny gave a wry snort. "Why waste the shot? You're already dead."

"Just the same," Mike said tightly from up where he stood beside Silent, "I'd blow the old coot's head clean off his shoulders." When Johnny and Sheila glanced at him skeptically, he shrugged his scrawny shoulders and said, "I ain't Mean Mike fer nothin'!"

Johnny turned back to Starrett just as the man's head exploded.

There was a loud thump, like that of a rubber ball being slammed against the ground. Johnny blinked, his mind slow to comprehend what his eyes saw, which was Garth Starrett's head snapping violently backward with a large, round hole in the forehead. Sheila screamed and lurched backward, away from the sudden carnage.

What sounded like a cannon blast reached Johnny's ears a second later, echoing hollowly.

"Leapin' hellcats!" Mean Mike howled, himself leaping two feet straight up in the air and landing in a crouch, raising his Spencer.

Silent Thursday merely looked from the mess that was once Garth Starrett's head toward the source of the shot that had just hollowed it out, laying the old man flat and unmoving in wide-eyed death between Johnny and Sheila.

The Morgan whinnied and sidled away, turning its head to gaze in shock at its dead rider.

Both of Johnny's Twins were instantly in his hands, his thumbs rocking the hammers back. He looked around, frowning. The sun was well above the horizon now, and at this altitude the light was lens-clear but glaring. The forested ridges around him were a gauzy blue-green, the sky impossibly blue above them.

The distant muffled thuds of a galloping horse sounded.

Silent lifted a thick arm and pointed toward the southeast. "There."

Johnny had just spotted it, too—a rider galloping up the nearest ridge in that direction. Man and horse traversed a clear, gravelly area stippled with mountain sage and then disappeared into thick forest peppered with autumn-dead aspens, and were gone.

Only faintly, Johnny could hear the man's horse snapping twigs and pine needles. The sounds faded quickly to silence.

"Who in the hell was that?" Mean Mike hissed, still holding his Spencer high across his chest.

Johnny looked down at the lifeless husk that was once Garth Starrett, for the past twenty years the most powerful, most broadly feared man in western Nevada, eastern California. There he lay with most of his head blown out, half-open eyes staring at nothing.

No one said anything. They just stood staring down at Starrett in shock.

CHAPTER 24

The old Chinese housekeeper, Woo, drove the two-seater chaise out of the east end of the Three-Bar-Cross's headquarters, then urged the sleek Morgan horse in the traces up the path that climbed the hill on which the Starrett family cemetery lay. Beside the diminutive old Chinaman sat his even smaller, grayer wife, Ling, bundled against the chilly, bright autumn mountain morning in a heavy wool coat, a gray shawl wrapped around her tiny, wrinkled head.

Murron Starrett sat in the chaise's second seat, between her children, Willie and Bethany, holding a hand of each in her lap. As she bounced along in the buggy, she stared over the heads of the Chinese couple at the stones mounted on the hillside peppered with sage, cedars, a few ponderosas, and evergreen shrubs.

At the very top of the hill, Garth had erected a large stone with the Starrett name chiseled proudly into it. Abutted by a large oak on each side, the stone was nearly as large as a good-sized wagon, and it was topped with the chiseled figure of a man riding tall on a tall horse—Garth Starrett himself sitting the proud horse proudly on a high ridge, gazing proudly out over his domain.

Smaller, pyramidal stones, one for himself and one for Murron, sat at the foot of the large family stone. To each side were the stones marking the graves of their two previously deceased children—the baby strangled during birth by Bethany's umbilical cord, and the boy, Wallace, who'd drowned in a bog while trying to free a mired cow and her calf.

Below those stones lay the still freshly mounded grave of Reynold Redstone "Rance" Starrett, as yet unmarked though Murron was sure that, had he himself lived, Garth would have erected a good-sized monument to the son he'd pinned so many hopes and dreams on. That was up to Murron now. She would leave Rance's grave unmarked. He didn't deserve a marker. He hadn't lived up to the Starrett name, which meant he didn't deserve to be memorialized. For the trouble he'd caused his family, his grave would remain unmarked.

That didn't mean, however, that his death wouldn't be avenged.

His killer must be punished as an example to others. The Starrett name needed to be upheld as a bastion against incursion. That was even more important now that Murron would wear the crown of the family name and business. She and her two surviving children would take over the ranch, and Murron had to make sure everyone knew that though Garth was gone, the Starrett empire was intact, the family impregnable.

Garth's business allies as well as his competitors would learn that Murron was an even more prized associate and formidable antagonist. The she-wolf is always the more savage protector of her den, leaving the male squirming under her glare.

Woo drew the wagon to a halt and engaged the brake. As he did, two Three-Bar-Cross hands pulled their buckboard up to the left side of the chaise. Garth's plain wooden coffin lay in the buckboard's bed, its bottom end abutting the closed tailgate. Both hands were dressed in their Sunday best, which meant that in addition to their usual wash-worn attire, they each wore a string tie. The ties were visible behind the open collars of their winter coats. It looked like they'd polished their boots and brushed their hats, as well.

Murron was more amused than impressed. She felt no affection for or loyalty to her husband's men, who were now her men but whom she would hold, as usual, at arm's length. They were in general as contemptible and as stupid as the cows they herded. Some of them came and went with the wind.

While they were here, they were sentimental and simpleminded enough to vow loyalty to the brand despite receiving little of that loyalty in return. (Garth had run off many men over the years who'd simply gotten too old or crippled from injuries acquired on the range or in the breaking corral to continue doing their jobs. He'd simply given them their time, one of the lesser horses in the remudas, and growled his adieus.) Like the cows themselves, the hands were a regrettable part of the ranching business, similar to rattlesnakes, coyotes, and saddle galls.

These two men looked a little puzzled as they climbed down from the buckboard. Murron knew why. The only mourners here at the "funeral" were her and what was left of her family, and the two

Chinese servants. The rest of the hands were at that very moment gathering in a large group on a knoll behind the bunkhouse to bury their own men who'd died hunting Shotgun Johnny.

Marshal Flagg had returned Garth's and Milo Channing's bodies to the headquarters, and Murron had sent out others to fetch the bodies of the remaining dead. In comparison to the small, grim gathering here on the Starretts' cemetery hill, the gathering on the hands' hill to the south resembled the grand parade of a deceased robber baron or head of state. The many plain pine coffins, just like Garth's own humble box, were being carried in a line up the hill from the several buckboards and saddle horses below. The hands' string ties whipped around their necks in the wind, and their freshly polished spurs and belt buckles flashed in the sunshine.

One man was playing a fiddle while another played a guitar. The strains of each instrument floated clearly to Murron's ears on the knife-edged autumn wind. One of the men, Curly Clarke, was a cook who doubled as a lay minister. Clad in a checked shirt, suspenders, and denim jeans, he stood tall atop the hill near the freshly dug graves, holding an open Bible in his hands and from which he was likely reciting scripture to his grieving brethren.

Murron had wanted to keep Garth's funeral simple. For one, she didn't feel like going to any bother for the man she'd neither loved nor respected for a long time, for the man who'd abused their youngest son so savagely only days before he'd died. Her second reason was that she had more important matters on her mind just now.

She knew that not holding a large, formal gathering

for a man of Garth's wealth and station didn't look "right." Word of Garth's death had likely spread far and wide. People, including some governors and senators, were likely wondering why they hadn't been summoned to his internment.

She would explain later. After her affairs here were in order and she was firmly seated as the grande dame of the Three-Bar-Cross, she'd throw a party and spew the silly nonsense that it was a celebration of her husband's life when, really, in her eyes it would be a celebration of the boorish old fool's having finally kicked off and turning the ranch over to her and her remaining children. They would run it far more effectively than he, a blustering drunk, ever had.

Murron felt her lips quirk with a smile.

How wonderful it was to not have to smell the sickly smell of him anymore, the reek of cheap whiskey oozing from his pores, and the smoke from his infernal cigars. Of course, a weakened version of the odor lingered, but it would gradually dissipate, and in the spring she would have Woo and Ling throw open the windows and give the house a thorough airing, ridding it of the last of Garth Starrett's lingering, abominable presence.

The two hands carried the casket to the freshly mounded dirt fronting Garth's marker. Flanked by her children and the two servants, Murron followed.

"Set it down there," she told the two hands, nodding at the side of the grave, opposite the side on which the dirt was mounded.

They gentled the casket down to the ground.

"I'll get some rope so we can ease it into the grave, Mrs. Starrett," one of them said, and started back toward the wagon.

"That won't be necessary."

Both men looked at her.

"I said rope won't be necessary," Murron repeated, more sharply. "I'll take care of the internment. You men may join the others. Thank you."

They exchanged puzzled glances.

"Good day, gentlemen," Murron said, smiling woodenly.

"All right, then, ma'am," one of the hands said. "We're, uh . . . we're sorry for your loss, Mrs. Starrett."

"Yeah, Mrs. Starrett . . . we're sorry—"

"Thank you, gentlemen," Murron said with another cold smile. "That will be all."

She ignored the puzzled glances cast her way by her two children and the Chinese housekeepers. The men pinched their hat brims to her and returned to the wagon. When they'd climbed into the wagon and started driving back down toward the headquarters, Murron stepped up to the coffin and the grave gaping on the other side of it.

Willie and Bethany stepped up to either side of her, each taking her hand. Woo and Ling stood on the other side of the grave, looking uncomfortable as well as befuddled. Woo held his bowler hat down in front of him. Ling was hunched deep down in her coat and shawl. The frail old woman looked as though the next slight wind gust would sweep her off to Las Vegas. The husband and wife, too, of course, were incredulous at there not being more mourners here today.

Murron hadn't bothered explaining why there weren't. She didn't have to explain anything to the people who worked for her. Not that it would have done much good had she tried. The Chinese couple had been in America for nearly twenty years, working at the Three-Bar-Cross for nearly ten of those years, and they still didn't speak or understand more than a few words of English. They communicated best through tone and gestures. Mostly, they didn't communicate with Murron at all. By now, they knew what she expected of them and when she expected it. Well aware of her mercurial moods, they danced around her in cautious silence.

Murron looked down at the coffin. She turned to Willie, who was sniffling, a few tears dribbling down his cheeks that still owned the swelling and discoloration they'd acquired when Garth had tried to beat him to death.

Yet here the boy-child was, crying for the father who'd never loved him.

Inwardly, Murron groaned at the boy's weakness. Would he ever make a man?

Garth had tried to make him one, but by doing so with verbal castigations and a bullwhip had only made Willie retreat farther into his prissy shell. He was a sensitive young man, one with aspirations toward becoming a poet. Not a cattleman. Murron had resigned herself to her youngest son's artistic ambitions, for she, like Garth, hadn't realized the responsibility that would soon fall upon his shoulders.

They hadn't realized that their oldest son, Rance, would never return to the Three-Bar-Cross. At least, not alive.

"Willie?" Murron said now. "Would you like to say a few words?"

Willie glanced at her. Tears rolled down from his wet eyes. His thick, pretty, dark brown locks blew around his fine head in the wind. He brushed his gloved hand across each of his classically sculpted cheeks, cleared his throat, sniffed, and said, "N-no."

He squeezed his eyes closed and sobbed.

Murron turned to Bethany, who stood gazing coldly down at the simple pine box, her unattractive face as expressionless as a frosty window.

"Daughter?"

Bethany shook her head.

Murron looked at Woo and Ling, who stood back from the grave, hunched against each other, crouched against the cold wind. They favored Murron with the same befuddled gazes as before.

"Mother," Willie sniffed, "whatever will we do now? Whatever will happen to us now that Father is dead?" He sobbed into his hands.

Murron looked at him pointedly. "Stop crying."

"What?" he said, making another strangling sound as tears rolled down his cheeks.

"I said stop crying." Murron turned full toward him, reached around behind his head, and pulled his chin up by a handful of his hair. "I said stop crying, dammit, Willie!"

"But Father's dead!"

"He's been dead for years. To me. To you. To Bethany!"

"Oh, Mother!" Bethany said, closing her hands over her mouth in astonishment.

"Now it's time for us to face facts," Murron said, spitting the words angrily into Willie's face, pulling his head back even farther so that he threw his pale, long-fingered hands on her arms for balance.

"M-Mother!" he cried, terrified.

"Oh, Mother!" Bethany moved up beside them both,

keeping both hands over her mouth. She appeared as terrified as Willie did.

The Chinese servants stared in hang-jawed shock on the far side of the grave.

Murron turned to Bethany and said, "You, dear daughter, will be sent off to San Francisco for the winter. I've already sent a letter to Senator Harrison McDougal. You'll stay with the McDougals, who have a daughter your age. They will help you shop for a suitable wardrobe or two and introduce you around to San Francisco society. You will not return to the ranch until you have found a suitable sire for my grandchildren. A young man from a respected, wealthy family. I want a minimum of two children from you, at least, including at *least* one boy."

"Mother, but look at me!"

"Yes, you'll need to take a little more care with your appearance. Losing some weight, washing your hair on occasion, and acquiring some stylish new clothes will help a great deal. Carry yourself with some pride, for God's sake, Bethany! Smile! Chin up, shoulders back. You'd be surprised how much beauty is in one's carriage alone!"

"Easy for you to say!"

Murron back-handed the girl. Bethany screamed and tumbled backward against her father's coffin.

The Chinese servants clung to each other, mewling.

Murron turned to Willie. "As for you, Willie, I've been far too easy on you. Your father was too hard. I was too easy. Off come the kid gloves. You are the male head of the household now, and it is time for you start acting like it. That means no more poetry. No more writing it, no more reading it. By day, you will study this ranch until you know it inside and out. By night, you will read the books in your father's library. If you don't do something . . . *anything* . . . very soon to prove to me that you belong here, I will kick you out to the bunkhouse, and that is where you shall remain, earning your pay along with the rest of the hands."

"*Mother!*" Willie shrieked.

"Oh no, Mother," Bethany said, slowly shaking her head, her cheeks mottling red. "You mustn't send Willie out to the bunkhouse. Why, the men . . . they'll . . ."

"He'll have to fend for himself out there and on the range, just like all the other hands. Your destinies are now up to you. It is time for you both to carry yourself like Starretts—with passion, pride, and vigor. You will set examples for your children. Yes, children—even for you, Willie."

Murron turned to the coffin. "Now, then, let's finish up this funeral nonsense and get to work!"

She crouched over the box, placed her black-gloved hands on the near side, and began pushing the vessel toward the grave.

"Help me here, dammit!"

Willie and Bethany stared at each other in wide-eyed shock.

"*Help me!*" Murron raged.

They both leaped into action, placing their hands on the coffin. Working together, the three of them scraped the coffin around the gravelly ground. It tipped sideways and dropped into the grave, landing on the bottom with a *crash!*

CHAPTER 25

Someone tapped on Johnny's door.

If not *his* door, at least the door of Sheila's bedroom, for it was here he'd spent the last several days, recovering from his most recent set of injuries. Instantly, the Twins were in his hands, the fog of his nap quickly lifting as his heart quickened.

On the door's other side, Sheila must have heard the shotguns' hammers click back. She said, "Stand down, Johnny. It's Sheila. You have a visitor."

She'd placed special emphasis on *visitor*.

She waited a moment longer before twisting the knob. The latch clicked and the hinges squawked. Johnny depressed the shotguns' hammers and returned them to their holsters hanging off a front bedpost to his right. Sheila poked her head tentatively into the room, looking a tad apprehensive. She knew he didn't stray far from the dual sawed-offs and that he had the reflexes of a cat. She also knew that, having escaped Starrett's posse and having left the rancher lying dead on the mountain beneath the New Penny Mine, he was expecting trouble.

She smiled when she saw his empty hands, then,

drawing the door open wider, said with a little too much brightness and cheer, "It's Miss MacFarland to see you again, Johnny!"

Johnny frowned as he propped himself on his elbows. "Oh?"

Glyneen MacFarland stepped into the room clutching her black medical kit before her. She wore a yellow winter coat and red knit mittens. Her pale cheeks were rosy from the cold. She smelled of the outside smells of cold wind, autumn leaves, and woodsmoke. It was late morning, or so Johnny thought, judging by the bright, crisp light angling through the near window.

Miss MacFarland smiled. "Hello, Mr. Greenway. I'm sorry. I didn't mean to wake you."

"I just laid down for a spell after breakfast," Johnny said, blinking the sleep from his eyes. "I didn't realize I'd nodded off." The wounds, none of which was serious, still caused him fatigue.

"I thought I'd check those wounds and rewrap that nasty one in your calf."

"I could have done that," Sheila said, a certain stiffness in her voice. "But . . . I suppose Dr. Albright wanted you to do it . . . just to make sure . . ." She let her voice trail off.

Miss MacFarland smiled. "Yes, Doc Albright sent me, Miss Bonner. I didn't come of my own accord, I assure you."

Sheila flushed.

Miss MacFarland glanced at Johnny. "The doctor wants to make sure there's no sign of infection in Johnny's leg."

"I see," Sheila said. "Well, good. I'll just . . ." She

stepped back to the door and, backing out of the room, smiling a little too brightly and stiffly, and pulling the door closed, said, "I'll just leave you two alone, then."

She drew the door closed, then, narrowing one eye suspiciously, opened it a couple of feet and left it there. She drew her mouth corners down, sheepishly, then offered another brittle smile, turned away, and retreated down the hall. Soon, Johnny heard her descending the stairs.

Glyneen turned to him. "Well, if that don't beat a hen a-flyin'!" she exclaimed softly in her petal-soft Southern accent. "She sure is protective." She set the kit on the side of the bed and pulled a chair up from the wall. "Or should I say *proprietary*?"

Johnny drew his mouth corners down as he sat up a little higher then rested back against the headboard. "I reckon that's my fault. My little display in the cabin the other day. I do apologize, Miss MacFarland. You didn't deserve that. You've been taking such good care of me, and that's how I repaid you. By using you to make my woman jealous."

My woman . . .

That had a nice ring to it, he vaguely thought. That's what she was, though, wasn't she? His woman. He was her man. He liked the sound of that, too. If only everything wasn't so complicated. He didn't know what Jonah Flagg was up to. He knew that Flagg was alive, because Sheila had seen him on the street. The marshal was staying awfully quiet. Too quiet.

The Three-Bar-Cross was awfully quiet, too.

Too quiet. It was the quiet before a storm. He could feel it building around him.

"I don't blame you," said Miss MacFarland. "Right

chivalrous, if you ask me. Trying to free her of you to keep her out of harm's way. I wish I could . . ." She stopped, shook her head, gave a dry chuckle. "Never mind."

"Wish what?"

She flushed as she opened her medical bag. "Oh, I don't know. I guess I wish that maybe someday I would meet a man who thought enough of me to do something similar." She smiled and shook her long, blond hair back from her face. She wore it down again today, curling over her slender shoulders. "What girl wouldn't?"

Johnny raised his brows in surprise. "You mean such a pretty girl as you don't have to fend off gentlemen callers with Old Hazel?"

"Pshaw! Charmer," she accused him. "I'm far too busy for gentlemen callers, as you call them, though it has been my observation that Hallelujah Junction is sorely lacking in gentlemen." She paused, drew a weary breath. "Besides, my dear widowed mother is right protective. I, in turn, am devoted to her. She is not well."

"I'm sorry to hear that. On all counts. I know about the lack of good male manners in these parts, since I've been guilty of it myself." Johnny gave a wry chuff. "I wouldn't be too envious of me and Miss Bonner, Miss MacFarland. Our situation is less than ideal."

"Yes, but then, aren't they all?"

"Some more than others."

"Let me see that leg, and then I'll run along and get out of Miss Bonner's hair."

Johnny tossed the covers back to reveal his

longhandle-clad legs. He'd kept his socks on, not having intended to doze off again but only lie here until his strength returned. He'd wanted to get into his clothes and boots and go down and repair a door on Sheila's buggy shed.

He was getting tired of lying around—mostly alone though today was Sunday, so Sheila was here with him. By the end of the day, he intended to head back to his own shack. He'd been staying here so Miss MacFarland didn't have to make the long buggy ride into the mountains where he lived with Mean Mike and Silent Thursday, and to be close to Sheila, as well. She'd given her housekeeper, Verna Godfrey, the week off.

He didn't know if Jonah Flagg had known that she and Mike and Silent had been on the mountain with him. He thought they'd been too far away for a clear view, especially with the lead having been swapped so quickly, men dying fast.

Just the same, he'd wanted to stay here. If Flagg had come for her, or sent others for her, Johnny would change the man's mind for him right quick—or turn the worthless badge-toter toe-down with a bullet. Mean Mike and Silent Thursday could take care of themselves.

Miss MacFarland had removed the bandage from Johnny's right calf and was examining the wound closely, both brows arched with approval. "Hmmm . . . not bad. Not bad at all."

"Looks good?"

"Indeed, it does. Doc Albright plucked the bullet out of there with minimal damage, it appears. It's healing well. I'll just apply a little more salve, wrap it one last time, and get out of your hair."

"You're not in my hair, Miss MacFarland. I'm in yours."

"Don't be silly. I'm sorry for all your trouble, but I've enjoyed coming over here." Miss MacFarland removed the lid on a tin box of White Cloverine and smeared her finger in the salve. Gently rubbing the healing substance into the wound, which had formed a nice scab over itself, she said, "Miss Bonner has such a nice home an' all, and you two are good people. There's a paucity of good people here in Hallelujah Junction."

She glanced at Johnny. There was a cast to her eyes he hadn't noticed before—a very dark one. One as bleak as it was sad. She smiled quickly to cover it, suddenly self-conscious, and returned her attention to his calf.

"You know that firsthand, do you, Miss MacFarland?"

She didn't say anything but just continued to spread the salve into Johnny's calf, which she'd laid across her lap as she sat there in the chair she'd drawn up to the bed.

Johnny placed his hand gently on her arm, frowning. "Tell me, Glyneen. Has . . . has something happened to you?"

She looked up at him and appeared ready to speak but then thought better of it. She forced a smile, shook her head, and said, "Never mind. It doesn't concern you."

"Has someone hurt you?"

She looked at him again, smiling warmly, as though she liked the way her name sounded, coming off of his lips. "No, Johnny. Never mind. Really. I shouldn't have said anything."

Johnny put some steel in his voice. "If someone has hurt you in any way, Glyneen, I want you to tell me."

She removed a spool of white felt from her kit. She cut off a length of the felt with a scissors and said, "If you insist, but please know—"

Sheila's voice cut her off. "Miss MacFarland?"

Johnny had heard footsteps on the stairs and now through the partly open door he saw Sheila's shadow sliding along the hall floor. Miss MacFarland had turned to the door, as well.

Sheila poked her head into the room. "When you're finished up here, and if you can spare the time, I'd very much like for you to join me for a cup of tea."

"Oh." The invitation seemed to have taken the young medical assistant by surprise. She glanced at Johnny then turned back to Sheila, hesitating. "Oh . . . you would . . . ?"

"Yes. I know you're busy, but I thought it might be nice if we could get to know each other. I don't know any other women around our ages in Hallelujah Junction." Sheila smiled, her cheeks dimpling beautifully. "Who knows? We might find that—"

"I'm sorry, Miss Bonner," Miss MacFarland said, snapping her bag closed and rising from her chair. "I'd really like to, but the time has gotten away from me. It must be nearly noon and I was supposed to meet . . ." She paused, smiling stiffly, hesitating again before saying quickly, nervously, "I was supposed to meet Dr. Albright. You know . . . for a . . . a meeting."

She turned to the door. Sheila moved slowly into

the room, frowning, sliding the door wide. "Oh . . . well . . . I'm sorry you can't stay."

"Maybe another time," said Miss MacFarland. She glanced at Johnny. "Good-bye, Mr. Greenway. I think you're well on the road to recovery. Let's not have any more setbacks, now, shall we?"

Johnny gazed at her curiously, puzzled by her sudden need to leave just when she'd been about to share some apparently important information with him. "But what about . . . ?"

"Later," she said with that too-bright, wooden smile again. "It'll keep. Good day."

She brushed past Sheila and headed off down the hall, saying over her shoulder, "I'll see myself out, Miss Bonner."

Standing by the door, Sheila stared after the young woman. She turned to Johnny, frowning, obviously as puzzled as he was. "What was that all about?"

"Your guess is as good as mine."

"I hope I didn't frighten her off. I hope she didn't think I'd come up here to make sure you two . . . well, you know . . . to make sure you two . . ."

"Yes?" Johnny said, arching his brows with feigned expectance. "To make sure she and I . . ."

"Oh, be quiet!" Sheila chuckled but her incredulity returned quickly as she glanced once more down the hall though she and Johnny could hear the front door opening and closing downstairs as Miss MacFarland left the house. "That was odd, though, wasn't it?"

"Yeah. She was about to tell me something. Sounded important, too."

"What do you suppose it was?"

"I don't know." Johnny turned to the window on his left. He could hear the rattle of wheels as Miss MacFarland rode away in her buggy. "She seemed on edge today."

"Well, she has an important job. And a hard one. She always appears on the move. I wish we could lure another doctor here. That might ease the strain on her and Doc Albright."

Johnny dropped his feet to the floor. "I'm sure it couldn't hurt."

"What're you doing?"

"I'm about to get up and go out and fix that door of yours. The one on the buggy shed. If I keep lying around like this, I'm going to get bed sores. I swear, in the past month I've spent more time on my back than not."

"You should stay in bed another day." Sheila sat down beside him. "Give that calf and those other grazes time to heal thoroughly before you start moving around."

"Nah, I gotta . . ."

He started to rise but she grabbed his arm, pulled him back down beside her, and wrapped her arm around his back. "Stay here. I have something I want to talk to you about."

"Not you, too."

Sheila pressed her cheek to his arm and smiled up at him.

He scowled down at her. "Uh-oh."

"What?"

"You got that look."

"What look?"

"That look that means trouble!"

Chapter 26

"I think you should let me make an honest man out of you," Sheila said.

Johnny scowled. "Huh?"

"Let's get married."

He just stared down at her, not sure he'd really heard what he thought he'd heard.

She pressed her cheek against his arm again, smiled again. "Why not? My father always said, 'Life's short and we're dead a long time.'"

Johnny turned toward her, placed his hand on her cheek, slid a strand of hair back with his thumb. "We'd never make it. Storm's a-brewing. You have to feel it."

"Starrett's dead."

"That's right. And so are a whole lot of other men . . . including two deputy U.S. marshals. If I wasn't so damn stubborn, I'd have left by now. By staying . . . especially staying here with you . . . I've been endangering you." Johnny had a hard time turning tail and running, even when he knew he should. He just couldn't abide running from a man like Jonah Flagg.

"Let's leave together."

Johnny laughed. "Where would we go?"

"I don't know." Sheila shrugged. "San Francisco."

"They'd find us there."

"Mexico City."

"Do you speak Spanish?"

"We'll have plenty of time to learn."

Johnny drew a breath. His heart fluttered. He'd be damned if he wasn't considering it. There was nothing he wanted more than to marry this woman and spend the rest of his life with her.

But could it really work?

"What about the bank?" he asked. "What about your house?"

"I'd sell both. In the meantime, Mr. Galbreath can take over my duties. He's a good man, knowledgeable enough to fill in for me as president until I can find a buyer."

Galbreath was the man, another of her father's friends—this one from Denver—she'd hired to fill the position of bank vice-president left vacant after the previous vice-president, George Poindexter, had been sent to federal prison for his part—along with Harry Seville and Louis Raised-By-Wolves—of robbing bullion as it made its way down from the Reverend's Temptation. Poindexter had betrayed not only Sheila's father but Sheila herself by acting as an accomplice in those robbery/murders, and he was now spending the first year of a fifty-year sentence in the federal pen in San Francisco.

Johnny's heart was beating quickly as he gazed into her eyes.

She smiled, laughed with delight. "My God, you're considering it."

It was his turn to smile. "Why the hell not?"

"This is your home," she pointed out. "I mean, you were raised in these mountains. You said it yourself—anywhere else you'd be a fish out of water."

"I can give it a try. What have I got to lose? There's too much trouble here." Johnny placed his hands on her shoulders. "I love you. I didn't think I'd ever use that word again, but there it is. I love you, Sheila. I want to marry you."

"Oh, Johnny—I want to marry you! And you're right. Why not give it a try? There's nothing but trouble here for both of us."

"How soon do you want to leave?"

The question seemed to take her by surprise. Her eyes opened wider, acquired a thoughtful cast. Her cheeks colored as her own heart quickened at the prospect of starting a new life elsewhere with the man she loved. Her time here in Hallelujah Junction had been one problem after another. She, too, was ready for a fresh start.

"Why . . . I don't know. I guess I'd probably need . . . I don't know . . . I guess I'd need at least a few days to get everything in order at the bank. I'd like to send out some letters to possible buyers. I know a man in San Francisco who might be interested, as he has another mine nearby."

"I heard you talking to Galbreath downstairs the other day. He said the Temptation has another bullion load ready for transporting."

"Yes, but . . ."

"You haven't found a guard yet."

"No, but I will soon."

Johnny shook his head. "I doubt it. Not someone

qualified for that kind of work, someone who knows that trail as well as I do."

Sheila frowned. "What're you saying?"

"I'll make the run. One last time."

"Oh, Johnny, you can't. You're in no shape to—"

"I'm just fine. And you need that gold. We'll need a stake. Besides, the town's too hot for me. My being here will only bring more trouble. Up there . . . in the mountains . . . is the best place for me right now. It's the best place for me for both our sakes. Flagg won't bother you if I'm not around, but he might if I am. Like I said, he's been too quiet. Everybody's been too quiet. Something's about to pop, and I think I can short-circuit it if I'm out of here for a while."

Sheila placed her hands on his face, splaying her fingers wide, pressing them into his skin with deep affection. Her brows were creased with worry. "Oh, Johnny—are you sure you're ready for another long ride? What if you get hit again?"

"Chances are slim. After what happened to Starrett. Besides, this late in the year most outlaw gangs have dispersed and headed down to Mexico."

Sheila pursed her lips. "I guess you'd probably be safer up there than down here . . . under the circumstances."

"I'll head out tomorrow. When I get back, we'll head for Mexico."

Her brown eyes smoldered. "Are you ready to learn Spanish?"

Johnny shrugged. "I already know a good bit. My folks spoke a mix of that and French. I learned Paiute and even some Ute when I was herding sheep with my family. I don't think Mexican Spanish can be any harder than that—eh, *mi amiga?*"

"No, no," Sheila said, placing two fingers to his lips and slitting her eyes coquettishly. "The word, I believe, is *mi amante.*" She kissed his lips. "My lover."

"I know. I just wanted to hear you say it." He gave a devilish grin. "Mrs. Godfrey's not around, is she?"

Sheila smiled. "No."

"Good."

She narrowed an accusing eye. "What have you got on your mind, bad boy?"

"Me? I got some of that *amante* on my mind."

She giggled.

Johnny wrapped her in his arms and drew her down to the bed with him.

Afterward, they snuggled together in the canopied bed in the small room, watching the light fade slowly in the single window and change the shapes of the shadows on the hardwood floor. The light turned from lemon yellow to a coppery gold.

The only sounds were the occasional hoof thuds of a passing rider, a dog barking in the distance, the creaking of the house's timbers as the temperature dropped, and Sheila's soft, love-husky voice as she told Johnny about the places to see—so many ancient cathedrals and Aztec and Mayan ruins—in southern Mexico.

She wanted to take him to all of them.

She'd made coffee downstairs and brought up a tray with two steaming cups and two steaming, butter-smothered cinnamon rolls, which she'd made that morning. In bed, under two heavy quilts, they sipped the coffee laced liberally with heavy cream, and nibbled the rolls, feeding each other, brushing and licking the frosting and crumbs from each other's lips and chins.

When Sheila shivered against the room's increasing chill, Johnny glanced at the small stove in the room's corner. He'd left the door open. He could see that the fire had nearly died. The wood box beside it was empty.

"I'll fetch some from the shed." He slid toward the edge of the bed.

"I'll get it," Sheila said. "You rest. That had to have taken a lot out of you," she snickered. "I know it did me!"

Johnny grabbed her arm and shoved her back down on the bed. He crouched over her, gazing into her satisfied eyes, her cheeks still flushed from the fulfillment of her desire. "I'm not a cripple."

She reached up and pressed a finger to his bottom lip. Her eyes crossed beautifully. "That was obvious."

Johnny winked. "Be right back."

"Hurry."

"You're insatiable."

"I am!" She laughed.

He left his pants hanging over the back of a chair and stepped into his boots. They were all he'd need; he'd make a quick trip. He had to get back to his lady, try to quench her thirst. He felt his body coming alive again to their remembered passion of only a few minutes ago.

He looked at the Twins hanging from the bed's right-front post. He started to reach for the shotguns, then, whether consciously or half consciously, he decided he wouldn't need them. He felt too at peace with the world to be able to imagine that peace being shattered.

He was only going for wood. He'd be back in a minute.

All was well.

He walked out of the room and down the stairs. Several dusty shafts of rich gold light touched with salmon bent through the parlor windows. He moved through the kitchen, past the ticking range and the oilcloth-covered table on which Sheila had left the pan of rolls to cool, and opened the house's back door, the glass pane in its upper half rattling softly.

He stepped outside, took a quick look around. The neighbor's cat sat crouched beneath the lilac bush near the privy. The cat's cream body was in vague silhouette, but the light made the cat's eyes glitter like gold dust. It must have had a mouse or a bird under there, or some other beast it was tormenting for its pleasure. The tip of its long tail curled.

Johnny stepped down off the small wooden stoop and followed the brick-paved path toward the shed, which lay to the right of the privy and was a lean-to addition to Sheila's buggy shed. He glanced at the door on the buggy part of the wood-frame building and cursed under his breath.

"That damn door," he said. "I should've fixed—"

He stopped abruptly when the cat gave a low, guttural groan and flicked its tail anxiously. His throat tightened when a man stepped out of the privy and onto the path before Johnny. Jonah Flagg was grinning broadly above his dark brown spade beard, and his eyes were slitted beneath the brim of his ragged hat. He cocked the Winchester carbine in his hands and, aiming it straight out from his waist, the bore centering on Johnny midsection, said, "Hold it right there, Johnny-boy!"

Flagg's five-pointed star, pinned to the left breast of his rat-hair coat, winked in the westering sunlight.

Fury flamed inside Johnny, and he pointed at Flagg threateningly. "Put that rifle down, you damn tinhorn!"

"Hold it, Johnny!" a man's voice sounded on his left.

Another man said on his right, "Hold it, Johnny! Don't make a move, or we'll dust you!"

Both men approached from each side. They were deputy U.S. marshals, their moon-and-star badges pinned to their coats. One on the left was Burton Antrim. The one of the left was Jeff Halsey. More foot thuds sounded behind Johnny, and he saw two more men approaching from the side of the house, moving up near the rear door.

They stopped side by side and loudly racked cartridges into their rifles' actions. One had a fat cigar wedged in the corner of his mouth. That was Saul Davidson, the oldest of the bunch and a man that Johnny had once respected. Maybe he still did. He didn't know. He hadn't seen the man in years. They must have been brought up all the way up from Colorado for this.

The man beside him, tall and gaunt and wearing a sheepskin coat, Johnny didn't know. He was young, likely fairly new to the service. He had small, nervous eyes, and his hands were shaking, making his Winchester shake.

A cold stone of dread dropped in Johnny's belly as

he glanced in turn at each maw aimed at him. They had him. They had him good.

Flagg laughed through his teeth. "There he is—the infamous, *notorious* Shotgun Johnny his ownself. Caught red-handed in his longhandles!" He threw his head back and laughed, his laughter pitched with raw mocking.

"Shut up, Flagg," regaled old Davidson. "Even half-naked, Johnny's three times the man you'll ever be fully clothed."

That squelched the laughter in Flagg's throat, wiped the smile off his ugly face.

"I didn't bring you federals in to insult me," Flagg protested, pinching his eyes with anger.

"Shut up," said Antrim. To Johnny, he said, "We're sorry to be here, John. Purely we are. But you killed two federals and Garth Starrett."

"I didn't kill Starrett," Johnny muttered halfheartedly, remembering the tall, black-clad rider galloping away from the mountainside that day. He knew it wouldn't matter that he hadn't killed Garth, though. No more than it had mattered that he hadn't personally killed Rance.

He'd come to the end of the trail.

Flagg walked slowly up to him, keeping his rifle aimed at Johnny's belly. "Down, Johnny. Belly-down on the ground. We're gonna truss you up like a hog for the slaughter!" His merriment back, he giggled girlishly through his teeth.

Behind Johnny, the house door opened. Sheila stepped out, horror in her eyes as she looked around and saw all the armed men surrounding her lover. She clutched only a blanket around her otherwise pale, naked body. "Johnny!"

"Stay there, Sheila!"

"Well, now," Flagg said, his lusty gaze stretching past Johnny to the beautiful woman in the doorway. "Lookee *there*!"

Johnny grabbed the rifle out of the man's hands and smashed the butt against Flagg's mouth and nose. He tossed the rifle away and raised his hands before any of the others were fully aware of what he'd done.

When Johnny stood holding his hands up, palms out, and Flagg was down on the ground spitting blood from his ruined mouth and broken nose, Saul Davidson doubled over in laughter.

CHAPTER 27

Murron Starrett rode low in the saddle and gave the horse its head.

The pinto galloped up the steep rise in the bright, clear sunshine, a cold wind blowing the woman's coal-blackhair laced with the silver that was a harbinger of an approaching old age.

Murron clamped her thighs against the horse's sides, wrapped both her gloved hands around the horn, holding on tight lest gravity should send her tumbling over the horse's tail to the trail. She smiled, feeling the horse's deep lunges, hearing the raking breaths and the clacking of the iron-shod hooves on nearly bare rock.

What a thrill it was to be out alone on a long, dangerous ride!

Somehow, she'd forgotten the value in a horseback ride in the mountains. Why? Surely, she could have saddled a horse, or had one saddled for her, and gone out on a run by herself among the forested ridges, thundering streams, and rocky crags. But she hadn't. Somehow, knowing that Garth had disapproved of her riding out alone . . . leaving him behind in his withering old age . . . had anchored her to the house despite her innate defiance at any man's shackles, even those of her husband.

Guilt was what it had been. An unconscious guilt that had held her captive in the featureless lodge that reeked of her husband's coming death.

Well, he was gone now. She hadn't realized how untethered that would make her feel, having been desperate for escape for so long to now be free and running without rein.

When the horse reached the top of the escarpment, it stopped of its own accord, front hooves plowing gravel, knowing that one more step would take it plunging down a steep cliff and into the Avalanche River winking below like a gold-skinned snake. The horse had been born and bred in this country and knew it well. Murron herself had ridden it out this way years ago.

Too many years ago now, but the horse remembered though Murron hadn't been sure it would, and her heart was still leaping to the thrill of a possible plunge the two hundred feet through cold mountain air to those frigid waters thrashing polished boulders.

She and the horse both shook their heads. Murron had worn her hair loose and free to blow about her shoulders, like she'd done when she was twenty years younger. She drew a deep breath, smiled at the electricity sparking in her blood, feeling as did the aging horse blowing now between her legs.

She turned to stare to the north. She could see the cabin down there in a thin spot in the dark green forest mottled yellow by changing aspens. A warmth grew in her belly. She closed her thighs against the horse's sides once more and said, "Come on, Pirate. Just a little farther now, Pirate!"

The horse plunged down the scarp's steep northern side. At the bottom it leaped a narrow gully then climbed the easier, opposite slope, weaving through pines and bulling through the underbrush. It galloped around the side of a bullet-shaped knoll then down the shoulder, through another stretch of forest, following an ancient wild horse and Indian trace and then one that migrating cattle and Three-Bar-Cross hands had deepened.

She drew rein in a small clearing in which a tidy, gray-aged log cabin sat under a shake roof liberally coated with blue-green moss and speckled gold with fallen aspen leaves. Three crows sat in a beaded black line atop the cabin's peak. Spying the interloper, they screeched their indignant complaints and flashed their inky black eyes as they took wing and, all three in a ragged line, banked out to Murron's right, banked toward her and behind and, climbing, alit in the naked upper branches of a towering fir.

This was a line shack that Garth and Ernie Wells, his first hired man, had built many years ago. They'd used it for hunting trips, during roundups, and for keeping an eye on the high summer pastures. No one had used it in years, and, in its moldering state, it looked like it. Murron had likely been the last one here, for she'd often stopped here during her rides for tea and a short nap . . . as well as for other things that brought a warm smile to her face and increased the warmth in her belly.

She rode up to the shack, the pinto's hooves *crunch-crunch-crunch*ing on the fallen aspen leaves. She swung down and tied the pinto's reins to the hitchrack.

She loosened the saddle cinch then walked up onto the small wooden stoop and flipped the metal latch. The door groaned as it sagged on its hinges, shuddering, and opened back into the cabin.

Murron poked her head in the door, looking around. "Hello?"

The place was empty save a mouse she heard scuttling across the floor.

She went inside and found the wood box full of kindling and split cordwood. Either she'd left the wood during her last visit several years ago or some other passing traveler had filled the box when he . . . or she . . . had left. Murron built a fire in the stove then found the teapot she'd left on a dusty shelf, and filled the pot from the rain barrel standing near the stoop. Returning to the cabin, she set the pot on the stove and added more wood to the firebox.

Soon the stove rumbled as the fire blazed, and the teapot purred.

Murron stood out on the stoop, taking the warm sun on her wind-burned face and watching the trail to the south, the direction from which she herself had come. Nothing out there. No one. She was alone. She removed her hat and lifted her hair, scrubbing luxuriously at her scalp, then let her still-thick tresses tumble back onto her shoulders.

When the pot sang, she stepped back inside and made the tea from a tin of Imperial Blend she'd also left on the dusty shelf. She let the blend steep in the stone mug in her hands, warming them as she drew the smoky-tart aroma deep into her lungs. She remained close to the stove, enjoying its warmth, having acquired a bone-deep chill during her ride and feeling it especially now that her perspiration from the ride turned icy beneath her heavy black cloak and riding skirt as her body had cooled.

She sipped the tea as she stood gazing out the sashed window to the right of the door, watching the breeze swirl the bright yellow and golden leaves around the pinto's hooves, the last leaves falling from the aspens ringing the clearing. Pirate stood hipshot at the tie rail, the breeze ruffling his tail. The breeze made a soft cooing sound beneath the cabin's eaves and whistled softly through cracks in the chinking between the logs.

Those and the occasional cawing of the crows were the only sounds she heard.

Until something thudded on the roof above her head.

Murron looked up at the ceiling.

It came again—the soft thud of something solid striking the roof. Whatever it was rolled down the north side of the roof then dropped with a soft thump to the ground.

Acorns?

But there were no oaks in the clearing. In fact, there were no trees of any kind near the cabin.

Murron continued staring up at the ceiling.

Another thud came, followed by the rolling sound and the soft thump as the object struck the ground.

Murron frowned. A vague apprehension touched her. She was sure the sounds were only a bird or a squirrel or some other benign creature, but they'd gotten under her skin. She set her mug of tea on the table and stepped cautiously out onto the stoop.

"Hello?"

She looked around. The pinto stared at her skeptically, one ear laid back.

"Is someone here?"

The thud came again—louder this time. It had come from her left. It sounded as though someone had thrown a rock against the east wall of the cabin.

Heartbeat quickening, Murron yelled, "Hello? Who's there?"

Then she thought: bear. A chill gripped her. She stepped off the stoop and moved around to the pinto's right side, where she'd strapped a sheathed Winchester carbine to her saddle. She'd always ridden with a gun of some kind. When she'd first come out here, after marrying Garth, he'd taught her how to shoot, and she shot well. At least, she had. She hadn't fired the old-model Winchester in years. She hadn't needed to.

But now . . .

She slid the rifle from the sheath, hefted it in her hands, and stared toward the cabin's east end. Nothing over there. At least, as far as she could see from this angle.

"Hello?" she called again.

Another, lighter thudding sound.

Murron looked up at the roof. A stone bounced off the roof, on the near side of the peak, and rolled down to drop over the side. It thumped onto the rotting wooden stoop.

Murron hardened her jaws in anger as she worked the carbine's cocking lever, racking a cartridge into the Winchester's breech.

Bears don't throw stones.

"Who's there?" she yelled. "I won't ask you again!" No reply.

The anger building in her, she stomped around to the east side of the cabin, holding the carbine straight out before her in both hands, her index finger curled over the trigger.

Rustlers, most likely. Despite Garth's best efforts, they were a dime a dozen out here. She would hire some good, no-nonsense gunhands as soon as this business with Shotgun Johnny was settled. She'd smoke them out and hang every one. They might have thought Garth was tough. Hah!

As she rounded the cabin's rear-east corner, a shadowy figure was running around the opposite corner . . .

"Hold it!"

Murron aimed and fired. The bullet tore a finger-sized chunk of wood out of the wall near the far corner, near where the intruder had been running a quarter second before he'd disappeared around the cabin's far end.

Murron cursed as she ejected the spent cartridge and seated a fresh one. Fury building in her, she ran along the rear of the cabin. She swung wide of the far corner, in case the rustler was waiting for her with his own gun cocked.

No one was there.

She ran back around to the front. Only the pinto stood before the stoop, prancing in place and whickering anxiously.

Murron looked around. "Where'd he go, boy? Where'd the son of a chicken-livered coward go?"

She gazed toward the east end of the cabin again. He had to have gone that way. There was nowhere else for the devil to go. He was playing with her. Toying . . .

That infuriated her even more. Rustlers likely

knew Garth was dead. They thought that she, being a woman, would be someone they could fool with.

"Come out here, dammit!" Murron shouted.

Squeezing the rifle in both hands, she began making her way toward the east end again. She was nearly to the corner when foot thuds rose behind her. She stopped and started to swing around with the rifle, but then the dirty skunk grabbed her from behind around her waist with one arm while ripping the carbine away from her with his other hand.

He laughed. He smelled like leather and tobacco. He laughed heartily as he picked her up off the ground and nuzzled her neck. She could feel the rake of his mustache.

"No!" Murron cried, trying to fight him off.

He laughed and nuzzled her neck. She felt the moistness of his lips and then he poked his tongue in her ear.

"Devil!" she cried. "Do you know who I am?"

Infuriatingly, the question was met with only more laughter.

He was a big man and he was dressed all in black. She could see that much when she slid her eyes to each side, to see behind her. His black hat tumbled off his head as he nuzzled her and lewdly massaged her body with his black-gloved hands. She could feel the lumps of several guns and knives pressing into her back, from where they were sheathed on his big body.

Murron kicked and flung her fists back behind her, trying to free herself. "Let . . . me . . . go . . . !"

Suddenly, he swept her up as though she weighed no more than a sack of flour. He draped her belly-down across his shoulder and, laughing, moved up onto the cabin's stoop. He ducked through the door, crossed the small cabin to the single cot, and tossed her down. She hit the cot on her back, and bounced.

He stood grinning down at her with his devil's dark eyes, white teeth showing beneath his black mustache that contrasted strikingly with the paleness of his long, fine-boned face. He was handsome if you looked at him a certain way, but he resembled a Mexican gargoyle if you just adjusted your view only slightly. He shrugged out of his black wolf coat and threw it aside to reveal the many pistols and knives bristling on his long, tall, black-clad body.

"You *pendéjo*!" Murron barked at him. "You scared the hell out of me!" She felt the heat again in her belly, smiled up at the man. "It's been a while."

"Years," he said in his heavy Spanish accent.

"Too many years." She raised her arms to him. "What are you waiting for? Get down here, El Cuchillo."

He laughed again.

He threw himself down on top of her, and she was his.

CHAPTER 28

Sheila gazed out the bank window, arms crossed on her chest, fuming.

Four men were erecting a gallows in the middle of the broad main street to her right. Two men were carrying wood planks from a dray and handing them to two others who positioned the planks and hammered nails into them. The four had been working since early that morning, and they already appeared to have the grisly, draconian contraption half-built.

Their breaths frosted in the cold mountain air around their heads as they worked.

A handful of young boys in wool coats and knit caps stood in a loose clump on the boardwalk on the opposite side of the street. They were eating hard candy out of paper sacks, watching the construction in wide-eyed delight while a young dog leaped and barked around them, wanting to play.

Sheila shuddered.

"Don't you worry, Miss Bonner," said Mean Mike O'Sullivan, who stood behind her, beside the hulking Silent Thursday, "me and Silent will go over to Flagg's office an' bust ole Johnny out of there. Them

U.S. marshals can't hold a candle to us! We'll fog it out of town and into the mountains. We'll meet you down on the border somewhere—Nogales, say—and head on down into old México. Them federals will never know—"

"No."

Mean Mike frowned at her. "Huh?"

"There will be no busting Johnny out of his cell. That would be admitting that he did something wrong. He did nothing wrong. He was only trying to defend himself against men out to kill him for a murder he didn't commit. He was working for me. He was only trying to do his job. For me. The reason he is locked up in that jail right now is all because of me!"

"No, it ain't." Mean Mike shook his head. "If you'll beg my pardon, Miss Bonner, the real reason Johnny is locked up in that cell is because of Flagg. He's a showboat, Flagg is. He's set his hat for the sheriff's job, an' he thinks a surefire way to get the votes he needs next fall is to hang in public the man he claims killed Rance Starrett an' then went on to kill his papa, too—old Garth, the most powerful man in the county. Maybe the most powerful man in northern California, western Nevada.

"Been here a long time, Garth has. Made a lot of friends. A lot of enemies. Cut a wide swath. Flagg— he's never made nary a track. Well, now, to his way of thinkin', he has." The diminutive graybeard wagged his head again and puffed the quirley forever in the corner of his mouth. "Yessir, he's plumb chompin' at the bit to wear that sheriff's star."

Standing beside Mike, bending his head low to see

out the window but still towering over Sheila and Mike, Silent Thursday grunted.

Mean Mike looked at him. "What's that?"

Silent Thursday dipped his chin, glancing at Sheila. She'd seen the men's reflections in the glass pane before her. Now she turned to Mike, frowning curiously. "What's he saying?"

"Uh . . . well, uh . . ."

"Spit it out, Mike."

Mike's cheeks reddened behind his thin, gray beard. He puffed the quirley, jetted the smoke out his nostrils. "Flagg . . . well . . . I overheard him talkin' one night over to the Silver Slipper. He claimed he was gonna . . . he was gonna . . . well . . ."

He glanced up at Silent Thursday but found no help from that quarter. His hulking partner remained customarily silent.

"Spit it out, Mike," Sheila said, tautly.

"Flagg, he claimed he's gonna marry you." Mean Mike winced as though slapped, puffed the quirley again, and looked down at the scuffed toes of his boots.

Sheila got the fantods from a nearly overwhelming wave of fury. For a second or two, she thought she was going to faint and fall to the floor like a gown tumbling from a hanger.

Mean Mike narrowed an eye at her and raised a helpful hand. "You, uh . . . you all right, Miss Bonner . . . ?"

"No." Sheila drew a deep calming breath, shook her head. "No, I am not all right." She turned to the door, stopped, and looked back at her bank guards. "Stay here. Someone might take advantage of all of the distractions around here to rob the bank. Stay here." She hardened her jaws and wrinkled her nose in barely checked rage. "Even if you hear Flagg screaming like a ten-year-old girl!"

Mean Mike and Silent Thursday shared a dubious glance.

Sheila stormed out of the bank and walked, swung right, and strode quickly up the street to the west. She walked stiffly, taking long strides, holding her chin down, lips pursed, as though trying to keep her head from exploding. Despite the cold and the absence of a coat, she could feel the blood rush into her cheeks. She was sure they were as red as apples.

When she reached Flagg's office, she stopped before the two deputy U.S. marshals sitting on the boardwalk in front of the building, one holding a rifle, the other a shotgun, both smoking cigarettes and sipping coffee from cracked stone mugs. They were dressed in heavy coats against the wintry chill. The larger of the two men sat with his chair tipped back against the jailhouse's front wall, but watching Sheila approach, he let the chair's front legs drop back down to the boardwalk with a dull thud.

His and the other man's eyes glinted lustily beneath the brims of their dark Stetsons, only pouring more fuel on Sheila's fire.

"Hi-dee there, purty lady," said the bigger of the two, and the one nearest to Sheila. The other man sat grinning in his own chair on the other side of the door from the big one, both men positioned to block it. "I'm sorry but I can't let you see the prisoner just now. He's with his attorney, don't ya know."

He smiled and his eyes roamed indiscreetly across the bodice of Sheila's rust-colored, long-sleeved gown trimmed with white lace.

"Some attorney," Sheila scoffed. "I'm not here to see Johnny. I'm here to see Flagg. Let me through."

She started to sidle between the two men, but the bigger man held out his arm to hold her back. "He ain't in his office."

"Where is he?"

The two men shared a sneering glance. "Where do you think?"

"The Silver Slipper."

The two federal marshals only broadened their smiles.

Of course that's where Flagg would be. The saloon was his second home. He spent more time there than he did in his office or on the streets preventing crime, that was for sure. The useless man let his two deputies do the brunt of the law work around Hallelujah Junction. The way the town was still growing, keeping the peace was getting to be a harder and harder job. The town needed a better marshal than Jonah Flagg.

Sheila wheeled and stepped into the street. She let a farm wagon pass, then two horseback riders, ignoring the lingering, lusty gazes of the men around her. She walked back east along the south side of the street and stepped into the Silver Slipper, which sat nearly directly across from the bank, beside another watering hole/house of ill repute—the Black Widow.

Closing the winter door behind her, Sheila squinted into the saloon's murky shadows. Instantly, she saw Flagg. It was easy to pick him out of the shadows because he was only one of three men in the place, not counting the bartender standing in place behind the counter running along the room's left wall, leaning forward to read a newspaper. Flagg was also easy to pick out of the shadows because of the bright white bandage he wore over his nose. The bandage stood out in sharp contrast to the shadows as well as to his dark and swollen eyes and dark and swollen lips, the injuries courtesy of Shotgun Johnny.

If she hadn't been so furious, Sheila would have smiled with satisfaction. Flagg looked miserable, sitting there at the table along the room's right wall.

He sat with two more deputy U.S. marshals. While the two lawmen played two-handed poker for pennies and nickels, Flagg sat glumly with no cards before him but only a half-empty beer mug and an empty shot glass. The beer mug had an egg lolling around near the bottom.

Flagg sat with his arms crossed on the table, running a finger around the rim of his beer glass. When he'd turned his head to see Sheila striding toward him, he turned his entire body in his chair and raised his brows.

His eyes, too, acquired that pathetic look of smoldering goatishness.

"Well, well, well," he said, grinning and kicking out the chair beside him. "Sit down and let me buy you a beer, purty bank lady." His grin grew ever seedier, making his badly swollen eyes shine like oil on dark water. "Or—maybe you come over to buy me one."

He winked then glanced at the two marshals, who'd paused their game to appreciate the comely female wares standing before them.

"Miss Bonner here," Flagg said, keeping his eyes on Sheila. "She fancies me, she does. In fact, we're fixin' to get married, her an' me."

Sheila chuffed. "You must be joking! Do you *really* think I would marry the likes of *you*, Jonah Flagg? If so, you must have been hit in the head way too many times, or, in addition to your simplemindedness, you're plainly insane, to boot!"

The two federal men chuckled.

Flagg's face flushed. At least, it seemed to but it was hard to tell after the battering Johnny had given him. His eyes narrowed and darkened a little beneath the brim of his badly weathered, funnel-brimmed cream hat.

"You're gonna need me when Johnny's dead," Flagg said. "You're gonna need a man to look after you, purty lady. A man to defend you against the brand of cutthroat that's been movin' into our fair, boomin' little city. Why, a woman without a man to protect her is a babe in the woods. No tellin' what might happen."

He'd spoken the words softly but darkly, with no little threat in his cadence. Obviously, he was trying to bully her into marrying him.

"You're a romantic devil," said one of the card-playing federal men. "I'll give you that, Flagg!"

Both men laughed.

Ignoring them, Flagg kept his battered face turned toward Sheila. "Johnny ain't gonna be around much longer. Why, in about two days, he's gonna be kickin' in the wind—guest of honor at his own necktie party!"

"You're an animal," Sheila said, seething, clenching her fists at her sides. "You cooked this whole thing up so you could make a name for yourself . . . and get your dirty hands on *me*. But I won't have it. I know I'm only a woman, Flagg, but as the sole banker in this town, I have power. I have sway with the town council. If you hang Johnny after you hold your kangaroo court day after tomorrow, I will see that you're fired and run out of town on a long, greased pole!"

She'd just gotten the last word out, her shout still echoing in the nearly empty saloon hall, when Flagg lunged forward, swinging his right foot from right to left and kicking Sheila's feet out from beneath her. The floor came up so fast that Sheila didn't have time to break her fall. She struck the floor hard on her head and left shoulder.

Bright red roses blossomed before her eyes.

"Damn, Flagg!" yelled one of the deputy marshals, leaping to his feet in astonishment.

"Pardon me, fellas," Flagg said, gritting his teeth as he glared down at Sheila with his swollen black eyes, his bandaged nose glowing white. He resembled nothing so much as a crazed goat. "Me an' my bride-to-be are gonna go upstairs and have us a little chat about what I expect from a *wife*!"

He grabbed Sheila's arm and pulled her to her feet.

"No!" she cried, trying to pull away from him.

She was too weak from her hard landing to put up much of a fight, and before she knew it, Flagg gave a loud, victorious whoop, crouching and pulling her onto his right shoulder.

One of the deputies laughed incredulously. "What the hell are you doin', you crazy . . . ?"

"Takin' my bride to the proverbial woodshed!" Flagg was hustling toward the back of the room, holding Sheila down tight on his shoulder. "You know what they say—spare the rod, spoil the bride!"

He laughed like a lunatic as he climbed the stairs at the rear of the room. Sheila struggled against him, groaning, but her head was still reeling from Flagg's unexpected assault. She knocked his hat off and pulled his hair, clawed at his face. When Flagg reached the first-floor balcony, he said, "Why, you little polecat—ain't you a *caution*?"

He swung sharply to one side, ramming Sheila's head against the wall.

That dazed her further, rendering her half-unconscious.

When the cobwebs had somewhat cleared, she found herself in a small room and lying belly up on a bed. Flagg was on top of her, grinning down at her, pawing her. She lifted her hands to try to fight him off but he was too strong for her.

"No," she moaned, her heart thudding when she saw that the door behind Flagg was closed. "No . . . stop . . . you pig . . . !"

"Here's how it's gonna be, see?" Flagg was the one seething now while squirming goatishly around on top of her, one hand around her neck, squeezing. "You're gonna get this through your thick head, purty banker lady—or you're gonna get your throat cut!"

Just then the door latch clicked.

CHAPTER 29

Flagg froze with his hand wrapped around Sheila's neck. He stared down at her, a sudden question in his swollen eyes.

Who was opening the door behind him?

Sheila looked over his shoulder. Her eyes widened in surprise to see Glyneen MacFarland step slowly into the small bedroom, extending an over-and-under derringer .44, which she clenched in both of her white-knuckled hands. Anger blossomed in the young woman's pale cheeks.

"Get off of her," she ordered through gritted teeth, her Southern accent especially pronounced in her restrained anger.

Flagg whipped his head around and grunted in shock. "Wha . . . ?"

Miss MacFarland blinked once. Her jaws were hard, her nostrils flared, her dark blue eyes glassy with fury. "Get your stinking filth off of her or I will drive two rounds through your ugly head!"

"Well . . . if it ain't the purty li'l gal from Tennessee!" Flagg removed his hand from around Sheila's neck. He raised both hands awkwardly as he lay sideways now on top of Sheila. "Hold on, purty li'l Southern gal. That peashooter's liable to go off!"

"I said get off of her!" Glyneen screamed at the tops of her lungs. "Or I will give you the bullet you deserve!" She paused, then added, quietly but with cold, certain threat, "For both Miss Bonner . . . and for me."

"Okay, okay!" Flagg rolled off Sheila, to her left. He rolled away from Glyneen, who had entered the room to stand just off the bed's right-rear corner, extending the stubby little, pearl-gripped over-and-under two-shot pistol at Jonah Flagg's head. Awkwardly, trying to keep his hands raised as if believing they would shield him from a bullet, Flagg scrambled off the bed, causing it to pitch wildly on its leather springs. He stepped back from the bed, backing into the opposite corner from Miss MacFarland.

"I'm off of her. I'm off of her! Now, put that gun down!"

Miss MacFarland kept the derringer aimed at Flagg, who appeared truly horrified, hands raised high in front of his face. He turned his head toward the curtained window behind him, cowering from the bullet he believed was imminent.

"I'm sorry," he croaked, one eye closed. "I'm sorry . . . if that's what you want to hear!"

"How would you know what I want to hear, you coward?"

"I said I'm *sorry*!" Flagg yelled, his own voice brittle and quavering with fear. "You, uh . . . you caught me on a bad night's all. I didn't mean . . . you know . . . I'd been drinking—all right? I'm sorry!"

"If you come around either of us ever again, or if I hear that you have another 'bad night' like the one last week . . . ever again . . . I will hunt you down and shoot you down in the street like the cowardly dog you are, Marshal Flagg."

Anger and humiliation seeped into Flagg's battered face, and he straightened his head to glare at the woman aiming the pistol at him. "Listen here, dammit, I'm—"

"Get out," the enraged young woman said tightly.

"All right, all right." Flagg edged haltingly down along the bed toward the open door. "Put the damn gun down. It's liable to go off."

"Oh, it's liable to go off, all right."

"Put it down!"

Flagg increased his pace until he fairly leaped out the door and sidestepped behind the wall to the door's right. He slid his head back into view, dung-brown eyes wide with exasperation. He lifted his arm to point from Glyneen to Sheila with an angry finger, threatening them both. "This ain't over! Not by a long—"

The derringer popped, flashing. Smoke puffed.

"Ach!" Flagg swiped a hand across his ear and looked at it. The palm was blood-streaked. "Jesus!" He whipped around and ran down the hall to the stairs, spurs ringing. *"Crazy damn women!"*

Ears ringing from the sharp report, Sheila looked at Miss MacFarland, still holding the smoking pistol straight out before her. The young woman opened her mouth and released a breath she'd apparently been holding. Lowering the pistol, she took a shambling step straight back, the blood rushing out of her face.

Holding the gun down before her now, she took

several deep, calming breaths then turned to Sheila. "You all right, Miss Bonner?"

Propped on her elbows, gazing up at her unlikely savior in shock, Sheila nodded dully, then managed a smile. "How 'bout you?"

The blonde appeared to think about that for a few seconds, then looked at Sheila once more, her own face shaping a smile. "Good. Yes. I'm good. That felt very . . . very good." She nodded as though to validate the statement. "Are you sure you're all right?"

Sheila sat up and swung her feet to the floor, wincing against the pain in her head. "I'm fine. My head just got banged around a little, is all."

"Let me take a look." Setting the derringer on a small table, Miss MacFarland sat down beside Sheila on the edge of the bed. She placed a hand on Sheila's left cheek, gently turning her head to face her. "Let me look at your eyes."

She placed both hands on Sheila's face and looked from her right eye to the left one, and nodded. "Your pupils are steady. I see no signs of a concussion. How bad does your head hurt?"

"Not bad. It's already fading, in fact. I think I'm mostly just scared. I don't know what I was thinking, confronting a man like that. I guess I didn't realize what he was capable of."

"Yeah, well . . ." Miss MacFarland looked down at the floor as though something was lying heavy on her mind.

"How did you know I was here?"

"I was just down the hall, tending one of the doxies. She's in the family way. I heard the commotion and when I looked into the hall, I saw Flagg carry you in here. I knew what he was up to. He's been up to it . . ." She let her voice trail off as though the words came hard. "Let's just say he's been up to it before."

"I tell you what," Sheila said, placing a hand on Miss MacFarland's arm. "I could use a drink. How 'bout yourself?"

The pretty blonde arched her brows in surprise. Then she smiled. "I don't normally imbibe, but under the circumstances . . ." She nodded slowly, her smile broadening. "Yeah, I could use a shot or two."

Sheila rose from the bed and gestured at the door. "I'm buying."

"Okay." Miss MacFarland laughed. "I'll be right behind you. I just have to fetch my bag from the other room."

Sheila walked down the stairs. The main drinking hall was empty. The bartender and both deputy U.S. marshals were gone. Just as Flagg was gone. Not a man in sight.

"Cowards," Sheila said.

Gaining the main floor, she walked around behind the bar and scrutinized the bottles arranged on shelves lining the back bar, on both sides of the beveled glass mirror. Footsteps sounded on the stairs. She glanced over her shoulder to see Miss MacFarland coming down the steps, holding her bag in her right arm. She'd donned a wool coat, and she held a pair of mittens and knit hat in her left hand.

"I didn't see your distinctive buggy sitting outside," Sheila said.

"I walked here from Doc Albright's office. My mother needed the buggy today. She sells eggs around town."

Sheila nodded, vaguely reflecting that she knew

virtually nothing about the woman. It seemed high time to remedy the situation. Sheila gave a wry smile. "Name your poison."

Miss MacFarland set her bag on a table near the front of the room, near the bar, and gave another deep sigh. "Something strong!"

"Let's have brandy." Sheila held the bottle up to show the pretty doctor's assistant. "It even has a label."

"Rare for around here!" The young woman laughed, then frowned as she glanced around the room. "Are we alone?"

Sheila grabbed a couple of goblets off a pyramid atop the bar then headed for Miss MacFarland's table. "Not a man in sight."

"Cowards."

Sheila laughed and set the goblets on the table. She popped the cork and started to fill a glass when the front door opened and the portly, bald Mort Stanley entered on a breeze gust laced with dead leaves. Stanley stopped abruptly when he saw that the only two customers were Sheila and Miss MacFarland. He'd lifted his hat a few inches from his head, and it froze there now, as the mercantiler looked around bewilderedly.

"The Silver Slipper is open for female clientele only, Mr. Stanley," Sheila said.

Stanley gulped. His heavy jowls were red from the cold and now from embarrassment, as well. "For, uh . . . how long?"

"Until we stagger out of here," said Miss MacFarland.

"Oh. Well . . . all right, then!" Stanley reset his hat on his head, swung around, and hurried back outside, jerking the door closed behind him.

Sheila and Miss MacFarland looked at each other and snickered.

Sheila filled two glasses, slid one over to her drinking partner, set the bottle on the table, then slacked into a chair. She picked up her glass.

"Cheers."

Miss MacFarland touched her glass to Sheila's. "Cheers."

They each threw down at least half their brandy.

"I needed that," said the doctor's assistant, setting her glass back down on the table.

"Me, too."

Miss MacFarland looked at her. "How did it start?"

"I had a tantrum."

"Because of Mr. Greenway? Being locked up, I mean? Awaiting Flagg's kangaroo court?"

"Mostly." Sheila polished off her brandy. "How 'bout you?"

"What's that?"

"How did it start with you? Flagg, I mean."

Glyneen stared at her for a long time, hesitating. Then she lowered her gaze to the table, and her cheeks turned a shade paler than normal. A sickly pale. She finished her own brandy, and Sheila refilled both of their glasses.

Glyneen leaned forward, her elbows on the table, one hand wrapped around the goblet before her. She hardened her jaws and narrowed her eyes with renewed fury. "He . . . had . . . had his way with me. By force."

Sheila placed a hand over her mouth. "No."

"I was late getting home. I'd helped Doc Albright with a complicated delivery—Mrs. Frieze over on

Hell's 's Knob." Miss MacFarland shook her head as though to haze herself back on track. "Anyway, I saw Flagg leaving a saloon as I rode through town. He must have seen me and took after me. He must have taken a shortcut, because he met me at the cabin I share with my parents. He was standing by the buggy shed as I drove into the yard."

Sheila drew a slow, deep, calming breath, steeling herself for what she suspected was coming.

"He scared the holy hell out of me," Glyneen said, flushing a little and gazing directly at Sheila. "I don't say those words lightly, for my folks raised me by the Golden Rule, Miss Bonner, but that's what he did, all right. The house was dark except for the one lamp Mama always leaves burning when I'm out working with the doc. I wanted to scream for help, but I was worried what Flagg might do to my poor old parents."

She paused, sipped her brandy, shook her head, drawing her mouth corners down with remembered terror. "I tried to fight him off. I really did. He hardly said a word. He just told me that good girls don't come home after dark. He told me he found my accent 'right fetchin'.' And then he went after me. I ran into the buggy shed, tried to lock him out, but he pushed his way inside, and . . ."

Her voice choked off in a sob.

Sheila sipped her own brandy, then slid her hand across the table. She placed it on one of Miss MacFarland's and squeezed.

The young woman sobbed again then brushed tears from her cheeks.

"Did you tell anyone?"

"Who was there to tell? He's the town marshal."
Glyneen stared down at her brandy.

"Your mother . . . your father?"

Miss MacFarland sniffed. "They wouldn't understand. Ma's very old, traditional. She just . . . she wouldn't understand. Besides, her health isn't good. The doc thinks she has a cancer."

"I'm sorry," Sheila said, meaning it.

"What brought you out here?"

"We followed Poppa after the war. First, Mama and I stayed home to tend my brother, Steven. He took shrapnel from a Napoleon cannon at Gettysburg. They sent him home because they couldn't heal him. Tending him is how I learned the healing trade. He came home just after I was born, but I tended to him as soon as I was able—eight or nine years old. To give Mama a rest.

"I learned from the older women who lived out amongst us in the hills and hollers I grew up in, near Ringgold, Tennessee. Those old gals practiced the ancient healing arts handed down to them from other women in their families. Few doctors in those hills back then. When Steven died, which we knew he would sooner or later, for the shrapnel had wrecked his heart, Mama and I followed Poppa out here. We had to leave Ringgold. Such a heartbroken place after the war . . ."

She sipped her brandy, set the glass back down on the table, and gave it a turn. "And . . . here I am . . ."

She looked over at Sheila, her wet blue eyes cast with dread.

"He's going to hang Mr. Green—" She stopped, shook her head. "Flagg—he's going to hang Johnny, isn't he? He's going to win. Just like the damnable Yankees who killed my brother!"

Sheila slid her hand back to her own side of the table. "I honestly don't know. I like to think that things usually turn out for the best, but now I'm not so sure." She finished the brandy and then refilled Miss MacFarland's glass as well as her own. "I do know this, though. Flagg will come after us."

"I know. I probably shouldn't have taken that notch out of his ear."

"Good shooting."

"No, I meant to miss!"

They had another laugh over that. The brandy was working its magic, but their laughter died quickly.

"What happens when he comes for us?" Miss MacFarland asked, haltingly, slowly turning her glass on the table.

Sheila sat up straight and drew a deep breath. "We don't aim to miss."

She held up her glass.

Miss MacFarland nodded. "It's hard to miss with Ole Hazel." She touched her glass to Sheila's. "Cheers."

CHAPTER 30

Homer Kinnon, Johnny's court-appointed attorney, cleaned his round, steel-framed spectacles with his tobacco-stained fingers and scowled at Johnny through the bars of Johnny's cell in Jonah Flagg's jailhouse office.

"Okay . . . now, now . . . tell me again, Johnny— where exactly are you sayin' Starrett's bunch jumped you . . . ?" He set the glasses on his nose, wrapping each bow around each ear and then touched the tip of his pencil to his tongue. "I need to get it all down here so's I can—"

"Never mind." Johnny lay back on his bunk, head and shoulders propped against the cold stone wall, rolling a cigarette. "Don't matter, Homer. Not one bit."

"What're you talkin' about—it don't matter?" Kinnon, who was as old as the hills and looked every year of it, hadn't defended a capital case in twenty or thirty years. In fact, Johnny had thought the attorney had been long dead until Flagg half dragged the poor old retired sot out of a whore's crib somewhere on the bad end of town, brought him into his office, and poured him a stiff cup of java to clear the old man's alcohol haze.

Glaring in astonishment through the cell door bars, Kinnon held up his lined, coffee-and-whiskey-stained legal pad covered with his penciled chicken scratch, and said, "You know what they got on you, son? They say you killed both *Rance* and *Garth Starrett*!" The penciled pages scratched as he gestured with the pad toward the window behind him. "You hear them hammers out yonder? You know what them carpenters are *workin' on*?"

Johnny knew all too well. He'd been hearing men building the gallows for his necktie party just outside the jailhouse for the past two days. Already townsfolk, whistling while they worked, were hanging bunting from telegraph poles and stringing banners across the main street at each end of town, advertising the hanging, which had been scheduled for the day after tomorrow though the federal judge hadn't even arrived yet and there wouldn't be a trial until at least tomorrow morning.

No, a jury hadn't yet been seated. Still, it was a lead-pipe cinch that hemp would be stretched the day after tomorrow.

The man who'd be stretching it would be none other than the notorious Shotgun Johnny. It was such a bonded fact that stringers from big eastern newspapers had been rushed to Hallelujah Junction to document the whole gala-like shindig—from the moment the condemned man is led up the gallows steps to the moment his feet stop kicking the midair two-step five feet beneath the platform.

It was such a certainty that the Hallelujah Junction Ladies' Sobriety League was just then printing up flyers to pass around to the crowd, urging the wretched sinners to resist temptation while at the same time the local saloon owners were expressing freight teams from Sacramento bearing tons of whiskey and beer kegs while every parlor girl in and around town was catching up on her beauty sleep so she was in top, indefatigable form on what would surely be the most lucrative day of the year—bigger than New Year's and the Fourth of July put together!

Food vendors were organizing, and a band had been commissioned. Johnny had heard the fiddlers and horn blowers warming up in a nearby saloon the past two evenings following supper. There was a definite excitement in the air. It could not be denied. And Johnny knew that the town would not be denied its hanging.

Never mind that Johnny was relatively well liked in these parts. But he *was* a Basque, you know. Not a white man at all. No, no—not really. He was one of those odd, reclusive mountain people who dress strange, talk even stranger, keep to themselves, and follow their sheep over hill and dale with no real and proper home. It hadn't helped him, of course, that he'd been making time with the most beautiful young lady in town. That rankled even his most ardent admirers enough that, well, who were they to protest a party?

Besides, everyone knew what happened when you messed with the Starretts. Well, it was happening now. The dark clouds of a surefire reckoning had gathered. Poor Johnny. Hey, save me a place up close to the gallows, will you, friend?

"All that hammer-poundin', you mean?" Johnny

said, blowing smoke rings. "Ain't that Rocky Burnette puttin' a new porch on the Black Widow?"

"Pshaw! You know what all that hammer-poundin's about. It's about . . ." Kinnon glanced over his shoulder at Jonah Flagg kicked back in his office chair, pretending to be asleep beneath his hat, and the two deputy U.S. marshals sitting around the potbelly stove in their fur coats, sipping coffee from steaming stone mugs and playing a desultory game of cribbage. "It's about them fellas playin' cat's cradle with your head!"

Jonah Flagg opened a swollen, black eye poking out from beneath his ratty hat and said, "You heard the man, Johnny. That's what it's all about, all right. Listen to that." Flagg grinned and gave a luxurious sigh. "Ahhh—music to my ears!"

Kinnon turned on the milk stool he was sitting on outside of Johnny's cell. "Marshal Flagg, is it not my prisoner's constitutional right to be able to confer with his attorney in *private*?"

"Nah," Flagg said, his eyes closed again, boots crossed on his desk, hands laced across his bulging potbelly. He had a big, white bandage over his nose, and his lips bristled with a dozen stitches. The broken nose gave him a high nasal twang. "The constitution's done been changed since you last practiced law, Homer. You wouldn't know 'cause you been three sheets to the wind for the past twenty years. Besides, I ain't listenin' to anything you been sayin'. I been asleep." He lifted his chin to call to the two federals. "Hey, Halsey, Antrim—you boys ain't been listenin' to Johnny and his lawyer's private conversation, have you?"

"Hell, no," said Deputy U.S. Marshal Jeff Halsey. "That'd be against the law."

"Besides," added Deputy U.S. Marshal Burt Antrim, moving a peg on the cribbage board while he rolled a sharpened match stick between his furred lips, "can't you see we're all involved in our game here?"

"Hey, Flagg," Johnny called from his cot.

Flagg looked at him, scowling. "What?"

"How'd you get that fresh bandage on your ear?"

Flagg's scowl deepened and his eyes darkened as he swept his hand across the fresh, bloodstained bandage over his right ear. The marshals snickered to themselves.

Flagg cast them a wicked glare then shuttled the glare to Johnny. "I cut myself shavin'. Now, shut up about it, or I'll grease you right there on the cot, and save the hangman the trouble!"

He pulled his hat down over his eyes again.

"Shavin', huh?" Johnny said, scrutinizing the man dubiously.

Kinnon grumbled and turned back to Johnny, who blew another smoke ring. The attorney wagged his head then, scowling, rose heavily up from the stool, and turned to Flagg. "Marshal, you said you have an eyewitness who will testify that Johnny shot Rance Starrett in cold blood. I think it's high time you produced this so-called witness of yours!"

Flagg poked his hat up onto his head again and turned his battered face to Kinnon and Johnny. "I got a coupla fellas out lookin' for him right now, Teagarden, too. He seems to have wandered away from Inter-Mountain despite the nice big three-room suite the town provided for him. He's likely over at one of your preferred haunts, Kinnon—a sour-smellin' whore's crib on the wrong end of town."

Flagg and the marshals chuckled.

Kinnon cursed Flagg tartly until the marshal looked at him crossways and said, "Don't you curse me, you old reprobate. If it weren't for me, you'd still be muckin' out saloons after dark for drinkin' money. The taxpayers are payin' you good to represent this cold-blooded killer though why the law thinks he needs defendin' after all his depredations is way beyond me! But since it says he does, you're here. Don't make me regret that fact or I'll . . ."

He stopped when voices rose just beyond the office door and boots drummed on the boardwalk fronting it. All heads turned toward the door as it opened and a tall man in a torn blanket coat came in, spurs ringing.

"We found him," he said as the door banged back against the wall. He grinned as he walked over to the fire and put his back to it, shivering. "Found him over at Miss Dove's place."

Behind the tall man a much smaller, older man shuffled in. Johnny recognized him as Winky Peters, the man who was said to have seen Johnny kill Rance Starrett in cold blood. Peters was in his late fifties though he looked at least seventy. His clothes were rags, including the rabbit fur hat with earmuffs hanging loose against his bony jaws, and his old wool coat, which bore the ancient sour stains of only God knew what, and even he didn't want a sniff. He was a little larger than Mean Mike, with a round owl's face and a single brow. A thin beard, like the coat of a mange-ravaged coyote, clung to his red-splotched, liver-spotted cheeks.

Two men followed Peters into the room. They,

like the tall man who'd entered ahead of them, were dressed in the worn, dung-splattered range garb of out-of-work cowhands likely wintering here in Hallelujah Junction. One more man entered behind them, and in his tailored outfit complete with steel-gray beaver hat and sleek cinnamon bear coat and black horsehair gloves, he looked like a golden goose swimming with mud hens.

This was the county prosecutor, Warren Teagarden.

"Miss Dove's place!" intoned Jonah Flagg, who'd climbed up from his chair and regarded his primary witness with amused incredulity. "Whatever possessed you to think you could patronize Miss Dove's whorehouse, Winky?"

Everyone around knew that Miss Sylvia Dove ran the toniest parlor house in Hallelujah Junction. Now, that wasn't saying much, of course. But the fact remained.

"That's what you get for stuffing his pockets full of silver certificates," chuffed Teagarden, shouldering two of his raggedy-heeled associates aside so he could soak up some of the heat from the potbelly stove. Apparently, it was a cold day.

"That was for room service over at the Inter-Mountain!" objected Flagg.

"Well, he decided to go over to Miss Dove's and get him some o' that high-priced stuff. When Miss Dove kicked him out before he even got beyond her porch, one of the girls slipped him a bottle, and ole Winky retreated to the woodshed for a party by himself— just him and a quart of labeled bourbon."

"*Labeled* bourbon?" Flagg asked.

"The girl must've felt sorry for him."

"Winky, dammit!" Flagg berated the little man who

stood looking around the room as though he'd just awakened from a dream and couldn't quite get shed of it. "You were makin' me as nervous as a cat in an attic full of rockin' chairs. You know you're the primary witness to Starrett's killin'. The judge needs you high an' dry! Now, for cryin' in Grant's whiskey, plant your skinny butt in the Inter-Mountain until I come fetch you for trial! If you want a woman, I'll send you a woman. Hell, I'd send you two or three at a time if I didn't think even one under the age of fifty would kill you!"

Laughter all around.

Even Johnny had to smile at that one.

"Hey, look at that," Flagg said when the laughter had settled. He'd glanced out the window and now turned full toward it, his back to where Johnny remained on his cot, resignedly smoking his quirley.

"Look at what?" asked one of the federals.

"That there." Flagg moved to the window to the left of his desk and whistled. "Is that who I think it is?"

"Is who, who you think he is?" Antrim said, and rolled the matchstick from one side of his mouth to the other.

Flagg sucked a breath and tightened his shoulders. He was turning his head slowly from left to right, apparently following someone moving in that direction along the street before him. "Sure enough. I do believe it is . . ."

"Oh, fer chrissakes, Flagg!" yelled Deputy Halsey.

Flagg turned, his blue eyes wide in their swollen sockets and his lower jaw hanging. "I heard he'd been seen in town though I ain't seen him myself . . . until just now. He done went into the Silver Slipper. Just seein' the man purely lifts the hair on the back of my neck." He shivered and swiped a hand at his collar, as though to dislodge a spider. "I swear if it ain't like havin' someone step on your grave, or feelin' a cold wind—"

Antrim waved a stick of split firewood and bellowed, "Flagg, if you don't come on out with it, you're gonna need another visit from Doc Albright!"

"Jose Ramon Cordobés," Flagg said, enunciating each name carefully and with no little dark foreboding in his softly pitched voice. *"El Cuchillo."*

No one said anything.

The two federals looked at each other.

"Ah, hell," Antrim said, and dropped the stick back into the wood box.

"He ain't what we're here for," Halsey said, flushing as he shifted uncomfortably around in his chair. "Besides, I don't get paid near enough to tangle with that rabid Mexican polecat. Maybe . . . if I was to get a raise . . . a big, *big* raise . . . I'd think about it."

Antrim turned the matchstick end over end in his mouth and grumbled, "Yeah, well, my wife's due to drop our sixth kid in a couple weeks, so let's forget about it an' get on with the game. Besides, I think Shotgun Johnny scrambled Flagg's brains around an' he's seein' ghosts. I heard the Arizona Rangers killed El Cuchillo down around the border a couple years ago."

"Ah hell." Flagg had returned his attention to the window.

"Now what is it?" complained Antrim in a huff. "Don't tell me John Wesley Hardin done just rode into town, now, too!"

"No," Flagg said. "Worse."

He turned to the federals sitting around the stove. "It's Mrs. Starrett. She just pulled up in front of the office. I think she's comin' in."

Antrim and Halsey stared at Flagg, expressionless.

Garth Starrett had been feared far and wide. But he'd been a newborn kitten compared to his wife. Joke had it that just whispering her name could make a baby cry in the next county.

Finally, Antrim spit out his toothpick, laughed, and turned to look over his shoulder at Johnny. "Hear that, Johnny? No point in finishin' that gallows. The she-wolf's here for blood!"

CHAPTER 31

Johnny blew one final smoke ring then dropped his cigarette butt into the chamber pot beneath his bunk. He picked up his makin's sack and started to roll another quirley. He didn't really want another smoke, just something to do.

As he pulled out a fresh Brahma Bull wheat paper, he watched Flagg move a little uneasily to the jail-house door and pull it open. She was standing there in the doorway as though she'd been waiting for one of her lessers to open the door for her, so she wouldn't have to soil one of her black-gloved hands on the knob.

"How do, Miss Starrett," Flagg said, awkwardly removing his hat and holding it over his chest. "Sure am sorry for your loss, ma'am. I mean, um . . . *losses*."

Murron Starrett looked at Flagg, whom she was nearly as tall as, then slid her moody gaze around him to the other men in the room—Johnny's so-called attorney, Homer Kinnon, the two U.S. marshals and Teagarden, the prosecuting attorney, as well as Winky Peters and the three out-of-work range hands who'd hauled him out of the woodshed behind Miss Dove's parlor house.

The men sat in awkward silence until Flagg loudly cleared his throat. All the other men in the room, except Johnny, snapped into action. Those who'd been sitting—the marshals—lurched to their feet and removed their hats. The standing men fumbled their hats from their heads, held them over their chests, and muttered their condolences to the most powerful woman in the county if not most of northern California and all of western Nevada.

Johnny slowly dribbled chopped tobacco onto the wheat paper troughed between his fingers.

"That sure is tough, ma'am," Flagg said in his halting, wheedling tone. "Losin' both your son and your husband . . . Mr. Starrett. I still can't quite wrap my mind around—"

She cut him off with: "Are you going to invite me in or make me stand out here on the street, Marshal Flagg?"

"Oh, Christ almighty—of course, of course. I mean . . . well . . . pardon my French, but do please come in out of the cold, Mrs. Starrett!" Flagg almost literally leaped backward, jerking the door along with him, raking the door against the toes of his badly worn boots and stumbling back onto his jangling spurs. "We got him all locked up. You can see for yourself. He ain't goin' nowhere. No, sir! The only place Shotgun Johnny's goin' is over to the Silver Slipper for his trial . . . just as soon as the judge arrives . . . and then straight from the Slipper to the gallows. He'll be dancin' with the devil by noon day after tomorrow, sure enough. You'll be resting easier once we get his filthy carcass in a grave up on Boot Hill, ma'am. Again, Mrs. Starrett, I sure am sor—"

"Flagg, would you please shut up?" she said, not looking at the town marshal before her but around the smoky potbelly stove and through the crowd of men standing stiffly around it.

She stared at Johnny rolling his quirley closed on his bunk.

Murron Starrett moved into the room, the men hastily, awkwardly making way for her. She was dressed in a long mink coat under which she wore a hooded black cape with a red inner lining. The hood was pulled up over her head. She wore her silver-streaked hair in a wind-blown mess tumbling down the front of the sleek, black coat. She was a handsome mature woman with crazy witch's eyes, and Johnny could not look away from those eyes boring into his as she moved through the room toward his cell.

As she did, he saw several of her ranch hands, who'd apparently accompanied her to town, one having driven her chaise, milling around outside on the boardwalk. A well-dressed gent stepped into the office, following Murron.

He wore a fox fur coat that hung to his knees, and a stylish beaver hat that matched the light tans and browns of the coat. What was really impressive about him were his combed sideburns and waxed handle-bar mustache, all of which were snow white, in contrast to the russet color of the man's handsome though aged face, the parchment skin drawn taut as a drum-head across the sharp, nicely chiseled bones.

He appeared somewhere in his late fifties, early sixties. A white-stemmed pipe with a cobalt china bowl protruded from a corner of his mouth. Instantly, the spiced aromatic tobacco filled the office as the man followed Murron in his leisurely gait, poking at the floor with a scrolled wooden cane capped with an obsidian horse head.

The other, more rough-hewn men in the room regarded the tony gent with quick, furtive, scowling glances, shuttling querying glances among themselves.

Murron stepped up to Johnny's cell and gazed in at him, her eyes piercing but a faint, bemused smile creasing her mouth corners.

"How are they treating you, Johnny?" she asked.

Johnny struck a match to life on a cell bar to his left. "Me, I feel like a robber baron holed up at the Park Avenue Hotel." He indicated the dapper gent standing to her left. "Who's your friend? I like his coat."

"This is Mr. Sterling Woodward from Reno. I've hired Mr. Woodward to be your attorney."

A silence so heavy came over the office that if it weren't for the sounds out on the street, including the hammer blows of the gallows construction, you could have heard a mouse fart beneath the floor.

Woodward narrowed his tobacco-brown, deep-set eyes in a bemused smile at Johnny and in reaction to the speechless reactions of the other men in the room. Beside him, resembling a scarecrow in contrast to the Reno attorney—one who'd seen more than his fair share of seasons in the cornfields, at that— Homer Kinnon made a whining sound deep in his chest. Flagg moved toward the cell, canting his head to one side and frowning—or what was probably a frown though it was hard to tell given the swelling around his eyes and nose.

"Uh . . . who'd you say he was, Mrs. Starrett?"

Murron turned to regard the men staring hang-jawed at her, and tipped her hand to indicate the dapper fellow beside her, who also turned to face the room. "I have hired Mr. Woodward to defend Mr. Greenway."

Homer Kinnon had finally conjured up enough gumption from what little remained inside him to say, "I'm . . . why . . . I'm . . . Johnny's . . ." Letting his eyes run up and down Woodward's well-attired frame, Kinnon let the objection trail off to oblivion, just as his eyes settled on the floor near the toes of Woodward's fox fur boots, and stayed there.

"You see," Murron continued, "I want to make sure that Shotgun Johnny is given a fair shake in court. I want there to be no question that, after the final fall of the judge's gavel, all has been done officially and properly, that the statutes have been followed to their last gilt letter. We wouldn't want anyone to call into question the veracity of these proceedings—now, would we Marshal Flagg?

"We are a growing city as well as a growing county, and we wouldn't want anyone to accuse us of allowing sham court proceedings—even when it comes to the murder of two men from a prominent family—now, would we, Marshal Flagg? That would be an insult to justice everywhere, and specifically an insult to the brand of justice we serve up here in Hyde County and in Hallelujah Junction. The West is growing more and more civilized by the day, and we here don't want to be called a backwater—now, do we? Holding back the refinements of progress wouldn't be good for any of us."

Flagg studied her closely, as did the other men in the room, as though they were awaiting the kicker of a joke. They seemed to be trying to figure out if she was kidding or not, or maybe just playing up the officiality of things for the dapper little gent in the fox fur coat and whatever eastern stringers might be scribbling in notebooks just outside the open door.

Surely, she wasn't serious.

Finally, Flagg laughed, as though getting the joke and wanting to play along.

"Hell, no!" he intoned. "Uh . . . pardon my French again there, ma'am. Rest assured that ole Shotgun Johnny is gonna get a letter-o'-the-law court trial over at the Silver Slipper in advance of our hangin' him. He's already got him a lawyer. Court appointed, don't ya know. Leastways, I appointed Mr. Kinnon on the court's behalf, just to save time. A man is supposed to get a fair and prompt trial. Leastways, that's what I always heard."

He glanced at the two U.S. marshals as though for corroboration. They just stood by the smoking wood-stove, still holding their hats over their chests, staring at him blankly.

The Reno attorney, Sterling Woodward, glanced out the window to the east. "I see that you're building a platform of some kind."

"That's the gallows we're gonna hang Johnny from," Flagg said, beaming unctuously at Murron Starrett, then stretching his lips in a toothy grin. "Just after we give him that fair trial, of course!" He rose up and down on his boot toes and winked.

"Do you know, sir," said Woodward, "that it is

Nevada territorial law that no gallows shall be built until a final verdict has been rendered? You see, by doing so you're prejudging the outcome. *Prejudgment* is not the way of justice."

"Oh hell, like I said—I'm just tryin' to save time." Flagg looked at Murron again. "I mean, everyone knows he's guilty as sin. I mean, he shot your son, Mrs. Starrett, in cold blood!"

"How do you know that?" Murron asked.

Flagg turned and looked around. Finding the man he was looking for, he walked around behind Winky Peters, who stood staring into space like a man in a trance—in a badly *hungover* trance, at that. Placing his hands on Winky's shoulders, Flagg walked him forward to stand before Mrs. Starrett and Sterling Woodward.

"Mr. Winky Peters, say hello to Mrs. Starrett."

"Hello."

Murron dipped her chin cordially. "The pleasure is all mine, Mr. Peters."

Smiling over Winky's head at Mrs. Starrett, Flagg said, "Winky, tell Mrs. Starrett about how you saw Shotgun Johnny shoot her son, Rance Starrett, in cold blood."

"Yep, I did, all right," Winky said. He glanced up over his shoulder at Flagg. "Marshal, can I go back over to the Inter-Mountain now? I could use a drink powerful bad!"

"Not just yet," Flagg said tightly. Returning his oily smile to Mrs. Starrett and the natty attorney, Flagg said, "Winky, tell Mrs. Starrett an' Mr. Woodward how it played out. You know—in Riley Duke's Saloon on the way up to the Reverend's Temptation Gold Mine."

"He shot him, sure as tootin'," Winky said, rubbing his dirty hands on the lapels of his ratty blanket coat.

"Who did?" asked Woodward.

"Huh?"

"Who shot who?"

"Johnny did. He shot . . ." Winky scowled up over his shoulder at Flagg again. "Who'd you say Johnny shot again?"

The other men in the room snickered.

Tightly, nostrils flaring, face flushing around the swelling and discoloration, Flagg said, "Rance Starrett, you imbecile! Just tell it how you told it to me and Mr. Teagarden!"

Woodward interjected with: "Is this your only witness to the killing of Rance Starrett, Marshal Flagg?"

"Uh . . . well . . . yeah. But he's just nervous, Winky is!"

"This man's testimony wouldn't hold up in court, Marshal," said Woodward. "He's obviously . . . unwell."

"No, no, he ain't. But he's just for starters. We got it all sewed up for your husband, Mr. Starrett."

"Oh? Do you have an eyewitness to his killing, as well?"

"Yes, ma'am, I do. Myself." Flagg smiled victoriously.

"Oh, *you*?" Murron said, smiling brightly . . . coldly. "Pray tell—what did you see?"

"I saw Shotgun Johnny shoot him!"

"With a shotgun?" Murron asked.

"Of course!"

"He wasn't shot with a shotgun." Woodward glanced at Mrs. Starrett. "It's my understanding Mr. Starrett was shot with a rifle. Probably a high-powered rifle."

"His head had exploded like a ripe cantaloupe," put in Murron, her voice taut. "Everyone knows Johnny doesn't carry a rifle—high-powered or otherwise." She glanced over her shoulder at Johnny still reclining on his cot, smoking, observing the proceedings in quiet fascination, not sure what in hell the lady and her expensive defense attorney were up to, but being visited by a chill breath against the back of his neck, just the same . . .

"You see, Flagg," said Woodward, "even if you did see Johnny shoot Garth Starrett, your catch-party was illegal."

"What?!"

Woodward now spoke to the prosecutor, Warren Teagarden, who stood several feet behind Flagg, staring at the floor and nervously tapping his left thumb against his hip. He looked as though he would rather be anywhere but where he was.

Woodward said, "You didn't have ample cause to go after the accused. It was his word against Rance Starrett's . . . or against that of the very undependable Winky Peters, who, I understand, spent several days in an oxygen-deprived, caved-in mine. Even if you had a signed warrant for Mr. Greenway's arrest, which I doubt that you did, since there was no judge here to sign one, it wouldn't hold up in court. In a proper court of law, a bona fide judge would dismiss the case before opening arguments."

"What?!"

"Vigilantism is against the law!" Woodward declared, speaking slowly enough that even an idiot could understand.

Apparently, it was too complicated for Flagg, however. The town marshal stared in hang-jawed shock at Murron Starrett, for nearly a minute making a strangling sound in his throat. "I . . . I don't understand. That there . . . Mrs. Starrett, that there is the man who killed Rance . . . an' Mr. Starrett. I mean, he's *responsible*, leastways. Look at him layin' there, lookin' all satisfied with himself!"

Johnny drew deeply on his quirley, blew the smoke at Flagg.

Murron didn't look at Johnny but kept her back to him. To Flagg, she said very quietly but firmly, "Turn him loose."

Flagg laughed. It was half a scream. "What?!"

"Turn him loose."

Lower jaw still drooping nearly to his chest, Flagg looked around the room as though for help. No one said anything. The others didn't even look at him. Well, one man did. That was Winky Peters, who'd been standing in front of Flagg, head hanging as though in shame though he couldn't fully comprehend what he should be ashamed about.

Now Winky, keeping his eyes on the floor, wheeled and scuttled mouselike through the crowded, smoky room and slithered nearly soundlessly out the door and into the street. He was followed by one of the U.S. marshals. Then the second marshal slipped out behind the first. It was as though they were the condemned men, and they'd suddenly found a way out of their own hanging.

That started a clearing of the whole rest of the room, the other men, including Teagarden and even Johnny's "attorney," Homer Kinnon, scuffling quietly, shamefully on out of the room and into the street, likely heading for the nearest watering hole or parlor house to distract themselves from the embarrassing situation they'd just endured in the jailhouse.

Finally, there were only Johnny, Murron Starrett, Woodward, and Flagg.

Flagg said haltingly, "I don't understand, Mrs. Starrett. I don't . . . I don't understand . . ."

"You fool," Murron said. "Do you think a public hanging is what I wanted?"

Flagg didn't have an answer for that.

Murron glanced over her shoulder at Johnny. She kept her voice down. She didn't want the newspaper scribblers scribbling down anything she said next. "That would be far too neat and simple. And *painless.*"

Johnny snorted, smiled. Now he understood.

He tossed his cigarette into the chamber pot, rose from the cot, and walked over to the door. He wrapped his hands around the bars and stared at Flagg. "You wasted your time, Flagg. That whole chase . . . all those men dead . . ." He glanced at Murron. ". . . Garth Starrett—dead. For nothing."

"Oh, not for nothing, Mr. Greenway. Garth and the others—they did it their way. They sought justice their way."

"Frontier justice," Johnny said.

"They sought frontier justice *their* way. And failed." Murron smiled but there was no humor or benevolence in it. Far from it. It was like the slash of a very sharp, very pretty knife. "Now it's my turn." She turned to Flagg. "Let him out."

She glanced at Woodward, then headed for the door. Like a well-trained dog, the fox fur–ensconced attorney was close on her heels.

Flagg moved up to the cell door. Expressionless, he poked the key in the lock, turned it. Johnny grabbed his hat off the cot. He turned to the door as Flagg opened it, staring glumly through the opening at Johnny.

"Don't look so sad, Flagg." Johnny moved through the opening and strode past the smoking woodstove as he headed for the open outside door. "It ain't over."

He stopped in the doorway and stared across the street busy with late-morning traffic. Instantly, his eyes picked out a tall man dressed in a black wolf coat and black leather trousers, standing on the board-walk of a saloon directly across the street from the jailhouse. The man wore a black, flat-brimmed, low-crowned hat. He had a long, marble-white face and a thick, black mustache.

He stared across the busy street at Johnny. As he did, he grinned and raised a half-empty beer mug in salute.

Johnny recognized him instantly. That was death standing there, grinning at him.

The sun glinted gold off El Cuchillo's beer mug as the man lifted it to his lips and drank.

"No," Johnny said with a long, weary sigh. "It ain't over by a long shot."

CHAPTER 32

Several days later, early in the morning, Sheila grabbed his arm. "Let's leave now, Johnny. Now. *Today!* Why wait?"

"Unfinished business," Johnny said as he tightened a pack mule's belly strap.

They were standing outside of his cabin. It was cold but the dawn was coming on clear. The air was touched with the pine tang of smoke unfurling from the cabin's chimney pipe. Johnny had saddled Ghost and the two compactly built pack mules he used on the bullion runs. They were short-legged, stout-hipped beasts, perfect for mountain packing.

Sheila had shown up a few minutes earlier, to convince him not to go.

"Johnny, let's—"

He turned to her, placed his hands on her arms. "We talked about this last night. We both agreed I should make the run. That Mexican killer will follow me. He's been shadowing me for the past week around town. He's trying to unnerve me while waiting for me to make one last run this year. When I do . . ."

"I know, I know. You explained it all very clearly to me last night. When he does, you'll lead him into the mountains and kill him, just like the others."

"It worked before."

"This is Cordobés we're talking about. El Cuchillo. Christ, what a nickname!"

"He's one man, Sheila. I know his reputation. No man who's worn the moon-and-star doesn't know it. He thinks he can run me down up there, kill me slow . . . for Murron Starrett." Johnny smiled, shook his head. "He'll try. And I'll lead him, just like I led her dead son, back to her ranch riding belly-down across his horse."

Sheila shivered and hugged herself. She wasn't cold. Just frightened.

"It all seemed a lot more sensible last night. Before I went to bed. After my head hit the pillow, I couldn't sleep a wink. I just lay there, imagining you two . . ." She turned to the northwest where the high ridges were starting to define themselves. "Fighting it out up there in those mountains . . . alone. With only one of you riding back alive."

She wheeled to him, placed both her bare hands on his cheeks. "Let it be you, Johnny."

"I will, honey."

She smiled. "I like the sound of that."

"You'll be hearing it a lot more often." Johnny smiled broadly, slitting his long brown eyes, which flashed warmly in the pearl dawn light. "When I'm back, we'll haul our tails down to San Francisco, get married, hop a steamer for Mexico, make a fresh start together. We'll be leaving clean. No loose strings."

"She'll send others."

"Not to Mexico."

Sheila sighed. Her pretty face acquired a pained expression. "I love you so much, Johnny. If you don't make it back—"

"I'll make it back, honey. I promise." He drew her to him, kissed her lips, then held her head close against his chest, feeling their heartbeats mingle.

The door scraped open and a raspy voice called out, "What the hell's goin' on out here? Sounds like a coupla sweet-talkin' teenagers who need the paddle taken to their *be*hinds. There's a coupla *hardworkin'* fellas trying to sleep in here!"

Sheila snorted a laugh. "Sorry, Mike."

"You'll be sorry iffen I take the paddle to ya!"

"You can't take the paddle to me, Mike. I'm your employer—remember?"

"Oh." Mike stepped forward atop the stoop, hacked phlegm from his throat, and spat it out over the porch rail. "I forgot. It ain't easy fer a man like me, workin' fer a woman. Especially one so purty and who's done set her hat for a rascal no-account half my age."

"I reckon the rascal no-account would be me," Johnny told Sheila.

"You were my first guess."

"What're you two doin' up so early? What you got the mules outfitted for?"

"I'm making the last run of the year."

"Well, why in the hell didn't you tell me?"

"Because by the time I got home last night, you and Silent—who isn't nearly so silent when he's asleep, by the way—were deep in your cups and sawing logs like it was going to be the longest, coldest winter ever. Do the barmen you work for pay you in *grog*?"

"No, but I wish they did so I wouldn't blow my wages so soon after I got paid. Hold on. I'll wake Silent, an' we'll ride along with you." Mike turned back to the cabin.

"No, Mike."

The little man was clad in the powder blue bathrobe he'd acquired from some doxie he'd spent a long winter with up in Montana. He wore the distinctly feminine garment around the cabin with nothing underneath but his longhandles, with no shame or self-consciousness whatever. "What do you mean— 'No, Mike'? No one says that less'n they wanna get kicked out with a cold shovel, consarn it!"

"No, Mike. You and Silent stay here and keep an eye on my girl here."

Sheila looked up at him, placed a hand on his chest clad in his buckskin mackinaw. "I think Mike has the right idea, Johnny."

"Mike's always got the right idea," Mike groused from the porch.

Johnny shook his head. "I want him and Silent down here keeping an eye on you and the bank. Someone might try to make one last play on it for the year. Especially if they know I'm up in the mountains, which most folks will realize when they don't see me around town."

Sheila gazed up at him. She hadn't told him about her run-in with Flagg in the Silver Slipper. Nor about Flagg's rape of Miss MacFarland. She hadn't wanted Johnny to be distracted and possibly let his guard down. Not when such a fierce killer as El Cuchillo was stalking him.

She was glad she'd kept the secret. If she hadn't, she had no doubt that Johnny would have killed Flagg, only adding to his problems. She was worried about another run-in with the demented town marshal. Still, she wished he'd let Mean Mike and Silent Thursday make the trip to the Reverend's Temptation and back, but she knew there was no changing his mind.

He was a stubborn man, Johnny Greenway. Maybe that was partly why she loved him. It wasn't often that you found a man who knew his own mind as well as Johnny did—especially one who'd been through as much adversity as Johnny had . . .

"You be careful," Sheila ordered. "Keep one finger on your trigger and an eye on your backtrail." She smiled at the old saying.

"I will."

"You got plenty of food?"

"Of course."

She smiled ironically, narrowing one lovely eye. "Warm socks?"

"All right, I'm goin' back inside before this gets all gooey again." Mean Mike hacked and spat again, cursed, and stomped into the cabin.

"I don't know," Sheila said, again casting her gaze toward the lightening ridges. "Awfully late in the year to be making such a trek."

"Several prospectors told me the snows are holding off. I should make it with no problem." At least, if he didn't make it, it likely wouldn't be because of the weather. Johnny frowned down at her. "Are you all right? It seems . . . I don't know . . . it seems like there might be more on your mind than Cordobés."

That's how well he knew her. He'd already read the trouble with Flagg in her eyes. She feigned a reassuring smile. She tightened her grip on his neck. "Only you, my love. I want you to make it down safe and sound. You've made a date with me, and I have every intention of holding you to it, Johnny Greenway."

"And I have every intention of keeping it." Johnny held her close again, kissed her, savoring the silky feel of her plump lips against his own, her particular female scent, the suppleness of her figure in his embrace. "This will be over soon. Before you know it, we'll have tied the knot and be steaming down Mexican way, planning our family."

"A family, eh?"

"Yeah. A big one."

"The bigger the better." She returned his kiss, clung to him so hard that he had to practically wrestle her away from him, chuckling. "I'd best head out before it's tomorrow!"

Johnny tightened Ghost's latigo straps and swung into the leather. "You'd best stay here until I'm good an' gone, in case he's on the prowl."

Sheila knew very well who Johnny meant. El Cuchillo.

She looked around, hugging herself again, against an inner chill. "I'll go in and swipe a cup of Mike's coffee . . . if you can call it coffee."

"Be careful—that stuff will melt a horseshoe!" Johnny pinched his hat brim and smiled warmly at his bride-to-be. "I'll see you in a few days, honey."

"I'm holding you to that," she called as he rode away.

* * *

An hour later, Johnny put Ghost up to the crest of a rocky ridge.

He rode twenty feet down the other side, ground-reined the horse and the two pack mules, then walked back up to within a few feet of the crest. Dropping to his belly and removing his hat, he gazed out over the lip of the ridge and back into the valley he'd just climbed out of.

He could see Bear Musgrave's old cabin straight off to the south—it was just a gray smudge in the blue-green forest from this distance. Beyond it and a little to the right lay Hallelujah Junction, barely visible between two high ridges. Mostly, he could see the pale wash of woodsmoke from chimneys. He could see the shimmering, royal blue thread of the Paiute River that skirted the little boomtown.

A sudden, unexpected wave of homesickness washed over Johnny. It was like an abrupt wind gust battering him violently. Odd how a man could fall so headlong in love with a woman that leaving her, for only a brief time, made him feel like clouding up and raining like a small child who'd just had his candy stolen.

Enough of that, you rascal no-account. You came up here to do a job. Two jobs. Don't lose your focus or that killer—a seasoned one, at that—will beef you from long range with that Big Fifty he's known to carry.

As Johnny studied the terrain around him, looking for any sign of El Cuchillo, he reflected at the number of men the killer had turned toe-down in these parts. Cordobés was a favorite regulator of the larger ranches and ranching associations. Johnny knew of at least three squatters he'd killed—men whose only transgression had been that they'd homesteaded on open range that a larger rancher or one of the associations unlawfully considered their own. El Cuchillo was known to be especially cold and sadistic. As a lesson to others like his victims, he'd skinned one husband and wife and left them hanging from their ranch portal. He'd shot the couples' three children, as well.

All the family's livestock, as well—including their dog.

Johnny had never had the opportunity to go after Jose Ramon Cordobés. He'd always been on other assignments when El Cuchillo had reared his pale death's-head, wielding his knives and Sharps rifle. No deputy U.S. marshal Johnny had ever known had wanted to go after the killer who was said to have come from a humble village south of the Yaqui River, in the state of Sonora. Other lawmen who had gone after him—at least those who'd caught up to him—had paid with their lives. Famously—or infamously, as the case was—El Cuchillo had cut off the heads of two U.S. marshals who'd caught up to him in a parlor house outside Tonopah, and mailed the heads back to the chief marshal in Carson City.

With their badges pinned to their foreheads.

That, of course, had made every federal lawman more than a little nervous about pursuing the gutless killer. The old joke was that if you drew that assignment, you'd pulled a joker off the bottom of the deck, and you'd best not only get right with your Maker but buy yourself a boneyard plot and a tombstone.

Johnny had to admit that after hearing all the savage stories of encounters with the man, he'd been just as hesitant as the others about taking on the infamous Mexican regulator.

He was no longer hesitant, however. Now he was the man's target. His resolve was unwavering. He had to admit feeling fear. No sane man didn't feel fear at such a time or in such a situation. But the fear was contained inside a box full of carefully modulated rage.

When the time came, Shotgun Johnny would take El Cuchillo down, as no man ever had. He'd buck out the chili-chompin' brute with four loads of buckshot and send him wailing deep down into the burning bowels of hell.

"Come on, killer," Johnny said now through gritted teeth, gazing carefully around him. "Let's get on with it."

No sign of the man, though. Johnny wasn't surprised. Cordobés knew what he was up to. The killer knew that Johnny was leading him off with the intention of killing him. He wouldn't show himself today. Maybe not even tonight or tomorrow. He might even wait until after Johnny had secured the gold from the Reverend's Temptation. That would make the most sense. Then he'd not only have a shot at Johnny and the bounty Murron Starrett had placed on his head, but the gold, as well.

With as much gold as Johnny would be packing, El Cuchillo could retire, though he likely wouldn't. No man who did what he did, in the ways that he did it, did it for money.

He did it for the pure sadistic pleasure of killing.

Johnny returned to Ghost and the mules. He mounted up and continued riding, trailing the mules by their lead ropes. He saw no sign of Cordobés the rest of that day or night. Nor the next day or the next night. In fact, it wasn't until two nights after he'd retrieved the gold and had started back down the mountain that he sensed any threat at all.

When he did, he quickly slid the Twins from their sheaths and kicked dirt on his campfire.

CHAPTER 33

The threat had come in the form of a chill breeze blowing against him, lifting chicken flesh along his spine.

Only, the night was as still as a held breath. It was very cold this high in the Sierra Nevadas, with a few inches of snow on the ground, but the air was still. Johnny had been listening to a hoot owl when the feeling had visited him. At first, he'd attributed the sensation to the owl itself but quickly nixed the idea. He'd heard owls before, and they'd never made him feel like someone had shoved a handful of snow down his shirt.

When he'd kicked the dirt on his cook fire, drowning the flames, he quickly stepped back into the shadows of the forest east of his camp. As he did, as if confirming the danger warning his body had given him, Ghost lifted his head sharply from his picket line and gave a loud neigh.

From far away came another horse's answering whinny.

Johnny smiled stiffly as he raised the barrels of both Twins. His sixth sense, the one attuned to danger, was alive and well. Tonight was the night Cordobés was going to make his play.

Blood quickening, Johnny stepped backward, keeping his ears pricked, his eyes flickering across the dark forest around him. He stepped sideways, behind a broad fir then turned and pressed his back against it, giving his gaze to the east, away from the fire, which he could still hear hissing and crackling as the flames died from oxygen deprivation.

He hadn't been sitting close to the fire, and he hadn't been staring into the flames, so his eyes were quick to adjust to the night's dense darkness. Stars offered a weak blue light. He could see the brush and deadfall around him, the spine-straight black trunks of the pines and fir trees, the occasional pale stem of a leafless aspen or birch.

His heart thudded slowly as he regulated his breathing, knowing he had to remain calm. A nervous man did not live when he was being stalked by such a killer as El Cuchillo. Cordobés was a calm, stealthy stalker, and only a man who matched his calm as well as his savagery could beat him at his own game.

That man was Johnny.

It had to be. He had a full life ahead with Sheila Bonner. He didn't deserve such a life, nor her. Not for the things he'd done in his past. But if he could make it out of this night alive, he'd know happiness again at last.

Shoving all of that to one side of his mind, he squatted low, pressing his back against the fir bole. He held the Twins straight up and down in front of him, his bare hands wrapped around their necks. He'd already cocked both weapons, and his index fingers were curled over a trigger of each. The guns were as cold as ice, but he ignored it.

He waited.

From which direction would he come? The left or the right?

Johnny was a little puzzled why Cordobés hadn't ambushed him by the murky light of early morning or late afternoon. He'd figured the killer would try to wound him then go to work on him with his famous knives. Murron Starrett would love nothing more than to hear how Johnny had been tortured and made to howl for hours on end, maybe for days on end. El Cuchillo had committed such atrocities before. In fact, he'd made quite a name for himself by doing so. His services were prized by men . . . and by at least one woman . . . who were especially eager to make their enemies suffer.

Johnny shoved those thoughts aside, as well. He had to be in the moment, all senses as well as his thoughts attuned to the here and now.

Then it came—a footfall in the forest to his left. It was a heavier tread than the one he'd have expected El Cuchillo to make, but, then, maybe all of the killer's past successes had made him overconfident.

Johnny turned his head to stare in the direction of his approaching assailant.

Another footfall. Then another.

Ghost whickered softly.

Silence.

The approaching killer had heard the horse, and he'd stopped.

Johnny winced against the cold burning his hands gripping the Twins. He was beginning to lose feeling in them. He blinked the thought away. He'd will enough feeling into his fingers to make them useful when they needed to be.

Johnny's heart quickened when the approaching killer took three more steps, each step a little louder than the last.

What the hell was he fixing to do? Waltz right into the camp?

There was a wild snapping crackling sound followed by a thud. Johnny stared in exasperation as the approaching man's silhouette fell to the ground about thirty feet away.

Johnny pushed away from the fir, dropped to one knee and leveled both Twins on the man improbably struggling on the ground before him.

"Hold it!"

A groaning sound. The man heaved himself to his feet, cursing.

"I said hold it!" Johnny repeated.

A rifle flashed, thundered. As the bullet tore into the side of the fir tree a few feet to Johnny's right, Johnny squeezed his right Twin's left trigger.

The shotgun's blast blew the night wide open. Johnny barely heard a shouted curse behind him. He wheeled to see another figure running toward him, two guns flashing side by side, resembling the glistening eyes of some charging animal. Johnny was aware of a burn across his upper left arm as he cut loose with both Twins, squeezing a trigger of each.

Another yell.

The man charging toward him wheeled off to Johnny's right and struck the ground with a mad thrashing of brush and twigs. The attacker lay writhing and groaning loudly.

Johnny wheeled to the first man he'd shot. That

man wasn't moving. Deciding he was finished, Johnny strode over to the gent howling in the brush between two mossy boulders. He stopped to stare down at the man who lay thrashing wildly, cursing and spitting like a wounded wildcat. He was dressed in a sleek rabbit fur coat and matching fur hat with earflaps. Judging by the shrillness of his voice, he was young. He also looked small.

Certainly not Cordobés.

"Who the hell are you?" Johnny asked, holding both smoking Twins on the wounded young man.

The young man groaned, sobbed. "It hurts. Oh . . . oh God . . . it *hurts!*"

Johnny cursed.

He holstered the Twins then reached down and grabbed the young man by one of his arms. He dragged the sobbing, screeching bushwhacker into his camp and deposited him by his smoking fire. Johnny stoked the fire back to life, and when a few orange flames began to flicker, shuttling light and shadows around the camp, he looked down at the wounded young man writhing on the ground before him.

The salmon flames caressed the soft, pale cheeks of Willie Starrett.

"Willie!"

"Oh God—I'm dying, aren't I?"

Johnny peered into the darkness where his second attacker lay unmoving. "Who . . . ?" He rose and walked into the darkness, stumbling around in the brush until he found the body of the first man he'd shot. He dragged this one—also light—up beside Willie. The licking flames touched the pimple-spotted cheeks of a boy roughly Willie's age, who Johnny knew belonged to a family of woodcutters who lived along the Avalanche River and supplied wood to the Three-Bar-Cross.

"Calvin Horton," Johnny muttered. Blood oozed from a corner of the boy's mouth, feminine-like in its plumpness and redness.

Johnny returned his incredulous gaze to Willie, who stared at him as though beseeching. So Willie had found a friend in this rough country. At least one. The woodcutters' son. And he'd partnered up with the Horton boy to . . .

"Help me," Willie cried, sobbing, his breathing growing shallow, his body relaxing. The light was leaving his eyes. "Won't you help me . . . please . . . ?"

"What the hell were you thinking, Willie?"

"I . . ." Willie swallowed. He was clutching his belly, which was a puddle of blood and oozing innards. "I just . . . wanted . . . to stay out of the . . . bunkhouse . . . !"

He'd barely gotten that last word out before he gave one final gasp, and his head fell to one side, eyes half closing. He stared opaquely at the leaping flames inches from his face, drawn and pale now in death.

Johnny sank back on the heels of his boots.

A fresh wave of anger rolled over him. "That damn woman," he bit out. "That damn crazy witch!" He punched his thigh in horror of what she'd done . . . of what she'd made him do.

But then his mind returned to El Cuchillo.

He looked around, frowning. Where was Cordobés?

If he was on Johnny's trail, why hadn't Johnny seen him by now?

Or . . . maybe he wasn't on Johnny's trail. Maybe

it wasn't Johnny whom Murron Starrett had sent him for . . .

The thought was as raw as the frigid air frosting in front of Johnny's face. He remembered her conversation with Flagg the other day in the jailhouse office in Hallelujah Junction:

Flagg said haltingly, "I don't understand, Mrs. Starrett. I don't . . . I don't understand . . ."

"You fool," Murron said. "Do you think a public hanging is what I wanted?"

Flagg didn't have an answer for that.

Murron glanced over her shoulder at Johnny. She kept her voice down. She didn't want the newspaper scribblers scribbling down anything she said next. "That would be far too neat and simple. And painless."

Johnny snorted, smiled. Now he understood.

Only, he thought he'd understood that day in the office. But he hadn't. Not fully. The pain Murron Starrett had wanted to inflict on Shotgun Johnny wasn't physical. That wasn't good enough for her. She wanted to inflict even worse pain on him.

Psychological pain.

The pain of losing someone he loved.

Johnny threw his head back on his shoulders and pounded his fists against his thighs. *"Nooooooo!"*

The echoes of his cry dwindled off between the stars as he gathered his bedroll and saddle and rushed over to where Ghost stood tied with the mules.

At the same time in Hallelujah Junction, Glyneen MacFarland stepped out of Doc Albright's office on the upper floor of the Johnson's Grocery Store and closed the door behind her.

Pausing for a moment on the upper landing of the stairs that ran down the outside of the building to a dark alley below, she put a hand to her mouth as she yawned. It had been a long night. A man had been brought down from the Big Tom Mine almost literally in pieces. There'd been a mishap with the dynamite the miners had been using to bore test holes around a new quartz deposit.

Doc Albright and Glyneen had done what they could for the poor, pain-ravaged man—only in his twenties. At least for now, they'd saved his life, and the doc thought he'd saved his legs, as well, but only time and fortune would tell in that regard. There was always the chance of infection.

Glyneen had assisted the doctor for the past three hours, and every minute of that time weighed heavy on her shoulders. She couldn't wait to fall into bed.

That thought in mind, holding her medical bag down low in her right, mittened hand, she walked down the stairs and into the trash-strewn alley. A cold wind funneled through the alley, blowing up old newspapers and dead leaves, chilling her to the bone. She shivered. A long winter ahead . . .

Turning toward the main street running through the heart of the town and paralleling the river, she stopped abruptly, closing a hand to her mouth to squelch a gasp. She stepped back into the shadows of the alley mouth as Jonah Flagg stepped out of the Silver Slipper Saloon hard on her left, on the same side of the street that she was on. She could see him clearly in the wavering lamplight issuing from the windows behind him and from the light of a burning oil pot to his left. He was maybe twenty feet away from her, no more. She was close enough that she could smell the smoke from the cigarette dangling from a corner of his mouth, hear his spurs ring and his boots scrape the floorboards of the walk fronting the saloon.

Glyneen stood frozen in fear, her heart racing. Everything about the man appalled her—the way his lips were always set in a leer, his almost insultingly casual way of moving, kicking his boots out to each side and raking his spurs and heels along the ground, his chin up, head and shoulders tilted back, potbelly gut stuck out like the prow of a ship cleaving hostile waters. She hated the whiskey reek of the man, which she could also smell now on the breeze, along with the fetor of his cheap tobacco.

Flagg stepped straight out to the edge of the boardwalk and stood there, tipping his head back and taking a deep drag off the cigarette. Blowing out the smoke, he stuck the quirley back into his mouth and then jerked both flaps of his open coat back behind his hips and reached down in front of him, bending his knees slightly.

Glyneen scowled, watching the man from behind his right shoulder, as transfixed as she was terrified. When she realized what he was in the early stages of doing, she grimaced.

Pig!

Stepping farther back into the shadows of the alley mouth, she heard the rattling sound of his water striking the street just beyond the edge of the boardwalk. She closed her eyes and pressed her head and shoulders back against the building behind her. The sound and the images in her mind sickened her. She'd never hated a man as much as she hated Jonah Flagg. The hate was mixed with a keen frustration, for there was nothing she could do to make sure that he was punished for what he'd done to her that horrible dark night a little over a month ago.

When the sound of him relieving himself faded, Glyneen turned her head to peer around the corner of the building. Flagg buttoned his pants then, standing with his feet spread a little more than shoulder-width apart, stood staring straight out into the street over which small snowflakes tossed by the breeze shone in the lights of the several saloon windows. He appeared to be thinking, pondering his next move.

Glyneen could hear him breathing as a sort of grunting and groaning, animal-like.

Suddenly, he whipped his head around to gaze back over his right shoulder.

Squelching another gasp, Glyneen jerked her head back behind the wall of the saloon, stretching her lips back from her teeth in dread. *Oh God—had he seen her?*

Her heart beat faster as she pressed her head and back and shoulders back against the wall.

"Hmm," she heard him say. "Hmm . . ."

A floorboard groaned, a spur rang, and a boot thudded.

Oh God—he was moving toward her!

For a second, her blood froze. She couldn't move. Then she somehow got herself farther back into the shadows and hunkered down low against the wall behind her. She sat down and drew her knees up to her chest, trying to make herself as small as she could.

Four more raking, jingling steps, then Flagg's shadow angled across the alley mouth. Glyneen glanced to her left and drew a short, quick breath when she saw him standing there at the corner of the Silver Slipper, facing her. She couldn't see anything more than his black silhouette, but he was staring toward her. It was so dark in the alley that she doubted he could see her.

No, he wasn't staring toward her. His chin was lifted and turned slightly away from her. He was gazing upward—at the top of the staircase rising to Doc Albright's door. She could see the pale bandage over his nose now.

Glyneen's insides recoiled.

He was wondering if she was up there still helping Doc Albright. He was wondering if she'd be coming down the stairs soon, dropping into the shadow-filled alley where he could attack her.

She knew that was what the man was thinking as surely as she herself was sitting there, frozen in terror, her blood having turned to ice in her veins.

She heard his animal-like, raking breaths, smelled his whiskey stench mingling with the smoke from his cigarette. She was so sick to her stomach that she worried she might vomit and give her presence away. But then he turned his head sharply left, staring up the street to the east. Then, after another ten or fifteen seconds or so of pondering, he stepped down off the boardwalk and tramped east along the street.

His foot thuds and spur jingles dwindled gradually.

Glyneen heaved herself to her feet. She was so stiff with lingering fear that she could barely walk, but she strode to the mouth of the alley in time to see Flagg turn the corner and head north up Third Avenue.

Fear refreshed itself inside her. This time, she didn't fear so much for herself as for Miss Bonner. Didn't Sheila live on the north end of Third Avenue?

Was Flagg heading toward her house?

raucous screech as it winged into the air over Tobias Miller's house to the south.

Probably hunting Miller's chickens. Sheila hoped the man, a widower who'd taken to drink, hadn't forgotten to close his coop up tight for the night.

She let out a relieved sigh then stepped back inside. Returning the lamp to its hook over the table, she said, "Just an owl, Cat. No monsters on the prowl tonight." She left the door standing half-open, in case Cat wanted to go outside. But Cat sat on the floor just in front of it, staring out with the same apprehensive expression as before.

"Do you want out?" Sheila asked. "Just remember the owl's out there." She knew Cat could elude the owl, however. He was savvy, Cat was. Few cats lived past their first or second years if they weren't savvy to all the predators that haunted this savage country. That went for humans, too.

A sudden knock sounded from the other end of the house, causing Sheila to give an almost violent start.

"Whoa!" She closed the door and pressed her back to it, frowning with foreboding. "Who could that be at this late hour?"

The knock came again, followed by a muffled female voice: "Miss Bonner?" *Rap-rap.* "Miss Bonner? Sheila, it's Glyneen MacFarland!"

Sheila hurried through the kitchen and into the parlor. Only one lamp was lit, on a table near Sheila's father's old oak rocking chair, so she stumbled over a pair of her own riding boots before she got to the door. Cursing under her breath, she opened the door to see Miss MacFarland standing on the porch in silhouette. She was bundled up against the cold, complete with heavy coat and knit cap, and she was holding a double-barreled shotgun in her hands.

"Glyneen, what on earth . . . ?"

Glyneen grabbed Sheila's right arm with her right hand, keeping her voice low. "Are you all right?"

"Am I . . . ? Yes, of course, I'm—"

"He's not here?"

"Who?"

"Flagg."

Sheila studied her for a moment, her own fear building again as she reflected on Cat's behavior only a minute ago. "Why do you ask?"

"I saw him headed this way. I hurried home and grabbed Hazel here"—she held up the shotgun in her knit-mittened hands—"and hurried over."

Sheila stepped back quickly, drawing the door wider. "Come in." When Glyneen stood before her, looking around the parlor, Sheila said, "You're sure he was headed this way?"

"He was headed up your street. He's drunk. I saw him stagger out of the Silver Slipper. He's got trouble on his brain, if I can read his mind. And I think I can. He's simpler than a McGuffey's."

"You can say that again."

Again, Cat made a low mewling sound in the kitchen.

"What was that?" Glyneen asked.

"My cat. He's been acting strangely and staring at the back door."

"He's out there, then," Glyneen said, fatefully. "Let him show his head and I'll give him a couple loads of buckshot! I'm right handy with this thing!"

"Let me check the back door," Sheila said. "I don't think I locked it."

Glyneen grabbed her arm. "Let me go first, then."
She raised the shotgun again.

Sheila nodded.

Glyneen followed the trail of guttering lamplight
into the kitchen and to the back door. She was nearly
to the door when it started to open.

Sheila stopped in her tracks, slapping a hand to
her mouth, stifling a scream.

Glyneen saw the door open at the same time Sheila
did and lunged toward it, ramming it shut with the
butt of her shotgun.

"Ow, dammit!" a man cried. "My *nose!*"

Glyneen had just reached for the locking bar when
the door exploded inward, glass raining from the
upper pane. She screamed as she flew back onto
the table. Jonah Flagg entered the kitchen, raging
through gritted teeth, the bandage over his nose
spotted red.

"You're gonna pay for that, you wicked little cata-
mount!" He looked at Sheila, who was scrambling
along the table to grab the shotgun that Glyneen had
dropped on the floor. "You're both gonna pay *big*!"

Sheila picked up the shotgun and began to raise it.
Flagg grabbed it just as she got a hammer clicked
back and drew back one of the hammers. The rifle
was angled upward toward Flagg's head when it dis-
charged, the thundering blast rocketing brutally
around the small kitchen, instantly filling the room
with the smell of powder smoke.

Flagg screamed as he jerked the rifle out of Sheila's
hands and tossed it out the open door behind him.
He screamed again as, bending forward, he clamped a
hand over the right side of his head, over the bandage
that covered that ear, which Glyneen had kissed with

a bullet only a few days ago. Blood oozed up between his gloved fingers.

This time that ear had been more than kissed.

Flagg screamed again, his glassy, red-rimmed eyes finding Sheila. She stood frozen in terror while Glyneen scrambled off the table, knocking Sheila's supper to the floor. Flagg stumbled toward Sheila, raising his hands like a monster from a child's nightmare, intending to wrap his hands around her neck and strangle the life out of her.

He'd taken only two steps before Glyneen grabbed the teakettle from atop the range and, lunging toward Flagg with a bellowing wail of unbridled anger, smashed the kettle against the right side of the marshal's head. Flagg stumbled sideways, screaming yet again, shriller this time, and now clutching the opposite side of his head from his shredded ear.

He fell sideways into the kitchen's shadowy corner, knocking pickle jars and airtight tins from their shelves. As he struggled to right himself, bellowing curses, he fumbled his right hand toward the Colt revolver housed in his thonged-down holster.

"Come on!" Glyneen cried, grabbing Sheila's arm.

Sheila was still somewhat in shock, her legs stiff, her knees unwilling to bend. She stared in horror as Flagg pushed himself off the wall, amidst the jars and cans raining around him, some of the jars shattering on the floor, and snaked the big revolver from its holster. "You whores! You'll *both* pay for that one!"

"Come on!" Glyneen screamed again and, tugging on Sheila's arm, began running toward the parlor.

Stiffly, haltingly, tripping over her supper plate, Sheila ran with Glyneen tugging on her arm. As they gained the kitchen doorway, Flagg wailed again. The wail was accompanied by the crashing blast of his Colt. Both women screamed as the bullet *whapped* loudly into the doorframe, peppering their cheeks with wood slivers.

They cleared the doorway and turned sharply to the right. After two panicked, lunging strides, hearing Flagg wailing and triggering his pistol again behind her, Sheila found herself on the stairs at the rear of the parlor.

"Come on!" Glyneen cried, tugging on Sheila's arm. "Hurry!"

Sheila's heart leaped when Flagg triggered another shot. The bullet caromed over her and Glyneen and thumped into the wall at the top of the stairs. Both women screamed again then wheeled to their left and ran down the hall and into the room at the far end—her father's old bedroom, which she now used as her own.

Earlier, Sheila had lit a lamp on the dresser, turning the wick down low. As she followed Glyneen through the half-open door, she slammed the door behind her and twisted the key, locking it.

A gun blast sounded in the hall.

The bullet tore through the door, making a ragged-edged hole and tearing out a six-inch strip of wood. Sheila flung herself to one side as Flagg, yelling insanely in the hall, triggered another round, another . . . another . . . and another . . . until there were four holes in the door.

Flagg's boots thudded loudly in the hall as he approached the door, shouting, "Witches! You're both gonna die!"

There was a loud *wham!* as he kicked the door, which lurched in its frame.

"You're gonna die, witches!"

Pressing her back to the wall beside Sheila, Glyneen said, "Is there a gun in here?"

Another *wham!* sounded as Flagg kicked the door again.

"Yes!" Sheila ran to the dresser, opened the top drawer.

"You're gonna die, witches!" *Wham!*

Sheila shoved aside several pantalets and stockings and pulled out her father's big, silver-chased, pearl-gripped horse pistol. She showed it to Glyneen, still pressing her back to the wall beside the door. "My father kept this for protection. He called it a Russian. I don't know if he ever fired it. I know I haven't."

Again, Flagg kicked the door. *Wham!*

"Is it loaded?" Glyneen asked, her eyes wide and round with terror.

"I don't know!"

"Let me see!"

Wham!

Glyneen grabbed the pistol and, like an old gun-hand, tripped a latch on top. The barrel dropped as the gun broke open to reveal all six chambers filled with brass.

"Yes!"

She snapped the pistol closed and hurried over to stand in front of the door, raising the heavy pistol in both hands, aiming it at the bullet-pocked upper panel.

Wham! The door was splintering around the lock. One more kick and it would spring open and Flagg would be on them.

Glyneen stretched her lips back from her teeth as

she ratcheted back the Russian's hammer. She waited for the next kick and the sudden opening of the door.

Standing by the open door of the dresser, heavy with terror, Sheila waited, too.

But another kick did not come.

Glyneen shifted her grip on the gun, frowning at the door.

When still another kick did not come, she and Sheila shared a puzzled glance.

They looked at the door.

In the hall there was only silence.

Then there was a thud. Not as loud as before. It didn't sound like a kick. It sounded like a body falling against the door. There was a high, almost inaudible gurgling sound just on the other side.

Sheila and Glyneen shared another befuddled glance.

Had Flagg collapsed against the door?

They waited nearly a minute then Glyneen stepped forward. When she held the aimed revolver a couple of feet from the door, standing at an angle to the side it would open from, she glanced at Sheila and nervously licked her lips. "Open it."

Sheila moved stiffly forward. She glanced at Glyneen standing to her left. Glyneen nodded.

Sheila twisted the key in the lock and slowly opened the door. There was a weight pressing on it from the other side. When it was three feet open, Flagg felt into her open arms, and she collapsed beneath the marshal's dead weight to the floor.

Groaning beneath the marshal's slack body atop her own, Sheila stared up in horror as another male figure stepped into the room.

He was a tall man dressed entirely in black, and his

eyes were as black as the black wolf's coat he wore. In one hand he held a knife. Blood dripped from the blade.

Cordobés sprang forward so quickly, catlike, that he grabbed the revolver just as Glyneen fired it, shoving it upward so that the round ripped into the ceiling. The killer gave a hard grunt as he ripped the gun from Glyneen's hands then gave another grunt as he smashed the back of his left hand against her face.

Crack!

Glyneen screamed and flew across the room before hitting the floor and rolling.

El Cuchillo turned and looked down at Sheila. Still holding the bloody knife, the blood glinting red in the light of the low lamp, his dead dark eyes not reflecting any light at all, he spread his black-mustached mouth in a catlike grin.

CHAPTER 35

Johnny galloped into Hallelujah Junction at midmorning of the following day. A couple of inches of powdery snow had fallen overnight, making the trek down out of the mountains at the pace he'd taken, and through two hours of full darkness during the wee hours of the morning, even more treacherous than it normally was.

He was trailing the two gold-laden mules and the horses of the two young men who'd ambushed him and who now lay belly-down across their saddles for their trouble.

Two more lives snuffed out because the Starretts wouldn't listen to reason. Because of some dark, twisted form of family pride.

The horses and the mules were blowing hard as he urged them north along Third Avenue, heads of the townsfolk around him turning as though on swivels to appraise his pack string tied tail to tail behind him, their gazes lingering on the two horses carrying the two blood-splashed bodies that Johnny hadn't even taken the time to wrap in their bedrolls.

He'd had only one thought on his mind. She was still on his mind, in every desperate beat of his heart.

Sheila . . .

Snow was still coming down, large flakes stitching the chill wind. It was a gray, cold day to match the darkness of Johnny's mood. As he drew up in front of Sheila's house, he scoured the ground outside the white picket fence with his gaze. There were no tracks in the freshly fallen snow. That didn't mean anything. Cordobés might have committed his vicious act before the snow had fallen. Hell, he could have paid his visit here anytime between when Johnny had left and now.

All Johnny knew was that it was more than likely that the man had been here and gone by now.

The possibility—the near certainty—of what Johnny would find inside wrapped an icy witch's hand around his heart, and squeezed.

He'd raced the wind to get here. He'd damn near killed the horses and the mules who stood wheezing behind him now, their lather steaming in the cold air. He'd nearly killed himself to get here, his mind stretching ahead across the lonely mountain miles. But now he paused at the half-open gate in the picket fence, reluctant to continue forward.

He no longer wanted to see what awaited him inside. He was sure what he would he would find, and when he found it, he would be ruined.

A hollowed-out shell.

He cursed and strode through the fence and up the unshoveled cobbled path toward the front door. He vaguely wondered why he saw no sign of Sheila's housekeeper, Mrs. Godfrey. Then he remembered it was Sunday. Mrs. Godfrey didn't work on Sunday.

He mounted the porch, wrapped his hand around the knob of the front door. It turned. The door wasn't locked. He pushed it open and stepped inside. He closed the door behind him, staring into the house filled with dark shadows tempered by gray prisms made by the winter light pushing through the curtained windows.

He called her name. Somehow, he knew she wouldn't answer. There was only his own voice here, swallowed by the shadows and the silence save for the metronomic ticking of a cabinet clock in the parlor to his left. It was cold in here. His breath plumed in the shadowy air before him. No fire had been lit. No fire had warmed the house for several hours.

Unconsciously, Johnny found himself stomping snow from his boots as he made his way into the neat house. Despite the cold, he sweated under his warm-weather gear. It was a cold, nettling sweat, oozing with each hiccup of his heart.

He called her name again as he turned to peer into the kitchen.

His breath caught in his throat when he saw the mess. The back door was open, swinging back and forth in the breeze. A good amount of snow had blown inside, dusting the glass and other rubble on the floor. There were cat tracks in the snow, leading outside.

Holding his breath, dread oozing through his veins like poison blood, Johnny looked around the kitchen for her body. Doing so, he spied a bullet hole in the door casing.

He'd been here, all right.

Johnny turned heavily. He had to check the upstairs. She was likely up there . . .

Just as the thought passed over his brain that was numb with terror, he heard something in the second story. He wheeled, pricking his ears. He heard it again. A thumping sound and a low groaning or moaning.

"Sheila!"

He bolted out of the kitchen, swung right, and was up the narrow stairs in three leaping strides. At the top, he swung left and paused. A body lay belly-down before him on the floor, all except for the boots inside the room at the end of the hall. Sheila's room.

As Johnny ran forward, he saw that the body was a man's.

Flagg's.

Blood had dried on the outside of the dead marshal's wool coat.

A moaning and thumping sounded again and Johnny turned to see a young woman on the floor to Flagg's left. For a second, he thought it was Sheila lying there in the misty shadows between the dresser and the bed, hog-tied, a bandanna tied around her head. But then he saw the blond hair of Miss MacFarland.

Johnny pulled his bowie knife from his belt sheath and dropped to a knee beside the struggling young woman. He pulled the bandanna out of her mouth, and she greedily sucked in a deep breath. As Johnny cut through the ropes binding her wrists together, she said in a pinched, fearful voice, shivering against the house's deep chill—"Cordobés!"

"Where's Sheila?"

"I don't know. He took her. He wants you to go after her."

Johnny cut through the ropes binding the young woman's ankles. "Are you all right?"

As she sat up, rubbing her wrists and wincing as the blood ran into them, she nodded. "He didn't hurt me." She licked dry blood from her bottom lip. "Not bad. He left me here to tell you he'd taken her."

"Is she . . ."

"She was all right, Johnny. At least . . . she was when he took her."

"He didn't say where they were going?"

"He said you'd know."

"Yeah." Johnny angrily tossed the cut ropes away. They slapped against the far wall and dropped to the floor. "I know where he took her."

He rose and grabbed a quilt off a chair. He wrapped it around Glyneen's shoulders. "I have to go."

Shivering, drawing the quilt tightly around her, Glyneen said, "It's a trap. You know that."

"Of course I do."

He rose and ran out of the room and down the stairs.

Twenty minutes later, he galloped out of Hallelujah Junction on a fresh horse from the livery barn. He'd tied Willie Starrett to the back of another fresh horse that now galloped just off the livery mount's right hip.

He'd left Ghost and the other blown-out horses and mules with the day hostler. He hadn't given any special instructions about the gold. He didn't give a damn about the gold. He'd hardly given it a thought once he'd realized that he'd been fooled, not understanding that Cordobés hadn't been sent here to kill him but to kill the woman he loved.

To kill her or worse . . .

He thought she was probably still alive. Murron

Starrett would want her alive. At least, until Johnny got to her. His reaching her would probably be her death sentence but what choice did he have but to go to her?

Rage fueled the long ride out to the Three-Bar-Cross. It fought out the cold, kept his blood boiling in his veins. He had to fight his impatience and not kill the steeldust gelding he was riding by trying to gallop full out the entire fifteen miles. Occasionally slowing to a canter was the toughest thing he'd ever done. A few miles from town, the fresh snowfall began showing the faint tracks of two horses heading toward the ranch headquarters.

Johnny's heartbeat quickened, pushing his dread-and-fury-poisoned blood faster through his veins.

He was not surprised he wasn't waylaid by Starrett's scouts. Under the circumstances, they likely would have been pulled back to the headquarters. Possibly, after all the men Johnny had killed when he'd led them into the mountains, their numbers had been so badly winnowed that Murron didn't have enough hands to spare for such chores, likely unnecessary with winter coming on, anyway.

His heart was firmly lodged in his throat when he galloped under the Three-Bar-Cross portal straddling the trail. Clouds hovered low over the headquarters' gray log shacks, including the long, L-shaped bunk-house.

Woodsmoke unfurled from the bunkhouse's chimney pipe. No hands were outside but lamplight shone in the bunkhouse windows. As Johnny swung his rental mount and the packhorse up the hill toward the lodge, he saw several faces looking out at him through the frosty bunkhouse windows. None of the hands came outside, however. They likely wanted nothing to do with this crazy, dark game Murron Starrett was playing. Riding for the brand was one thing, kidnapping a woman with the intention of murdering her in front of the man who loved her was another thing altogether . . .

Johnny rode on past the two hitchracks standing at the foot of the wooden steps terraced into the steep hill beneath the sprawling house. Pulling the pack-horse along by its lead rope, he continued on up the hill, the house looming and gaining dimension before him. He was maybe a hundred feet away when he jerked back suddenly on the steeldust's reins, stopping the horse in its tracks.

His heart stopped. Or he thought it did.

His mouth went dry. His tongue turned to leather.

Murron stood before him, ten feet away. She was dressed in widow's weeds with a black hat and a black net veil. Black gloves on her hands. She held a Winchester carbine in those black-gloved hands, at port arms across her chest. Her hair was down. Snow clung to it and the breeze nudged it.

Behind her stood Cordobés.

El Cuchillo.

He wore his own traditional black garb. His face looked especially waxen in the pearl light of this wintry day. His wolf coat rippled in the wind. He held a long-barreled, black Colt .45 barrel up in his right hand. In his left hand he held the long leather bridle ribbons of Sheila's sorrel gelding. His black eyes, as black as his coat and his mustache, but without any light in them, were slitted. Like a cat's long, evil eyes.

They rolled to one side, toward Sheila sitting on the sorrel's back. A noose was knotted around her neck. The end rose straight up above her, tied around a log beam jutting out from beneath the lodge's porch roof.

The sorrel lifted its head, whickered, shifted its position. Sheila straightened in the saddle as the noose drew taut around her neck, her own face pale and drawn in terror.

CHAPTER 36

"Don't." Johnny swung down from the saddle. He took two steps toward Murron Starrett, who adjusted her grip on the carbine in her hands. "She had no part in the killing of either your son or your husband."

"I know." Mrs. Starrett glanced at Cordobés, who stood there like a wax, black-attired statue, a faint grin of raw evil quirking his mouth corners. "El Cuchillo killed Garth. I sent him to make sure Garth's posse didn't kill you. I wanted the honors of doing that." She smiled coldly. "In my own way. Slow-ly."

"I didn't kill Rance. I told you that."

"Oh, don't try to explain to me how unfair it is, Johnny!" Murron chuckled dryly. "So much of life isn't fair. Why should you get to live in happiness when I can't?"

Johnny glanced at Sheila. "How is her death going to help you?"

Sheila said tightly, "Go, Johnny. Ride away. She's sick. They both are. You can't help me."

"Quiet her," Murron told Cordobés.

El Cuchillo shook the bridle ribbons slightly. The sorrel whickered, started forward.

Sheila sucked a sharp breath and leaned back in the saddle as the noose tightened. She grimaced.

"Don't!" Johnny pleaded, taking another step forward and holding up his right hand, palm out. "Kill me! I'm here now! Kill me! *Hang me!*"

"No." Murron shook her head slowly. "You and I will live to fight another day, Johnny. I want your remaining days to be as painful as mine are. There's nothing really quite as painful as a mother's pain . . . except possibly a lover's."

"Do you know where your other son is, Mrs. Starrett?"

"Willie?" Murron's face tightened a little. "He ran away. He often does. He'll be back. He always comes back."

It was Johnny's turn to offer a frigid grin. "Not this time." He gave the packhorse's reins a fierce tug. The horse lurched up past him toward Mrs. Starrett and stopped on her right, as though to purposefully display its grisly cargo. Willie's curly head hung down over that side of the horse, his slender arms dangling toward the ground.

Murron stared in shock. For a few seconds, Johnny thought her stormy, dark blue eyes would tumble out of their sockets. She turned to Johnny, wide-eyed and frowning. Tears now glistened in those large round orbs, stormy with unchecked madness. "Why . . . ?" It was barely audible. "Why . . . ?"

"He and a friend bushwhacked me on my way down from the Reverend's Temptation. Said he was only trying to stay out of the bunkhouse."

Johnny knew this would be his sole opportunity.

He had to make his move or he'd be out of chances and Sheila would be dead. As Murron Starrett staggered with a mother's heavy bereavement toward her son, Johnny saw that Cordobés was looking at the dead boy, as well. He'd taken his eyes off Johnny.

Johnny's hands dropped to the Twins a quarter second too late.

Murron just then whipped her head toward Cordobés and screamed, "*Kill her!*"

At the same time, screaming, she aimed her carbine at Johnny.

Sheila screamed as Cordobés triggered his .45 into the air and released the sorrels' reins. Even as Murron Starrett's bullet ripped into Johnny left side, he watched in horror as the sorrel lunged forward, neighing shrilly.

Sheila was jerked back off the saddle.

"No!" Johnny raged, drawing both Twins.

He aimed the left gun at Murron, and triggered both barrels as, bunching her lips, she rammed another cartridge into her Winchester's action. The double-ought buck ripped through the gun and into the woman, hurling her backward in shreds. Johnny threw himself forward as El Cuchillo extended his .45 straight out from his shoulder and fired.

The round screeched over Johnny's head as he hit the ground on his belly. He extended his right-hand Twin out in front of him, angling it up, and squeezed both triggers at the same time.

Ka-booommmmm!

Both barrels ripped into Cordobés, picking him up and throwing him violently back against the porch. He bounced off the porch timbers, dropped his pistol, then fell to his knees. His now-hatless head lolled around on his shoulders. His chest and belly were shredded, blood and viscera bubbling out of his shredded wolf coat. He looked down at the mess the buckshot had made of his person, and then at Johnny, and said, "*Eso . . . duele.*" ("That hurt.")

He fell straight forward and lay quivering.

"*Sheila!*"

Wincing against the burning ache in his left side, Johnny heaved himself to his feet and looked at where he'd expected to see her dangling from the timber. She wasn't dangling, kicking, dying as he'd feared. She was on the ground, just now sitting up and wincing as she clawed at the noose, trying to lift it from around her neck.

"Here!" Johnny jerked some slack into it and ripped it off her head. He grabbed her shoulders and stared into her eyes. Miraculously, she stared back at him. Undeniably albeit improbably alive. Her expression was as puzzled as his own.

They both looked up to see the severed end of the hang rope dangling from the timber. It had been cut about two feet beneath the porch roof. The severed end danced in the wind.

Sheila looked at Johnny. "Did you . . . ?"

"No," Johnny said. "It wasn't—"

"Now, was that about the finest shootin' you ever did see?" said a familiar, raspy voice to Johnny's right . . . Sheila's left.

They both turned to see Mean Mike O'Sullivan strut toward them in his bandy-legged fashion, holding his Spencer repeater in two hands straight across his body. He wore a ratty buffalo coat and a coonskin cap pulled low over his ears. The hulking Silent

Thursday trailed him, as usual, making him look even smaller than he was.

"Yessiree!" Mike intoned, cackling. "That was some purty fine shootin' for an old man—wouldn't ya say? I made that shot from a good seventy-five yards out."

"Forty," Silent quietly corrected him.

"Yessiree, a hundred yards out if it was twenty!" Mike insisted, ignoring the giant beside him. He grinned proudly down at Johnny and Sheila. "I may be old"—he indicated his eyes with the first two fingers of his left hand—"but I still got the peepers of an eagle-eyed owl!"

"Mike, you old devil," Johnny said, his face breaking out into a broad, relieved smile, "where in the hell did you two come from?"

"We seen you ride out of town like a bat out of hell. We was on our way over to check on Miss Bonner, an'—"

"Why in the hell weren't you keepin' an eye on her in the first place?" Johnny said in sudden exasperation. "I told you when I left tow—"

Sheila placed two fingers over his lips. "I told them to go about their business. Like you yourself, I thought El Cuchillo was after *you*, not *me*."

"Yeah, see there?" Mike said, indignant. "She told us to go about her business, ya contrary no-account. I oughta put the whup-ass on ya for thinkin' we was negligentable. I would, too, if your girl wasn't here to see the disgrace of it. Anyways, we was gonna check on her when we seen you ride out of town like—"

"I know, I know," Johnny said. "Like a bat outta hell."

"So we saddled up and followed ya, decided to

steal up real quiet-like. An' good thing we did, too."
Mike looked up at Silent Thursday as though for
corroboration.

The big man, clad in a striped blanket coat and a
ragged red knit cap, merely shrugged and looked
around. His breath plumed in the air around his
huge, rough-hewn, red-hatted head.

"Johnny," Sheila said, looking at the bloodstain on
his coat. "You're hit."

"Just a graze. I've cut myself worse . . ."

He let his voice trail off then looked back at the
house, frowning.

"There's one more Starrett," he said.

Sheila nodded. "Leave her."

"Why do I have a naggin', dark feelin' I'll be sorry
for doing so?"

"Just the same, Johnny," Sheila said, placing her
hand against his cheek. "Leave her."

"Maybe she'll be smarter'n the rest of 'em," opined
Mean Mike, also staring darkly at the front of the
lodge where a round, pale face had just pulled back
from a window.

"Maybe smarter," Johnny growled. "But she's still a
Starrett."

"Come on, Johnny," Sheila said, rising to her feet
then tugging on his arm. "Let's get back to town. We
have a wedding to prepare for, remember?"

Johnny smiled as he rose. He took her in his arms,
kissed her, then drew her taut against him despite the
burn in his side. "How in the hell could I forget?"

"Ah, jumpin' bobcats!" Mean Mike said. "Come on,
Silent. Let's fetch the hosses before these two make
me sicker'n a june bug dipped in honey!"

"Yeah," said Silent, trudging after the bandy-legged little oldster. "All right."

"That was a good seventy-yard shot, too, even if you say it wasn't," Mean Mike protested as they walked away.

"No, it wasn't."

EPILOGUE

Two weeks later, Sheila yelled up the stairs, "Johnny, the stage will be pulling up to the Wells Fargo office in fifteen minutes!"

"Comin', honey!" Johnny made one more scrape down his lathered cheek with his razor then dipped the razor in the water-filled porcelain washbowl on the marble-topped stand before him.

He dried his face with a towel then quickly dried the pearl-handled razor, as well. He closed the razor, placed it in its leather case, then dropped the case in the accordion traveling bag standing open on the bed.

"You can't possibly make yourself any handsomer," Sheila called, teasing. "Now, get down here and escort your bride to the . . ."

She let her voice trail off as the sound of horse thuds, muffled by another couple of inches of new-fallen snow, sounded on the street outside the house. The thuds drew near. They were accompanied by the rattle and creak of a buggy. Suddenly, the thudding and rattling stopped. Men's voices rose.

Splashing shaving tonic on his cheeks, Johnny

moved to the window, edged the curtain aside with his hand. He frowned, and a chill rippled down his spine. Three well-dressed men bundled in fur coats against the high-country chill were climbing out of the two-seated chaise parked in the street fronting the house. Four more men, clad in high-crowned Stetsons and frost-rimed furs, rode up behind the chaise on horses shaggy with their winter coats.

Johnny recognized several of them. One of the three in the chaise, an older man, was Mica Severance, the newly seated chief U.S. marshal for the districts of northern California and Nevada. Another, older, man climbing out of the buggy was Nevada territorial senator, Webster Downing. The third was Fred Castle, mayor of Hallelujah Junction.

Deputy U.S. Marshals Saul Davidson and Burton Antrim were among those swinging down from the horses—Davidson puffing a fat cigar. When he'd tied his horse to the hitchrail, he walked side by side with Antrim, following the older men along the path toward the house. Two younger, tall, and erect young men followed close behind Davidson and Antrim; they were likely also deputy marshals.

A small army.

The blood quickened in Johnny's veins. He and Sheila had lingered too long. The law had come for him. The federal law. The Starretts had wanted blood, and now Uncle Sam wanted its own portion, as well. No doubt as a consequence of the federal badge-toters who'd died giving chase in the mountains a few weeks back.

"Well, damn . . ." Johnny muttered as a knock sounded on the front door.

Frisco. Marriage. Mexico. They had been a nice

dream, anyway. Why had he thought he'd ever be able to escape his fate?

Sheila called in a voice far less perky than before, "Johnny . . . ?"

Grimly, he responded with: "Coming, honey."

Johnny looked at the Twins hanging from a wall peg by the door. He started to reach for them but then thought better of it. He'd run from Fate long enough. The time for running was over.

He shrugged into his black suitcoat, pulled his black slouch hat off another peg, then walked out of the room. He was descending the stairs as Sheila stepped back from the front door, and five of the seven men entered the winter-dark parlor. The two younger deputies remained on the porch. Johnny could see them milling beyond the front windows, talking and lighting cigars.

They'd be summoned if they were needed . . .

They wouldn't be.

Chief U.S. Marshal Micah Severance walked through the foyer area between the kitchen and the parlor and, holding his hat in one gloved hand, met Johnny at the foot of the stairs. "Hello, Johnny. Been a while."

"Hello, Marshal." Johnny had met Severance a time or two in Carson City, when he'd been an underling of the chief marshal at the time. Severance was a crisp, neat man in his midfifties, of average height, and still, it appeared despite his heavy bear coat, without a single pound of excess flesh. His carefully trimmed pewter mustache matched the color of his still-thick, wavy gray hair combed back from a widow's peak.

"We'd like to have a conversation with you, if you wouldn't mind?"

Johnny gave a slow sigh, stretched his lips in an ironic smile. "Why not?"

Severance turned to Sheila, who, looking stricken, remained by the door, staring toward the well-dressed group who'd gathered before her, shifting awkwardly and holding their hats in their hands. "Ma'am, do you mind if we sit?"

Sheila shook her head and closed the door. "No. Go ahead."

Severance moved into the parlor area and sat in a brocade armchair, his back to the front window. Mayor Fred Castle and Senator Webster Downing drifted over to the sofa that sat against the far wall, facing the foyer. Since there were not enough chairs for all of the visitors, Saul Davidson and Burt Antrim remained standing in the foyer. Davidson had tossed away his cigar before he'd entered, and now he and Antrim stood near Sheila by the door, holding their hats, cheeks rosy from the cold they'd left outside.

They all appeared grimly businesslike.

Johnny glanced at Sheila, who returned the look with a grave, fateful one of her own. Her traveling luggage was piled on the other side of the door from her. She strode down the foyer to squeeze Johnny's arm reassuringly then stepped into the kitchen doorway, where she remained, hands clenched together before her, waiting with dread. She was dressed in a natty traveling gown and mink fur coat complete with matching fur traveling hat. She wore pearl earrings, and the pearls shone in the gray light from the window.

Her attire as well as Johnny's looked silly now. Silly in its futility. Naive. They weren't going anywhere. Well, Johnny was. But for where he was headed he certainly didn't need his freshly laundered suit and freshly brushed hat, which he hooked over the newel post of the railing now as he walked into the parlor. Since Severance didn't appear willing to start talking until Johnny was seated, Johnny sat in a chair facing Severance, his back to a small fire popping in the brick hearth. The stairs were to his left.

"All right," Johnny said, clearing his throat. He was leaning forward in the chair, elbows on his knees. "Let's hear it."

Severance had been holding a leather satchel. Now he opened the satchel on his lap and dug out a large manila envelope. He glanced at where Davidson and Antrim stood in the foyer, and said, "Would one of you please give this to Johnny?"

Both men hesitated, glancing at each other, then Antrim stepped forward. He accepted the envelope from his boss and walked the twenty-foot length of the parlor and handed the envelope to Johnny. Antrim resumed his position in the foyer beside Downing, both men's faces stonily expressionless.

"Please," Severance said, nodding at the envelope in Johnny's hands. "Take a look."

Johnny saw that his name had been carefully typewritten on a white label attached to the envelope.

"Well, this looks all very official." He opened the envelope and pulled out its contents. There was a good half-inch sheaf of paper and another, smaller envelope with something hard inside that made it bulge.

Johnny expected to see warrants for his arrest, but as he flipped through the typewritten pages, frown lines dug gradually deeper across his forehead and into the skin above the bridge of his nose. Scowling, he looked incredulously across the room at Severance.

"I . . . don't understand."

"What's to understand? The president of the United States had granted you clemency for past—um . . . shall we say . . . *indiscretions*? The killing of the men who murdered your family is what I'm referring to. I've added an apology on behalf of the federal lawmen who pursued you through the mountains last month. If they weren't dead, they'd be fired. What they did wasn't sanctioned by my office. It was an illegal pursuit without just cause. You killed them and the others in self-defense. They were led by that madman, Garth Starrett, who accused you of murdering his son without evidence. Rance Starrett was a known criminal in this area. Good riddance to him and his ilk, is what I say!"

Johnny just stared in shock at the man.

"Also," Severance continued, "I was granted permission by the United States Marshals Service to reinstate your deputy's commission. In addition, you'll find there when you look deep enough a generous offer made to you by the Hallelujah Junction Town Council. What the federal and city governments are offering you, Johnny, is a return of your deputy U.S. marshal's commission as well as the job of city marshal of Hallelujah Junction.

"I thought"—Severance glanced at Mayor Fred Castle sitting on the sofa beside the senator—"and the mayor agreed that since you seem to be well rooted here in Hallelujah Junction"—now he glanced at Sheila standing in the kitchen doorway and looking as though she were about to faint—"that you might as well oversee the town in addition to this neck of the

Sierra Nevadas. You have proven yourself quite, uh . . . well . . . *capable*, shall we say?"

Severance raised his brows, and for the first time the hint of a smile curled the corners of his thin-lipped mouth beneath the pewter mustache.

Johnny fingered the small envelope containing something hard inside.

Severance said, "That is the moon-and-star that was *wrongfully*, to my mind, taken from you after you gave the killers of your family the only justice they deserved. It is yours if you choose to accept our offer."

Johnny shook the moon-and-star out of the envelope. It lay faceup in the palm of his hand.

His heart thudded heavily. For a few seconds, his vision blurred.

He glanced around the room. Both Saul Davidson and Burt Antrim were smiling at him. Johnny looked at the mayor and the senator. They smiled then, too.

Mayor Castle said, "Take your time, Johnny. I heard by way of the grapevine that you were planning a little trip." He glanced at Sheila and his brown eyes glittered. "To San Francisco, I believe?" He pursed his lips, shrugged. "I see no reason why you can't still make the trip and do whatever it was you intended to do there. I've held the stage for you, by the way. In the meantime, you can consider our offers."

"Of course," agreed Severance. "When you return to town, you can wire me your reply. Just say yea or nay."

"Yea or nay . . ." Johnny said, staring down at his old badge in his hand.

"You and Miss Bonner will want to discuss it—I'm sure," Torrance added.

"Yeah," Johnny said, jostling the badge in his hand. He turned to his bride-to-be. "I'm sure we will."

TURN THE PAGE FOR AN EXCITING PREVIEW!

**EVERYTHING IS BIGGER IN TEXAS.
EVEN DEATH.**

Lone Star Sheriff Cullen McCabe has always
been a risk-taker. But sometimes, taking a risk
means taking a bullet—unless you kill first . . .

THE SCAVENGERS

Sheriff McCabe knew he'd make a lot of enemies
when he agreed to be a special agent
for the Texas governor.
But now that he's managed to keep the peace
in the hopeless town of New Hope,
he's hoping he can go home to Two Forks
and get back to business as usual.

No such luck.

The corrupt marshal of East City, Micah Moran,
and his murdering band of kill-crazy cutthroats
are running wild, leaving the folks in East City
in a deadly grip of terror. Now, Two Forks
will have to wait because Micah Moran and his evil
gang need to be taught some manners—
with McCabe's own brand of retribution.

**National Bestselling Authors
William W. Johnstone
and J.A. Johnstone**

THE SCAVENGERS
A Death & Texas Western

On sale now, wherever Pinnacle Books are sold.

Live Free. Read Hard.
www.williamjohnstone.net

CHAPTER 1

"Look who's comin' in again," Alma Brown whispered softly to Gracie Billings when the cook walked past her on her way back to the kitchen. Gracie paused and looked toward the front door. It was the second time this week that Jesse Tice had come in the dining room next to the hotel, appropriately named the Two Forks Kitchen. He had become a regular visitor to the dining room ever since his youngest son was killed there some weeks before. Usually, he came in only once a week. "Wonder what's so special about this week?" Alma whispered. They were never happy to see the old man because he made their other customers uncomfortable as he hovered over his coffee, a constant scowl on his unshaven face, while he watched the front door and each customer who walked in. Coffee was the only thing he ever bought. Everyone in town knew his real purpose in haunting the dining room was the chance to see the man who had killed his son. Cullen McCabe was the man he sought. But McCabe was a bigger mystery than Jesse Tice to the people of Two Forks. Everyone knew Jesse as a cattle rustler and horse thief whose three sons were hell-raisers and troublemakers. Cullen McCabe, on the other hand, was a quiet man, seen only occasionally in town, and seeming to have no family or friends.

Alma's boss, Porter Johnson, owner of the Two Forks Kitchen, had talked to Marshal Woods about Tice's search for vengeance against McCabe. Johnson was not concerned about the fate of either Tice or McCabe. His complaint was the fact that Jesse used his dining room as his base for surveillance, hoping McCabe would return. "Doggone it, Calvin," he had complained to the marshal. "I'm runnin' a dinin' room, not a damn saloon. Folks come in here to eat, not to see some dirty-lookin' old man waitin' to shoot somebody."

Marshal Woods had been unable to give Johnson much satisfaction when he responded to his complaint. "I hear what you're sayin', Porter," he had replied. "I reckon you just have to tell Tice you don't wanna serve him. That's up to you to serve who you want to and who you don't. I can't tell folks where they can go and where they can't. As far as that shootin' in here, I told him right from the start that that fellow, McCabe, didn't have no choice. Sonny started the fight and tried to shoot McCabe in the back, but he just wasn't quick enough. I told Jesse I didn't want any more killin' in this town, so I'd have to arrest him if he shot McCabe."

Looking at the old man now as he paused to scan the dining room before taking a seat near the door, Alma commented, "One of us might have to tell the ol' buzzard we don't want him in here. I don't think

Porter wants to get started with him. He's probably afraid he'd start shootin' the place up."

"Maybe we oughta hope McCabe comes back to see us," Gracie said. "Let him take care of Jesse Tice. He took care of Sonny proper enough."

"Meanwhile, I'll go wait on him and take his order for one nickel cup of coffee," Alma said. She walked over to the small table close to the front door. "Are you wantin' breakfast?" she asked, knowing he didn't.

"No, I don't want no breakfast," he snarled. "I done et breakfast. Bring me a cup of coffee." She turned and went to get it. He watched her for a few moments before bringing his attention back to the room now only half-filled with diners. He didn't see anyone who might be the man who killed his son. The major problem Tice had was the fact that he had never actually seen Cullen McCabe up close. When he and his two sons had gone after McCabe, he had circled around them, stolen their horses, and left them on foot. Still, he felt that if he did see him, he would somehow know it was him. When the marshal tried to talk him out of seeking vengeance for the death of his son, Jesse was tempted to tell him that McCabe was a horse thief. He thought that would jus-tify his reason for wanting to shoot him, but he was too proud to admit how his horses happened to get stolen. Every time he thought about the night he and his two sons had to walk twenty-five miles back home, it made him bite his lower lip in angry frustration. When Alma returned with his coffee, he gulped it down, having decided there was no use to linger there. It was already getting late for breakfast, so he thought he might as well go back to join Samson and

Joe, who were keeping a watch for McCabe in the River House Saloon.

It had been several days since he returned to his cabin on the Brazos River after completing his last assignment from the governor's office. The long hard job in the little town of New Hope had turned out to the governor's satisfaction, and Cullen figured it would be a while before he was summoned for the next job. For that reason, he hadn't bothered to check in with the telegraph office at Two Forks to see if he had a wire from Austin. He needed to do a little work on his cabin, so he had waited before checking with Leon Armstrong at the telegraph office. When he was not on assignment for the governor, he usually checked by the telegraph office at least once a week for any messages, and it had not been quite a week since he got back. Halfway hoping there might be a message, he pulled up before the telegraph office and stepped down from the big bay gelding. He casually tossed the reins across the hitching rail, knowing Jake wouldn't wander, anyway.

Leon Armstrong looked up when Cullen walked in and gave him a cheerful greeting. "How ya doin', Mr. McCabe? I got a telegram here for you. Figured you'd be showin' up pretty soon."

"Howdy, Mr. Armstrong," Cullen returned. "Has it been here long?"

"Came in two days ago," Armstrong said as he retrieved the telegram from a drawer under the counter. "Looks like you're fixin' to travel again."

Cullen took only a moment to read the short

message from Austin. "Looks that way," he said to Armstrong, and folded the message before putting it in his pocket. "Much obliged," he said, and turned to leave. It seemed kind of awkward that Armstrong always knew Cullen's plans before he did, but since he was the telegraph operator, there wasn't any way to avoid it.

"See you next time," Armstrong said as Cullen went out the door. As curious as he was about the mysterious telegrams the big quiet man received from the governor's office in Austin, he was reluctant to ask him what manner of business he was engaged in. And after the altercation between McCabe and Sonny Tice, he was even more timid about asking. For the most part, McCabe had very little contact with anyone in Two Forks except for him and Ronald Thornton at the general store. McCabe had an occasional meal at the Two Forks Kitchen and made a call on the blacksmith on rare occasions perhaps, but that was about all.

Cullen responded to Leon's farewell with a flip of his hand as he went out the door. All the wire said was that he should come into the capital. That's all they ever said, but it always meant he was about to be sent out on another assignment. So, his next stop would be Thornton's General Merchandise to add to his supplies. As was his usual practice, he had brought his packhorse with him when he rode into town, in the event there was a telegram waiting. Austin was north of Two Forks, while his cabin was south of the town. So, by bringing the packhorse with him, there was no need to return to his cabin. Taking Jake's

reins, he led the big bay and the sorrel packhorse up
the street to Thornton's.

Jesse Tice and his two sons came out of the saloon
and stood for a while on the short length of boardwalk in front. Looking up and down the street,
hoping to catch sight of the man who shot his
youngest, Jesse figured it another wasted day. Both
Samson and Joe were content to participate in the
search for the man called Cullen McCabe as long
as their watching post was always the saloon. There
was not a great deal of gray matter between the ears
of either Joe or Samson and what there was seemed
easily diluted by alcohol. Neither son carried the
same driven desire their father had to avenge their
brother. They generally figured that Sonny was
bound to run into somebody he couldn't outdraw
in a gunfight and the results would be the same.
"How 'bout it, Pa?" Samson asked. "We 'bout ready to
go on back to the house?"

"Hold on," Jesse said, something having caught
his attention at the far end of the street. At that
moment, Graham Price, the blacksmith, walked out
of the saloon, heading back to his forge. Jesse stepped
in front of Price. "Say," he asked, "who's the big feller
leadin' them horses to the general store?" He pointed
to Thornton's.

Price paused only long enough to say, "His name's
Cullen McCabe." Having no more use for Jesse and
his sons than most of the other citizens of Two Forks,
he continued on toward his shop. Had he taken the
time to look at the wide-eyed look of discovery on
Jesse Tice's face, he would have regretted identifying

McCabe. As luck would have it, Jesse had asked one of the handful of people in Two Forks who knew McCabe's name. As Price crossed to the other side of the street, he could hear the excited exchange of conversation behind him as the three Tice men realized their search had paid off.

Joe, Jesse's youngest, now that Sonny was dead, ran to his horse to get his rifle, but Jesse stopped him. "Put it away, you damn fool! You're too late, anyway, he's done gone inside the store."

"He'll be comin' back out," Samson insisted, thinking the same as Joe. "And when he does, we can cut him down."

"Ain't I ever learnt you boys anythin'?" Jesse scolded. "And then what, after ever'body in the whole town seen you do it? Take to the hills with a marshal's posse after us?"

"Yeah, but he shot Sonny right there in the dinin' room, and ever'body seen him do it," Joe declared. "Marshal didn't arrest him for that."

"Sonny called him out," Jesse said. "There's a difference. You pick him off when he don't know you're waitin' for him—that's murder, and they'd most likely hang you for it."

Confused now, Samson asked, "Well, ain't we gonna shoot him? Why we been hangin' around here waitin' for him to show up, if we ain't gonna shoot him?"

"We're gonna shoot him," his father explained, impatiently. "But we're gonna wait and follow him outta town where there ain't no witnesses."

"What if he ain't plannin' to leave anytime soon?" Joe complained. "I'd just as soon step up in front of him and tell him to go for his gun—see how fast he is when he don't know it's comin'. Then it would be a face-to-face shootout, and like you said, that ain't murder. Hell, I'm as fast as Sonny ever was," he claimed, his boast in part inspired by the whiskey he had just imbibed. He didn't express it, but he was also thinking about gaining a reputation by gunning down the man who killed Sonny.

Jesse smirked in response to his son's boastful claim. "You don't know how fast McCabe is. You ain't never seen him draw." He had to admit that it would give him great pleasure to have the people of Two Forks see McCabe shot down by one of his boys.

"You ain't seen me draw lately, neither," Joe replied. "I know how fast Sonny was, and I know how fast I am. I'm ready to shoot this sidewinder right now."

"He is fast, Pa," Samson said, curious to see if Joe could do it. "He ain't lyin'."

The prospect of seeing McCabe cut down before an audience of witnesses was too much for Jesse to pass up. Joe was right, he hadn't seen how fast he was lately, and he knew both his boys practiced their fast-draw on a daily basis. There had always been a competition among all three of his sons, ever since they were big enough to wear a gun. Sonny had been the first one to actually call a man out, though, and that hadn't turned out very well. But the fact that Sonny's death didn't discourage Joe was enough to cause Jesse to wonder. "All right," he finally conceded. "We'll go talk to Mr. McCabe. He owes me for three horses he stole. We'll see what he has to say for hisself about that. Then, if you think you can take him, that'll be up to you. If you don't, we'll follow him out of town and shoot him down where nobody can see us do it." They hurried toward Thornton's store, concerned now that McCabe might finish up his business and leave before they got there.

Inside the store, Cullen was in the process of paying Ronald Thornton for the supplies gathered on the counter when Jesse and his two sons walked in. He had never had a close look at the old man or his two boys, but he knew instinctively who they were, and he had a feeling this was not a chance encounter. He decided to treat it as such until he saw evidence backing up that feeling. He purposefully turned one side toward them while he gathered his purchases up close on the counter, so he could keep an eye on all three. Jesse took only a few steps inside before stopping to stand squarely in front of the door. His sons took a stance, one on each side of him. Thinking the entrance rather odd, Thornton said, "I'll be with you in a minute, soon as I finish up here."

"Ain't no hurry," Jesse said. "Our business is with Mr. McCabe there."

Thornton was suddenly struck by the realization that something bad was about to happen. "Clara," he said to his wife, "you'd best go on back in the store-room and put that new material away." When she reacted with an expression of confusion, he said, "Just go on back there." Seeing he meant it, she quickly left the room.

Up to that point, McCabe had not reacted beyond pulling a twenty-pound sack of flour and a large slab of bacon over to the edge of the counter, preparing to carry them out to his packhorse. "What is your business with me?"

"Maybe it's about them three horses of mine you stole without payin' me for 'em," Jesse snarled.

"I figured we were square on that count. I paid

you the same price you paid for them," Cullen said, guessing Jessie and his boys had most likely stolen them.

"I'm callin' you out, McCabe," Joe blurted, unable to contain himself any longer.

"That right?" McCabe asked calmly. "What for?"

"For killin' my brother," Joe said. "That's what for."

"Who's your brother?" Cullen asked, purposefully trying to keep the young man's mind occupied with something other than the actual act of pulling his weapon. He had faced his share of gunfighters in his time and it was fairly easy to read the wide-eyed nervousness in young Joe Tice's face. The fact that his speech was slurred slightly also suggested that alcohol might be doing most of the talking. Cullen understood the obligation the two brothers felt to avenge Sonny's death, no matter the circumstances that caused him to be shot. There was a chance, however, that he could talk the boy out of a gunfight, so he decided to give it a try.

"You know who he was," Joe responded to Cullen's question. "Sonny Tice. You shot him down in the Two Forks Kitchen."

"So, you're Sonny's brother, huh?" Cullen continued calmly. "Yeah, that was too bad about Sonny. I could see that he wasn't very fast with a handgun. I think he knew it, too, 'cause he waited till I turned around and then he tried to shoot me in the back. He mighta got me, too, but somebody yelled to warn me, so I didn't have any choice. I had to shoot him." He could see that his calm rambling was confusing the young man. He had plainly expected to see a completely different response to his challenge to a face-off. "Yeah, I felt kinda bad about havin' to shoot poor Sonny," Cullen went on. "I've seen it before; young fellow thinks he's fast with a gun and ain't ever seen a man who's a real gunslinger. You must figure you're faster than Sonny was, but I don't know about that. Judgin' by the way you wear that .44 down so low on your leg, I don't see how you could be. How many men have you ever pulled iron on?"

"That don't make no difference," Joe protested. "That's my business." He was plainly flustered by the big man's casual attitude.

"That's what I thought," Cullen said. "This is the first time you've ever called anybody out. Well, we'll try to make it as quick and painless as we can. Let's take it outside this man's store, though." He pulled the sack of flour and the slab of bacon off the counter. "Here," he said, "you can gimme a hand with these supplies. Grab that coffee and that twist of jerky—save me a trip back in here."

Clearly confused by this time, Joe wasn't sure what to do. Accustomed to being ordered around all his young life, he did as McCabe instructed and picked up the sack of coffee and the beef jerky, then started to follow Cullen out the door. Caught in a state of confusion as well, Jesse finally realized that McCabe was talking Joe out of a face-off. "Hold on there! Put them damn sacks down," he blurted, and pulled his six-shooter when Cullen started to walk past him. It was not quick enough to avoid the heavy sack of flour that smacked against the side of his head, creating a great white cloud that covered him from head to toe when the sack burst open. With his other hand, Cullen slammed his ten-pound slab of bacon across Jesse's gun hand, causing him to pull the trigger, putting a bullet hole in the slab of side meat. The hand that had held the flour sack now held a Colt .44, and Cullen rapped one swift time across the bridge of Jesse's nose with it. Stunned, Jesse dropped like a rock.

His two sons stood paralyzed with the shock of seeing their father collapse and Cullen was quick to take advantage of it. "Unbuckle those gun belts, both of you." With his .44 trained on them, they offered no resistance. After laying his slab of bacon on the bar, Cullen took both belts, then picked up Jesse's gun. "Pick your pa up and get him out of here. Take him home and he'll be all right," he ordered, while covering them with his Colt. "There ain't gonna be no killin' here today. And if you're smart, you'll just forget about gettin' even for your brother's mistake. He made a play that didn't work out for him. Don't you make the same mistake." Still numb with shock from the way the confrontation with McCabe turned upside down, Joe and Samson helped their father to his feet. Jesse, unsteady and confused by the blow to the bridge of his nose, staggered out the door with the support of his sons. They managed to get him up in the saddle and he promptly fell forward to lie on his horse's neck. Still covered with flour, he looked like a ghost lying there. Watching the process from the boardwalk in front of the store, Cullen said, "I'm gonna leave your weapons with the marshal and tell him to let you have them back tomorrow." There was no reply from either of the boys and Jesse was still too groggy to respond. Cullen continued to watch them until they rode out the end of the street. It occurred to him then that he hadn't taken their rifles from their saddles. *I hope to hell they don't think about that,* he thought.

"I reckon you're gonna need some more flour,"

Thornton commented, standing in the doorway of the store. "Maybe some bacon, too."

"Reckon so," Cullen replied. "Flour, anyway. The bacon looks okay. I'll just cut that bullet hole out of it—might flavor it up a little bit."

"I'll tell you what," Thornton said. "I won't charge you for another sack of flour. That coulda been a bad situation back there, and I wanna thank you for preventing a gunfight in my store."

"'Preciate it," Cullen said. "Now, I expect I'd better get movin'. I'm takin' the road outta here to Austin, and that's the same road they just took to go home. If you don't mind, you can get me another sack of flour and I'll take these guns to the marshal while you're doin' that." He started walking down the street at once and called back over his shoulder, "Sorry 'bout the mess I made in your store."

Still standing in the door, Thornton looked back inside. "Don't worry about that," he said, "Clara's already sweeping it up."

Marshal Calvin Woods was just in the process of locking his office door as he hurried to investigate the shot he had heard several minutes before. Seeing Cullen approaching, he feared it was to report another killing in his town. When Cullen told him what had taken place, the marshal also expressed his appreciation to him for avoiding a shootout with Jesse Tice and his sons. Cullen left the weapons with him, then returned to the store to tie all his purchases on his packhorse. Ronald Thornton stood outside and watched while he readied his horses to ride. When Cullen stepped up into the saddle, Thornton felt prompted to comment, "It looks like Jesse Tice ain't gonna let it rest till he either gets you, or you cut him down."

"It looks that way, doesn't it?" Cullen replied. "I reckon killin' a man's son is a sure way to make him an enemy." He wheeled the big bay away from the hitching rail and set out for Austin.

Thornton's wife was waiting for him when he came back in the store. "Well, you don't know any more about that man than you did before, do ya?" She shook her head impatiently. "You and Leon Armstrong are gonna have to get together to gossip over McCabe's visit to town today, I suppose," she said, referring to the many discussions the two had already had, trying to figure out the man's business. "I'm not sure I like to see him come in the store," she concluded as she pointed to a bullet hole in the floor. "It seems like everywhere he goes, somebody starts shootin'."

"In all fairness, hon," Ronald pointed out, "it's people shootin' at him, and not the other way around."

"I don't care," she said. "It liked to scared me to death. I was sure one of us was gonna get killed and right now I've gotta go to the house and change my drawers."

Thinking it not smart to take another chance on a showdown with Jesse and his boys, Cullen nudged Jake into an easy lope as he set out on the road to Austin. He remembered all too well the day he was forced to shoot Sonny Tice. At the marshal's urging, he had hurried out of town, only to find that the trail to the Tice ranch forked off the road to Austin a couple of miles north of Two Forks. He had managed to pass that trail before they found out he was heading to Austin. It was his intention to do the same today. As he rocked in the saddle to Jake's easy gait, he kept a sharp eye on the road ahead of him. In a short while, he came to the trail leading off to the west and the Tice ranch. He rode past it with no incident, so he hoped that would be the end of it. Time would tell, he told himself, but he was not going to count on it. He had not only killed Jesse's son, but what might be worse for a man like Jesse Tice was the fact that he had made a fool of him twice. There was also the matter of three horses Cullen had taken from the ambush site. *There ain't no doubt*, he told himself, *that old buzzard has plenty of reason to come after me.*

CHAPTER 2

It was time to be thinking about some supper by the time Cullen rode into the capital city of Austin, but he decided it best to take care of his horses first. So, he rode past the capitol building to the stable at the end of the street, operated by a man he knew simply as Burnett. Cullen stepped down from the saddle at the stable door. Having seen him ride up, Burnett walked out to meet him. "Mr. McCabe," he greeted him. "You ain't got no horses to sell this time," he said, glancing past Cullen to see only the one packhorse.

"No, I reckon not," Cullen answered. "Ain't run across any lately. I'd like to leave these two with you overnight. And I'd like to sleep with 'em, if you don't charge too much."

"Sure," Burnett said with a wide smile. "I reckon I charge a little bit less than the hotel does, unless you want clean sheets." He chuckled in appreciation for his humor.

"I 'preciate it," Cullen said. "Maybe you could recommend a good place to get some supper. Last time

I was in town, I ate in the dinin' room of that hotel near the capitol, and it wasn't to my likin'."

"You shoulda asked me last time," Burnett said. "I woulda told you to go to Pot Luck. That's a little restaurant run by Rose Bettis between here and the capitol building. That's where I go when I take a notion I don't wanna cook for myself, the Pot Luck Restaurant."

"Restaurant," Cullen repeated. "That sounds kinda fancy." He thought of the place where Michael O'Brien had taken him to breakfast before and all the diners dressed up in suits and ties. Since Burnett said it was back the way he had just come, he commented, "Sounds like I shoulda noticed it on my way down here."

Burnett laughed. "Nah, Pot Luck ain't fancy. It's anything but. It's just a little place next to the hardware store. I ain't surprised you didn't notice it, but if you're lookin' for good food at a fair price, then that's the place to go."

"I'll take your word for it," Cullen said. He followed Burnett into the stables, leading his horses. He unloaded his packhorse and stacked his packs in the corner of a stall. After checking Jake's and the sorrel's hooves, and finding them in good shape, he asked Burnett what time he should be back before the stables were locked up for the night.

"You've got plenty of time," Burnett assured him. "I don't usually leave here till after seven o'clock. I ain't got a wife to go home to, so I ain't in any hurry to go home." Cullen told him he would surely be back before then and started for the door. "Tell Rose I sent you," Burnett called after him.

Cullen found Pot Luck next to the hardware store

and he was not surprised that he had not noticed it when he rode past before. A tiny building crammed between the hardware store and a barbershop, the name POT LUCK RESTAURANT was painted on a four-foot length of flat board nailed over the door. A little bell over the top of the door announced his entry when he walked in and paused to look around the small room, half of which was taken up by the kitchen. A long table with a bench on each side, and a chair at each end, occupied the other half of the room. A man and a woman, the only customers, were seated at the far end of the table. They both stopped eating to stare at the man who appeared to fill the doorway completely. A short, rather chubby woman standing at the stove, whom he assumed to be Rose, turned to greet him when she heard the doorbell. She paused a moment when she saw him before she brushed a stray strand of dull red hair from her forehead and said, "Welcome. Come on in." She watched him as he hesitated, still looking the place over. "Since you ain't ever been in before, and you ain't, 'cause I'd re-member you, I'll tell you how I operate. I don't have no menus. I just cook one thing. It ain't the same thing every night, but I just cook one supper—just like your mama cooked for you. Tonight, I'm servin' lamb stew with butter beans and biscuits, and you won't find any better stew anywhere else in town. So you decide whether you wanna eat with me or not." She waited then for his reaction.

"I don't recollect if I've ever had lamb before, but I reckon this is a good time to try it," he decided.

"If you don't like it, you don't have to pay for it," Rose said. "Course, that's if you don't eat it."

"Fair enough," he said.

"Set yourself down and I'll bring you some coffee, if that's what you want." He nodded and she suggested, "You'd best set in the chair at the end, big as you are." He took his hat off, offered a polite nod to the couple at the other end of the table, then sat down in the chair.

The lamb stew was as good as she had claimed it would be and the serving was ample for a man his size. The coffee was fresh and hot and she brought extra biscuits. The price was more than fair at fifty cents, considering prices for most everything were higher in a town the size of Austin. When he was finished and paying her, he asked, "Are you open for breakfast?" She was, she said, opening at six o'clock. "Then I reckon I'll see you in the mornin'," he said. "By the way," he thought to say as he opened the door, "Burnett, down at the stable, sent me here to eat."

The night passed peacefully enough as he slept in the stall with Jake, who snorted him awake at about half past five when the big bay heard Burnett open the stable doors. Knowing Michael O'Brien usually came into his office at eight, Cullen decided he would buy himself some breakfast at Pot Luck before he saddled up for the day. He was sure he would prefer eating breakfast with Rose than going to breakfast with O'Brien at the Capitol Diner, where all the customers were dressed up like lawyers. As it turned out, Burnett went to breakfast with him and they took their time drinking coffee afterward. It was a rare occasion for Cullen, but he had to kill a lot of time before O'Brien would be in. Rose's breakfast was as good as her supper had been, so Cullen knew where he would be eating every time he came to Austin in the future. And that would depend upon whether or not he still had a job as special agent for the governor. He still could not know for sure how long the arrangement would last. Granted, he had received nothing but satisfied responses so far, but knowing it to be an unusual position with no formal contract, it could end at any time.

After leaving Pot Luck, he went back to the stable, loaded his packhorse, and rode back to the capitol building. He was still a little early for O'Brien, but Benny Thacker, O'Brien's secretary, was in the office, so he took a seat in the outer office and waited. He refused the offer of a cup of coffee from Benny, since he had drunk what seemed like a gallon of it at Pot Luck. He sat there for about fifteen minutes, conscious of the frequent glances from O'Brien's elf-like secretary. He wondered why the shy little man seemed to be so intimidated by him. Then he recalled the last time he had been in the office. He had walked in just as Benny was coming out and they accidently collided, the result of which nearly knocked Benny to the floor. Further thoughts were interrupted when O'Brien walked in the door. He started to give Benny some instructions but turned to discover Cullen sitting just inside the door when Benny pointed to him. "Cullen McCabe!" O'Brien exclaimed. "Just the man I wanna see. Have you been here long?" Before Cullen could answer, he asked, "Have you had your breakfast?" He hurried over and extended his hand. When Cullen shook it, and said that he had already eaten, O'Brien said, "Benny could have at least gotten you a cup of coffee while you waited."

"He offered one," Cullen said, "but I've had more than I needed this mornin'. Thanks just the same." Impatient now, he was anxious to get down to business. "Have you got a job for me?"

"Yes, sir, I sure do," O'Brien answered. "But first, let me tell you Governor Hubbard is well pleased with the success of this arrangement." He winked and said, "You did a helluva job in New Hope. He's started claiming that the creation of your job was his idea, even though it was mine right from the start. Nobody had even thought about appointing a special agent who reports only to the governor until I suggested it." Without a pause, he went right into the reason for his summons. "This is a special assignment the governor wants you to investigate this time. So let's go on in and I'll let Governor Hubbard explain the job."

Cullen followed O'Brien into the governor's office and the governor got up from his desk and walked around it to shake hands with Cullen. "Cullen McCabe," Hubbard greeted him just as O'Brien had. "I'm glad to see you," he said. "I was afraid my wire hadn't reached you." He smiled warmly. "I'm glad to see you got it." He motioned Cullen to a seat on a sofa, while he sat down in an armchair facing him. "The job I've called you in for is one of special personal interest to me." He paused then to interrupt himself. "You're doing one helluva job, by the way," he said, then continued without waiting for Cullen to respond. "This is a slightly different situation than the problems you've handled up to now. We've got a little situation about a hundred and twenty-five miles northwest of here between a couple of towns on Walnut Creek."

"Where's that?" Cullen interrupted, not having heard of it.

"Walnut Creek is a healthy creek that runs through the Walnut Valley. It's a branch of the Colorado River. I'm sending you to a little town on the west side of that creek, called Ravenwood. It was named for a man who owns many acres of land next to the creek, Judge Harvey Raven. He gave the land for the town to the county officials, along with about one hundred acres for county government business. Of course, the idea was to make Ravenwood the county seat. The problem, though, was that there was already a town of sorts on the east side of the creek where a lot of settlers had farms and homes. They didn't like it much when the county took Raven's offer. Next thing you know, they started having trouble about the water rights. One thing led to another, and pretty soon there were some shots exchanged between the folks that built up Ravenwood and those that wanted the town left on the east side of the creek. So the east-side folks created their own town and called it East City."

The governor rambled at length about the troubles between the two towns, a characteristic Cullen assumed was common to all politicians, but he wondered what it had to do with him. "What, exactly, is it you want me to do?" he asked when Hubbard paused for breath.

"I'm getting to that," Hubbard said. "The problem lies in East City. It's become a town of saloons, brothels, and gambling halls. The mayor contacted my office. East City's crime is spilling over to the other side of the creek, so the folks in Ravenwood petitioned my office for help, also. I sent a delegation up there to meet with the city officials. They concluded that the town was justified in their complaints, but they couldn't recommend any plan of action to improve the situation. We sent a company of Rangers up there to maintain the peace. They set up a camp and stayed for three days. And for three days everything was peaceful. As soon as they left, East City went back to business as usual."

"Ain't there any law in the towns?" Cullen asked.

"Yes, there is," the governor answered, "in both towns. Ravenwood has a marshal and East City has a marshal and a deputy. The problem is, the East City marshal seems to be in control of the whole town and is nothing more than an outlaw, himself. And the town has become a haven for every other outlaw on the run in Texas. As far as we know, the marshal in Ravenwood is an honest man."

"What do you expect me to do," Cullen asked, "if the Rangers couldn't fix the problem?"

The governor glanced at O'Brien and winked. "What you always do," he answered then. "What you did in New Hope and Bonnie Creek—look into the situation and see if there's anything you can do to improve it."

Cullen shook his head and thought about all Hubbard had just told him. "I don't know," he said, not at all optimistic about reforming two towns. It sounded to him that the governor needed a negotiator, and that label didn't fit him. The next best thing was to make one of the towns a permanent Ranger headquarters, and he was about to suggest that when O'Brien interrupted.

"Just ride up there and look the situation over," O'Brien said. "We trust your eyes more than the

Rangers'. If nothing else, you can at least report back with a more detailed presentation of the facts."

Cullen shrugged and shook his head again. "Well, I can do that, I reckon. It's your money. I'll see what I can do."

"Good man," Hubbard exclaimed with a grin. "I knew I could count on you. There's a check for your expenses already in the bank. You can pick up your money today. Think you'll be ready to leave in the morning?"

"I expect I'll leave today, just as soon as I pick up my money at the bank," Cullen said.

"Excellent!" Hubbard responded. "Come, I'll show you where you're going." He walked over to the large state map on the wall and pointed to two small dots that looked to be in the very center of the state. Cullen stood for a few minutes studying the route he would take, noting the rivers and streams. When he was satisfied with the way he would start out, he turned and said he was ready to go. "It's early yet," the governor stated. "If you'll need a little time to get ready to go, maybe you'd like to have dinner with me."

"Thanks just the same," Cullen responded, "but I'm ready to go now, soon as I pick up the money at the bank." He didn't think he'd be comfortable eating with the governor. He imagined it would be more awkward than it had been with O'Brien in the Capitol Diner. He shook hands with both of them and took his leave after they wished him a good trip.

O'Brien and the governor stood at the office doorway and watched Cullen until he reached the end of the hall and disappeared down the stairs.

"Might be a waste of time sending him up there," O'Brien commented.

"Maybe," Hubbard said, "but I've got a lot of confidence in that man. Besides, it's a helluva lot cheaper than sending a company of Rangers back there for who knows how long."

Visit our website at
KensingtonBooks.com
to sign up for our newsletters, read
more from your favorite authors, see
books by series, view reading group
guides, and more!

BOOK CLUB
BETWEEN THE CHAPTERS

Become a Part of Our
Between the Chapters Book Club
Community and Join the Conversation

Betweenthechapters.net

Oh no.

Glyneen drew a deep breath, trying to calm herself down. It didn't work. Her knees felt like oak knots. Finally, she managed to stumble forward and then to walk east along the main street. She felt strong, invisible hands trying to hold her back.

She bulled through them and headed after Flagg, hoping that she might somehow be able to arrive at Miss Bonner's house ahead of Flagg, in time to warn Sheila that the mad marshal of Hallelujah Junction would be calling on her tonight.

CHAPTER 34

Sheila stared into the steam rising from her teacup.

On the table to the right of the cup sat a plate of food—fried chicken with potatoes covered in milk gravy and canned beans from Verna Godfrey's garden.

Verna had left the meal on the warming rack for Sheila, who had not yet eaten more than a few bites since she'd set it there a full half hour ago, after she'd arrived home late from the bank. She nearly always worked late, but for the past few days she'd been working even later than usual to help keep her mind off that over which she had no control—namely, what was happening with Johnny and Cordobés in the northwestern mountains. She hadn't seen the dark-eyed Mexican killer in town since Johnny had left, so he'd gone after Johnny, all right.

El Cuchillo was hunting Johnny, like a mountain lion coldly, doggedly stalking its prey . . .

Despite her trying to distract herself, the thoughts were always there—lurking in the back of her mind like shadows shunted by the light of a weak lamp. Nagging, cloying, worrisome . . .

Nearly a week had passed since Johnny had left. The trip took roughly six days, depending on the weather and if any owlhoots were haunting the trail. Those six days were nearly up. If all had gone as planned, Johnny should be riding down out of the mountains by late in the day tomorrow.

If all had gone as planned, and Cordobés was dead . . .

What if it was the other way around? What if instead of Johnny riding down out of the mountains with El Cuchillo tied belly-down across his saddle, it was . . .

"No," Sheila said aloud, shaking her head and lifting her teacup to her lips. "Stop it, now. All you can do is wait. And hope."

She sipped the tepid tea and set the cup down on the table.

Across from her, a guttural meow rose.

That would be the half-wild cat that had come with the house. Sheila's father had taken in the cat when he'd found it prowling around the yard one winter, so skinny that its ribs had shone through its charcoal-colored fur. Her father had never given the cat a name but only called it Cat, so Sheila had stuck with tradition.

"What's the matter, Cat?" she asked. "Do you need to go outside?"

In good weather, Cat stayed inside most of the day and stalked the town by night, meowing to come inside very early in the morning for his milk and whatever leftovers Sheila had saved from her previous evening's meal. It being colder now, and him being a very spoiled, plump cat, indeed, Cat had cut his time outdoors in half.

Plump as a baby pig, he sat on the chair across the table from Sheila, on the old buckskin blanket her father had provided for Cat's comfort. He'd been curled into a tight ball, enjoying the warmth from the range, when Sheila had sat down to her meal, but now she saw that he was sitting up, staring at the outside door to Sheila's left. His hair was lifted, both ears pricked.

Again, he gave that mewling groan that cats gave when they were troubled and which always placed a cold hand on the back of Sheila's neck.

She frowned at the door, peering outside through the upper sashed glass panel.

"What is it, Cat?"

Cat sat erect on the chair, staring at the door.

"Is someone out there?"

Apprehension poked at Sheila's nerves. But it was probably only a raccoon or maybe a coyote prowling around the neighborhood trash piles.

A low strangling sound made its way up from Cat's throat. What he sensed must still be out there . . .

Sheila rose from her chair. She removed the lamp from the hook hanging over the table and moved to the door. She opened the door, stepped out onto the small wooden stoop, held the lamp high, and looked around.

"Hello?" she called. "Is anyone out there?"

She moved the lamp slowly from left to right, pushing the darkness back to reveal the shadow-limned shrubs, stacked firewood, overturned wheelbarrow, the privy to the left, and the woodshed to the right. Beyond stood a murky black hedge.

A shadow moved on Sheila's right. She swung her head toward it with a startled gasp. The owl gave its